Spanish José the Come Up Disclaimer: This is a work of fiction and this statement is included to inform the reader that any celebrity name(s), business name(s), locations, and organizations that are stated in the content of this book are real. However, they are used in a way that is purely fictional.

I0601949

Jazzy Kitty Publications
Presents...

Spanish José
the Come Up

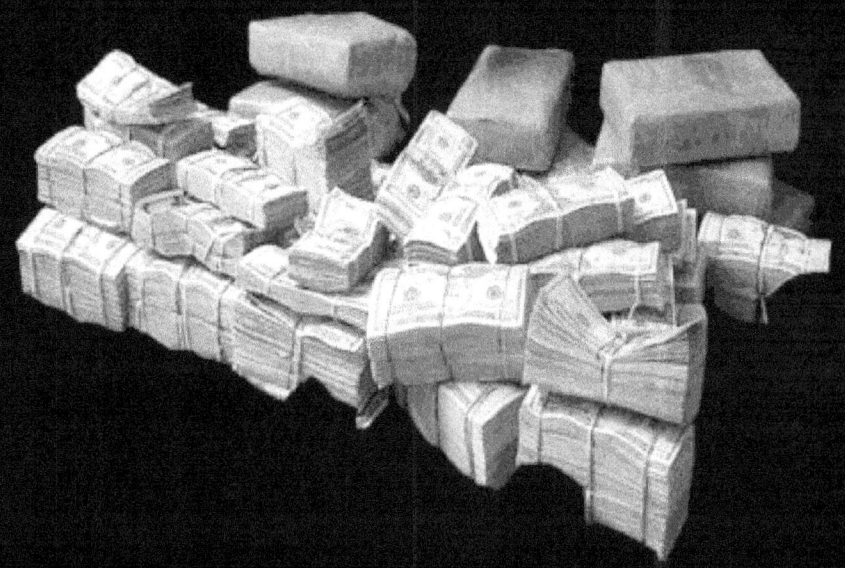

J. Rice
Vol. 1

Spanish José the Come Up

Written by J. Rice

Vol. 1

Cover Created by Jazzy Kitty Publications

Logo Designs by Andre M. Saunders

Editor: Anelda L. Attaway

Co-editor: J. Rice

© 2019 J. Rice

ISBN 978-1-7324523-6-7

Library of Congress Control Number: 2019939411

Published by Jazzy Kitty Publishing & Marketing LLC Dba Jazzy Kitty Publications utilizing Microsoft Publishing Software and Book Coverly. Please be advised this book has strong language and content. Parental Advisory is suggested due to mature content. Disclaimer: This is a work of fiction and that any celebrity name(s), business name(s), locations, products, and organizations while real are used in a way that is purely fictional.

ACKNOWLEDGMENTS

Acknowledgements are meant to shine light on the people who have shed light on my dark life thus far.

First, I would like to thank God our Father in Heaven for never giving up on me. Growing up I always thought that I was cursed because I never felt that I received blessings. I think these last 3 ½ years I received the appropriate blessings needed to live a blessed and modest life. Thank You Jesus! If there are angels in Heaven, I know Gracile Harris Rice is amongst them; Gracile you are missed so much! I couldn't ask for a more wonderful stepmother. Jada and Tee Tee, I do this for us my sisters who rode through the storm, thank you.

To my other sisters, Pudda, Muddy, Niaja, all of my nieces, nephews, my lil brother Brandon, and Porsha, I love you all.

I want to thank everybody, aunts, uncles, cousins, sisters, and my grandmother R.I.P. Thanks to my mother for reminding me to love all of you whole heartily because you're family. Every chance I get I try to influence and motivate all my sisters, brothers, nieces, and nephews to never give up!

Next, I would like to thank a few people who have made being me worth it! Eugena, Sherell, Markelin, Marta, Catrina, Mom Mom Shirley, and the Wright Family, I love you ladies since 94'. When we met it's been love on all levels, you women will always be remembered as Drew's family.

Ebony and Jaunita Richardson, you two were there from the beginning of my transformation from a boy to a man. Y'all were my sister and mother, when I left home at 14.

Sonya, Miss Dora, Isis, Pooh, Terry, Miss Mike, and Shay, the beautiful women of the Walston Family. Y'all asses are wild, but you all are down to earth and define the meaning of hustle hard.

Taylor, JoJo, Janay, Yonnie, Lexi, Kiearian, Keeli, Daisy, Ashlee, Yadi, Sadi, Betsy, Tata, Lil Jessies, Jessie, and Anthony. My Spanish family, Pretty, Princess, Shariyfa, Alicia, Laura, Quadia Jasmine Ann, Tiffany, Camilla, and Margret Stewart love y'all.

And my daughters mother, Kara, I apologize for my absence leaving you to raise our child alone. You're doing a wonderful job raising her and I promise I got her when I touch!

Special thanks to these women because you all have made an impact on my life whether good or bad. I wish all of you the best in life.

Thanks to my lockdown homies, a special thanks to my artist, he made see my vision blossom. Thanks to Joel Ortiz, Eddie (40) Rigdon, Show stopper, Young Hoc, Dawger, Beans for 6th (my celli) who would listen to every chapter I finished. My man "B.R." from Layfette Apartments it's been 2300 since we were teens. Fats from Eastside we were each other's motivation (can't wait till you drop... you're up next). Shamar Harris from Chester, you're a good brother and your knowledge could be used to help free a lot of Black and Latino brothers physically and mentally. Kadeem lil bro get home to those beautiful twins and thorough wife of yours. T.Q. from the mag-life, Amillio (Lito), MacLaden (Mr. Amin) hope to see overturn your conviction, Alpha, Twizz from 30th, Jai, Ball-out from Concord Ave, Ears Montana, Roe Rock, Jarreau Ayers (hold ya head cousin) you gotta let me pen the story! Chico go home to ya wife and kids, we to old now plus, she still loves you, she's just frustrated.

Thank from North, thanks for the insight on Fort Dix. Oh, my man from Virginia Gee and his talented wife Ms. Sherell, somebody give this woman a deal! Thanks to Killer, Shafee, Pop, and the rest of 8th Street. Spider, Big Marv from Eastside, Ponyboy from Dover (BBMG) check 'em out! My man

Roc from Vandever Ave, my man "Co" from West, good dude, listen out for the album when he touches. Buc from Jersey, D. J. Hud, youngin go home and get focused jail is not for you. Old Head Bump, Mike, and my White boy since 2004 Mike Wilson. Belvee from 20th, Zell from Brookmont, Smoke, Chevy, and Gottie. Rt. 40 niggas, Trot from Belvedere good dude, 6-9 from 30th, Fresh from North. My man Snipes, Butter, Keem, B-more, Mere, and Jewels from Scott Street. Brothers like K.G. from Riverside, Fella, Pee Wee, Coop, Lips, Bud from the original 26th St (Bucket). They say they knew me before I jumped off the porch. LOL! And to all the stand-up dudes behind the prison walls praying for a change, it is possible. You can achieve if you do believe, just look at me!

Also, to Akbar Hassan el it's been years since we've spoken. I know we have a lot to talk about and I promise that when I touch, I will carry the weight of holding you down like a true friend. I will stand here and rep for you until our dying day.

Thanks to Cynthia Bright, Richard Jackson, TDM Mixtapes, Wyse Shemeek, Golden Child Records (Blood Nimrod) For U Entertainment, Flava Clothing, Blue Chip, and everyone who played a part in my music career back in the day. F-Sar Records, my folks in Seaford, Laurel, Bridgeville, and Rehoboth! They call me J. Rice one of the state's nicest (R.I.P.) Dwayne Perkins thee nice thee nicest period!

José Reyes thanks for the translation of the Spanish.

Ride for life! Thanks for everything Kieshaun & Lauren, Ooch, it's a pleasure to call you friends.

Thanks to Miss Sherry Rose, you planted that spiritual seed long ago. You showed me another way besides the streets and I thank you dearly; and remember that my God is an Awesome God! Your love is the definition of God in the flesh, there should be more like you.

Thank you, Ms. Nancy Hanley for helping my daughter with her reading and writing; you're an awesome grandmother!

Thank you to a very close and special friend for helping me through these dark days. When I was forced to do this time without having an intimate relationship God brought you, a friend from my past who never knew I was checking her out the whole time. You've been here solid as a rock; your demeanor and maturity keep me attracted even though your 11 years my senior. I've grown to love you unconditionally and if your reading this I plan to hopefully fulfill both of our dreams and make you my wife someday. Frances, it's team us and I'm not perfect but I'm damn sure gonna try my best to keep you smiling, love you Baby!

If it weren't for my brother Nathaniel who regardless of my continuous fuck ups never turned his back on me. While I'm locked down, he handled the majority of the finances needed for this book to come to life. Not just that, while mommy worked, he was home helping me with reading, writing, and counting at 10-years-old; now, look at you. My brother is a Lt. Colonel (Boss), ya hard work paid off bro. I'm far from dumb, thanks for everything, I owe you big!

If y'all didn't know, back in 2011 I was diagnosed with Uveitic Glaucoma which unfortunately caused me to lose my sight 20/200 way passed legally blind. I only saw dark gray along with cataract in both eyes. Thank you Dr. Carolyn Glazier-Hockstein, Scott Fuddenberg, Jeffrey Minkowitz, and the entire staff at Eye Physicians and Surgeons. After four years of blindness, four major eye procedures, needles injected into my eyeballs, they worked together to restore my sight. Even when I wanted to quit and said fuck it, Dr. Glazier you never gave up, you're the best! This book was written with your entire staff on my mind. There has to be a God to bless people with the ability to make the blind see, I can see now.

Miss Annette Robinson, I owe you my life because you put yours on pause to provide for the three of us. I never understood when I was young the importance of school and staying out of trouble. Now, as I sit in this cell, I can hear your voice and see your tears. I plan to change the course of my life with Spanish José. Making you proud of me was always a part of my plan. I've let you down so much, I can't blame you for losing hope if you have. I just want to thank you because regardless if I may have felt that it was right or wrong your method actually worked. I finally got the picture that no one is gonna give me anything, I have to work for anything I want in this life, period!

My precious daughter Hope, you're my reason for breathing, writing these books, and trying to make a change for the better. It's no one's responsibility to raise you but mine and that's what I plan to do. I love you more than myself and its time I show it. Daddy loves you!

I haven't met you personally yet but thank you so much Mrs. Anelda Attaway aka Jazzy Kitty. You've given me life once again; the life of a writer sounds intelligent and cool. You've made it possible for unlimited possibilities to happen for me. All I must do is work hard and go get it! I promise that we are in this for the long-haul, let's surprise ourselves with a bestseller!

I would like to thank a good friend of mine "Ya Favorite Author" Jerz Toston. You walked behind these walls, so you felt my pain and then gave me a chance to change my life forever. You and Tambra are good examples for Black couples to learn from, like James and Florida Evans!

With that, let's get it the Fuck On! Spanish José!!!

TABLE OF CONTENTS

TABLE OF CONTENTS

INTRODUCTION

Am I the plug? Nah, but I serve enough playas to be looked at as one. Am I paper chasing? You motherfucking right! I don't plan on stopping until I got half a million and at least a legitimate business, word! Would I say I have it all figured out? Hell no! One thing I've learned in the street life is that you can never for one second think you can out-think the opposition. Stick to the script, stay low-key, and keep stocking. Ship the flamboyant lifestyle, reward yourself when you retire.

Always make sure those you surround yourself with are loyal and treated fairly. Crush all competition, annihilate them if it's needed. Never burn your bridges and take care of home first.

Finally, Fuck what the next man may think or feel when it comes to your money or product. Always go with your first thought or your gut intuition. Once you have applied these strategies and mental notes to your game plan, it's only one thing left for you to do... that's come up!

CHAPTER 1

José Only Knew the Crack Game

"I was ashamed my crew was lame." The Notorious B.I.G.'s Sky's the Limit crept through the sound system invading the air awakening José from his sleep. Releasing a burst of oxygen and stretching brought him to life. Sitting up now, he glanced over at the chocolate dime who was still in a deep sleep. With a slight nudge and a tug of the blanket, it was a sign that it was time for her to arise as well. With no conversation between the two, they both got dressed in silence.

After she was completely dressed like it was a regular routine she walked up to José, kissed him on the cheek, and then said her goodbyes. After she was gone, José finished completing his hygiene. Once that was taken care of it was time to get to work. Heading towards the kitchen he grabbed an old dinner plate. Next, he went to the dirty clothes hamper and then emptied it. Finding what he was looking for he grabbed the two gray socks and then went straight to the dining room table. Removing from both socks, José dropped two palm size balls on the plate.

The only work José knew was the crack game and to be only 18 and moving 4 ½ ounces a week, all pieces he was good at the moment. He moved anywhere between two to three ounces every three days. He would never buy the whole 4 ½ at once. I don't know why? I guess he liked to move like that. Preferring to use 12 x 12 skinnys on the breakdown. Off the two ounces of crack sitting on the plate in front of him, José would make a sum of anywhere between four to five grand and just a few days. After shorts and play money, he would usually make four grand off the two. Scoring each ounce at 800 apiece and 400 for the half, that made it a lite two grand he was grabbing with. So, he doubled his money with ease, that was the whole plan. Stuffing each of the tiny bags to capacity and burning the tips was a task within itself. Once it was finished though he would reap the benefits.

José wasn't your typical everyday hustler. He didn't stand on your corner all day competing with the others, chasing the smokers down tryna promote his product. The product he had was pure cocaine no cut and once he hit the kitchen, he performed his magic... walaal, straight butter, moonrock, or drop. These are just a few names that the fiends called A-1 crack. With this shit he had, all José had to do was show his face and the money machine started.

After packaging the last bit of his product José grabbed his Timbs, T-shirt, and his Beretta 9mm. Before he walked out the door to hit the spot, he dropped to one knee and said a quick prayer then bounced.

"Poppie can I get four for 30?" asked the half-dead looking fiend.

"Nah, I need 35... you know this already. I don't know why you keep coming up short," José said looking the fiend up and down.

The fiend scrambled through her pockets quickly tryna locate her last five dollars. Sure, that the amount was correct he dropped the stones into her hand, scanned the premises, and then stepped in the opposite direction swiftly. This type of transaction happened all day long as the poppies face was seen. They loved him; he had the best work on that side of town quiet as kept.

Wilmington, Delaware nicknamed Murdertown U.S.A. was never really known for any of the professional sports players that may have come from there. It was known for the gun violence that plagued the 41-block war zone.

A spike in shootings and a major increase in the city's homicide rates put Delaware on the map for the worst reasons. With little to no nightlife that left the city open for the wolves and hyenas to roam and that they did. On any given day or more like every day innocent civilians were gunned down so you be damned if you do and damned if you don't.

Where I came from was the Westside of Wilmington but to the hustlers it was called the Hilltop. I grew up here, moving from one block to another here you learn to do one of three things fast; hustle, fight, or fix a car. Unlike most Spanish dudes I couldn't fix a motor for shit, so I adopted the other two. Knowing so many people was sort of an advantage in my line of work. I was blessed to be able to bounce from block to block. Mingling with the niggas and bitches, showing love to the neighborhood elders and children opened the door for me to slide from one house to another when the law came through on their bullshit. The strategy best used was buying a few dinner platters off the older women, dropping a hundred or so on one of the females on the block to help towards their electric bill. Also, buying the little girl's ice cream every now and again, and then I might pay for lil man to get a fresh cut. These things made me loved and known, yeah everybody knew Spanish José from the Hilltop. As cool as I was, you need to know that I always kept that torch on me and I had a team that was vicious as a junkyard dog.

"Swoop!"

"Oh Oooh!" the small group yelled.

"Bet 50 nigga."

"Bet it... nigga don't talk my ears off."

"My shots butter... double or nothing."

"It's a bet."

This nigga's shot looked like Dennis Rodman's. The group got quite long enough to watch Carlos release the ball with rhythm.

"Swoop! Pay me nigga!" Betting 50 a shot on the milk crate that was nailed to the telephone pole was a game that showed off ones skill.

Carlos and Andre, these two knuckleheads where my two closest friends. I've known Carlos since kindergarten and Dre since first grade. We all happen to link like a bike chain and have been inseparable ever since. With me and Carlos being Rican and similar features like skin complexion and built a lot of people often mistaken us for being brothers. That was because of his dark-colored skin tone. Dre was Spanish as well but was always mistaken for being Black. That was because of his dark complexion. He was Dominican born there raised here and from the day he started Pulaski Elementary it's been on!

Last but not least, my man Castro. Castro was the only nigga that I would trust with my life. Yeah, he's Black, straight from the gutter inner-city Black kid. I liked him from the start because Spanish people are big on loyalty and Castro has broken bread with the squad since middle school. Plus, I don't know who his connect is, but he always made sure our lives were safe. With that being said damn near any kind of torch you needed Castro could get it.

"What up?"

"What up José," Carlos and Andre said in unison giving their friend dap at the same time.

"Chasing a dollar and a dream… while at the same time shooting for the stars. I see Carlos still living out his hoop dreams on this milk crate again."

"Nigga I just raped him for a lite hundred. Would you like to lose your money too?" Carlos asked twirling the ball in his hand preparing to shoot!

"Nigga I'm not betting ya Bum Ass. I came outside to make money not to lose it."

"José you talked to Castro yet?"

"Nah, it's still early he probably laid up boo loving... he'll probably hit me in a few. How long y'all been outside?"

"We been out here since seven, you know we got to come out early to eat Spanish José," Carlos said jokingly.

"You about to force me to start selling heroin. Can I eat with you?" Andre asked.

"Y'all can't expect to pay 500 an ounce of some cooked-up bullshit and make money; it just doesn't happen that way. For the last time, quit being cheap and spend the money, go in with me when I go to copp and you won't be having any problems."

"Man fuck dat, I'm gonna continue to pay five for this bullshit, sell it, and then do it all over again. When the fiends stop buying it, I'll go grab a pound or two of chow then move that," Carlos said pulling out a few jars of sour diesel.

"Well, I see you got some chow that means the coke money done slowed up... I'm gonna support ya movement, let me get a 20."

"Listen playa, I'm gonna make it regardless if you copp or not... this Shit I got is GAS."

"I hope you do, you got if not one of the easiest jobs in America... Los you can sell drugs for a living, you don't have to do shit but have the drugs," José said bursting into laughter.

"So, what you doin today?" Andre asked.

"Trapping until I knock off this "gee pack" then after that, probably have Summer come through."

"What's up with her cousins Hope and Treasure? You were supposed to have been set that up," Carlos said.

"Yeah you right, I forgot, my bad, when I see her tonight, I'll be sure to put in a word for y'all niggas... see if we can set something up for this weekend."

Money came and the coke went fast. The trio bounced from block to block busting sales and politicking with a few associates. While in traffic the crew ran into Bunny. Now Bunny was caliente hot! She was a mixture of Roslyn Sanchez and Mariah Carey. She was in her late 20s but was always mistaken to be in her early 20s. All three of the crew wanted to fuck her simple as that but never got further than a smile and an occasional hug. She had a body like Mariah and her face like Roslyn that made her equivalent to a dime plus ninety-nine. On the low, Bunny had a thing for José and wanted to give him the pussy but knew he was off-limits because he messed with her little cousin Summer. Bunny is what you might call in an O.G. Diva. Since back in the day when she was in her teens all the big-time hustlers wanted her. Only a few had bagged her, but all wanted her. With her being the hot topic, she was always in the IN crowd and that's what made her that number one diva.

"What up Dre, Los, and José."

"What up Bunny... how you?"

"Chilling, just taking a walk so I can blow this chow."

"Bun, you know I got that gas on deck just so you know," stated Carlos.

"That's whaddup... but how much you payin' for an ozone?" Bunny asked.

"I'm grabbing two pounds for 58 and it's that sack."

"Boy, you still getting them young boy prices. Come fuck wit ya baby Bun Bun and I'll throw them at you for 24 apiece... and whatever you grab I'll throw on top. Here taste this, this the loudest of the loud."

"Word? Let me get ya number, I'll hit you soon as I'm done."

"I know that's probably the best thing you could do right now cause that coke ain't gonna do it," José said jokingly.

"A José, did you talk to Summer?" Bunny asked.

"Nah, not today... why what's up, everything cool?"

"Yeah, I was just asking... since ya name seems to be ringing bells up in Roxanne's salon."

"Oh really... that's funny cause I never stepped foot inside there. So, how and why was my name coming up?"

"You know, girl talk."

"Oh well... on that note, I don't want to know. But on another note, I'm gonna definitely holla at you about that bud look. I've been thinking, it's time to fuck this shit up wit everything."

"A'ight... holla at me when you ready poppie, get my number from Carlos."

Stepping away, José took a mental note of two things Bunny had said. His name ringing bells in the salon and the prices on the pounds of bud. Getting back to work, he mixed and moved until his pocket full of stones became a pocket full of cash. The more José thought about his current situation he knew Andre was joking when he said it, but even a lil bit of dope wouldn't hurt either. Never one to leave people behind he was definitely gonna holla at his crew.

"Pardon me sexy… can I get a second of ya time?" Strap confidently asked.

"Nah, I'm good thank you though."

Summer was in a hurry to make it to the Villa on the Market Street Mall to grab two pair of the Air Jordan's No. 9's. She was getting a pair for herself and a pair for her man. They were limited and were first come first serve so she didn't have time to stop and chat.

"Damn shawty, a second isn't even a full minute."

Summer stopped for a hot second, spun around on her toes, smiled briefly, turned, and then kept walking. The half-ass diss bruised Strap's ego, he just knew that he could get any woman he wanted. If it wasn't because of his looks it was definitely his money. I guess this time neither would work, Summer was focused on one thing and it was those Jordan's. After being the first in line to get her shoes, she was relieved. Happy of the fact, engulfed in her bags looking at Strap waiting in the same place she left him. Feeling in high spirits now, she decided to hear the heathen out for fun!

"Shawty, can I get a minute now?"

"Boy, first you asked for a second, now it's a minute. Boy, what do you want?" Summer asked in a joking manner.

"You know what I want every time I see you, a shot at the title."

"Boy didn't I tell you that I have a man for the umpteenth time."

"Yeah, you keep saying that, but I never see you with him."

"I didn't think or know you were suppose to."

"I'm just saying, I think you're making that shit up… a nigga would've seen y'all together at least once."

"Boyyy... go head, you probably know him anyway."

"Who ya man?"

"Spanish José."

"Spanish José from the Hilltop?"

"Yup, that's my boo."

"I see you like fucking with the manager when you could be fucking with the boss."

"Boss... how are you the boss and you work for King? Boy bye."

"You don't believe that yourself," Strap said walking off.

"You Broke Ass Nigga, you couldn't even smell my panties."

As the sun fell, the crew made their way back to the safe haven. 2nd and Scott where they had the most stash houses and chill spots to lounge at. Along with the homegirls and the kids that sit outside all day Castro had known one of the landlords, so they got the hook up on a one bedroom. The four all pitch in a buck twenty-five apiece for rent; then an extra fifty for electric. They had a warm cozy hideout to beat the heat. The crew nicknamed it the Batcave. This was not a trap house, so it had the amenities of an apartment. Sofa, TV, dishes, food, and a king size bed for the bitches they brought through. Blunt after blunt and round after round of Bombay Sapphire had the crew feeling real groovy. Castro had slid through after being M.I.A. all day. He had the latest on everything that was going on around the way. Supposedly two hood rats had gotten into a fist fight over one of the girls' fucking the other girls man. This is the typical shit that goes on around the way. The tricky part that I'm having a hard time figuring out is whose man he really is. One minute he's here and the next minute he's there; and they both know and they still stay with him. These girls need to get their minds right, seriously. Next, he mentioned something about a group of Spanish guys from out of town who had moved on Pleasant Street. They were said to be holding pressure on the hustlers in the hood and they're selling every drug. That type of information was always good, but it was no worry to them. With no hesitation, all guns will squeeze at the drop of a dime. For anyone trying to stop or slow up the team's cash, it would only lead to one thing… warfare.

Leaving the Batcave feeling groovy José had to make one quick stop before he took it in for the night. With all the wrong he had done in the streets as far as the drug selling and gun-toting there was one place he felt peace.

"Hey, ma."

"José... boy, come over here and give me a hug!" Miss Valdez said excited to see her son.

"How's ya day... where is Felix and Sammy?"

"Felix is upstairs playing that damn game and ya older brother is gone. I don't know what the hell he's doing but his ass is always gone. So, what about you mister? You rarely come and visit ya mother anymore. I hope you're not still selling them drugs boy?"

"No ma I'm chilling."

"Yeah whatever, you can tell me whatever you want. Answered this question, how in the world you paying for an apartment and ya yellow ass ain't got no job and no SSI check? You must think my head spins off and on."

"How's ya day?" José asked trying to skip the subject.

"It's s going good… looking over some bills, preparing dinner for ya brothers. It would be nice to have you come sit down with your family once in a while and have a home-cooked meal."

"I'm sorry ma, I've been really busy lately. I promise to start coming over more often to spend time. Can I please have a plate to go?"

"Yeah boy… you lucky I love you."

"Thanks, ma... I'm going to come get Felix this weekend and take him to get a haircut... here take this too." José handed his mother $200 and gave her a kiss on the cheek.

"Son, I want you to be careful out there in them streets... I love you," Miss Valdez said giving José a hug.

Before José left his mother's, he stopped and played a quick game of John Madden with his 10-year-old brother. Felix was the youngest of the three and had been diagnosed with autism at birth. Between José, his mother, and older brother Sammy, Felix had the world and they made him understand that by being at his call whenever he needed them. Passing his younger brother, a $10 bill, José grabbed the Puma Sports bag from out of Felix's closet and then hit the door. Making it to his apartment before Summer arrived gave José time to take a shower, buss a grub, and then count his stash. Emptying the sports bag on the coffee table in front of him he also placed the remainder of the product on the table as well. Flipping through the stacks of cash, one count then another equaled a total of $13,500. Plus, the three-grand worth of crack and the 700 he made today gave him $17,200. He was cool with the sum but definitely wanted that to double in a hurry. A knock at the door brought him out of his trance. Summer had arrived and was upbeat and jubilant. With bags in her hands, smiling from ear to ear happy to see her man she rushed him. A hug and a kiss on the cheek was her greeting.

Summer had gone over her days' events, including her run-in with Strap. José couldn't help but laugh at Strap's comment. People always tried making themselves out to be more than what they were when it came to trying to impress Summer. Who could blame anyone for not wanting Summer? She's standing at 5 foot 3, black hair in the wind, her copper-colored eyes, and milk chocolate complexion.

The night was mellow, José sat watching New Jack City on DVD plotting on how he wanted to execute his next move. Wanting to be up early, José headed to the bedroom with Summer right behind him.

CHAPTER 2

José's Plan

"Yo how much you think in up in there?"

"About a cool 25 grand, he gettin' a couple dollars."

"25? Come on nigga we can go in there right now."

"Nah chill, pump ya brakes, I've been watching the spot and we move out when I'm ready."

"A'ight it's ya lick... but I'm definitely with scommie."

Rakmeef and Twink sat with their eyes focus like a lion stalking its victim behind the tinted-out windows of the Lincoln. These two were some of the cities most feared stick-up kids. There were plenty of rumors that they had more than a dozen homicides. They were questioned a few times, the detectives at the W.P.D. were familiar with the two but never had enough to stick on them. With the two-running pressure on the city like they did they had made mad money in a short time. Ready to war with anybody and any set Rakmeef and Twink played for keeps. Blowing on an entourage filled with grape Kush they studied the cars on the block, neighbors, and kids. Anything and everything that could become hindrance they wanted to know about, just in case they had to shoot-it-out.

Sammy bagged a customer's groceries for the hundredth time that day. Angelina's corner store was a little convenience store that was in the hood. She'd been there for years and known Sammy since he was a child. With Sammy being one of the few kids in the neighborhood who was honest, hard-working, and respectful it earned him a job. Angelina had taken Sammy under her wing like one of her own and would do anything for him. If it meant anything to her, she would see to it that he stayed out of trouble.

Her name was well recognized and her influence was strong. She was known to be kind-hearted, but no one ever tried getting over on her. Maybe because of her fathers' underworld ties or her husband's political connects. Whatever it was they knew not to cross Angelina.

Sammy would stay until the end of the night to help clean up the store. He was in charge of stocking the shelves but had strict orders to never go into the basement for anything. If he needed something that wasn't in the back room, he would either ask Angelina, Ivan, or Noel. Those were the only people allowed in the basement. Sammy never asked why he just followed his orders and did his job; that's why Angelina loved him. Ivan and Noel were her handymen, but you never saw them fixing anything. They were more like security for the little kids stealing chips and juices. The most work either of the two did was unload about 30 boxes a week from off the distribution truck. It came twice a week, 15 boxes on Monday and 15 on Thursday. Those boxes went straight to the basement.

At the end of every night, they would all close up together and leave together. With all three being licensed to carry weapons every night they had three torches rested on their hips as they locked up. Sammy wanted to ask why they felt the need to carry the guns but decided to mind is own business. The weird thing about it was seeing the weapons made him feel safe.

On his way home, Sammy would encounter tricks and fiends of all kinds. Only living four blocks from the store sometimes seem like miles. Someone was always begging for loose change or one of the neighborhood tricks we're trying to get a date. He would always kindly decline the offer and continued his way.

When he got home, he would first go in and check on his mother, next he would head into Felix's room. Most of the time, they would both be asleep so he would take a shower, grab a bite to eat, then call it a night.

Pleasant Street had transformed from a dry and desolate block to one of the Hilltops most money-making strips. The reason for the rush was the strip was supplied with damn near every drug; crack, heroin, weed, pills, meth, and acid. They even were rumored to be pushing mushrooms from the block. Wanting all money, they even opened a late-night bootlegger. The Reyes family had moved from Redding PA to Wilmington a few months earlier. Since then, cash has picked up and the family is chewing. With a total of 40 in all including kids they had at least 15 houses on the block. Each house had its own purpose and would be used to store work on some days and on others used for shelter. The head of the family was Priscilla Reyes. The 60-year-old mother and grandmother had been running the operation for the last 20 years. She had taken control of the business after she had her own husband killed in order to take over. No one to this day knows the true story behind Oscar's death. All they know is since his demise Priscilla has held the crown. She's dangerous and will cut the head off anyone who tries to stop her family. Her motto was "Wisdom can rule a kingdom for generations." With that being said, that's just what she did. She ran her operation with her five son's and five daughters. Out of her 10 kids, Alex Reyes was probably the most vicious of them all. He was a no-nonsense type of guy. His zero tolerance for drama only meant that if you brought drama, he would go out of his way to end it. Some had to learn the hard way though. Those guys aren't living to tell the story.

Traffic was flowing and money was coming, this was just another day for Alex until an unfamiliar face appeared to be posting up on his block. Without thinking the matter over, he grabbed the piece of 4 x 4 that was lying on the pile of trash then made his way to the corner. Observing the unfamiliar face make hand to hand transactions fueled his anger even more. At about the same time he made it to the corner he made contact with the unfamiliar face. Ignoring Alex, Ivan continued to make sells to the fiends as they came. Feeling disrespected without warning Alex attempted to swing the 4 x 4. Before he could get a full swing, Ivan had pulled the .45mm from his waist and now had it pointed directly between Alex's eyebrows. The only words that were spoken were clear, cold, and deadly.

"It's time to relocate papa!"

Knowing he was no match at that present time, he decided to use his better decision-making skills and stay quiet. Ivan's look was a look that spoke in volumes but he wanted his words to be felt because if he was nothing else, he was a cold-blooded killer.

"I think you and your family have the wrong impression, this block is taken so if you don't want any innocent causalities of war, I suggest y'all all pack up and leave."

After stating his business, Ivan tucked his torch, turned, and walked away without looking back. Alex stood frozen for a brief second internalizing the warning he had just been given. Since coming to Delaware his family hadn't ran into any problems but it was something about Ivan's demeanor that made Alex carry this treat as one that shouldn't and wouldn't be taken lightly. Before he could act on anything or anybody, he had to find out who the cocky scar faced poppie was. Next, he would inform his mother of his encounter and see just how she wanted to handle things. José was ready, he had a correct count on stash. His next move would be to have a meeting with the crew. If they could all muster up five grand apiece and he put up 10 that would give them a $25,000 total. He needed his plan to work in his favor for them to take all their hustling to the next level. He figured if you spend 15 grand on soft (coke) he could get 18 ounces. Once that is cooked, he should have 24 ounces of good crack. Split the 24 between the four and each would come off with six ounces apiece. They all had to bring a gee back off each ounce. That would make the total 24 grand. Next, with the 10 left from the crews' pot he would holla at Bunny and grab about three pounds of loud for 7200. Bunny was also advertising that whatever was brought she would also throw on top. That would be a good six pounds of loud that they would have. They would all get a pound and a half to move and with the flow of money that comes for the bud, they should have no problem getting rid of it. Finally, with the last 2800 José wanted to get involved in the dope game. On a day to day basis, he watched as the constant money flow would just pass him by because of his unwillingness to participate. That was all about to change in a matter of days. With 2800 he knew he could score at least 20 sticks of dope. Not really having the clientele he preferred to only grab that amount. If the team agreed to give his plan a try, they all would be in position within a month's time. The only other person he needed to inform about his power move was his peeps Fat Papi.

Later that evening while chilling in the Batcave, José decided to take a shot at the crew. Everyone was in attendance and they hadn't even started getting fucked up. Once he had their attention he spoke to his peeps with assurance and certainty about his plan. Besides a few questions and concerns, everyone seemed to go along with the plan. With the crew planning to attack the Hill as hard as they plan to, excitement filled the room. No more every man for himself, it was now a certified team thing. That meant everyone involved would see paper. Entourages filled with Sour Kush and shots of Henny had all those niggas on fade mode. The five grand apiece was of no concern to any of the crew members, so they planned to meet up the next day at noon to break bread with José. Everything is going as planned so José proceeded to move forward with his plan. Grabbing his phone, he called his man Fat Papi.

"Yo papa what's good?" José asked.

"Nothing everything good, how bout you?" Fat Papi replied.

"Living I can't complain... but look, I need to see you tomorrow any time after two o'clock."

"A'ight what you need ya usual?"

"Nah, that's why I need to see you."

"A'ight just hit me up when you ready."

"A'ight cool."

With the hard part of the plan seeming to be behind him, José relaxed a little. Even with things looking on the upside he just never knew what could go wrong. So, while things were looking good, he was calm and a little excited.

That night Castro had a few of his female friends come through to show the crew a good time. The Dime Divas stripped teased, pranced on their toes, and swayed their hips from left to right. Before long, right there in the one-bedroom mancave, a full-fledged orgy had transpired. A lot of touching and sucking, moaning, and fucking was taking place. By the end of the night, all that could be done was handshakes and smiles. Satisfied with the way the night turned out, they all made an agreement to meet the following day at noon and then they all went separate ways.

Before heading home, José wanted to stop by his mother's house to drop off some "dough" and to holla at his older brother. He'd remembered his mother mentioning that Sammy had been staying out all day and didn't know his whereabouts. José knew Sammy was a good guy and wasn't into anything illegal, but he just wanted to make sure his older brother was okay. Walking onto his mother's block out of habit he would scan the whole block; the cars, people walking and sitting. If you didn't know any better, you would think he watched the leaves as well. Stashing most of his money at his mother's was something that he really didn't like doing and was about to switch that spot up A.S.A.P. He felt that it wasn't wise with that being the thought he had to change places. Walking onto his mother's porch he was surprised to see his brother Sammy sitting alone eating a dish that his mother had prepared for him.

"What's up big bro?"

"Nothing... busting a grub. It's almost midnight, what you still doing outside?" Sammy asked stuffing a fork full of chicken and rice into his mouth.

"I just came through to check on you... I haven't seen you in a while plus, ma said lately you've been gone all day so I'm checking on my big bro."

"I've been working over at Angelina's on Delamore Place... I'm trying to save some cash so I can get mom and Felix off the Hill you know."

"What, have you seen something you like yet?"

"I've been looking at a few places but..."

"But what?"

"The price is kinda high."

"How much they want?"

"I got 20 another 20 plus the loan and we got a three bedroom out Newark... Word!"

"Damn that's fucked up, Sammy you doin this for ma and you didn't even think to include me in."

"Ya line of work isn't guaranteed, José... mine is and that's what the bank wants to see."

"Well, how about I help you out with the other 20 grand; let's say by the first of the month. You do whatever you gotta do to make sure that ma gets off the Hill... deal?"

"No strings attached José."

"None."

"A'ight... let me know when you'll have it and I'll move from there."

"Sounds good to me big bro. Well, let me go put this up so I can get out of here."

José dashed in the house and in a minute or so later he was back on the porch. Taking the safety off his torch José leaned over to give his brother a hug and then walked off. Sammy worried a lot about his younger brother. Knowing that his line of work brought a lot of unwanted attention Sammy could only continue to do right and pray for his little brother.

"Yari, Silva go get your brother Alex and tell him to get everyone together; we're having a family meeting."

Priscilla Reyes sat alone at her roundtable fuming. She didn't know who the idiot was who pulled a gun out on her son, but she wanted a name. What she didn't realize was that the name of the man she was hunting had just as much power as she did in this city, if not a lil more. She wouldn't be starting a war with Ivan she would be warring with Angelina and their war she just might not be ready for.

Early in the a.m. like usual José hit the block to knock off his rocks. Knowing that by 12 everyone from the crew should've dropped off their part of the cash, he just waiting for his phone to ring. Wanting to grab a bite to eat he went to Yummy Bites and grabbed a breakfast sub and an orange juice. While waiting on his food he ran into Bunny, she was looking fly as hell even on the am. She was accompanied by some Spanish dude who had a rugged fly guy look who kept quiet but was watching José closely. Not one into making new friends José ignored Bunny's attempt to introduce the guy and went straight for the gold.

"Yo Bunny what's good?"

"Shit... chasing change, how bout you?"

"I'm tryna holla at you later today on that bud look."

"What you tryna get?"

"First, are they still for 24 apiece... and second, are you still gonna throw on top whatever I grab?"

"Yeah, the price still the same... and for you, whatever you grab I'll match lil cutie."

"A'ight cool, I'm gonna need three of those, sometime after two."

"José you got my number just call me when you're ready."

By the time José had finished politicking with Bunny his food was done. He grabbed his grub and took a stroll through the hood making sells and eating at the same time.

It was now 10:30 a.m. and Dre and Carlos had hit José's phone trying to locate his whereabouts. José ended his early morning stroll and headed to the Batcave

CHAPTER 3
Copp & Go

Carlos, Dre, and Castro beat José to the Batcave and were ready to see what today's events would bring them all. Each man recounted their stack of cash over and over as if a bill had somehow slipped away on the last count. José had finally arrived and you could tell he was the man of the hour by the looks on all of their faces. They sat down and got straight to business. Counting out 15 grand four times everyone was certain that the money was correct. Next, José called Fat Papi and arranged to meet with him at 2 p.m. Altogether he was spending 17,800. Fifteen for the soft and 2800 for the dope. Since Summer had a car when he decided to meet up with Bunny, he'd have her take him. Now that all the cash was there no work jitters sat in. To keep everyone cool, Carlos rolled up some sour then got high. Before meeting with Fat Papi, José stopped by his mothers and grabbed his two Puma sports backpacks. For some reason, they brought him good luck so over the years he kept them. Never knowing what to expect in a drug deal José checked the safety and the magazine on his torch. Whenever he met Fat Papi he met him alone so today will be the same as well. He'd normally come to wherever José was at but today Fat Papi told José to come to the garage. He knew exactly where it was, it was only a three-block walk from the Batcave and since he was sure he'd be okay he stepped off solo. Besides, if anything went wrong going to or from it would be nothing less than a shootout.

In front of the garage sat a Midnight Blue Mazda Rx-7 blasting Tego Calderon's latest hits. Walking in the shop he didn't notice anyone at first until the dirty mechanic that was under the car changing oil stuck his head out.

"What's up poppie, how can I help you?"

"I'm looking for Fat Papi I was supposed to meet him at two."

"What's ya name?"

"José."

"A'ight... hold on let me see."

The heavyset Spanish mechanic got on a walkie-talkie and within seconds Fat Papi's voice came back through in Spanish telling José to sit tight he'd be right down. Within minutes, Fat Papi appeared from a backroom looking just like his name, Fat Papi. Fat Papi was a big guy, he resembled the Spanish rapper Big Pun in every way. He had his size, looks, and he even wore the few gold chains like the rapper did. Whenever Fat Papi saw José he would smile. He loved the young man's ambition and he liked how he only followed his plans and no one else. Out of breath with a pint of shrimp fried rice in hand Fat Papi motioned for José to come to the back of the shop. When José walked into the back room, he damn near had a stroke or better yet a heart attack. There were two desks that looked as if they belonged in an office. On one desk there sat bricks of cocaine four rows of five and on the other sat what looked to be at least a hundred sticks of heroin and two whole bricks that hadn't been touched yet. José had been in the game for a minute but had never seen that much product. He did know that if he got busted in that room with all that work, he'd be buried under the jail. It was no time to think about the downside, he was there for a reason and that was to copp. José had one routine and he wasn't about to change that today. Copp & Go was all that was on his mind at that present time.

"Yo José, what's good? How can I assist you?" Fat Papi asked still eating.

"I know I normally grab two ozone's, but I'm ready to come up so, me and my crew got a couple ones to spend with you."

"How much y'all got?"

"I'm trying to get a half a brick for 15 gees and about 20 sticks for 2800."

"You got damn near 18 grand right there walking up and down these streets bro?"

"Yeah but I also got this," José said lifting his shirt exposing the butt of his gun.

"Cool... I like how you move youngin."

"So, what's the verdict, Papi."

"Yeah, I can definitely do that for you, but the only problem is I don't have a half a bird. So, I guess your gonna have to take this whole one and you owe me 15 grand... you think you can handle that poppie?"

Not one into taking fronts, José knew this was a come up. He knew they could flip the brick in no more than a week tops. So, he went with his gut and made the best move at that time.

"A'ight it's a deal... I'll have ya money to you in no longer than a week."

"Cool, just be safe... there's no hurry, do you youngin."

Fat Papi counted out 20 sticks of dope and then grabbed a brick from the other table. José handed Fat Papi the money and the exchange was made. Placing everything in the backpacks José did what he said he was gonna do Copp & Go. Before leaving he called Castro's phone to let them know that everything was a green light and that they should come and meet him. With no questions asked the call ended and they were in route to meet him. As soon as the crew met up, they went straight back to the Batcave to handle business. Pyrex pots, baking soda, and ice cubes were the three main ingredients and they had all three. With José being a master chef, the cooking of the cocaine was left up to him. They all had a job if it was nothing but getting fresh ice cubes. Yo Gotti's "Standing in the Kitchen" played in the background which made the moment more surreal. Whipping four and a half at a time was his strategy. Off the 4 ½ he would bring back six ounces of raw crack. With a wrist like that he could bring back 48 ounces off the whole brick and that was the plan. The process was time-consuming but once they started, they did not stop. Since Dre was more familiar with dope fiends and he wanted to get involved in the dope game they agreed to let him control and build the dope clientele. Once the traffic was coming that's when they would all join in. Carlos would do the same with the bud, direct all traffic to that one spot. Once the block was jumping, they would all join in. José and Castro would bring all the crack money to the strip. They planned to fatten the bags and keep good crack. Instead of moving around they will post up on 2nd and Scott. Everyone even agreed to bring all the money back to the pot for the first three flips. That would just put everyone in a comfortable position since everything was being broken down to the dime. If all went well, they should at least be sitting on close to a hundred grand. That's a 75 grand profit and that's not bad for the first flip. After the cooking was done the bagging came, they would all chip in for that dreadful process. Before they got started José decided that he wanted to make all his moves before sundown. He first called Summer to have her come scoop him, then he called Bunny. She was ready and waiting plus she had the extra three she promised. She had José meet her on Lancaster Ave. and Franklin.

Once again, Bunny was accompanied by the same Spanish guy that she was with earlier. This time he seemed a little more relaxed, so José acknowledged him.

"What's up."

José knew Bunny so that was who he did business with. Bunny made small talk with her lil cousin Summer while she counted the money out. Once the total was correct the Spanish guy in the back seat handed José the Hefty scented trash bag. Inspecting the contents of the bag, making sure that everything was good both parties said their goodbyes and then parted ways. It was something about Bunny's friend that rubbed him the wrong way, so he knew he had to watch him closely.

Summer dropped José back off on 2nd and Scott and from there he stepped back to the Batcave. When he walked in it was business as usual, everyone was still bagging. After the crack was done, they would all sit down and bag up the bud. They wouldn't hit the block until all the work was bagged. They planned to swing all the phone money to the block and catch all stragglers. It might be slow in the beginning, but it'll be a gold mine at the end.

After bagging up a half brick of all dimes they took a smoke break. That was just the excuse they all made up so that they could test the smoke. From the time José laid the pounds on the table the smell was invading their nostrils they had to see what it was heading for.

Getting back to work it was 11:00 p.m. and they had cleared 30 ounces, so far, the count was $64,000. Minus 15 for Fat Papi and 7200 for Bunny that would still leave them 41,800 off the 30 ounces. That's not even including the last 18 ounces, six pounds, and 20 sticks of dope. The way things were looking they had made a serious come up.

A day later and with all the work bagged up they had a grand total of $135,685. It was time to collect all the paper, bagging everything up just made the pot bigger than what they expected. Everything was bundled in "gee" packs ready to be moved, in the a.m., the operation would begin. For the time the work was cool at the Batcave, but that spot would definitely have to be switched. José knew his work was getting moved A.S.A.P. and he knew just where it was going. When all else fails Taylor and JoJo would ride out for their homie José. They smoke, drink, ate, and hung out and if any of them needed anything they all had each other's back. To make things better since they had an apartment on a side block with little to no traffic coming to their crib, he would give them 200 apiece a week and nail money. They were what you would call friends when José was doing a lil 18-month juvenile bid both Taylor and JoJo made sure he had mail, magazines, and a visit once in a while. Since then he treats them like sisters. He made a mental note to call them first thing in the morning. For now, the crew would enjoy the rest of the day and smoke. All the money that called or came through they promoted that they would be on "2nd" starting tomorrow. They seemed more ready than ever. The only problem they seem to have was the more their faces were seen the more they came familiar to the law. The way José saw things were like it wasn't a plan to stay on the block forever it was just until a steady flow generated through each person's phone. The rest of the day was spent on 2nd and Scott. Weed, smoke, women, and kids made the strip populated and live. Since Felix was always stuck in the house under his mother José gave his mother a break and took Felix for the remainder of the day. The look in his little brother's eyes spoke in volumes. Felix was having so much fun playing with the other little kids. Reminding himself that the upcoming week and that he was taking himself and Felix to the barbershop. José loved his younger brother and even with his disability, he tried to keep him active and involved. There was no limit when it came to Felix. José had a surprise for his lil brother, he knew Felix would love it because every time José came around, he gave him props on it. So, with that being his lil man he was definitely watching out for him.

"Knock, Knock, Knock."

"Who is it?" the voice on the other side of the door asked.

"Heat Pro... we're here to take a look at the heating system." The man was in shock and surprised to see two 40 Calibers aiming directly at his face.

"Back the Fuck up and get the Fuck on the floor! Who else is in this Mothafucka?" Rakmeef asked with venom spilling from his lips.

"My-my son is upstairs... please what do you want? I have nothing."

"Yo Twink go get that lil mothafucka and bring him downstairs," Rakmeef said giving orders like a drill instructor.

Twink ran up the steps and within seconds he was coming back down with a frightened teenage boy.

"Now this is how we gonna do this, you got three chances to answer my questions or you and ya son will end up dead. Where's the cash?" Rakmeef asked calmly?

"Man, I swear, I don't know what you're talking bout."

Rakmeef looked at Twink and with no hesitation, the 40 Cal smashed hard into the side of the teenage boys head. The hit split the boys head instantly causing a non-stop flow of blood and a gash that would need staples.

"Now question number two. Where's the cash?"

"Man please, I'm not lying its nothing here I swear to God."

This time Rakmeef smacked the father in the mouth with the butt of the gun knocking out all of his front teeth. Blood was everywhere and both Rakmeef and Twink's adrenaline was pumping so it was time to turn up the heat. Twink grabbed the duct tape and taped the son's wrist and ankles together. The look he had on his face was sinister. You could tell they were about business and if anything interfered, they would pay the ultimate penalty.

"Now for the final Fucking time! Where's the cash?"

"Man, if I had any cash here, I would've been gave it to y'all... I swear to God that the cash isn't here."

Without any words, Twink left the room and walked into the kitchen. He came back with a broom in hand. When the victims saw the broomstick, they started pleading. It didn't matter the damage would soon be over.

"Please man... leave my son out of this he's a kid."

Twink grabbed the kid and threw him forcefully on his stomach. With no emotion, he stripped the boy of his jeans. The boy became frantic. He began squirming and tears filled his eyes instantly. Realizing that his son was about to be violated in the worst way the dad finally gave in and told them where the stash was.

"Okay man... I will tell you... just leave my son alone."

"That's what the Fuck I'm talking bout!" Twink shouted excitedly.

"Where that Shit at Playboy?" Rakmeef asked.

"It's upstairs in the bathroom vent... take all of it just don't hurt my son."

Twink disappeared up the stairs and into the bathroom. When he returned in one hand, he was holding what had to be at least 20 ounces of cocaine. The other hand close to 50 grand in it. Feeling okay with the "lick" they just pulled off they began packing the work and money in their duffle planning to leave. Everything seemed to be going as planned except for one thing, their faces were seen. Knowing this could cost them their lives if they let them live; they knew what had to be done. With no hesitation both Rakmeef and Twink lift their torches. Blocking out all pleas and cries they let off two shots apiece silencing the two victims. The lick was a good one and it only added to what they already had. Rakmeef set a goal to have a million off robbing niggas in the game. He planned to reach that goal. With a lil less than a 150-grand saved he was still hunting and hungry.

It had begun to get dark and it was time for José to get Felix in the house before the sun went completely down. When they arrived at their mother's house Miss Valdez was just finishing dinner. He finally put his affairs to the side and sat down to have dinner with his family. He loved his mother's cooking and whenever he got the chance to have some, he appreciated it. José looked at himself as his families protector. He would exceed any level to make sure they were happy and safe. As usual, his mother preached to him about the dangers of the street life, but just like any teenage boy who was knee deep in the game, it went in one ear and out the other. Miss Valdez's biggest fear was that José would be tragically killed like his father. José's father was a kingpin in the early and mid-90s, he was supposed to be going to make a deal when his own friends had set him up, robbed, and killed him. Losing any of her kids were a mother worst nightmare and that's something Miss Valdez prayed on every night.

After dinner José helped with cleaning the kitchen and dried the dishes when he was done, he went upstairs to Felix's room. He had to get at least one game of "2K16" in before he left. With Felix having autism one might think he was slow. He would fool you if you let him. Any video game you put in front of him he would play it until he mastered it. So, when José or Sammy may have thought they had an easy win they had another thing coming. Before they got started José removed his 18-karat rose gold Cuban link and placed it on his little brother's neck. Felix was hype! He couldn't stop jumping around, giving his older brother hugs. José knew he'd be excited; he's been wanting one since José first brought it. Felix took off down the stairs, you could hear him explaining to his mother about the gift he had just received. He came flying back up the steps in game mode. He had no smile or a grins just a blank stare. He grabbed the controller and nodded his head for José to grab the other. When the game started it was on! By the 4th quarter, the score was 75-98. Felix had a comfortable lead and wasn't letting up. You could see the frustration in José's eyes. To make the matter worse, Felix would taunt his brother after every three-point shot or slam dunk. With 1:20 left in the game it was clear José had gotten crushed. Once the game was over José peeled his brother off five ones, then headed downstairs to say goodbye to his mother. Wanting to drop his work off with Taylor and JoJo early that next morning he decided to call them while he walked home. After chitchatting for a sec and promising them to 200 a week they agreed. With everything going great it was only one thing that would set this night off right. The only thing on his mind was some pussy so he called his girl Summer.

CHAPTER 4

The Dough Boyz

The next morning had arrived and it was on! On his way to Taylor and JoJo's spot with a half of brick plus six, 24 ounces bagged up in all dimes made him anxious. Making it to his homegirls spot safely, once he arrived, he removed the gee packs from the sports bag and placed them in his safe. 48 grand was his total, he grabbed two gee packs that he planned to take with him to the block. He rolled up a Dutch Master filled with sour and smoked with his two sisters. He never once crossed the line with either of the girls, that's why Summer never argued the fact that he hung with them. Now don't get me wrong both girls were hands down beautiful with bodies to match. Taylor was a light brown skin shorty that stood about 5'6" and weighed about 155 lbs. solid. Breast and ass should have been her middle name because she was stacked. Now JoJo was a drop dead gorgeous 100% Dominican. She was about 135 lbs. and her body were evenly proportioned. Everything was just right on her from her head down to her size 5 ½ feet. Making small talk while they puffed, José almost forgot that he had one more surprise for the girls. They were both the girlie-girlie type but could switch to Cleo from Set It Off in a heartbeat. So, when the two twin compact .380 came out of the sports bag they damn near knocked José down to get their hands on them both. José had grabbed them off Castro just so the girls had a little protection. You never know and José wasn't into taking any chances. The funny thing though, the girls were war ready. They gave off the vibe that a shootout would be just as exciting as having an orgasm so if it happened, they would love it. Crazy, is all José would say about the two.

The girls got ready for work and José hit the block. He was out there earlier than any of the other crew as usual. He beat the high school kids going to their bus stops. As soon as he post up a sale came, it was a 40 sale. He always considered it to be good luck when he made a sale as soon as it came on the block. That was a sign that he would have a good day. To José trapping was his favorite past time, however knowing that he was wheeling and dealing with a brick plus, he went straight into beast mode. He was never the one to compete or fight to earn cash, it normally just came. However, with his new agenda, quota and goal he set for himself it was on! Like usual, he floated through all the Hilltop blocks and made dough but with every fiend, old ones and new ones he had just met, he would pass off his number. He would promote his block, his product, and then slide.

By 9 a.m. the whole squad was in go mode and the block was awake. The normal flow of traffic came plus a few stragglers. Once they took a look at the chunky rock-like substance that resembled peanut butter they knew it was oils! It was crazy how such a little mineral could take a person to deep space nine and have them spending their whole check. José simply embraced it and kept on slingin. The fiends would copp, then 30 minutes later they would return with two or three other people trying to purchase the oils. Most people would normally spend 50 to the least. See, you had junkies robbing, tricks fucking and boosters thieving. With all that going on even the bottom of the barrel kept little cash on their person. Then with the White people from the suburbs who owned their own companies that would take a chance and come into the hood to purchase, it made the Hill a gold mine. I mean, those Crackers would spend on an average day at least three to 500. And if it was a great day, you might run them up to a cool $1500. Now you do the math, three a pop, 10 White fiends, that's three grand plus the locals and stragglers. That's just me! It's about a hundred of me on the Hill baby, in other words, money is the motto! The way things were looking José would be done his first gee pack by noon. By the end of the night, it was possible he could clear five grand. That would be good considering it was all dimes. See, José's way of hustling was simple, his mindset was simple, keep a good product and stay consistent and you wouldn't lose. All drugs from bud to acid sold itself, so as long as you had the gift of gab, the ability to network, and you're a peoples person it should be no problem with you making cash. Now, on the flipside of things, I don't know if the females in the hood had a six sense or what, but I swear for some odd reason that when Carlos came out so did the bitches! I mean it was clear that the bud game was soon to be his. I mean, women from everywhere were talking about the size of the loud sacs on 2nd and Scott. You knew what that meant if the broads were promoting it, that the niggas were sure to follow. Eventually, either two things would have to happen, one, he would have to hire a few workers and do 24-shifts or sell weight. Fuck, he might just have to do both.

Carlos already had bud clientele, then with him being in one spot, he didn't miss a dime that walked through or pulled up in a car looking to grab some green. Carlos was in heaven even though his squad was one and no one was considered the lease just because he sold all the bud, he had all the attention of the bitches, he was the man. By the end of the first night, he had dumped almost 2 ½ pounds. That was just parts of the hill, that wasn't even the whole Westside or the rest of the City of Wilmington. His plan to expand would be happening soon and he couldn't wait. Surprisingly, Dre was the most shocking story of the day. Not really knowing the effects that heroin had taken on the state as a whole we had seriously overlooked the dope game. What a big mistake, that they planned not to make ever again. Between a few players that grabbed a couple of whole sticks on the humbug and the junkies who grabbed their bundles at 25-40, the "d" was flowing.

Dre had sold every single bundle of dope. He had already hollered at José so that he could hit up his connect before the end of the night so that he could be ready for the next day. Dre saw the future and it looked bright and when it was all said and done, he had one person to thank, the mastermind José. Castro was the hit and miss type. He had a spot in New Castle that did a pretty number on a day to day basis, but his main job was security. To put it simple, keep the squad with more artillery than the armed forces.

Later that evening, they all met up at the Batcave. They discussed the days' events and so on. How they would direct all the traffic to the middle of the block, in which they would use the alleyways for quick escapes if needed. Lighting Jacks a nickname for the law hadn't made their presence known so far, but with the constant rush of people moving up-and-down and in and out of the block they were sure to show their badges soon. I mean you know what they say, the more money the more problems and with that being said if they started eating too much out comes the haters. José had made the move needed to ensure that Dre would be straight for the next day. Fat Papi insisted on throwing José another 20 on top of the 20 he had just purchased. He really didn't understand how fast the dope would move and that Fat Papi was just trying to save him a trip back to see him tomorrow. Oblivious to what was going on around him he declined Fat Papi's offer. Making it back to the Batcave and dropping the sticks of dope off to Dre, José was ready to bounce. He called Summer and just like always his girl was on her way.

Thirty minutes later, Summer pulled up bumping to Daddy Yankee, hitting the horn, checking herself out in the rear-view mirror.

"Mami hot," José said leaning over the seat to kiss his girl.

"Hey boo... how was your day?" Summer responded.

"It was jumping... long but jumping!"

"Well, I'm glad you're done for the night because I missed you."

"I missed you too babe... let's go grab something to eat."

"Where you wanna go?" Summer asked.

"Don't know... Shit, let's try the Cheesecake Factory I heard they have some good stuff, plus I gotta taste for some Cheesecake!" Summer smiled at her man and then pulled off.

At the restaurant, the two talked while they waited for their food. The conversation wasn't anything in particular just gossip. Summer did most of the talking, she had the who's and how's on everything. One could sense that she was just glad to be hanging out with her man. The food finally arrived and it looks scrumptious! With all the running around José had done today etiquette was out of the question. The good ol' fashion throwdown and scrape the plate with the dinner roll was the only reasonable solution. Being the skinny fat kid that he was even after devouring his main course with a double cheeseburger on the side, he still made room for a slice of Chocolate Chip Cheesecake. When he finished, he was stuffed. It was only one more thing that could top the night off. Paying the tab and leaving a generous tip like he always did José and Summer exited the restaurant.

In the parking lot while emptying the guts out of his Dutch Master he ran into Strap. No words were exchanged just a stare down and a sly smirk by José. With Summer being with him and Strap being accompanied by two females he figured now wasn't the appropriate time to confront the issue at hand, Summer. Only being 18 and Strap being 10 years his senior he figured it to be pure jealousy because he was a has been who worked for the next man. Unlike José who controlled his own destiny and still had the potential to bubble. If it wasn't that it was plain old lust. I mean, Summer was 18 so she was legal, but a nigga damn near 30 keeps harassing her; it's like he's a stalker. José knew he wasn't about to be going back-and-forth or fist fighting with the nigga over something that was his. So, at that moment knowing the kinda guy Stapp was and the crew he ran with, he made up his mind. He would try to holla at Strap once and pull him up on his disrespect. If anything, other than a mutual understanding occurred he would kill him!

The ride home was silent, he was in deep thought. Summer planned to relax his mind a little. Summer Hernandez was what you would call drop dead gorgeous!!! At 18-years-old the half black and half Dominican beauty was flawless. Inheriting her mother's Dominican traits with fine curly strands, light brown eyes and affluent tongue in the language along with her father's black genes with a smooth chocolate skin tone with the measurements of 36C-26-44 and standing only 5'3" and weighing 140 lbs. she was caliente! To put the icing on the cake she worked as a dental assistant during the day and went to school at the local university studying Geology at night. With the beauty came the brains, Summer was an all-around dime.

When they finally made it to the apartment José was relieved. He couldn't wait to kick the Foam Posites off his feet. Needing some much-needed relaxation he went straight to his room to strip out of his clothes and into his basketball shorts and slippers. José sparked up his Dutchie and surfed through the channels while Summer headed for the shower to unwind a little. On Channel 6 Action News the anchorwoman Sharrie Williams was speaking on the recent spread of the epidemic of heroin in the tri-state region. The effects it has caused in the community and the alarming rise that have councilmembers worried. Statistics are showing that there has been a 15% rise in overdoses from the drug this year. All stemming from the prescription painkiller Percocet that spiraled out of control over the past recent years. Recent seizures by local and federal agents have obtained over $10 million cash in the three neighboring states and over several hundred arrests. Heroin is this new era's drug of choice. José was sadly mistaken about the drug, but after seeing the segment on the news he definitely wanted in! So, caught up in his thoughts he never noticed Summer walk into the room standing butt naked, José almost dropped the Dutch that was between his lips. She seductively walked up to him and then straddled his waist. Wrapping her arms around the back of his neck and placing a sensuous kiss on his lips, she gyrated her hips in a circular motion on his meat stick. He took the privilege of fondling one of her busky breasts in one hand then placing the other one in his thirsty mouth. Soft moans escaped her mouth quietly, all she wanted was for the moisture between her thighs to be pampered. An orgasm or multiple ones were all that was on her mind and she was going to get one! She knew this little antic would have her man hitting that phat ass of hers all night long and possibly until the bird started chirping. He came out of the shorts fast as lightning and laid down on the bed gently but didn't waste a second diving face first into her sweet tasting fruit basket. Her moans became louder as the seconds passed. She locked her soft thickness around his neck and closed her eyes as his tongue flickered across her clit continuously and rhythmically causing her to gush in his mouth. That was only the first nut of the night and she wanted more. Being the freak that he was, he turned her over onto her hands and knees and sucked her pussy from the back causing her to start bucking her phat ass up against his face. Soon she was arching her back and busting off in his mouth again. Summer is what you would call a creamer, her nut was thick, white, and creamy. At the sight of it, that sent José into pro-mode; he lifted her up and guided her slowly down onto his thick and throbbing meat stick. She was so wet and her swollen lips were so sensitive that she finally got all of José's 10 ½ inches to the bottom and she was cumming again! She started slowly but then began bouncing that ass up and down faster and harder. José gripped both cheeks to go in as deep as he could. His thrust became more powerful from the bottom as they looked into each other's eyes. Summer's ride game was awesome but when she was horny words couldn't describe that nana. José confessed many of times that Summer's hole was a perfect fit. Being caught up in the moment he got a little aggressive and pushed her from off top of him. Hurrying to get in her favorite position face down ass up, she couldn't wait for poppie to enter her from behind. He gripped his shaft and pushed his way into her love hole in one swift motion. Her moans were soft and angelic, beautiful and powerful described how he thought he was making love to Whitney Houston the way Summer was singing with passion. His strokes started modestly but then more forcefully they came. Pounding away into a land of bliss sweat began to steadily drip from his muscular chest down between her chocolate ass-crack. At the sight of seeing her fluffy ass bounce and roll like an ocean wave José was on the verge of busting but he withheld. Losing track of her nut count and wanting her boo to get his after hitting that G-spot for a good 45 minutes she reached under and back then started lightly tapping his ball-sac. She knew that would do the job as he repeatedly long stroked her hole; as juices were flying and he was now grunting. Grabbing hold of her hips as he entered the final moments he pulled on her hair, smacked her ass hard and bit down on his bottom lip. A light drop of blood he could taste, just as she was cumming for the umpteenth time he released stream after stream of warm creamy seed into his wifey. Loving the episode that just took place they laid in each other's embrace. José sparked his bud and took a few puffs while he rubbed his girl soft ass. Before he knew it, he was slowly getting erect again, round two!

Across town on the Northside of the city Market Street was live as hell! Blocks were in full swing and the playas and hoes were out. Traffic was backed up for a good three blocks, systems were cranked up to high velocity and rims were shining. The bitches were definitely choosing and they had their eyes on one team in particular. The Dough Boyz were a team of young rich niggas who operated under the watchful eye of Amin Wiggins a.k.a. Strap. Strap was a mid-level drug pusher who moved about two bricks a week on the Northside. At one point before he caught a four-year prison term at James T. Vaughn Correctional Institute, he was a heavyweight. Back then, him and his then right-hand man King had a plug with some Albanian mobsters who flooded them with more than enough cocaine to supply the whole northern part of Wilmington. Money was made fast and power was gained but his downfall came when unlike King who was cool, calm, and dangerous Strap ran things with an iron fist. He instilled fear into people which soon lead to a two-month investigation. One evening while making drops around the city the local vice squad swarmed his Range Rover and recovered 126 grams of powder cocaine. With that being his second violent felony, the first for possessing a firearm by a person prohibited he was sentenced to six years in prison. Earning good time released him back to the streets in four. While he was bidding, King had found a Mexican connect and expanded his empire enormously. He was no longer local nor did he directly deal with the guys from his hood anymore. But when Strap touched, he did what close friends do, watch the fuck out! Giving him money, clothes, and cars, it wasn't long before Strap wanted back in. King not thinking twice gave his friend five bricks, Strap's failed attempt to move them was of no worry since he was just getting started King thought. After two more failed attempts and a lost almost 15 bricks total instead of killing his childhood friend, he sat him down and talked to him seriously. The end result, Strap taking his last 20 grand and copping a brick off his friend. Since then, he's been maintaining a cool two to three bricks a week. With a three-man team including himself, his team was doing good. With the money once again came the arrogance that all the bitches loved but the niggas hated. The Dough Boyz were the most talked about crew in town and Amin Wiggins a.k.a. Strap was the main topic.

CHAPTER 5

The Crime Scene

"Boss look what we have over here," Detective Chad Stevens said.

"Looks like the entry wound is in the back of the head… execution style."

"Have you found anything?" asked Senior Detective Steven Baldwin.

"Nothing… no forced entry… can't call it a home invasion… seems like they walked right through the front door."

"It doesn't make sense, the child was killed, but for what? Wrong place wrong time is the only other reason I can think of," Detective Baldwin spoke while intently scanning the crime scene.

"Hey Boss, take a look at this," one of the uniformed officers called out to Detective Baldwin from an upstairs bedroom, "while looking around I discovered this Macy's shopping bag and these sneaker boxes… this looks to be 2 ½ bricks of cocaine and from what I see right there with those two boxes of hundreds and those two all fifty's that has to be close to 300 large!" The uniform officer said like he had just cracked the case. What he failed to realize was finding the money and drugs wasn't cracking the case, finding the killer was.

"Bingo! Now we have a clue of why those two victims are dead," Baldwin said.

"Why would they kill the kid though Boss?" asked Detective Stevens.

"It could have been numerous reasons… one, maybe they weren't wearing mask… no witnesses left behind, or they were just cold-blooded killers," Baldwin spoke solemn, "the only people I know that's ruthless enough to wipe out a 13-year-old kid is Zy'Kim Harris and Anthony Jones a.k.a. Rakmeef and Twink!"

"Who's that boss?" asked a curious Detective Stevens.

"Two scumbags I've been trying to take down for at least a half a dozen or so bodies that I know of!" Baldwin snapped, "I want you to get on Deljis find those two guys most current addresses and put an all-points bulletin out for them too... If nothing else, we'll at least get to question those two assholes. And if they didn't have anything to do with it, they'll be fine."

Detective Baldwin had a good feeling that his gut was pointing him in the right direction. Now all he had to do was find Rakmeef and Twink. When law enforcement officers couldn't find their suspects, they turn to the streets and went to their trusted informants. Ramone was a dope shooting, coke sniffing fiend who would do anything to get his next fix. He went as low as fucking men in the ass to get high. He was a gay junkie and Detective Baldwin really despised the low life. But dealt with him because he seems to have the lowdown on any and everything from who was selling, thieving and shooting. He was reliable, he helped crack a gun ring that nabbed 150 guns. Getting a 150-assault rifles off the streets got Baldwin the promotion to Lieutenant and Senior Detective. Now he was looking for Ramone to find out his latest issue, the double murder. It wouldn't be hard to find him either, he normally roamed the Franklin Street area. This being the spot that the fiends call Dope Man Heaven. The biggest supply of heroin could be found in this section of the city. Franklin Street was on the Westside, the Hilltop to be exact. Knowing he couldn't just roll up and talk with Ramone, Baldwin would jump out, frisk him down, and then secretly tell him to call him by nights end. Ramone would play unwilling but always seem to call. They always met somewhere on the outskirts of the city. This time he had him meet up at a Seasons Pizza Parlor about five miles outside of the city on Marilyn Avenue. Sliding into the booth at the back of the restaurant Ramone scanned the dimly lit joint just to make sure he wasn't being watched or followed. Not waiting to be offered a slice Ramone quickly snatched a slice of the vegetarian pizza off the tray and gobbled it down without catching a breath in between.

"So, what's up Baldwin? What's new on the agenda?" Ramone asked wiping the crumbs from the corners of his mouth.

"Same ol' same ol'… looking into that double murder that happened two weeks ago on Clayton Street. I have my suspicions but that's about it right now."

"Let me guess… if I'm accurate, a double murder execution style, a little boy and no evidence. The only people that are brutal and good enough in your mind is Rakmeef and Twink," Ramone said chomping into his second slice within a matter of minutes.

"Correct, I just can't prove it yet, but when I do these assholes are going down… so I need you to hit the streets hard and find something out for me. If you can do that, I'll give you a hefty allowance this time around."

Ramones eyes twinkled at the sound of a hefty allowance. Detective Baldwin would normally give Twink between two and three hundred dollars. So, he figured this info could earn him at least five big ones. That's not including the $50,000 reward that the victim's family was offering. This could be Ramones big break, he just had to find out something that could implement the two goons or find the killers responsible. Before leaving the restaurant, Detective Baldwin slid Ramone a crisp 20 across the table and then reminded him to keep in touch.

Jesenia and Glady ran their early morning errands as usual. Stopping at the Krispy Kreme doughnut shop to grab a half a dozen glazed donuts and coffee first. Next, they would drop the kids off at daycare and preschool afterward. After their motherly duties were taken care of for the morning, they would then go to the grocery store, laundromat and the pharmacy for their mother. The two sisters were quite, conservative and alluring. Being twins made things more animated when people especially men saw the two 23-year-olds in public. They would lust first and then fall in love with the two Puerto Rican goddesses. Being identical in every sense of the words from head, waist, ass, and feet to even weighing the same you'd never tell the two apart unless you were family. The two could have easily been mistaken for the Urban supermodel Elba Everlasting. Men tried every trick in the book to get their attention, money, clothes, cars, and jewels. Some even went as far as trying to fly the two out of the country on vacation numerous times. What these guys didn't know was that Jesenia and Glady were accustomed to the finer things anyway. Their family was affluent and very dangerous! They had adapted to the family's ways and now the two sisters had achieved a level of comfortably that most men and women dream of.

When the sisters first came to Delaware, they frequently surveyed the area. After visiting a few Spanish and Mexican salsa clubs, then a couple of upscale clubs that cater to the White college kids and businessmen it was time to put their plan into motion. After about six months of moving and shaking the Twins were moving 3 to 5 thousand pills a month apiece from Perc 10s, 15s, and 30s to Zanex, Tramadol, and Oxycodone. They even pushed ecstasy but only from ladies night on Thursday to club night on

Saturday. They had the pill game on lock in both New Castle and Kent counties. They even had people coming from as far as Sussex county to copp. The sisters had the whole state and were good. With money seeming to be the girl's main priority the only thing that tends to distract the two mami's were young pretty thugs. They loved younger guys around the age of 19 or 20 with that pretty boy swag. They fell for them every time.

After running the errands, they stopped to get some gas. They both saw the two thugs at the same time and both hollered Damn!!! Hopping out of the Acura TL like two twin Video Vixens they knew all eyes were on them except for the four eyes of the two young thugs. The youngins simply glanced over at the two bombshells and kept it moving. Not being used to being rejected especially since coming to Delaware they both put a little more strut in their step like they were on the catwalk. It worked; the two thugs zoomed in on the phat asses then moved in like two timber wolves stalking their prey.

"Senorita," the two thugs said at the same damn time.

"Ay poppie," the girl's said to them smiling from ear to ear.

"Let me talk to y'all for a minute if that's okay?" replied the short stocky one.

"Which one?" Glady asked.

"I mean y'all twins... I guess it really don't matter."

"It does matter... I mean, we are twins, but we do have different personalities."

"Twins and I'm kind of the upbeat type, how bout me and you get acquainted sexy."

"A'ight... I'm feeling that... but behind all that thickness there has to be a name so what's yours?"

"Carlos... and yours?"

"Glady... and this is my little sister Jesenia."

"How's that ya little sister and y'all twins?"

"Because I was born four minutes before her that's why."

"Oh... okay sounds good to me."

"So, who's ya friend? Ya brother or something... and why is he so quiet? What, he scared of my sister? She won't bite plus she likes tall dark men."

"Shut up Glady," said Jesenia embarrassed that her sister had just exposed her hand so soon.

"Nah, he ain't my brother... he Latino though, he Dominican... that's my man Dre... and trust me he ain't never scared. Your sister might not be ready for a seasoned vet like my boy. You know what they say, Dominican men are the freakiest men on earth," Carlos said chuckling a little.

"Never known for being the bashful type Dre gently grabbed Jesenia's hand and led her away from Glady and Carlos. She excepted the invitation and followed him to a more discreet location where they could get to know each other better.

After the introductions were done, they all exchanged numbers and planned to meet up with each other that upcoming weekend. The Twins were ecstatic that they had met two handsome well-groomed Latino men. Since coming to Delaware they've been all about business, but these two pretty thugs had somehow broken the barrier in two ways. One, they would be the first to get a chance to entertain the Twins from out of Delaware. Two, they were the first two poppies to give them that pulsing sensation between their legs in a whole year!

The elderly woman with 20/70 vision due to her advanced stage of Uveitic Glaucoma scanned through the Delaware News Journal local section hoping to catch up on the city's current events. Sipping on a fresh batch of Folgers out of her world's number one Abuela coffee mug that she received years ago on Mother's Day from her grandchildren, Priscilla Reyes waited patiently for the rest of her family to arrive. The meeting she had arranged today normally took place after the family dinner that was held every Sunday evening. Due to a sudden increase in a few of the products that they were moving and word floating around about unwanted investigation things had to be addressed and quickly. Plus, she wanted info on this guy who pulled a gun out on her son Alex. One thing Priscilla did not play was someone threatening her kids that meant grandchildren and all. As time passed by everyone had finally shown up to their mother's main house except the two youngest who were out doing Lord knows what. Deciding not to hold everyone hostage while waiting for her daughters she started the meeting.

"Good morning everyone, I know this is a spur of the moment meeting, but things are happening and it needs our attention immediately. A few things first, our shipment of snow has been up to 25 squares a week now and our manteca shipment is also being up to 15 squares a week. The reason being, Edwin has been dealing with some guys in Chestertown Maryland who have constantly been purchasing 5 to 10 squares of snow a week. That's at least 20 extra squares a month to the least. And Alex and Hector have been and have finally negotiated a deal with the Garcia family back in Redding to supply them with at least 25 to 30 squares a month of a manteca. All the other operations seem to be moving steadily however, I'm kind of worried about the mushrooms and acid cash flow. Remember, all money isn't good money. And since we've journeyed into these uncharted waters we've been seeing and dealing with those fucking spoiled little White brats. They come and buy these drugs that they really can't handle and then they go back to their neighborhoods and commit heinous crimes such as murder, rape, and arson. When they are asked why they did it, they blame it on the drugs. Which in turn, points back to us which then starts the investigation which none of us need. Remember, we have these little ones to look after so one mistake could cost us a whole lot."

"Mama. how do you know that we're being watched?" Chomo asked.

"I have my sources... just like I have people that watch y'all I have people watching this block and they're saying that on numerous occasions they've seen unmarked vehicles sitting a few blocks away. White guys in plainclothes with binoculars watching, unfamiliar White girls' trying to buy snow and all sorts of work vans suddenly have appeared. Just keep your eyes open, be smart and use common sense and we should all be fine. Why haven't Silva and Yari finished those bales of smoke yet? Alex, I told you to oversee them because they're too kind-hearted."

"Mama, they actually just finished them a few days ago. I have Solongel helping them get more acquainted with the right people."

"Who's Solongel, Alex?"

"Oh, I'm sorry mama... Bunny."

"Oh okay, that's good just watch over them."

"I will mama."

"So, what's this I hear about this asshole pulling a gun on you Alex?"

"Mama. I don't know the puto was selling on our territory and when I saw it, I went to approach him," Alex said with his strong Spanish accent.

"Alex, how did you approach him? And do not lie to me."

"Uh... you know mama, I just went to talk."

"But?" Priscilla added.

"I grabbed a 4 by 4 board from the trash and stormed his way," Alex said knowing his mother wouldn't approve of his approach.

"Alex, how many times have I told you about approaching situations in this manner... you're so quick to react and so slow to think shoot! I think I'm gonna take you off of block patrol permanently," Priscilla said sternly.

"But mama," Alex pouted.

"No buts... I told you time after time to curb your attitude and you still want to do things your way. You're just like your father, hardheaded. Alex what you do not understand this is not PA. You don't know whose territory you're on. Just because we moved in without any problems doesn't mean that this wasn't being occupied. Have you ever wondered why this one block generated so much cash flow so quickly? Not because we came in with the product because after doing my research this block was one of Wilmington's most lucrative blocks at one time. Once a block is known for business even if it dies down a little it only takes a little boost to get it moving again," Priscilla spoke like giving a history course on urban wealth and finances, "so what do we know about this guy? Who is he and where is he from?" Priscilla inquired.

"Mama I don't know anything about the man all I remember is the huge scar on the left side of his face and him telling me that it was time for my family to relocate."

The rest of the family sad quietly they could see that their mother was about to blow a fuse and they didn't want to be nowhere around. Their mother was old, but she could be demonic if pushed to the limit.

"You mean to tell me that you anger so easily and you're ready to whack someone upside the head so quickly, possibly kill them too but almost a week later you don't know anything... you're a Fucking runaway train and I'm bringing it to a halt right now!! You are relieved of all your family duties, business affairs, and financial earnings until this "Maricon" is a dead man." Priscilla said as she slammed down her fist to end the discussion.

Alex lowered his head in defeat. He knew better than to try and go back and forth with his mother. Edwin and Chomo were to oversee Alex's dealings until he handled the situation at hand. Hector being a human Presa Canario was put in charge of block patrol for the meantime. Block patrol was the overseer of the block, security for the safe and stash houses, and most importantly the security of the kids and Queen Priscilla. Yari raised her hand and waited to be called upon.

"Yes, dear?" Priscilla questioned

"Mama, apparently Ashlee who lives up the street said she was out there the day the guy did that to Alex. She said she knew him and that he was some crazy dude named Ivan from a few blocks away. She said it he's dangerous and deals with some serious guys that deals a lot of product throughout the city. Apparently, this used to be his place of business but now he's all over the place. She said the only thing that will come out of this mama is a war, bloodshed, and casualties."

Priscilla had to think quick but wisely. A master at the game she played, she refused to lose. Focusing her attention back to her son Alex, she spoke.

"How is it that your sister who wasn't involved in this confrontation has more intel on this guy than you? How is it that after a week you haven't been out looking for him? Because you let your anger put you in a situation that you're really scared to face. Now what you're going to do since you put me and my grandchildren in harm's way, you're gonna call Ellé. Ellé was Priscilla's oldest, who handled the finances and ran the family businesses. Whenever the call was made Ellé would book flights for the entire family to go away to Puerto Rico for a week or so. That was enough time to handle whatever needed to be handled.

"Tell her we're going on vacation but you Alex will stay back to handle your business. And if you can't handle it by the time, I get back I just might have to call Amillio." Priscilla finished speaking then got up out of the chair and then left the room.

Alex was fuming! He had to find this son of a bitch fast before Amillio and his wrecking crew came to Wilmington and caused an all-out war! The first person he called was Bunny, he knew if anyone knew this dude Ivan she would. She practically knew the whole city! After a few moments of conversing Alex knew more about this Ivan guy. But he was also informed that any dealings other than business would be somewhat of a foolish move. Bunny made it clear that she wanted no part of the situation. She knew better, Ivan's reputation for beating murders and shootings stem back to the middle of the 90s. Maybe that's because she secretly knew Ivan's ties to Angelina and knew that Angelina's political connects ran deep in the state of Delaware. Bunny never mentioned Angelina's name once throughout the whole conversation. Choosing her battle wisely and not really knowing the extremity of the beef that's cooking up in the streets, at that exact moment Bunny decided it would be best to distance herself from Alex a little. She knew that money would still blow her phone up for the bud, so she needed to link with a playa that could get her at least 20 pounds a week at the same price or better. The only person that came to mind off hand was this new dude who had been trying to holla at her for a while. He was real laid back, quiet, and discreet but he was getting major paper! From what Bunny knew, the one time she went to chill with him she was impressed. At first, she took him to be involved in corporate America. He was clean-cut, wore fitted jeans, and a Polo button-up minus the jewelry that would give off that the person was a flashy big shot. He had mediocre written all over his face. But when they pulled up to his four-bedroom, two car garage home with an Audi A-8, and a new S-500 Mercedes Benz parked in the driveway she became curious. A little investigation and tour of his mancave resulted in finding out that he had no children and was in no relationship, that was a huge plus! Then the array of jewelry sprawled across his dresser and jewelry chest that looked to cost well over a hundred plus grand, she finally asked what his profession was. One of three things entered her mind, he either was an executive in corporate which she hoped for, a party promoter or he was involved in the music industry. The latter two she opposed due to the enormous amount of women he would've had to deal with. Bunny wasn't going to be played or end up on this niggas thot list. She was completely wrong about the six-foot one brown skin gentleman.

Without answering her question, he took her the hand then led her to a customized wine cellar he had built just after he bought the house. Before entering the wine cellar, he asked her not to look at him differently once she saw what she was about to see. Once he opened the door to the climate-controlled room he instantly burst into laughter after seeing Bunny's expression. Her jaw had damn near dropped to the floor! She was in awe! She was staring at a room about the size of a jail cell that was filled to capacity with several types of exotic weeds. It had to be at least a ton and a half. This man had all this at 26, he was a major plug in the bud game and moved to Delaware from North Philly to change sceneries. And this is who she was going to contact, MacLaden from North Philly!

CHAPTER 6

Sammy and Angelina

Angelina was busy ringing up a customer at the register when Sammy walked in to start his shift.

Buena's dias... como estas," Angelina spoke

"Bien, bien... y tu," Sammy replied.

Around the store they only spoke Español it was a form of tradition to embrace their culture. Every now and then the neighborhood kids come to hang out with Sammy, Angelina, Ivan, and Noel. When it wasn't too busy, being the loving person that she was, she would pull out her little marker board and teach the Black kids Spanish and the few White kids in the neighborhood how to read and write Spanish. All it took was a little hug and smile for the kids who didn't receive them from their own parents at home, a good home cooked Spanish meal like patellon and a whole bunch of juice and snacks to have most of the kids visiting Angelina's once a week. Angela didn't mind though she loved kids and only wanted the best for all of them.

Ivan and Noel hadn't yet arrived, which made Angelina a little uneasy. Though she was a kind-hearted woman the heroin and crack epidemic had some of the most upright people turn into downright crooks over the years. That was the main reason her husband hired Ivan and Noel to protect his wife at all costs. Their undisclosed amount had to be a nice penny with both guys living on the riverfront in the luxury condos. Though outwardly Sammy was never inquired, but inwardly he wondered what other businesses Angelina was into. I mean, over the years he has been to her house a few times that was marvelous! It was an eight-bedroom, Victorian style pad with two movie theaters and an inground pool. Along with other amenities that would have Angelina's house showcased on an episode of Lifestyles of the Rich and Famous. Not to mention over the years, her expensive taste in luxury cars from Jaguars to Maserati's. All this from one corner store on the Westside of Wilmington. She had to own more than just one store. Whatever she did had Angelina in a position to make it possible for others to see financial gain and she wouldn't like to have it no other way. Still, with no sign of her two bodyguards, it showed that Angelina was beginning to become worried. See, today the New York deliveries were coming, beings though he wasn't allowed in the basement it would complicate matters. When other distribution trucks came throughout the week Sammy could help unload but that was it. He would bring the boxes in the store and Ivan and Noel would take it from there. But on Monday and Thursdays when the New York trucks pulled up he had strict orders not to bother with unloading. Now that Ivan and Noel were absent, he could tell that Angelina was on edge. Just as a customer was walking out the air brakes from the delivery truck could be heard.

"Shit!" Angelina snapped.

"What's wrong? You know I don't mind handling that for you boss," Sammy offered.

"I know but..."

Just when Angelina was about to start explaining her situation to Sammy the delivery driver walked in. The driver spoke to her in a low tone then began walking out. Angelina had locked eyes on Sammy and began heading directly towards him. As she rubbed her hands together feverishly, she began speaking Spanish to Sammy. But before she could go into detail in walked Ivan and Noel looking apologetic. Angelina gracefully smiled at

Sammy and turned around rapidly and start cursing the two idiots out in Spanish for being tardy. After her brief tongue lashing and erratic hand gestures to show her signs of disapproval she went right back to her kind, patient, and loving self. She went back behind the counter while Ivan and Noel went to retrieve the boxes from the truck.

Sammy had been working for Angelina for years now and she wanted to tell him the truth but then rationalize with herself and concluded that the less he knew the better off he was. I mean, he made 16 dollars an hour, he worked 12-hour shifts, five days a week. So, he made great money to be a cashier, bagger, stock boy, and janitor. She knew that he was saving to get his mother a house out of the hood one day and she would be a silent backer. Plus, he received a check so he could file taxes at the end of the year. As far as anyone was concerned Sammy had a legitimate job working for Angelina.

The day went on and the flow of traffic was steady. Ivan and Noel were running errands for Angelina all day while she played phone tag all day. Missing and making calls, arranging appointments, then running back-and-forth from her office to the basement all day. Mondays, Thursdays, and Fridays especially on the 1st and the 15th we were the busiest. That's when Sammy basically ran the store himself.

By the end of the night, everyone would be tired as hell. Just like usual they will pull the gates down while all three stood as guards, guns in holsters watching their surroundings.

Afterwards they would offer Sammy a ride, he would decline, and they would part ways. The night breeze was so lovely, so Sammy opted to walk a different way home. Walking through his hood he felt safe always plus the fact that from the age of 8 to 16 Sammy trained and went on to become a Golden Gloves Champion. The whole hood knew that and knew he could cause havoc real fast if provoked so they left the 21-year-old well-mannered youngin alone. Walking down the block and noticing the huge crowd of guys Sammy thought wisely and began to cross the street until he heard his name being called.

"Sammy! Yo Sammy!"

He turned to see who it was that was calling his name. He still hadn't seen who it was until the figure stepped from out the crowd. His younger brother had the whole crowd around him. José was in the midst of the action. Sammy should have known, the only time he ever really got stopped on his way home was whenever his younger brother spotted him. Never getting the chance to see his brother as often as he wanted because of his work hours and José's involvement in the streets so whenever he ran into him, he would stop and kick it.

"What's up, bro?" José said happy to see his brother.

"Chilling, just getting off work… bout to head home."

"Is mom and Felix okay?"

"Yeah, of course... but you should stop by a little more, you know she's worried about you out here."

"I know papa... I just been so busy lately I've let myself get sidetracked a little."

"It's cool, you know I'm gonna hold it down though."

"That I do know," José said seriously.

"I see you took Felix to the barbershop too... who cut his hair that line is sharp! I might need to go see homie."

"I took him to see Malley at His Image on Lancaster Ave., he nice, he's the one that's been dicing my shit," José said posing a little.

"Why you give that boy that chain? He ain't took it off since he got it. He wants to wear it to school but ma won't let him. She scared he might lose it."

"It was a gift... you know that's my lil man."

"Yo where you get those kicks, the fly as hell?" Sammy inquired.

"What these? Oh, these the new Kobe Bryant's they just came out... you like them?"

"Yeah, they soft." José went in his pocket then peeled off a buck fifty and handed it to his brother.

"Nah, I'm good José," Sammy said refusing to take the money.

"What, you're my bro... this shit ain't about nothing, money comes and goes. Now go to Sports Connection in Adam Four Shopping Center and get yourself a pair. Just don't get the same color papa!"

"You sure José?"

"Look, man you're my brother, I gave Felix the chain and I'm giving you the money for a pair of sneaks it's no big deal.... but what's up with the house for ma, we still on for the end of the month?"

"Yeah, if you gonna be ready... I'm just about ready," stated Sammy.

"I'll definitely be ready... I can't wait to see ma's face when you give her the keys to her own house and her own land."

"I know, she'll probably cry... oh before I forget, she wants you to stop by for dinner this Sunday... she wants you to bring Summer too. She needs a female presence around; I think she's tired of us guys always around."

"You just gave me an idea Sammy! I'm gonna have Summer take ma on a little outing Sunday morning. Maybe to the mall that'll be good!"

"That'll definitely make her day bro." While they were talking a fiend walked up.

"José you got me for a buck twenty," the anxious fiend stuttered.

"Hold on bro," José told Sammy then turned his back to make the drug transaction.

The fiend hurried away clinching his palm tightly. José turned back to Sammy and could see the look of concern on his brothers face.

"Bro I'm straight... stop worrying, you and ma scare me sometimes when y'all worry so much," José said jokingly.

"I know man, I just wish you could do something different... you remember what happened to papa... ma would be crushed if something happened to you out here."

At the thought of his father, José became silent. He was only 10 when his father was killed but he remembered all the details about his death. The mood was solemn for the moment then José broke the silence.

"Look, bro I'm good and well protected," he said lifting his shirt exposing the handle to his torch, "but forget all that right now I only get to chill with you once and a while and since Hell will probably freeze over before we hang out again. What we drinkin'?"

"What?" Sammy asked.

"What... are... we... drinking?" Joss repeated slow and retarded like.

"Nah, I'm good."

"Nigga you drinkin'... now what you drinkin' is the question. Look after you drink this bottle with me then you can slide... deal."

"A'ight... but what's new?"

"You got Cîroc, Belaire, and Crown Royal Apple and we can still get your favorite Bombay Sapphire."

"You remember that?"

"Yeah... but for real, I've been fucking with this new champagne called Branson B. Cuvée... the shits light but it'll creep up on you plus you can still function in the am... Mr. Workman.

"A'ight lets get that, but after I drink it, I gotta be heading home to make sure ma and Felix are good."

"A'ight." Sammy threw his arm around his younger brothers shoulder and they walked to Tony's liquor on 4th Street while chit chatting like brothers do.

The portable ghetto blaster pumped Yo Gotti's classic album "I Am" out of its speakers bringing life to the rather dull city block. At 8:30 a.m. the only life outside on the Eastside were the low class, single parent mothers heading to there just above average places of employment. Struggle was evident on the Eastside. The rowhomes were cluttered together, barely able to be identified by someone unfamiliar with the area. The widespread of drugs and guns plagued the community as well as young girls having babies early as 13. That just made it harder for their mothers who were probably only in their late 20s themselves. Babies having babies was the saying that quickly gained attention throughout the urban areas worldwide. With all that could be said about the Eastside of Wilmington, the one unanimous thing that the city residents were certain of was that the Eastside was the home of two vicious mothafuckas named Rakmeef and Twink. Rakmeef sat on the stoop eyeing the block in both directions. Not really the hustling type I guess he just really didn't have the patience for it. But with all the work they accumulated during their heist it had to be sold. Making it damn near impossible to resist, they stuffed every bag and sold the weight for some of the lowest prices in the city. Even though their hustle may have only been part-time the junkies still dealt with them. Either because of how good most of the product they were getting was or they just feared the two goons. Whichever reason it may have been they both still seen paper. The only downside with Rakmeef and Twink's hustle was with all the people they had robbed and possibly killed they were always on high alert and playing cat and mouse. Rumors linger that they had over a half dozen contracts on their heads but whenever someone came to cash the check they always seem to escape with their lives and the assailants turned up dead. With so many attempts on their lives, they didn't trust a soul and always kept a torch on them. Now, to make matters worse, the word around the way was that the law was looking for the two of them. They found this out through a couple of people who have been stopped and questioned by the Vice squad. Not to mention, earlier this week while driving back to their old trap house they witnessed themselves the S.W.A.T Team, armored truck in all kick in the front door to the pad. Good thing the place was clean, the only thing in the house was two beds, living room set, TV, Xbox, and electric the bare necessities. They quickly grabbed another pad on Pine Street and rented another spot in Fairfax to stash the product and guns. With that, everything was back to dream chasing. They could only imagine what the law wanted. They probably got a tip about one of the bodies, but most of them were done with no witnesses. So, it's either a tip was dropped or their just being harassed. Whatever it was they wouldn't find out until they were caught and that just wasn't in the plans.

Twink was upstairs getting his dick sucked by one of the neighborhood thots while Rakmeef sold weed, coke, and dope. See the Eastside was closer to Downtown Wilmington closer than any other side of town, so everyone from lawyers to teachers would go to the Eastside to grab the drug of their liking.

While making one of his numerous sells, a thick chocolate brown eye amazon who looked to be in the medical field from the skintight neon pink scrubs she was wearing approached him. She was bad! Shorty had to be a good 5'11" and weighed a good 165 lbs., the only problem was he had never ever seen her before. So, her reason for approaching him still was uncertain. That was until she went into her shirt pocket and pulled out two crisp 20s.

"You gotta 8th of loud?"

"Yeah, I got you sexy," replied Rakmeef.

"Okay good, cause I have to take a piss bad... Shit! I can't hold it, I gotta go. Is it alright if I go in one of these alleyways?"

"Shit, I don't give a Fuck... go in this one, that's my alley."

"Well, can you show me the way, cause I don't wanna get caught."

"Yeah, no problem plus, I gotta go back there to get the bud anyway."

Rakmeef pointed to a spot in the corner of the alley while he retrieved the bud. Shorty who was far from shy dropped her pants quickly exposing a phat soft looking chocolate heart-shaped ass. She glanced back at Rakmeef cracking a little smile while teasing him by shaking her ass from side to side a little. Caught in the heat of the moment, Rakmeef grabbed his dick that was quickly getting harder by the second then gave a crooked smile. Now, he remembered that he didn't even know shorty and that he was slipping. It was too late! The barrel of the gun was tapping the back of his head. The Amazon pulled her pants up walked over to where Rakmeef was standing then kissed his lips softly. She then stepped back to see the look in his eyes. He knew he was dead. Then she grabbed the bud out of his hand, placed the money in his pocket and grabbed a handful of his dick.

"Um, we might have to fuck him on the other hand," said the amazon. Then from behind him, laughter occurred, then a slap to the back of the head. Rakmeef flinched then turned around to see is young girl Bree.

"I got ya bitch ass… caught you slipping nigga," Bree said jokingly.

"Nah, not really," Rakmeef said nodding his head signaling her to turn around.

There stood Twink with two .45 calibers pointed directly at Bree and her girl with a smile on his face.

"What's popping lil nigga?" Twink asked.

Bree is what you would call a dyke/butch. She was a woman who acts and dress like a man. She loved the same sex and flaunted her many trophies around the way. Men of all ages envied her because of her skill to pull some of the baddest bitches and have them open off her tongue. They never tried anything stupid though because Bree was a shooter simple and plain. She will kill you and get away with it and since she was knee-high following behind her cousin Twink, she's been a menace. She's been dying to get down with Rakmeef and Twink for years, but they refused to put her in the line of fire. She's what you would call an ace in a hole, if they ever really need her, she'll be on standby.

"Who ya girl tho?" asked Rakmeef.

"She gotta mouth ask her... but you ain't hitting that, that's my pussy nigga," Bree said.

"Shit, we family we can share," Rakmeef said looking the Amazon in the eyes seductively.

"Nigga you're too aggressive... you wanna knock her walls down and all that extra shit. You gotta learn to be gentle with the pussy, nurture it like an infant," Bree spoke.

"Nah, you gotta tighten your abs and squeeze ya ass cheeks together and push that warm, thick mothafucka all the way up in her until it touches the bottom and she started squirting and shaking," Rakmeef said still eyeing the Amazon.

"Um, Um, Um, it sounds good, but this cookie will definitely have to be eaten before you ever get to feel how wet this pond is. Then once you get it, after the first few times you're gonna want to knock this soft ass up and all that other boogie shit that follows... oh yeah, my name is Nyomi."

"Yeah, well newsflash shorty, me and my man "Black mamba," Rakmeef said grabbing his dick, "ain't in the business of playing house or having kids... so miss me with the bullshit."

"I sense some sort of competition!" Bree said instigating.

"This pussy is fat, wet, and ready for war," Nyomi said grabbing Rakmeef's hand pulling him towards the house.

"Let's go... this is the type of morning that has a playa creating new tricks and going for the gold," Rakmeef said palming both of Nyomi's soft round ass cheeks in his hands.

Twink and Bree post in the alley smoking a swisher sweet filled with LA Confidential. They laughed at their two friends for the way they went about seducing each other. But really found it funny how the whole episode was set up by Bree. She knew Rakmeef, he was like a brother, so she knew he had a thing for chocolate drops. So, she knew once he saw Nyomi he would bite! She was cheesing with her hair in disarray while Rakmeef stood in the doorway shirtless and smiling. Once again, he had prevailed!

CHAPTER 7

Get Paper!

Almost two weeks had passed and the squad was doing what they had set out to do and that was get paper! The first flip was a good one. It took about 10 days to flip the brick of crack, but they had to re-up at least three times on the bud and damn near every day of the heroin. After shorts and play money, they were left with 128 grand. They would have had a lot more for the extra flips, but they paid Fat Papi and Bunny what they owed them.

It was time to re-up again and to be sure they wouldn't have to keep returning to purchase more work he was going to grab heavy this time around. He had already discussed with Fat Papi the price for the whole brick and he would give it to José for 25 grand. José was sure he was grabbing two of them for 50 gees plus, he wanted to take a chance on the dope and copp up, so he decided to get 200 sticks. That would put his total at 68 grand and if he could get Bunny to give him 10 lbs. for 22 grand things would be straight especially if she still throws 10 on top of that. The squad's stash was now at 28 grand but after this flip, all should be well. José made his move more anxious than he was the first time, he put the call into Fat Papi.

"Yo dimelo," spoke Fat Papi

"Yo que tas pasando?" José inquired.

"Tranquillo."

"Yo toy ready."

"Tan rapido!"

"Ya tu sabe... que toy siendo!"

"Tato pue que nesescita."

"Nesescito dos plato y que tas pasando con los otro?" José inquired.

"Ya tu sabe tato bien!" Fat Papi replied.

"Ta bien pue voyahora." José hung up from Fat Papi then immediately called Bunny.

"Dime."

"Que tas pasando fea?"

"Tu sabe, fea no soy!" Bunny shot back.

"Nah, beautiful I'm just playing but I need you though."

"What's good poppie?"

"Nesecito diez por venty-dos."

"Well, I've been dealing with this dude from North Philly and I can get them for you for 18 apiece. If you grabbin' 10 or less, but I can get them for 15 if you grab 20 or more."

"Well, get me 12 then... he probably ain't throwing nothing on top yet huh?"

"Probably not, but I'll definitely let him know that you can move it and see where it goes from there. Well, I am more than certain he's gonna fuck with you off the strength so when are you gonna be ready?" Bunny questioned.

"Whenever you are," José replied.

"Alright, give me about an hour."

José decided to waste time by strolling through Scott Street and seeing who was outside. Janay was a tall light skin honey who was actually a close friend of José, she was sitting on her front step with her one-year-old daughter. Janay was a loner who stayed to herself most times. Years back the two had a fling once or twice but nothing ever came from it. José confessed that Janay's twatt was fat, wet, and one of the best he had ever had on many occasions. On days like today, the two old friends would flirt with each other and smoke a Dutch. Today seems to be different though, she had a glossy look in her eyes and she looked to be staring off into the distance. She had tears in her eyes and something was wrong. José cracked the Dutch Master then filled it and rolled it up.

"What's up with you… why are you crying?"

"I'm not crying."

"Girl, I know what misty eyes look like… now hit this and tell me what's going on," José said passing Janay the Dutch.

"Everything… everything is wrong José. I'm working 40 hours a week at this dead-end job, I'm not getting anywhere. Social Service keep cutting my food stamps, I am not getting no help from my family and I never get a break… I don't even have enough money to buy her a pack of diapers, let alone buy her anything for her birthday," she said sobbing loudly.

"When's her birthday?"

"Tomorrow… September 14th."

"Where's her a dad at… I know he around right?" José asked in a concerned manner.

"Boy, he ain't been around since I had her. It's all good though when she grows up to be something special, he's gonna be sick!"

"Look, Fuck him, if he ain't taking care of his responsibilities he's less of a man. Here take this."

"What's this?" Janay asked looking at the wad of money José handed her.

"Enough to get some diapers and something nice for her birthday. And this should be enough to get yourself something nice. Now stop crying girl."

"Ooh, I Swear to God José I will pay you back as soon as I get it."

"Girl, you alright, it's a gift from me to her. That's like 350, that should be enough right?"

"That's more than enough... thank you," Janay said throwing an arm around his neck, "I love you José."

"Now, don't go getting all emotional on me. Nah, but seriously, I love you too homie."

"You know you were my first and you can have it whenever you want."

"I remember and I also know how good that shit is that's why I'm staying far away from that," he said pointing down between her thighs.

"Boy, your silly as hell."

"No, I'm using my head... and not my little one. But look, I gotta handle something so I'll come see you later or tomorrow a'ight."

"Okay and thank you so much again. And José be careful, the streets are talking and they're saying that those Scott Street boys are on the come up. And Spanish José got it on smash!"

"Word!"

"Yup!"

"Thanks for telling me... but listen, I gotta go I'll see you later," José said giving her a hug and a peck on the cheek then stepped away.

Heading to Taylor and JoJo's to get the money for the bud, he considered bringing the whole 100 grand so that he could grab everything all at once. After a split decision of thinking and knowing that would be a foolish move, he decided on grabbing the bud first then going to see Fat Papi. When he made it to the spot Taylor was gone. JoJo had just finished showering and was walking around butt naked. She hadn't heard him come in, so she was shocked just as much as he was to see her in all her thickness. Inwardly he was like damn! Outwardly all he could muster up to say was ill stink butt.

"Boy, yeah right, this body smells like Kiwi Strawberry," JoJo said strutting into her room.

"More like grandma's chitterlings. Where Taylor at?"

"Boy, you wish you could smell it… she went to the mall though… why?"

"Girl beat ya feet, Lil Miss No Booty… and while you're at it get dressed, we're going out to eat."

"Where we going? Hold up, what you up to and how much am I getting paid for taking you?" JoJo asked.

"Damn, why I gotta be up to something and why I can't just take my homegirl out to eat?"

"Because I know you, José Valdez."

"A'ight look I gotta make two stops but we are gonna meet my folks at T.G.I. Fridays first. So, we mind as well get something to eat while we're there. Then we'll drop that off and slide to the next spot. So, you'll be spending some time with me today and for your trouble, I got a cool 500. Don't tell Taylor then she's gonna want 500 also.

"Five hundred and a free meal… shit I'm getting dressed now. Should I dress casual or should I throw that shit on… meaning heels and all?"

"What's already understood doesn't need to be explained," he said going to his safe.

Thirty minutes passed and JoJo stepped out in a perfectly fitting catsuit, open toe heels, makeup, and accessories on, she was ready to roll! T.G.I.

Fridays was packed to capacity, waiters were moving to and from, bartenders were mixing concoctions and the atmosphere was family friendly. No one would have ever imagined a $22,000 drug deal was about to occur. Just as expected, when JoJo walked in heads turned, men and even a few women had to get a good look. Carrying a large Coach bag that contained over 200 Benjamin Franklins and her compact .380 JoJo played the part of Nina Ross. When they arrived at the table Bunny and a dude who looked to be in his mid-20s was sitting with her. I could see that Bunny was feeling good by the smile on her face. Bunny and JoJo already knew each other from the neighborhood so they exchanged cordial greetings. She then introduced me to her friend who sat quietly.

"José this is my boo, Mac… Mac this is my youngin I was telling you about José," she said smiling like she was happy to be introducing the two.

"Bunny told me you got some pretty nice numbers depending on what I grab."

"Yeah, shit can get lower than you can possibly imagine if you're consistent and loyal… I mean whatever kind of loud you want and the amount of it I'm sure I can cover it. What else are you into… is this ya only line of work poppie?" Mac asked.

"Nah, I got my hands in the few things but that's here or there right now."

"Where are you from, I can hear ya up north accent?" asked José

"I am from North Philly, 28th and Birch."

"Okay."

"Where are you from Wilmington?"

"The Hilltop."

"I heard about y'all Wilmington niggas… y'all gun happy gunslingers!"

"Only when provoked," José said jokingly.

The meals had come and everyone ate while having a general conversation. The two females excused themselves from the table and headed for the restroom. Mac invited José to Philly whenever he wanted. Promising that the nightlife there was much more exciting than Delaware's nightlife as a whole. José promised to take him up on his offer on a later base but wanted to know what could be done to get whatever he brought matched on a front as well. Mac looked him in the eyes and told him that he had to grab at least 50 to get a front of the same amount. He also let him know that if he grabbed 50 at once his price would drop to 12 a pound. If he ever happened to grab a hundred or better depending on the quality, his price would be an astounding $800-$1000. Those prices were the prices he knew he needed to fuck the city up.

Bunny and JoJo had finally made it back to the table. After a little more convo both groups paid their tabs and left. In the parking lot as they walked along José was impressed with Mac's snowflake white Aston Martin convertible on 20s. Uninformed that the deal had already taken place when the two girls went to the restroom José was looking confused until JoJo grabbed his hand and told him that she had already taken care of everything. All José could do was smile.

Rhianna's "Work" blasted through the speakers of JoJo's cherry red 2015 Toyota Camry as they cruised down Concord Pike back into Wilmington. Hidden behind the tinted windows assured them that they were incognito as they moved the work from one spot to the other. Instead of dropping the bud off at the Batcave he dropped it off at JoJo's when he went to grab the cash for Fat Papi. Grabbing both of his Puma sports bags, his new .45 cal "judge" and the cash he was in and out of the house and on his way to the shop to meet Fat Papi.

As usual, when they pulled up all that you heard was Tego Calderon playing loudly throughout the shop. Just like the many other times, Fat Papi was eating a large Stromboli. José was accompanied by JoJo and her .380. When they walked in Fat Papi damn near choked on a piece of Stromboli when he saw JoJo's sexy ass. See, Fat Papi was a money getting' mothafucka, but his only downfall was his weight. True, women liked big men but poppie was huge! He had to weigh at least 450 lbs. and his dress game was on "E". Knowing he couldn't get many women from looks, he spent major cash to get a shot of pussy. Thinking JoJo was young and naïve he tried his luck by placing a few stacks of money on the table in front of him. She wasn't hardly impressed. She was focused on one thing and that was being an extra pair of eyes, ears, and gun for José. José inwardly smiled to himself because he had heard about Fat Papi and his fetish for young Spanish women, but he also saw how down to ride his homegirl was. She kept her hand inside her Coach bag the whole time clutching her torch. José introduced JoJo to Fat Papi, they exchanged greetings then she remained silent with her eyes locked on the mechanic and Fat Papi the whole time.

Walking to the back room of the shop a familiar scene appeared, both tables were filled with bricks of cocaine and dope to the max. Each table had about 20 bricks apiece on them. Fat Papi seem to not worry about the mass amount of work up in the shop at one time.

"Yo poppie you wild… you got all this work sitting up in here," said José.

"Papa this shit will be gone in two maybe three days tops," replied Fat Papi.

"Damn, you be moving this shit that fast," said José.

"Yo, this shit moves like water José no lie!" Fat Papi boasted.

"Damn, I'm trying to get to this level."

"You can papa just keep doing what you're doing… wait on the other hand, if you do that you might put me out of business, damn," Fat Papi said playing around.

"Not if, I'm copping off you right?" José asked.

"I guess you're right, so what can I do for you José ?" Fat Papi asked.

José went into his sports bag and pulled out several stacks of money. This time a lot more than any of the previous times, Fat Papi was shocked but also impressed with the youngins drive to get money. Counting out 50 grand of all 50s the table looked like it was about to overflow with cash. José pointed to the bricks of cocaine then threw up dos. Fat Papi went across the room to the desk and grabbed two whole squares.

"Shit, I can throw you one if you want since you showed ya worth," Fat Papi mentioned.

"Word… damn, that would be nice. How much you want back?' José inquired.

"Give me 25," Fat Papi responded.

"Ah… do I really want to be in the hole for 25 grand? Shit, we still got 28 put up and everything is a come up," José thought to himself, "Fuck it, let me get that."

Fat Papi tossed him three bricks of soft and José stuffed them in his sports bag then handed it to JoJo who was still silent.

"So, what's up with the rest of the paper?" Fat Papi asked.

"I'm trying to get 200 sticks of dope," said José.

"How much you got?"

"That's 28 grand right there."

"You might as well grab a half brick for 25.9," Fat Papi informed him.

"I don't know the first thing about cutting that shit plus, the bagging process is much longer than coke or weed. Plus, I don't have a place or the people to do that shit, but I will keep that shit in mind for future endeavors," José said reasoning with Fat Papi.

"A'ight, papa but because you good money give me 26."

Fat Papi handed José four large plastic Ziplock looking bags that contained about 50 sticks apiece. They wouldn't fit in the sports bag so Fat Papi gave him a large size duffel bag to conceal all the work.

The deal was sealed and everything was good. On the way out of the shop Fat Papi finally inquired about the silent assassin that had accompanied José to the meeting.

"She's my homegirl… what you like what you see poppie?" José asked.

"Yeah, papa I would love to take her out and get to know her better."

JoJo looked back over her shoulder and without breaking her stride or missing a step she turned her head in his direction and left with four words.

"Only in your dreams," JoJo said rolling her eyes in disgust.

Those were the only words she spoke until she got to the car. In the car before pulling off José could sense that she was nervous. He giggled out loud then asked her what was wrong?

"OH MY FUCKING GOD! Boy, you just grabbed all that work plus, the shit at the house. You got a half million in drugs José... you need to be careful, you were fine with what you had, so why all of sudden you wanna become big time?" JoJo asked sincerely.

"I don't know... I guess I gotta a lot of people to look after and that small change wasn't enough plus, I got my two lil sisters who gotta stay looking good so I gotta go hard," he said rubbing her leg then handing her a thousand dollars, "thanks for hanging out with me today girl."

"Anytime big bro," she said then pulled off.

When they arrived at the house Taylor was home.

"Where y'all been?" she asked curiously.

"Out and about... I got to finally pack my heat and hold bro down," JoJo said excitedly.

"What... what happened?" Taylor asked.

"He went to cop his work and I went along... I was up in that bitch like Nina Ross clutching on my shit, word!"

"Damn, José that's fucked up I wanted to go too!"

"Should have been home and you could've gone... but no you wanna be in the mall spending money. You lucky I love you, here I got a gift for you," José said handing her five Benjamins.

"Shit, thanks I needed this... a bitch is broke."

"You only broke because you choose to spend rather than save. Start saving girl," he said giving Taylor a bear hug.

José went to the table then placed all the contents on top of it. The three of them sat and looked in silence for a good minute or two. That was certainly the most work José had ever owned at one time and prior to JoJo going to the shop with him, her, or Taylor had never seen that much work before in their lives. They both had a strange feeling that they will be seeing a whole lot more in the near future. José was more focused on the heroin that sat in front of him. This one drug, if only he could find the proper place and people to package and cut it, he could easily see 1 million in no time. For the time, he had to get to work and this is the most dreaded part of the money process, cooking, and bagging. He called everyone up and had them meet at the Batcave. With his new shipment being a heavy one bagging everything up in dimes would take them damn near a month to move the crack alone. So, instead of selling all three in pieces, he decided to bag up "ballgames" with the extra bricks. Ballgames were the nickname for eightballs which were 3.5 grams of crack. They were sold in the street for 150 apiece. They would put the grand total off that brick at 43,200 without adding any extra cut to stretch it. He packed everything back into the bags then had JoJo take him to the Batcave.

As soon as the squad arrived, they went to work! Carlos and Dre immediately started bagging dimes of bud. Scales were blinking, bags were being stuffed and sealed, pots were bubbling with coke. French Montana's "Schemin'" was playing, it was sort of like a get money theme song. Money didn't stop, on some days like these, they would throw the youngins packs on a 70-30 deal. It wasn't a need to complain because so much money flowed that they would leave the block at the end of the night with like 5 to 600 apiece. Dre would occasionally have to run out to drop off a few sticks. Now that he had enough work to cover almost any order that came through the block, he started promoting heavy. Plus, they discussed dropping the prices a few dollars to really make it go. Playas that were grabbing five to 10 sticks could now grab 50 to 100 sticks if they wanted. All José wanted was for everybody to see cash. After this flip he would grab one more time and then they would start dividing the loot. Locked in José had Summer make a pot of "Arroz con Gandules" for everyone. They all loved this dish and besides, they were stuck in there until they finished everything. So, morning, noon, and night they would sit cooking, bagging, and smoking. Between the four of them, they had to bag up 96 ounces all dimes. Bagging up to two grand off each ounce would give them somewhere around a 190 grand off the two bricks minus the 25 grand for Fat Papi. That would give them a 18,000 profit off the 3rd brick. Then if they sold each stick of dope for $250 that would be 50,000 minus the re-up, that would be 24,000 profit and he figured he'd probably need to re-up faster than he expects. Then 12 lbs. in all dimes is 53 grand, subtract 22 and you're left with 21 grand profit. That puts the total at 235 grand. From 98 grand to 235 thousand, that's a 137 grand plus the 28 grand from the first flip they would have $164,000 stashed between the four of them. That's not even mentioning the last flip before they split the money up! As planned the big spenders were phone clientele so that money never got away. The block money was left to the youngins only until they finished what they were doing. Four days and at least 80 blunt roaches later the task was complete, they were finished. Now that the hard part was done a surge of energy ran through the squad. It was time to get back to the basics, getting money.

This time they all hit Scott Street like runaway trains, they all had green vision. Each morning they would hit the block around 6 am. All together and hustled all day long. The only breaks that were taken were shit breaks and an occasional pussy break. They also knew that they were missing the most money on the graveyard shift but reasoned by saying they needed a break and they only dealt with phone money after 10 in the evening.

As the cash flowed, José watched the block and the people on it, he knew soon he would have to definitely hire workers if he planned on having any longevity in the street life. The dimes were moving now that the fiends knew the block to go to and that product was oils.

Three days into the money and they had sold all but 20 ballgames. Wanting to keep that money coming, he went and paid Fat Papi and Fat Papi threw another one. Dre had knocked off close to a hundred sticks. Carlos, as usual, did his thing knocking off 9 lbs. so quickly and Castro made the piles of dimes decrease at a rapid pace.

Within a week the heroin, weed, and two bricks of ballgames would be gone. They figure it will take at least two weeks to bang out all the dimes which they were cool with as long as they had what was in demand, the weight! The team kept grinding and just as expected José went to see MacLaden before the end of the week grabbing another 12 and hitting Fat Papi up for Dre and the heroin. They damn near dumped everything twice except for the dimes in one week. That was an extra 45 grand on top of the 235 placing them at 280g's!!!

Being a man of his word, just like he promised Sunday morning José came to spend the day with his mother and to catch a true home cooked meal. Summer, of course, was there with her man. When Miss Valdez seen her, you would have sworn she had seen a long-lost daughter. Her eyes became big as coins and a smile that could soften any thugs heart. She ran up to Summer and hugged her tightly and started spitting Español at a rapid pace. She loved Summer like her own daughter. José had been dealing with her since he was 14 and she was 15, so she's been around for quite a while. Miss Valdez headed straight for the kitchen but was stopped.

"Ma... go get dressed Summer's taking you somewhere," stated José.

"Where?"

"Ma please go get dressed."

"Okay," Miss Valdez said heading up the stairs.

15 minutes later, Miss Valdez came back downstairs wearing a blue and yellow Sunday dress, black stockings, and white Nike's. She looked like a peacock; José couldn't help but laugh out loud. She sensed that he was laughing at her and caught a quick attitude.

"Boy, what are you laughing at? I know you're not laughing at my dress cause my dress looks nice," she said rolling her eyes at her son.

"José be nice, I think it's cute... I like it Miss Valdez," Summer added.

"Thank you, Summer... my son has no respect. Boy, I used to dress your little Latin ass."

"I'm sorry ma it's only a joke... here this is for you," he said handing her some money.

"What's this for?"

"For your trip to the mall with Summer... a little shopping spree."

"Thank you, honey!!! I needed this... can I get my nails and feet done?"

"You can get whatever you want ma!"

"Well, in that case, Summer we better be going so that we can shop til' we drop," Miss Valdez said smiling from ear to ear locking arms with Summer leading the way out the door.

"See you later babe," Summer said blowing her man a kiss then vanished through the door.

Once they were gone, he went to check on Felix who was still asleep. Letting him sleep, José went back downstairs and turn on Telemundo.

Sammy was at work, so it wasn't really nothing to do except lounge. Around 11 Felix had awakened and José prepared him a light breakfast; a bowl of cereal and jelly on toast. Once he finished eating it was on! They headed upstairs while Felix set up the game system, José grabbed his stash from his little brothers closet. He still had five grand on tuck and prided himself on never having to touch a dime of the squad's money cause he hustled hard to get what he had. And at that moment, he said a quick prayer to ask for protection from whatever is awaiting him in the future. The joystick controller broke his daze and the video screen lit up. Picking it up from his lap he went into war mode as the video game Tekken started. Going for the kill José started off punishing his little brother who was no match for the three and four kick combination. After about the third straight game of losing Felix sat the controller down momentarily, walked over to his dresser then placed his favorite necklace on his neck. Felix called it his good luck charm and it must've been because from the time he placed it on his neck he went bananas. For the next hour, he demolished his older brother. José couldn't get one combination off and a few of the rounds Felix upsets him by winning with flawless victories. José threw the controller on the bed and gave up. José reached in his pocket and gave his brother five ones.

"All the money I give you, I hope you save some."

"I do... I only spend it when I go to the store."

"You go to the store every day... how much money you got saved up?"

"I don't know, like $20 I guess!"

"Twenty dollars that's it! Let me see your piggy bank."

"It's right there, count it for me... I can't count that high yet."

"Let me see, 5, 10, 15, 20, 30... one, two, three. Boy, you got 50 dollars here. You better start paying attention in school and stop playing this video game so much. If I tell mama you can't count to 50, but you can beat all these games she's gonna take the game," José said in a concerned tone.

Felix looked at him strangely for a second then spoke, "Listen, José I'm 10-years-old I can count to a hundred or even a thousand duh!"

"Well, why did you say you couldn't?"

"If you were dumb enough to believe me... why not let you count it."

"Gamed by a 10-year-old," was all José could say.

It was about noon when Sammy came home from work. The two brothers talked for a while. José informed him that in two weeks he was sure to have the 20 grand his brother needed to purchase the house for his mother. Sammy said okay but just wanted his brother to be safe. José then went to the porch to make a few calls. After the calls were finalized and the squad was all in agreement. They concluded that for the next two weeks they would do all-nighters. Sleep would have to come whenever it came or when the body shuts down. For now, they were once again in beast mode, but this time it's for 24 hours a day, 14 days straight. His main focus was the two bricks of dimes that he wanted to get off in less than two weeks, all the weight will keep getting flipped in the process. He really didn't need the squad out there with him but since they all wanted to get at a dollar so be it.

For the late nights, Castro would have to bring the choppers or Mac 10's out. Regardless, they'll be playing the alleyways so the torches will still be on the hip.

Summer and Miss Valdez had finally made it back from the mall. With bags and smiles, Miss Valdez was ecstatic. One could see that it was the most fun she had in a long time. After showing everyone in the house her hands and feet, her new outfits, and her costume jewelry she went straight to the kitchen. By six that evening, everyone was sitting at Miss Valdez table stuffing their faces with her famous Sancocho. After dinner, Summer helped Miss Valdez clean up the kitchen while Sammy, José, and Felix were dozing off in the living room on the sofa, just like boys do!

The week had started and with the squad doing all-nighter catching mega paper, shit was gravy. I mean fiends would spend hundreds like 10 back to back to back.

After about 11 days all the dimes were gone and the squad was exhausted. Taking a day to relax and regroup everyone chilled out, the next day except for the meeting they had at Miss. Valdez's house in the basement. Whenever they met there it had to be important. So, when everyone got there, they were anxious to see what was going on. Explaining to them the values of loyalty and hard work José mentioned the extra flips they had also made that week which they made off the weed, dope, and coke. That would have been an extra 60 something grand added to the 280g's that put them at 340g's in three weeks! Knowing he said he wanted to flip three times before they split the cash, he changed his mind due to the amount of cash they had and nowhere to keep all that money. So, the meeting was necessary. Laying a $100,000 to the side first to continue with the same flip they've been doing, José passed all three of his homeboys six blocks of money apiece. They all looked shocked, happy, and surprised all in one.

"What's this?" Castro asked.

"That's your cut... everybody's the same amount, no one person has more than the next," responded José.

"How much is it?" Dre asked."

"60 grand... and that's in three weeks. If I must say, that's the best any of us has ever done and it's all because of teamwork my niggas."

"60, I'm cool with that, now I'm ready to add to that. So, when are we grabbing again?" Carlos asked.

"I'm calling my people tonight so probably tomorrow, but in the meantime, start looking for a car. We definitely can't be waiting anymore." With that the meeting was over, everyone went their separate ways.

After everyone had gone, he went upstairs to Sammy's room and threw the two $10,000 wads of money on his bed then said, "Go get ma her house bro."

CHAPTER 8

Fat Papi and His Mechanic is Killed

Priscilla Reyes had boarded the plane with her family in tow. You would have thought that the airport was hosting the Puerto Rican day parade with all them Spanish people in the building. The family's luggage had to be over eighty suitcases and carry-on bags. The kids were ecstatic to be going to the island of sun. All they could think of was fun, fun, fun. While everyone anticipated the events of the trip Priscilla thought of her son. She loved Alex very much and knew that when she passed, he'd likely take her position as the boss. However, his anger would certainly cause havoc for the family. With the families worth being estimated at close to $15 million in 20-years, she was serious about letting all of her hard work and mind power go to waste because of her son's childish behavior. Still, she worried, back home in Redding PA, she ran things with an iron fist. No one dared to question her decisions in the several surrounding counties. This time things were different; she was out of town with her whole family in a city with the nickname Murdertown USA. She knew nothing about the people she was dealing with and from what Alex told her they knew everything about her. For the time being, she could only hope that when she stepped off the plane returning from Puerto Rico that Alex would have the situation resolved. Priscilla said a silent prayer while looking out the window of the plane. In the meantime, she couldn't wait to sip on a Seagram's Bahama Mama on a beach with white sands and ocean blue water!

Back in Wilmington, Alex patrolled the blocks searching for Ivan. Ivan wasn't your ordinary block boy so finding him outside on the block would more than likely be impossible. He's been looking for him the past two days and hasn't had a clue. Ivan seemed to be invisible. Alex even went through the blocks Ashlee told him about. These were where he frequented the most. His hangouts were even ghost town. It was simple, when Alex ran into him, he would kill him. Despite what his mother said to handle the situation, his way of handling things was murder. Not fearing retaliation from the low-level drug pusher, he thought killing Ivan would be a here today gone tomorrow type of thing. Little did he know that if they even heard of an attempt on Ivan's life, they would hold pressure on Alex and his family until they were all gone! He thought he had seen him while riding through the Hill one day entering a cornerstone. When he hopped out of his whip and walked in the store with his torch out, he startled the woman behind the counter and the young man who was also sweeping. That was it though there was no sign of Ivan. Alex apologized sincerely walked out the store fuming then hopped in his ride and pulled off. His family would be gone for 10 days and he wanted blood badly as he became frustrated thinking of Ivan. He had been calling Bunny and she'd been avoiding him for some strange reason. He figured it had something to do with Ivan. Cause ever since he inquired about him, she's been distant. She would still stop by from time to time, but she seemed on edge. He remembered Bunny telling him to leave Ivan and his people alone, but he waved her off.

After cruising through the city blocks of Murdertown most of the day he decided to stop to get a bite to eat at Tropicana a Dominican restaurant on 4th and DuPont. Deciding to call it the night, he grabbed a platter of bacalhau and a few pataleios to go. Heading back to Pleasant Street, Alex rode through West 3rd and Conrad Street to see if Santos the owner of a few garages happened to be outside. It must have been a gut feeling of his intuition because when he drove past one of the many Spanish owned mechanic shops there stood conversating with two men was Ivan! It was on! He wanted to jump out right there and get busy. He could taste the bloodshed on the tip of his lips. Instead, he used his brain, he quickly circled the block and found a parking space. Taking the safety off his .44 Desert Eagle, loading four hollow tip shells into his pistol, and gripping his sawed-off 12-gauge Remington, Alex threw his hoodie on and stepped out of the car. He tucked his weapons and then walked towards the garages.

The crack smoke lingered throughout the abandoned house while the fiends walked around like zombies in a trance-like state. In the basement of the Bando, Ramone was bent over a cum stained sofa getting penetrated from behind by one of his dope fiend lovers. It smelled horrible down there, between funk, piss, sex, ass, and shit you would have thought you were either in a Port-a-Potty or the city dump. After another ass whipping lust session, Ramone wanted to get high. His anus was sore and the only thing to ease the pain was a few bags of caution. Caution was the latest batch of heroin to invade the streets and take the addicts by storm. They loved it, it was for both shooters and sniffers, Ramone would shoot though. If he couldn't find a vein he would go as far as shooting up in his dick. He was a disgusting motherfucker! As he prepared his syringe for his next fix in walked Abbee. Abbee was a one-time prom queen turned heroin addict. Even in her addiction with her busky breast, plumped ass, and light brown skin she was still a number one pick amongst the tricks looking for a prostitute to have a little fun with. However, Abbee also knew the latest going on in the streets on a higher level, unlike Ramone who could give you the rundown on the street corners. She, on the other hand, had the inside scoop on the major dealers and their crews. You know, young guys and late nights when they can't find a sexy young girl to satisfy their cravings. They find thick good-looking tricks like Abbee to substitute. Quite as kept, she had probably popped that pussy and sucked about half if not damn near all them young niggas dicks on the Hill during her late-night stroll. Anyway, she always had her own money to spend, kept her appearance up, and never disrespected herself by doing some of the degrading things that some of the heroin addicts did to get high. Just those things alone drew all types of people to her. Which equaled lots of money and return meant seeing her youngin Andre who had that dark soul in at the time. As she prepared to sniff her dope, Ramone decided to see what he could find out about his two little friends.

"So Abbee what's going on?" Ramone asked.

"Shit chillin' getting money popping this pussy, driving these tricks crazy."

"Girl, your ass is bad... I wish I had what you got between ya legs because I know you've made triple if not quadruple what these other tricks made with a lot less bodies," Ramone said in a transgender type of voice.

"I guess you can say that, but you don't know the things I have to go through with these young guys and dealers. They wanna fuck me in my ass... that's not gonna happen. Then they wanna gang bang me, two and three niggas at a time. I had to pull my blade out on a few of them, I've had so many guns pulled on me it's ridiculous. Hey, this is the life of a superstar, high profile trick," Abbee said while giggling.

"So, what's going on round the way? Did you hear about the man and the little boy who was murdered a few weeks ago? That was sad."

"Yeah, that Shit was Fucked up... that was Big Jake and his son Lamar. The little boy was either 11 or 12, they didn't have to do that to the poor kid. You know I happened to be walking down the street when that shit took place," said Abbee.

"Were you? Uh-Uh!" Ramone said egging on.

"I think I know who did it too. I'm not sure, but I saw them leaving right after the shots went off."

"Who girl?" Ramone questioned.

"Those grimy ass stickup kids. They said when the police went in the house, they found like a quarter million in cash and a few bricks! That means those niggas killed them for nothing," said Abbee.

"Those? Who are they Abbee?" Ramone asked wanting to know.

"Them two niggas from Eastside, them killer mothafuckas. What's their names, Rakmeef and Twink? Yeah, I saw them two crazy mothafuckas walking straight off the porch. Those two niggas scare me for real though. I hope they didn't see my ass because I'm not getting involved in that shit," she said worriedly.

"Jackpot! Girlll I'm about to get 50 grand. That guys family has a $50,000 reward for the arrest of the suspects plus, this detective I know has been trying to pin them for a while now," said Ramone excitingly.

"You better split that shit down the middle a bitch needs a cut for her information these days," said Abbee eyeing Ramone suspiciously.

"Girl I'll take care of you. You might have to talk with my Detective friend though."

"I will for that money... when?" she asked.

"I'll let you know in a few days," said Ramone just before he pushed the syringe into his veins and then drifted away into a world of darkness.

While Ramone sat nodding off into another world Abbee thought about pulling out her straight razor and slicing the rat from ear to ear. Over the years she's done many of things, but snitching was always out of the question. The thought that Ramone would even think that she would snitch pissed her off. Instead of getting her own hands bloody she knew exactly how to kill a rat, poison him. Not until she paid her high school sweetheart Rakmeef a visit over Eastside. Instead, of getting high she packed up her things and left the bando.

"What's good papa?" Fat Papi said answering his phone.

"You know, getting money tryna stay low key," José shot back.

"Low key? Papa, I hear ya block is crushing them so how you low key?"

"I guess I'm not anymore. So, what's the deal?" José asked.

"What you need?" Fat Papi asked.

"The usual... I got 76 and I hope you're gonna show the same love you've been showing too. I got plans with the extra shit," said José in boss mode.

"Of course, I got you, just come through I'll be waiting."

Since meeting the Twins Jesenia and Glady, Carlos, and Dre have been talking to the two on the phone almost every day. Both young men have been very interested in the Twins and vice versa. The conversations started off cordial but quickly turned to an explicit manner. Before long, they were talking about pussy eating and dick sucking with no filter. Carlos and Dre wanted to meet up with the Twins soon to fulfill each other's lustful desires. They had to wait though because the Twins were out of town with family for a week or two. With money came women so Carlos and Dre wanted more money. They were determined to get to the top of their hustle. No one could stop them and that's what drove them to push José into grabbing more of both products. Quiet as kept, the Twins had Carlos and Dre wanting to venture off and go solo just so they could be the king. What they didn't know was that the Twins were princesses soon to be queens of their respected castles and were looking for two young kings to reign supreme. Knowing José wouldn't grab more weight than the usual they started planning a way how they could get more money on the side. After brainstorming, Carlos came up with a plan that would most likely put them in a comfortable spot!

Fat Papi had just finished placing his new shipment of work in the back room of the shop. He normally had 20 bricks of cocaine and 20 of dope alone with 400 sticks already packaged. This load was lighter tho he got 20 bricks of coke and 10 bricks of dope with 250 sticks. Stepping out of the back office his mechanic Raúl was preparing to leave for the night when a young Spanish guy who neither men had seen before walked in. He removed his hood that covered his face revealing an expression that revealed danger was near. Noticing that the man had his hand tucked under his hoodie that was now revealing what looked to be the handle of a "shotie" they knew something was up. Fat Papi knew he couldn't make it to his arsenal of guns, so he played it cool. Thinking this was robbery he tried to talk some info out of the man to stall time and to remember as much as possible.

"Yo, we closed papa," said Fat Papi to the assailant. The man stood there and looked around the shop like he was looking for something.

"Yo, my man you good... we closed. Can I help you with something?" Fat Papi spoke again.

"Where's Ivan?" Alex asked growling.

"Who?" Fat Papi asked.

"You heard me puto!" Alex said gripping his Desert Eagle.

"Hey boss, I'll see you in the morning," Raúl said making an exit for the door.

Alex swiftly pulled his torch out and pointed it at Raúl who was visibly shaken by the guys' actions.

"Ya Fat Ass ain't going nowhere til' you or fatso over there tells me where the Fuck Ivan is. I just saw him here so where the Fuck did he go?" Alex said in a sinister tone.

"Look, my man, I don't know what business you and Ivan got to discuss but that ain't got shit to do with us so all I'm saying is leave me out y'all Shit. I just fix cars around here, now you walk up in my place of business with your gun out looking for one of my customers. Poppie you're wilding," said Fat Papi bouncing from one foot to another.

"So, he's one of your customers, right?" Alex asked.

"Yeah, why?" At that very moment, he knew he made a mistake that just might cost them both.

"So, if he's your customer you can call him, tell him something came up and that he should come pick his car up now," said Alex.

"Like I said, I run a business here papa I ain't getting involved in nobody's street shit," said Fat Papi rubbing his hands together.

"Yes, you will or you're gonna die," Alex said devilishly.

Fat Papi knew that if he called Ivan back, they would both be killed and if he didn't, he'd still be killed. So, he had to think fast and try to find a way out of this mess he was caught up in. Catching a bullet wasn't in his plans but he was out of arms reach of the .357 magnum that sat about five feet away and a mechanic job box. Making eye contact with Raúl, Fat Papi tried to cause a distraction by hollering Fuck You puto and throwing a handful of wrenches at Alex then taking off towards the job box. The wrenches caused him to duck only for a split second. Raúl's fat ass tried to make an escape but was too slow. Before he could take a full three steps, BOOM! Alex let one shot off to Raúl's stomach dropping him to his knees. From the look on his face, he was already dead, but Alex threw two more shots just to make sure. BOOM! BOOM! One hit Raúl in the neck, the last one smacked him directly under his eye. His body slumped to the ground and the blood from his wounds covered the shop floor.

By this time, Fat Papi had made it to the box just in time. Alex had sent one flying past his head slamming into the wall followed but another one. Fat Papi grabbed his .357 and without aiming he fired blindly into the shop. Letting off five shots as he tried to make his way to where his big arsenal was stashed. Not thinking, he let off two more shots just as Alex had let off four hitting Fat Papi in the hand.

"Oh Shit Mothafucka! I'm gonna kill ya Bitch Ass!" Fat Papi screamed out.

"One of us ain't leaving this shop Fatso!" Alex responded back.

"That's you Mothafucka!" Fat Papi said jumping up to let off another barrage of bullets.

CLICK, CLICK, CLICK, his gun had run out of bullets and he was still a distance away from his other gun stash. He knew he had fucked up, his .357 only held seven shots and now he was empty. Before he could run or take cover Alex appeared with a shotie in hand rushing towards Fat Papi,

BOOMMM! The first shot to his chest sent him flying backward onto the hood of a car. Fat Papi was fighting to hold on to what little life he had. He was fighting a losing battle though. Alex then walked up on him and put the shotgun to the side of his head then spoke his next words as calm as a patient father talking to his son.

"Fatso you should have just called him." BOOMMM!

Covered in blood Alex grabbed a towel, wiped off his face, threw the towel in a plastic bag along with his gun, and then walked out the shop like nothing ever happened. No one happened to be outside when he stepped out of the shop except for some kids who was about a block away heading in his direction. Alex turned around and went in the opposite direction, then a few seconds later he vanished in the dark.

After gathering together, the re-up money and his .45 caliber "judge" José was ready to meet Fat Papi. Refusing to except no for an answer, both Taylor and JoJo wanted to ride out with their homie. Refusal wasn't an option, so he let them ride along. He decided to have them wait in the car while he went inside though. The girls were furious. As usual when they didn't get their way they started bitching and complaining. José simply blocked the two whining friends out of his mind. He had his mind made up that he would attend this meeting alone. Having Taylor park a block and a half away, he took the safety off his baby cannon and then threw his hoodie on. He tried calling Fat Papi to let them know he'd be there in about two minutes, but he didn't answer. Saying Fuck it, he looked at his two friends and told them to leave if he's not back in 15 minutes. Of course, they snapped like two emotional down ass chicks like Taylor and JoJo would do.

"Fuck Naw Nigga we ain't going nowhere! If ya Spanish Ass ain't out of there in 15 minutes we gonna set it off up in that Bitch, Word!" JoJo said.

"Fucking right, we hittin' everything in that piece or they gonna hit us," Taylor added.

"Yo Thelma and Louise calm the Fuck down. I'll be out in 15 minutes damn," José said smirking and shaking his head at his two friends.

"We love you poppie but remember what we said, you ain't out in 15 minutes we coming in," the girls said in unison.

"I love y'all too," José said getting out the car walking down the block towards the shop.

In the city of Murdertown when the sunset anything was bound to happen. So, on his way to the garages, José kept his eyes and ears open. The night seemed solemn though, it was too quiet, and everything seemed to be standing still. The only movement noticeable were the multi-colored leaves fumbling across the street and some dude who seemed to be walking in his direction then suddenly turned around and went the opposite way. It was never like Fat Papi not to answer when José called and José never just popped up. Since he had just spoken to him no more than a half an hour earlier, he assumed everything would be cool. Another thing that stuck out was that there wasn't any music playing. At any time, you could walk or ride by and hear music playing throughout Fat Papi's garage. José walked up to the door and knocked twice only to get no answer. He tried calling Fat Papi's phone once again but received no answer. However, he did hear the phone ringing from the inside of the garage. He had a strange feeling but still, followed his intuition and turned the doorknob and walked in the garage. What José saw left him frozen and traumatized for a good three to four minutes. Laid stretched out in the middle of the shop what look to be a shot to the face and stomach was Raúl, Fat Papi's mechanic. Whatever happened had to be personal because Raúl was legit, he just worked on cars and got paid by Fat Papi weekly. He supported his wife and five kids off the 800 a week he made at the shop. Breaking his trance, José slowly began to maneuver around the shop until he laid eyes on who he expected to be Fat Papi. The body was blown open exposing his insides and where his head and face were was now shreds of meat plastered to the windshield behind him.

"Oh, Shit! Damn papa!" José mumbled to himself.

He walked cautiously around the shop making sure he didn't touch anything. He tried replaying the scene over in his head like an F.B.I. analyst. Nothing! The only thing one could make of this mess so far was that it was a gruesome murder. He had seen enough and was ready to bounce but walking past the desk that Fat Papi would always be sitting at eating when he stopped by, he remembered that Fat Papi always had cash in there. Grabbing a handy cloth from off the top of the desk he began opening the drawers. Opening the last one, the bottom drawer his eyes lit up instantly! "Bingo!!!" he said removing his sports bag from his shoulder.

This nigga had stack after stack sitting in the desk. He had 40 stacks of two grand wraps, it was 80 bands! Losing track of time and finding the dough had him wanting to search some more. He then walked towards the back office but was stopped when he noticed a single black locker slightly opened. Opening it he was stunned to see all sorts of guns. He had to be looking at a minimal of 15 guns, a few assault rifles, riot pumps, and all kinds of handguns. For the hell of it, José threw three pieces in his bag along with the cash. He was about to go into the back office when he was startled from a noise coming from behind him.

"Yo nigga what the Fuck Yo!" Taylor said stunned with her gun out.

"What the Fuck happened in here boy?" JoJo asked.

"I thought I told y'all to wait in the car and to leave if I'm not back in 15 minutes," José said.

"I thought we told you if you weren't back in 15 minutes, we were coming in... and it's been 20," they both said tapping their watches.

"Yo José what the Fuck happened?" JoJo asked.

"I don't Fucking know. All I know is, I walked up in here and they were laid the Fuck out. Fat Papi is laid over there with his face blown off!" he said.

"Shit, nigga we need to get the hell out of here then," Taylor suggested.

"I'm about to, I just want to check the back office... he usually keeps work back there," José said then walked into the back office, "Oh Shit!" José said running out of the back office with a look of excitement on his face!

"What!" both girls said in unison.

"Jo, go pull the car up front and turn the lights out, make sure nobody's watching either... hurry up! Taylor come help me grab this shit," José said darting back to the office.

Grabbing the four large duffel bags that sat in the corner of the office José and Taylor started stuffing the bricks of coke and dope into the bags. The dope was marked with a caution stamp and his normal Darksoul stamp. He loaded the package sticks into another duffel bag then hit the door. When they stepped out into the night air JoJo was waiting. No one seemed to be roaming the block on this particular night. Throwing the bags in the trunk they hopped in then pulled off. And now that they were safely away, he could calm down but the only thing they had him puzzled was whoever killed Fat Papi and Raúl left everything; money, drugs, and guns. Signs like that meant that whatever the reason was it had to be personal. José was glad he hadn't walked into the massacre and happy as hell about his major come up. What he didn't know was that everything he did at the shop would soon be revealed.

Alex had finally gotten some blood on his hands in Wilmington. A double murder was his kind of introduction to the killing game and the city where they kill for a sport. He was still upset though; he wanted Ivan and had only missed him by mere minutes. They would meet up one day and when they did Ivan had better be ready for war. Not knowing his next move, he decided to get acquainted with the fiends. Now, they should be able to lead him directly to the man he wanted to see.

Back at one of the stash houses on Pleasant Street, Alex sat alone in the dark eating his Dominican platter with the same bloody clothes on. Once he finished eating, he pulled a cigarette out of his pack then dipped it into the yellow liquid substance. Removing the filter from the cigarette, he sparked the embalming fluid and puffed away. As his head began to spin and his eyes closed his last thought was of him standing face-to-face with the scar-faced thug who pointed the gun at him.

"I'm gonna kill that maricon!" Then he dozed off.

CHAPTER 9

The Work

At Taylor and JoJo's, the three of them seemed to be lost in their own thoughts. Seeing Fat Papi with his head blown off and his mechanic gunned down effortlessly shook the two young girls seriously. That had them questioning if they wanted to really be involved in the gangsta shit! José was kind of shaken himself, he knew the work from the shop belonged to someone, he just didn't know who. As he put all the bricks both coke and heroin on the living room floor along with his new guns and the packaged product no one in the room could believe their eyes.

"Yo, word José that's a lot of shit. How much can you make off all of that?" Taylor asked being nosy.

"I know that off the heroin alone just selling weight I'm sure that's a half-mill easy… with the coke that's another half so I should see somewhere around a good million strong. That's not even including the sticks. Dre is gonna love me for this one word!" José said excited knowing that his boy would have all the dope he needed to get on top.

"Nigga you make me wanna hit the block word, but I'd been done blasted me a mothafucka for playing with my cash word. Don't let this pretty face fool you," JoJo said so cool.

"I'm sure I'm gonna make more because some of this shit is getting broke down and bagged up. Far as the dope goes, I'm gonna have to find somewhere to package this shit," thinking for a few seconds it came to him, "yo, I'm gonna need all y'all too sometime this week," José spoke.

"For what?" the girls asked.

"We going to the Sheriff Sale... we goin house shopping. Y'all think a few of your hoodrat friends wanna earn some money bagging dope up for me?" he asked.

"How much they gettin' paid cause them bitches need some dough anyway," Taylor said.

"Word," JoJo added.

"First, I gotta go talk to my man Rosé Roho, he's the only nigga I can think of offhand that can cut this shit properly and still have this shit fire," José said.

"We know that nigga Rosé'... he fine with the capital F," the girls both agreed.

"That nigga is Dominican and Black I think... he can get it!" JoJo said laughing.

"Look at y'all... thots, we tryna get money," stated José.

José grabbed his phone and made his calls then they packed the work back into the duffel bags. Hitting the door with his two trusted companions behind him they hopped in JoJo's car and drove directly to Miss Valdez's house. Once they arrived everyone greeted Miss Valdez and Felix then headed to the basement.

After waiting for nearly an hour the whole squad was in attendance. Now they could begin the meeting and first he wanted to give each member of the crew their share of the 100 grand and the re-up money. Questions were asked but he didn't have an answer, so he showed them. He had the girls lay the bricks on the pool table that sat in the middle of the floor. Every one of his homeboys' mouths hung wide open! More questions came but he decided that the less they knew the better off they were. José had explained how he planned to move all the work by sticking to the script while politicking with a few heavy hitters to get some of the weight off. Just looking at the bricks you could see the hunger in their eyes especially Carlos and Dre. It was on and now they were all gonna come up. The meeting had finally ended and everyone had left except for JoJo and Taylor so they packed everything back into the bags. He wanted to keep the work at his mother's for the night but quickly decided against it. So, they returned to the girls' apartment.

His safe was too small to put all the work in it so he placed it in the bedroom. Before he left, he opened his sports bag and pulled out 10 stacks of money.

"That's 20 grand... y'all get 10 apiece, thanks for everything. I love y'all.

"We love you too boy... be careful," they said together like they always did.

Summer was pulling up just as José was stepping out of the apartment. Getting in the car he finally got the chance to unwind. He started calculating his savings in his head. Forty from my stash plus, the 25 from the re-up and the 80 grand from the shop should give him a buck twenty-five. He smiled to himself thinking about his earnings, always on top!

"What's up baby... why you smiling?" Summer asked.

"Oh nothing, just thinking but what are you doing tomorrow?" he asked.

"I'm free tomorrow... no work or school. Why?" she asked.

"I want you to take me to get a car," he stated.

"Okay, but what kind of car are you trying to get?"

"Don't know yet... something fast though," José spoke.

"Well, babe let's get some sleep and I'll take you wherever you wanna go in the morning."

The next morning, José was up and ready. Summer was still asleep so, José went and cooked a small breakfast; eggs, sausage, and waffles with a glass of Tropicana orange juice. He knew that would awake her out of her sleep. The smell of an early morning aroma lingering throughout the apartment it brought Summer out of her slumber. Being awakened to breakfast in bed instantly put a smile on her face. Covered by nothing but a blanket while she picked through the plate of food José ate her basket of goodies out! His tongue was somewhat magical and she was getting wetter by the second. She couldn't take it anymore, so she laid her plate to the side and grabbed both sides of his face and pushed his tongue in deeper.

After a few minutes of tongue fucking her asshole, he climbed on top of her and entered her. There was no time for lovemaking, she was wet and horny. And he wanted a nut, so the only solution to their problem was a powerful early morning quickie! The session had ended, now they were moving around getting prepared for their day. While Summer fixed her hair in the bathroom mirror José put on a black and red Polo Sport sweat suit and a pair of black and red Jordan 13's. Keeping the 25 from the re-up at the crib he planned to use that for his purchase.

They hit the door and was on a mission, they stopped by a few car lots and browsed the scene but didn't see anything he liked. They stopped at a Spanish restaurant for lunch and had a quick bite to eat. The Lechon Asado was great! Then they were back on the hunt for his ride, they made it to Pennsylvania Avenue where multiple dealers from Cadillac to Lexus were on showcase. After an hour of searching, they still had no luck! See, José didn't want anything too flashy or to up to date. He wanted speed and power and most of these luxury cars lots didn't have that. Deciding to go to a used car lot in Newport Delaware where most of the cars were still in good condition and the price ranged from anywhere between five to $15,000. The selection of vehicles varied from pick-up trucks, SUVs to contemporary cars and a few luxuries. The selection of muscle cars is what caught his attention. The selection was a huge one to browse through. After 30 minutes of searching, he had found what he was looking for. It sat alone in the corner screaming his name!

"Babe I want that!" he said pointing to the muscle.

"You like that one babe? It's cute, you'll look nice in that," Summer encouraged.

"How much they want? Damn, they only want $9200. I'm getting this today. Where's the salesmen?" José said excitedly.

After all the paperwork is done, he was about to hop in his new muscle car and peel out until he saw another beauty. He always wanted one of these and with it costing 10 grand he had Summer put it in her name for him. The platinum color paint job along with a 22-inch chrome Ashanti rims the Mercury Marauder was his. He had to drop one of his new cars off, so he took the navy-blue SS Impala to Taylor and JoJo's spot. He planned on keeping that basic except for the tinted windows and the souped-up engine along with the customized stash boxes that can hold close to 50 bricks. That car would be strictly to grab his work in. No one would ever know he even owns the car.

Now that he parked his Impala, he went back to pick up his Marauder. When he got behind the wheel he was out! Summer went and parked her car and rode out with her man. He immediately went to get a sound system in his wheels. Once that was done, they rolled around the city blasting Don Omar, José would stop and politick with a few acquaintances he hadn't seen in a while. He promoted his work mainly the coke beings though he hadn't figured out what to do with the dope yet. A few guys were dabbling in some major weight so they exchanged numbers with guarantees that they would be in touch soon. This is exactly what he wanted, to turn up on a whole new level. His only worry was if he sold out to fast who could he go to for the re-up at a nice price. He knew someone to get the dope from and probably could find coke as well, but will they be able to cover the order if he needed it. It had begun to get dark outside and he wasn't strapped so he headed back to the Westside where he felt most comfortable. He stopped on 2nd and Scott for a hot minute and happened to run into Carlos who had went and purchased a car as well. Carlos grabbed a 2017 Lincoln Continental even though the car was nice José thought it was a little too new and flashy, but he kept his thoughts to himself. Since they started seeing a couple of dollars Carlos seemed to be getting big headed. His new flamboyant lifestyle was altering his thinking.

Having Summer hanging out on the block was a strict rule of not to do so after politicking with Carlos for a lil bit they said their goodbyes and then parted ways. Everything seemed normal pulling up to their apartment so when they got to the front door and seen it slightly ajar Summer panicked. José didn't have his torch on him, so he had to be cautious. He sent Summer back to the car and told her to wait there. Once she was safe, he stepped into the apartment quietly. What he saw was foul, whoever broke in had ransacked the apartment. They turned furniture over, pulled all the dishes and utensils out of the drawers, they even pulled all the couple's clothes out of their dressers and closets. Nothing was missing because he kept nothing there except for a light five grand he already had put up just in case Summer needed anything. What had him puzzled was the fact that not too many people knew where he stayed but when you live in the city it's possible that anyone could have seen him coming to and from. Giving Summer the okay to come into the apartment he could tell she was visibly shaken and wanted to calm her. While they put things back in their place in silence she began crying.

"Summer what's wrong?" he asked his girl.

"Poppie I'm scared... what if I was home when whoever came in here showed up!"

"More than likely they were watching me or the house, you're good Mama," José said.

"But babe, now you have to be careful, somebody might try to hurt you," Summer said concerned.

"Look, I'm cool but to make you feel safe go find us a house for $1200 a month somewhere in Concordville. That should be far enough in the cut to be able to spot someone following us home. I'll give you the money tomorrow, now calm down. And you might gotta start carrying a little pocket rocket too," said José.

"Babe, if you get it, I'm carrying it and if somebody tries something, I'm gonna use it!" Summer said seriously.

Late that night while Summer was asleep, José tried but couldn't come up with an individual that would have run up in his spot. Then he thought of how his block and team were doing numbers right now and figured one of the many bitches or niggas who were probably pillow talking and his name came up which led to this current event.

"Well, I just gotta move quieter... it's time to disappear."

Miller Road Diner was the meeting location for Ramone and Detective Baldwin. Weeks had passed since the snitch had met with the detective; however, Baldwin was more than certain that when he received a call from Ramone his informant had some info. Pulling into the 24-hour diner that was off Philadelphia Pike in a discreet location he scanned the parking lot which was just a police procedure and then made his way into the diner. When he approached the table where the frail-looking, half dead, malnutrition fiend sat eating a chicken finger and French fries platter Detective Baldwin just shook his head. Ramone looked as if he hadn't eaten in months. Baldwin slid into the booth across from Ramone and waited for the information to be dispensed so that he could catch a break.

"What's up, Baldwin... what's new?" Ramone asked with a mouthful of fries.

"You tell me, Ramone, it's been a few weeks since we last talked. I hope you have something good for me, buddy," Detective Baldwin responded.

"So, how much was the reward that the family was giving up for the capture of the persons involved?" Ramone asked ignoring Baldwin's last question.

"$50,000 plus, what I'm gonna give you, now stop fucking around. Do you have any info on this case or what?" Baldwin asked getting agitated.

"Yeah, I got something... I might, no I'm sure I have an eyewitness seeing your two boys leaving from the house right after the shots were fired, but to get her to talk she wants in on that reward money," Ramone said still stuffing his face.

"Who is it?" questioned Detective Baldwin.

"Can't tell you all that... we gotta arrange another meeting and also to ensure her safety as well as mine along with the money and I'm sure she'll cooperate," Ramone spoke.

"It's a female?" Baldwin asked.

"Yeah, but it's a million females out here before you get any bright ideas," Ramone said putting a halt to his plans.

"Well, as soon as you see her you call me and we can meet up and we'll handle all of the business of statements, protection, and earnings. Do we have a deal?" Detective Baldwin asked.

"Yup!" Ramone replied while wiping his mouth with his filthy hands.

Detective Baldwin paid for his meal, then like usual handed Ramone a 20 then left the diner.

"If you just sign where both of the X's are the paperwork will be finalized and you will be the proud owner of your new house Mr. Valdez."

Sammy felt great! He had set out to accomplish a goal and he finally achieved it. Years of working, saving while still providing for his brother and mother had finally paid off. He planned to move his mother and brother into their new house in the next few weeks. Excited about receiving the keys to the home he called his brother and wanted him to come with him to show their mother her new home. José agreed to meet his brother at the old house and take them to the new house himself. Meeting at Miss Valdez's house, the brothers kept the secret from their mother while she got dressed. They had her believing she was being taken to dinner by her son just cause. While she picked through her clothing José found Felix something comfortable to wear. Once they were ready, they left the house getting into José's new car which surprised them all to see that he had such a nice car. Cruising down the highway Felix was amazed at all the cars he had a chance to see while Miss Valdez questioned her two sons over a dozen times about the restaurant they were going to. Getting off on the Newark exit they passed University Plaza and all the mainstream restaurants. This only bought more questions from their mother. They turned onto Old Baltimore Pike and drove for a quarter mile until they turned into Salem Woods housing development. The houses were middle-class living, one and two car garages, front and back lawns with three bedrooms and a finished basement. It's a nice environment for kids to grow up and escape the dangers of the city. Felix would be able to play outside without his mother having to worry about a stray bullet hitting her child.

When they pulled into the driveway their mother had a look of confusion or her face. The modern styled home with its lavender window shutters and white vinyl siding which were their mother's favorite collaboration of colors was modest Miss Valdez sat admiring the house. Until Sammy got out of the car and signaled for her and Felix to follow and when they walked up the front steps he turned around and handed her the keys. She was still confused and not sure what to think until Sammy spoke.

"Ma you've been wondering what I'm doing all day well, this is what I was doing. Me and José thought it was time for you to get out of Wilmington so those are the keys to your new house, we love you," Sammy said holding back his tears.

The tears filled Miss Valdez's eyes instantly as her two oldest sons hugged her unconditionally.

"It's beautiful you guys... can we go in?" Miss Valdez asked.

"Ma it's your house, you can do whatever you want," Sammy replied.

"You two aren't playing games, are you?" she asked.

"No ma, it's really yours," José said.

"So, when can I move in?" she asked.

"Whenever you want… I just have to rent a U-Haul," Sammy replied.

"Don't worry bout that bro, find out how much it cost and I'll take care of it. She can move next week if she wants," José said matter-of-factly.

They toured the whole house from top to bottom, Felix was excited as well. He had every right to, his new room was almost twice the size of his old one and it had two windows facing the backyard, unlike the old one that had one window that viewed a row of abandoned garages. Miss Valdez fell in love with her new kitchen that had an island that sat directly in the middle of the floor along with a sliding glass door that led to a patio attached to the back of the kitchen. Just like usual, José would have access to the basement and whenever he decided to sleep over that would be his resting place. After excepting her overwhelming surprise, she had become hungry so just like they promised they went to Harry's Savoy Grill and ate dinner.

Carlos and Dre knew that whatever José had done to get that amount of work that they were about to come up. There was no way they could lose with all that work. Jensena and Glady would be back in a few days and even though they had money Carlos and Dre wanted to splurge a little. José would have to start breaking down this work so that the money can keep flowing. The way they looked at it was the more money the more expenses. So instead of really saving for a rainy day, they lived every day like their last. With strong thoughts of going solo, they'd discussed just copping the weight off José then scratched that plan thinking of the original plan of coming up. Everyone would see cash and no one is considered the least was the motto so with that the two friends awaited the call from José.

Poncé Puerto Rico was the city that Priscilla Reyes was born and raised in. Mediocre and small but polluted by gangs and drugs made this spot a place where tourists should stay away from. With her father being blind and her mother raising 12 kids on her own and Priscilla being one of the oldest she turned to the streets fast. In her younger days, she would have been considered eye candy. Standing five foot even with a bra size 34DD and a tiny waist and an even huskier ass she was stacked. Her blue eyes and her short-cropped hairstyle and pouty lips gained her attention from the locals and tourists. By 16 she was hot! This gained her privileges such as being invited to the hottest clubs, hotels, and resorts on the island. With a need to make money to help her family she started pushing bud. Before long with her knowing all the people she did it didn't take long for her to become one of the main suppliers on the island. With her eight brothers being well known for the havoc they caused all throughout Puerto Rico her security was tight. Around this time, she had just turned 19 with the face of an angel and a body of a goddess, a heavy hitter named Estevez had been trying hard to get with her. After numerous failed attempts and months of rejections, Priscilla finally let him take her on a date. However, this wasn't an ordinary date. They flew to Miami Florida for the week and relaxed on the beach, shopped all day, and partied all night. She was blown away and needless to say when they got back to Puerto Rico they were like J-Lo and A-Rod, inseparable.

Six months later, she was pregnant with her oldest child Ellé and the following year Amillio was also conceived. By the time she turned 25 she had five children and along with her children's father who supplied over half of the island with cocaine, she was a made woman. At the age of 30 with the authorities cracking down on the flow of drugs entering and leaving the country and with Estevez being one of the authorities main focus; he decided to pack up his family and move it to the United States.

As soon as they made to the states residing in Los Angeles first, they married. With his connections back home in Puerto Rico, it didn't take long for Estevez to get plugged into the underworld. Within no time, he had surpassed the local pushers and moved his wife and kids to a better living. However, with the money came power, and with the power came the ruthlessness. He would sniff coke and beat on Priscilla mercifully. He would beat her while she was pregnant, or he would rape her in front of the kids while they looked on in horror. With all the money and nice things, they had, you would have thought she was happy. She was the opposite, she felt trapped. She was emotionally scarred and she knew that if she tried to leave with the kids, he'd probably kill her. So just like her days back on the island, she began pushing bud. And just like on the island between her looks and personality she was chewing a little. The beating and rapes continued, just not as much because she'd be gone just as much as him. The beating would occur when he would be high and would accuse her of cheating with one of the many playas, she dealt with in the bud game. He would swear that the kid she was carrying at the time wasn't his and would try to fuck it out of her. Over the years she had several miscarriages but has never once blamed her husband for the deaths. Even after all the beatings she had taken, being in her late 30s she still looked great! It wasn't until her 40th birthday while she was pregnant with her two youngest, the Twins that she knew it was time to escape. After her 40th birthday, he raped and beat Priscilla for allegedly having an affair with one of his workers while she was three months pregnant. He went as far as having his workers fuck her at gunpoint while he watched. That crossed the line in her mind. She had never been with another man but now she had been violated and wanted out, but she had come up with a plan. Rosa, one of the girls she'd been supplying with bud for years and was in her mid-thirties had been trying to get her to go out to the club with her for years. After she had the Twins and healed properly, she took Rosa up on her offer and went clubbing. Clubbing for a few weeks put Priscilla back in high spirits and it showed in all her dealings. The kids were happy; the bud was moving rapidly, and she felt sexy. Since she began clubbing, her and Estevez had become somewhat distant lovers. They would make love maybe once or twice a week after her club nights which she liked caused that's when she wanted it the most. She assumed that her husband was having an affair because he started staying away from home for a few nights out of the week. She didn't mind because she had also met a 29-year-old Cuban man named Sonny that she had been talking to as well. After a few weeks of cat-n-mouse sneaking around the city having lunch and dinner dates she finally gave in. Priscilla had finally had sex with another man willingly after only being with her husband. It felt great and she couldn't resist, every chance she got she met her young Cuban lover. Now, it was time to put her plan into action before she coward out.

One day while her husband was gone, she went to his stash house. Since she was the only other person besides him who knew where it was located. Checking on the stash reassuring that he just received a new shipment she was surprised to see 50 squares of "white girl." Estevez normally only received 20 to 25 a month so this was a surprise to see this amount of work. Then she went to check the second safe which held the currency. She was shocked, to say the least! Now, her husband had his family living better than most musicians were, but Priscilla had to be staring at anywhere between one and a half to 3 million in cash. She knew they had enough to leave the game alone especially with her 300 grand she had saved but she felt a tinge of betrayal. She had convinced her young Cuban lover one day after a steamy sex session that he should help her rob her husband of all his money and drugs then they could flee the state with the kids and be together. He agreed and was ready to do it as soon as possible so that they could stop sneaking around. She called her husband while lying next to her lover and told him that Rosa's cousin wanted to buy a few squares if he was willing to deal with him. Knowing it would have to be worth his while she told him that he had $170,000 for 10 squares, he jumped on it. The meeting place was an old run-down warehouse on the outskirts of the city close to the airport. It took Estevez a little over an hour to get everything together in the midst of handling other things. That was good because that gave Priscilla time to get the money from her stash to make the buy seem real. Her young Cuban lover was clueless all he knew was that he would meet with his lovers husband to buy a few bricks off him. He met Priscilla at the warehouse and about 20 minutes later Estevez arrived. Being the flamboyant gangsta that he was Estevez stepped in wearing caramel colored designer slacks a silk Calvin Klein button-up to match the slacks with a chocolate brown square toe Havanna Joe to compliment his outfit and the enormous amount of gold he wore. He walked as if he owned the world and the way he kissed her and palmed her ass added to his boss demeanor. Like the loving wife that she was she embraced her husband's attention and grabbed his crotch. Just like the days back in Puerto Rico she stood behind her man representing him like a wife should do. The two men became acquainted with each other and then they talked numbers. After the count of the money which took close to an hour Estevez went to the trunk of his car and retrieved a large size garbage bag that contained the 10 bricks. Priscilla had placed the money inside a large Polo duffle she had bought along. While the men closed the deal, Priscilla rummaged through her Chanel bag and when Estevez turned to leave POW! A shot ripped through the shoulder of her husband's silk shirt. With a shocked expression on his face, he started to watch her. POW, POW, POW, one to the chest, stomach, and neck Estevez dropped and he was unresponsive. Tears filled her eyes as she stood trembling with a smoking pistol clutched in both hands. Her young Cuban lover was in shock but tried his best to hide it as he walked over to Priscilla and placed his arms around her for a minute. She cried and he held her because he was in love with the older woman. They broke their embrace, Sonny her lover went to grab the squares, then headed for the car, and then he was stopped in his tracks.

"I can't, I just can't," Priscilla said through her sobbing and tears.

When her lover turned around, he never had a chance. The bullet crushed his skull with the force of a hippopotamus's bite. Directly between the eyebrows, he died instantly.

Priscilla wiped her eyes, grabbed the bag of bricks, looked at both her husband and lover and simply said it in a cold calculated way, "I just can't let you live." From that day on, she has killed, ordered murders, and tortured people of all kinds if you dared to test Priscilla Reyes.

CHAPTER 10

Ivan in Mourning

West 4th Street between Monroe and Adams seemed to be busy with a constant flow of traffic from sunup til sundown. From men and women heading to the bus stop as early as 4:30 a.m. to prostitutes and junkies scrambling to make a buck all day long; the workflow, school kids, addicts and local winos made this block pop! Considered as "down bottom" which is the bottom part of Westside just like the Hilltop this section of the city was plagued with violence as well. Wherever you had drugs and violence in the city you were sure to find a major player somewhere in the midst. Now over the years Westside as a whole has had a few heavy hitters R.I.P. Moegood, Coco, Bear, Quinton, Artega, and there were more. The Hilltop had so many poppies who had that work in it was ridiculous but Gill, Layton, Robb, and Tone all those niggas were O.G.'s who surpassed the level of regular money-getters, they were major players. Now since this dope epidemic has spread like a wildfire, the nigga fucking it up "down bottom" is my man from elementary school and just the person I need to see. I've been floating through his block on a regular for the past few days and haven't caught him, so I took a chance and stopped by his mother's house. She knew me since I was a kid, but I haven't seen her since I was 13 so I hope she remembers me. To my surprise when she opened the front door, she knew exactly who I was and was more than happy to see me.

"José... boy look at you, you're getting big and handsome. How have you been?" an excited Miss Pam asked.

"I'm doing fine, I was just stopping by to see how you were doing," replied José.

"I'm doing okay... how's your mother?" asked Miss Pam.

"She's good and my older brother just bought her a house out in Newark, so I guess she's excited," replied José.

"What! I know she's so happy... I wish Ra'mee brought me a damn house with his tight ass!" Miss Pam snapped.

"Where's he at right now?" José asked.

"His ass is down in my basement with one of them fast ass little girls... I don't know why he keeps bringing their stank asses here when he has his own house in Middletown. He should be entertaining those hoes there," she continued to fuss, "go head down there Baby these hoes probably wouldn't give a damn anyway."

Before entering I knocked to make my presence known but that didn't stop whatever was going on. I could hear the moans and skin smacking while I walked down the steps. When I reached the bottom, there sat Rosé on the edge of the bed being straddled by one of the thickest Black woman I had ever seen. She continued bouncing that soft looking ass up and down on Rosé's shaft. Noticing that I was watching, she began to put on a show and grind slowly and then lifted and dropped it even slower. Rosé continued until he got his nut, then pushed the woman from off top of him. I just shook my head while my friend threw on a pair of basketball shorts. The tall lanky kid could've easily been taken as a college athlete of some sort, but he wasn't, he was a plug.

"José what's up with you poppie?" Rosé asked embracing his friend.

"Trying to catch up with you nigga," José responded.

"Well, you better keep pumping then nigga... anyway what's the reason for this visit?" Rosé inquired about while rubbing his chin.

"I kinda need to holla at you alone," José shot back.

"Go upstairs with my mom for a minute," Rosé told the woman he was just fucking.

She got up without a word and left the basement with a switch in the hips that could rival Tyra Banks.

"So, what's good poppito?"

"Look, I just got my hands on some "d" and I don't know how to cut the shit probably to keep it fire... and I was hoping you could show me since this is your line of work and your heavy in this shit," José stated his case.

"First, friend or not to show you I'm gonna have to charge you... not a lot, but I'm gonna have to charge... business is business," Rosé said seriously.

"Cool," José said rubbing his hands together.

"A'ight so when do you wanna do this, how much you talking bout cutting and my price is a stack to show you the correct way and where do you plan on doing this shit at?" Rosé asked pulling his shirt over his head and sparking his cigarillo.

I'm ready right now and if you up to it we can cut up a brick and I got a spot to handle the work. Do I need any tools of any sort?" José asked anxiously.

"Yeah, I need you first to pay me 15 to cut a whole brick... that shit is gonna take forever. Next, I want you to stop by Rite Aid and grab some baby laxatives then go to G.N.C. or any nutrition shop and get some B-12 and I'll call my folks to see if they got any fetnayl."

"How bout I give you a stack? You walk me through the process hands-on and I'll pay you a stack to help me cut up 4 ½," José said taking control.

"Sounds good to me," Rosé responded.

"Let me ask you something else... how much you payin' for a square of "d"?" José inquired.

"56, but it's A-1 Shit poppie!" Rosé said boasting.

"Well, the Shit I got is A-1 and I can get it to you for 50 flat," José said convincingly.

"You bullshittin'... well, if it's what you say it is and you can get it at 50 get me two right now!" Rosé said getting hype.

"Well look, if you tryna get two of those your gonna have to give me about a half hour. Let me go put everything together and go grab up the ingredients. On that thought give me four hours... and let me get ya info so I can hit you with the address when I'm ready for you," José said while giving Rosé dap and a half hug."

After leaving Rosé's spot, José headed straight to Taylor and JoJo's, when he arrived the crib was silent and dark, so he knew he was there alone. Not wanting to waist anytime he went to his work stash that was in the extra bedroom and grabbed three squares of "d". He then went into his safe and grabbed his "judge" and was back out the door. He hopped in his SS Impala and head over to Upper Oak Street, which was still in the city, but it was off Broom Street on a nice little quiet block. This is one of the two homes José had Taylor purchase for him at the city's sheriff sale auction. The house only needed minor repairs such as a few holes in walls, light plumbing work and a few broken windows. After a trip to Home Depot and around the clock working the house was up and running in a week tops. He would have to move someone in there preferably a female since females would be doing all the bagging and packaging. He arrived on Upper Oak Street he grabbed the work out of the stash box then headed inside. On the inside there was the essentials water, electric and cable. There was really no furniture except a wrap-around sofa José got for the low from his poppie Alex that worked at Brandywine Furniture. Besides that, there were two, one in the dining room the other in the kitchen rectangular cherrywood tables that included six seats per table. Instead of going to three different store his man Pooda turned him unto a spot over Southbridge that had everything he needed including Bonita & Quanine the original cut for the heroin. Tucking the work away and only keeping his cannon on his waist he then text Rosé the address. Fifteen minutes later Rosé was knocking on the front door. When he entered, they gave each other the hood greeting, a stern handshake while embracing each other with the other arm. José did inform Rosé that no guns were allowed in the house except his so Rosé returned to his car and tucked his pistol. Now it was time to get down to work and Rosé walked José through the steps a few times. He even let him do it on his own to see if he really understood what he was doing. He caught on fast and with the two of them cutting the dope they actually finished the whole brick. The biggest surprise of the afternoon was how the one brick was now two bricks and a quarter one! That meant they profited a brick and a quarter off one. If sold as weight that's an extra 65 grand at least. Now they had to see just how good it was! Just their luck Rosé's phone had went off! When he answered he told the caller to meet him on Broom St. A few minutes later, Rosé left only to return 15 minutes later with a huge grin like the Grinch who stole Christmas on his face.

"Yo, José it's on Word!" Rosé said anxiously waiting for the next move to happen.

"What's the verdict papa?" José asked growing excited.

"My fiend Bill just did a tester... he's a shooter, anyway that nigga shot that shit and went straight under. When he came through, he said the shit was damn near a perfect 10. The dude normally grabs four or five bundles at 40 apiece but after hitting that shit, we drove down to the Cumberland Farms Convenient Store and he hit the ATM. That fiend spent 400 for the 3 ½ grams I had on me. The shit's fire José if all this Shit is the same, we on one," Rosé said more serious than ever.

José changed his mind and gave Rosé the 15 for his services, then put the two and a quarter bricks into Ziplock bags.

"So, do you got that for me cause I'm ready to hit the ground running," Rosé proclaimed.

"Yeah, how bout you?" José questioned.

"I got the paper right here."

Rosé pulled out 10-$10,000 bundles of money. He began counting and when he finished José counted next. After everything was good, José retrieved the bag with the work and handed the exact same work to his friend. The deal went good and Rosé had left so José called Taylor who was with JoJo as usual and had, them come to "Hell's Kitchen" the name he gave the house on Upper Oak Street since it would be used for the purpose of manufacturing the work. When his two homegirls arrived, he got straight to business.

"So, what have y'all two thots been doing all day?" José said jokingly.

"First off, if Imma thot I'm the sexiest thot you know Word!" JoJo said in her defense.

"Hold up, Jo this nigga was the same nigga rubbing our feet and cooking us dinner... you tender dick if you doin all that for some thots," Taylor added to the assault on José.

"I did that cause you'll always remember me for that and no nigga can take my spot in y'all lives. I'm here forever," José said showing off his sexy smile.

"So, how is it possible for you to have a wife and get in house pussy but we can't even have a jump off come over from time to time and tap this soft ass," JoJo said emphasizing by grabbing her ass cheeks.

"You know why Jo so stop talking crazy (referring to the work and money) but if you need love, I wouldn't mind touching that soft little body of yours," José said seriously catching JoJo off guard.

JoJo got up from her seat and stood in front of José and told him he can have it whenever he wanted it in a playful manner but deep down inside, she met every word. She loved José more than he knew.

"Look at y'all two... go get a room. Boy, you gotta girl anyway my dawg ain't playing second to no one! Plus, I think she looks better than Summer anyway. How bout you José?" Taylor asked waiting for a response.

José looked over at Taylor then at JoJo who looked kind of skeptical to what his answer might be. True JoJo did have Summer beat all around, body and face. Now Summer was bad hands down so if JoJo had her beat all around that should really explain how beautiful she was. Never one to let his true feelings show he did what he does best and evaded the question.

"No comment," he said smiling at JoJo then changed the subject, "so what's up with y'all girls? Did y'all find out if they wanted to work?" José asked.

"Yeah, I talked to the Twins, Keya, Keisha, Mere, Mook, Janae, and

BeBe they were down since it was for you. They all wanna know when they start and how much you paying?" Taylor asked wanting all the details.

"To start, I'll give them 500 hundred for every brick they break down and bag up plus, they can smoke bud whenever their working for free," José said trying to bargain.

"Shit, that sounds good I might gotta get in on that," Taylor said.

"Nah Sis, I'm gonna give y'all two a stack apiece each week to hold it and drop it off to them as needed. No niggas are allowed here period! And where are the Twins staying at now?" he asked.

"With their grandmom on Union Street," Taylor replied.

"Good, see if they wanna move in here A.S.A.P., I don't want the house empty, but I don't want a lot of traffic either. Neighbors don't worry about a lot of females like that, it's the men, music, and weed that draws the heat. So, see what's up cause I need them to start working tonight if they can," José said like he was about his business.

While in the middle of talking his phone went off! It was Rosé letting him know that everything was good on his end and that he wanted to meet up with him the upcoming weekend at the Hookah Lounge with his team. José accepted the offer then ended the call. Now, all José had to do was call his team and let them know they'd be back on in the am. He had to stop by JoJo's and Taylors to grab a brick of white girl to cook up so that he would also be ready for the morning. Deciding to grab two bricks of coke instead of one he went to the Batcave and begin the process of standing in the kitchen. With the bud already situated and the "d" being taken care of while they spoke all hands were in on the baggin' up of the coke. As usual, one brick and 12 ounces were being bagged up in all dimes and the other brick plus, was bagged up in ballgames. With all the coke he had he would definitely sell a few whole squares. Tallying up all the money he spent on the two houses, the two cars, the money he gave Summer for the apartment plus the money he had to pay to fix the houses, pay the bitches for bagging up then the bags and utensils needed to package the shit his stash was light. So, he knew he would definitely be going hard all that week. Good thing Rosé spent that hundred grand just to keep him comfortable.

Ivan was mourning the death of his younger cousin Fat Papi who had been brutally murdered earlier that week. Angelina had personally stopped by the shop to view the horrific scene once she received the call from Ivan. Knowing Ivan had just lost his closest cousin she sent him home. When Ivan left, she looked and went into the back office. There was an extra door in the office that she seemed to be focused on and when she opened the door, she found exactly what she was looking for! Leaving the back-office Angelina called her own personal cleanup crew. She gave them strict orders to clean the place out of all guns and money but to leave the bodies. Once that was taken care of, call the police from a "burn out" phone to report the murders, and then get rid of the phones. Fat Papi is what she considered a close associate and Ivan's family, so she wanted answers and she hoped that she'd soon have some. Ivan had been M.I.A. and was asking a few people he dealt with if they had heard anything but everyone, he asked had no info on the double murder. The murder had him on edge seriously, he didn't know a thing, what it was about or who it was. All he knew was that they had to take the work his cousin had just grabbed because it was gone when he got there. Pulling up on 2nd and Van Buren Ivan stopped by LaFlores corner store to get a bite to eat. While waiting two kids walked in behind him who looked to be Hispanic but were dark as Black people. They were talking in Spanish about how fly Ivan's burgundy and tan Bo Jackson's were. Looking down at the two youngsters shoes he smiled inwardly, thinking of his younger days when he couldn't afford sneakers. He went in his pocket and pulled out two crispy Benjamin Franklins and handed them to the boy and girl and he also paid for their snacks they had in hand.

"Gracious," the two kids said excited to have just received the money.

"No gracious!" Ivan replied with a smile.

"Why do you say thank you and you gave us the money?" the kids quizzed.

"Because seeing you two reminds me of where I came from... remember to never forget where you came from," Ivan said patting the young boy on the head.

"Hasta luego!" the two kids said running out the store and then down the block.

Ivan's mentality was rather you were Puerto Rican, Dominican, Mexican, or Cuban if you were Spanish it was all good and all love unless you forced his hand. He dealt with other races too especially the Blacks which he had no problem with it was just he loved whatever you wanted to call them Latin, Spanish, Hispanic, all the same and as a whole culture. Getting his food in leaving LaFlores he was shocked to see the two kids returning with their mothers. Of course, the mothers wanted to know if he gave them the money and why? He explained he wanted the kids to buy themselves a pair of sneakers since they were admiring his. So, indulged into his conversation with the mother he almost didn't notice the man walking down the block with his baby Cannon out until the little boy alerted him.

"Oh Snap!" the little boy said with a look of panic on his face.

Ivan, off instinct immediately grabbed the Glock 19 from under his shirt and spun around quickly. The mothers tried grabbing their kids, but the first shot burst into the wind. BOOM! With no time to think Ivan let off three shots in succession causing the man to finally take cover, but he continued to fire back! Taking cover Ivan noticed that the little girl had been shot and it looked pretty bad. She was bleeding heavily from a gunshot wound to the upper torso or arm area. Wherever it was she wasn't moving her mother was hysterical as she cuffed her child. Ivan knew he had to get out of there before the law showed up so he "turned up." He rose in the direction of the shooter but went the opposite way of the kids and their parents. BOOM, BOOM, BOOM... BOOM, BOOM! He let his torch blow and this caused the shooter to come from out of hiding and try to escape. That was all he needed because when he got a good look at the shooter, he recognized him immediately.

"That's that bitch ass puto from Pleasant Street," Ivan said fuming through clenched teeth.

The sirens could be heard approaching quick so Ivan had to go. He wanted to stay in check on the little girl but knew that he couldn't. So, he gave her mother his apologies then hopped in his car and left! The first thing he did was let Angelina know what had just happened and who was involved. Next, he went on Delaware Online to see if anything on the shooting came up. It did but it was too early for details later that evening he watched the news and still nothing on the little girl. Then he received a call from Angelina the next morning who informed him that she was coming to pick him up. When she got there Ivan got in her Bentley Coupe and they pulled off. Twenty minutes later, they were at the Christiana Hospital heading to I.C.U. Before going to the unit Ivan stopped at the gift shop and brought balloons, candy, cards I mean the works for the little girl. When they stepped on the floor everyone noticed the huge selection of "Get Well Soon" balloons. Stopping at the desk the receptionist pointed them to room 215. When they entered the father was holding the daughters hand who was awake and smiling. The mother made eye contact with Ivan instantly. She stood to greet them both as Ivan handed her the gifts. Angelina had known the family for a while and when she heard Maria was shot in the middle of the shootout she wanted to apologize personally. Along with an undisclosed amount of cash for the hush, they were now standing in the room. Ivan walked closer to the bed and when Maria saw him her eyes grew wide as never before!

"Wow, it's you! Man, you were shooting like the Cowboys vs. the Indians," Maria said grinning ear to ear.

"Are you okay? I'm sorry this had to happen to you," Ivan said sincerely rubbing her head.

"Yeah, I'm okay, it hurts a little but I'm kind of a tomboy, so I'll live. I did lose the money you gave me for the sneakers though," she said seriously.

"Don't worry bout that kiddo!" Ivan said pulling two crispy Benjamin's out of his pocket and then handed it to her.

"Gracias," Maria said happily.

"No gracias," Ivan replied winking his eye at her.

They talked for a little while longer after Angelina spoke with Maria's mother and father. Just like she agreed she gave them an envelope containing $10,000 and then they left. After knowing Maria was still alive

Ivan relaxed a little. Just as soon as they stepped out of the hospital though Angelina transformed.

"I want you to go through Pleasant Street and give them a going away party for everyone except women and kids until I say otherwise."

CHAPTER 11

Picking Up Where Fat Papi Left Off

Alex was upset that he didn't expect the unexpected. He thought when he saw Ivan walking in LaFlores that he had the drop on him but to his surprise, Ivan was strapped and ready for war. Alex knew the little girl was shot in the process of the shootout but didn't give two shits. He considered it a casualty of war and that comes with the game. His mother would be back sometime the next afternoon and he had missed his target. He also knew that Ivan had identified him so he would have to go all the way in. Taking no chances with his new adversary Alex put the price of a "gee" for anyone with the whereabouts of Ivan and was correct. What he didn't know was about the same time he had put that word out in the streets it had already got back to Ivan. Now he wouldn't have to look for him because Ivan was coming directly to him and his family.

Ivan had received a call from a loyal customer named Pedro who copped weight off him on the regular. Word had been said by one of his friends that some new dude named Alex was asking around about Ivan and was giving a $1000 with the correct info on his whereabouts. Talking with Pedro Ivan found out that Alex and his family had a much bigger operation than he expected and that it was rumored that the whole thing was ran not by Alex but his mother, some old woman named Priscilla. Deciding to stay at his second apartment out Glasgow Ivan headed to the parking garage in the basement of the condo. As he walked to his 2015 Black Range Rover, he was sidetracked by a beautiful looking Spanish woman who had to be in her early 40s. She had to live in the building but with so many floors it was easy not to know her.

As she walked to her Smoke Gray RX470 Lexus Jeep Ivan approached her. Catching her off guard startled her and Ivan immediately apologized.

"Como le va?" Ivan asked cracking a smile.

"I'm fine and yourself?" the woman replied returning the smile.

"Are you new in the building? I don't think I ever saw you before," Ivan asked.

"Not new, I've been here a while now at least a year... and I've seen you a few times though," she stated rubbing her hair gently.

"What's your name if you don't mind me asking?" Ivan asked.

"You can call me LeLe and what's yours?" she asked in return.

"Hoviare... that's my real name but you can... on the other note, just call me Hovi. I mean I was kind of in a rush and it looks like you're heading out as well so if it's okay maybe we can exchange numbers and later this week we could get together for lunch," Ivan said in a saucy manner.

"Sure, I'd love that, I haven't been out in a while... so here's my card with all my contact info and be sure to call me," she said while getting into her Lex Jeep and pulling out of the parking garage.

Ivan stood looking at the card that had her profession being a financial advisor. He hopped in his Range and headed to Glasgow with his new friend LeLe on his mind.

"Umm! Umm, Slurp, Slurp, Slurp! Was the sound of the amazing head Rakmeef was getting from his high school sweetheart. With enough saliva to cover his dick balls and her tiny hands along with the powerful lockjaw she had Abbee was sucking his dick like she was French kissing a popsicle. She caressed his balls with one hand while pumping a nice size amount into her mouth with the other one. Abbee was a master of the art and could actually make a nigga cum in less than five minutes but with Rakmeef she loved pleasing him. So, she took her time and twirled that fat dick all around on her tonsils, her gag reflex was perfect so she would try to stuff his whole cock down her throat but could never get the whole thing.

"Damn, boo boo you still the best... I miss this Shit right here," he said while rolling his head back.

"Umm, I miss sucking this big mothafucka that's why I came to see you Meef," Abbee said in between sucks and licks.

"Damn, boo boo why ya Sexy Spanish Ass have to go and start getting high?" Rakmeef asked sounding all emotional and shit.

"Come on Meef, why you always go there? I got my own spot, more money than most of these hustling niggas out here, I still look good and I don't have any STDs," Abbee said pulling out the results from her latest doctors visit and smiling while handing him the paper to view.

After a thorough look, he handed her the paperback, then stood her up from her knees and lowered her down onto his dick in the reverse cowgirl position. Rakmeef watched his dick appear and then disappear between her plump tan cheeks. She was loving the multiple orgasms he made her have when they made love. Because that's just what Rakmeef would do when he sexed Abbee. After he got his nut she sat on his lap and rested her head on his shoulder then spoke to her high school sweetheart.

"Meef, I got something to tell you and I don't know how you wanna handle it... but you gotta handle it fast," Abbee said catching Rakmeef off guard.

"What's up boo boo?" Rakmeef asked looking Abbee directly in the eyes.

"Well, I was on the Hill earlier and this bitch ass nigga named Ramone said he saw you and Twink leave the house where that guy and little boy was killed on the hill. He said he witnessed y'all leave right after he heard the shots babe," she said fumbling with her fingers not making eye contact.

"Okay, that's a lie cause I haven't been over Westside in a minute, but thanks for letting me know," Rakmeef said while fondling her titties.

"Babe, that's not all though!" she said in her strong Spanish accent.

"What else is it then?" he asked growing impatient.

"He's working with this detective and he's supposed to meet with him to make a statement on y'all and if y'all get convicted he gets 50 gees... I think he said the detectives name was Baldwin or something like that," she answered.

At the mention of Detective Baldwins name Rakmeef had become uneasy very quickly. He knew Baldwin had a hard on for the two hyenas since they were in their teen when they were acquitted on their first homicide.

"Boo Boo what's his name... the fiend?" Rakmeef asked.

"His name is Ramone babe and I can't stand the rat bastard... you should let me handle this for you," Abbee said meaning every word to prove her loyalty.

"I need you to handle something else for me... I'll take care of Ramone... where he be at and what he look like?" he asked.

"He always on the Hill and he's a faggot so he likes to dress in women's clothing or skintight jeans and shirt and shit," she said giving up the details.

"A'ight good, me and Twink are gonna pay homegirl a visit," he said.

"So, what you want me to do Rakmeef?" she asked sincerely.

"I want you to go check into the Gateway Rehabilitation Center down in Delaware City and get yourself cleaned up. For real, if you get yourself together and stay clean, we might be able to work on us again... but you gotta fall back with all the bullshit or it's nothing. It takes up to six months to complete, I'll make sure you have what you need and I'll visit you every weekend. And when you get out, we can get apartment down there to keep you away for a while, deal?" he asked.

After thinking about it for a minute she made her mind up and decided to go away to rehab. She knew the withdraw would have her sick as hell, but she was ready for a change in her life. Plus, she loved her some Rakmeef so when he said he was willing to take a chance on her once again she was also willing to take a chance on change. She decided to throw her work away she had copped earlier and smoked a blunt and sipped some Henny with her babe. The weed had her high as the sky and the only thing that she could think of that always brought the two ex-lovers together was their past.

"Babe, do you ever think of the baby?" Abbee asked sadly.

"All the time, my baby would have been seven this year," Rakmeef replied genuinely.

"Yup, she would've looked just like her daddy too," Abbee said turning to face Rakmeef.

They sat quietly for a minute then he kissed her on the lips and laid her down. Then he whispered in her ear "I love you always" and then entered her once again. Regardless of her reputation or addiction, he loved Abbee because she was his first love and they had a baby together. Unfortunately, the baby died unexpectedly from SIDS (Sudden Infant Death Syndrome). They were young when it happened, like 18 to be exact so the stress broke them apart and led to Abbee getting high. Now seven years later, Rakmeef was ready to get his boo-boo back and make shit right once again. First, he had to handle a rat and shake the law.

All the work hadn't quite been bagged up, but the morning had come and it was time to get money. Carlos had the bud jumping as usual and Dre had finished the sticks José had gotten from the shop, but the girls were working and they had a good amount of sticks prepared. He hollered at a few playas about the work so in no time was the weight moving. 4 ½ soft here and nine ozones of hard there, even a brick sale came before mid-afternoon. The dimes and ballgames were still moving with excellent timing. Castro went to his stash and even decided to grab a brick and a half of soft which cost him 37 grand. Then to top it off to make the day even better two young niggas who were 16 from Cash Avenue named Reese Real and Jugstar had been riding through the city trying to find a plug on the "d" and ran into José while they were at Scott Market on 5th and Scott. They were looking to grab nine ozones of "manteca" and they had 15 grand so José served them as well. They already knew how to cut and bag it, so they were straight, after grabbing they rolled out. With all the movement he did he just threw the money in his car trunk. Wanting to count it he walked off the block to where he parked his car then popped the trunk. After counting the cash quickly, he knew he had roughly made over 80 grand today and that didn't include the dimes, ballgames, Dre's dope cash and the bud money. This and he hadn't even cut all the bricks of dope yet or cooked up the coke. He sold two bricks of dope and cut one up which came back to two and a quarter. That gave him more than he started with. So, he decided to step on five bricks of "d" and bring back 11 and a quarter and sell the other five to Rosé if he needs them. And with the coke he would cook up 10 squares and stretch them to almost 13 ½ squares and sell the rest as raw power. With the money from today and what he got from Rosé and his stash; he was sitting on a little over 200 grand.

Everything was going well; the block and the people seem content and José was coming up. While the kids played out front on the sidewalk and José sat on the steps with Janay who was on her way to Hell's Kitchen for work, they noticed a 2016 Dodge Charger the "Hellcat" coasting down the street. When it passed by slowly José and Janay noticed the guy staring at José. Feeling unsafe, Janay got up from the steps and walked on her porch. José jumped up and darted in the alley, grabbed his Glock 40 with a 36-shot clip and then exited the alley. Seeing José exit the alley the guy got out of his vehicle and first lifted his shirt revealing that he didn't have a weapon and then proceeded to walk towards José. Poppie had a rugged fly guy look, he wore a silk peach and gold Versace see-through linen shirt that was buttoned up halfway exposing his chest hairs. A peach-colored fitted Versace jean with the white and gold Versace belt with the gold Medusa head on it, a pair of powdered peach and gold colored Versace loafers to match the outfit. Poppie had a lot of "moda" a Spanish word that means fashion, style or mode.

"Como esta?" the man asked José. José nodded his head in return acknowledging the stranger.

"Is your name José?" the stranger asked intently.

"Who wants to know papa?" José replied showing no emotion.

"Oh, excuse me, I'm stepping on your turf not even introducing myself then asking a bunch of questions... my fault my name is Angel," he said extending his hand.

José shook His hand then asked what he could help him with.

"Look, poppie if you don't mind if you're not busy maybe you could take a ride with me... it just may be beneficial to you in the long run," Angel said heading to the car.

José looked at Janay then back at Angel and decided to see what was up with him. He was strapped so if anything, funny took place he would shoot his way out or die trying. Once they pulled off Angel got on his phone and told someone on the other end that he had met up with José and that they were on their way. That made José feel unsafe and Angel could tell so he reassured him that everything was okay. Riding for a few minutes, José realized he was heading to Greenville Delaware. This is where the millionaires lived and when they pulled into the wraparound driveway with a six-car garage and all types of foreign cars from a Rolls-Royce Phantom to a Ferrari and a two million-dollar Bugatti, therefore, he knew that whoever lives here had a million dollar plus bag! Walking up to the door of what seemed to be a compound instead of a mansion, José was amazed by the 12-foot high European crafted doors. He looked around at the scenery and was very impressed but also curious about the reasons for being here. When he stepped through the double doors into an extraordinary looking foyer that had charcoal gray granite tiles with faces of the Greek gods and goddesses that were engraved by hand, he stood still in shock admiring the work. When he walked up the five steps to reach the main landing he was blown away! He watched as a mother, a great white shark, and her child swam around freely underneath his feet. Schools of colorful fish, seahorse, jellyfish, and four dolphins moved about without a worry in the world.

Whoever's house this was had the entire floor which had to be at least 4000 square feet customized into an aquarium. The cathedral ceilings and abundant windows to invite the sunlight to bathe on the open hardwood floors with beautiful paintings and flowers throughout the place gave it a castle-like aura. Receiving a tour of the house José was impressed with the five bathrooms, two and a half baths, a library with built-in shelves, home theater, game room, wet bar, gym, and wine cellar. The kitchen was decked out with commercial appliances it had a center-island sink and granite countertops. The wrap around staircase leading directly to the master suite that had a huge pink and gold marble bathroom and double walk-in closets. That was just on the inside, on the outside there was a custom-made pool designed in the letter A, a hot tub, an outdoor kitchen with a fire pit and a guest house and another garage that held five more cars. José was done, this was the way he wanted to live.

This guy must be some sort of entertainer or musician cause he was loaded," José thought.

"Yo, how big is this shit?" José asked seemingly stunned.

"8,375 feet to be exact... it's sitting on 4.2 acres but who's counting," Angel said chuckling.

"Damn, I want some shit like this one day," José confessed.

"And you can ultimately have it one day if you work hard and smart," Angel said.

"So, what's up poppie, why'd you bring me all the way out here? I know it wasn't to give me a tour of up ya spot," José said wanted to get down to business.

Just then a woman stepped out onto the balcony and motions for us to come inside. Due to the sun shining directly in his face, he couldn't make out who it was. When they entered the house in the distance a shapely woman was approaching the two. From the low-cut top and short cut bottom he could see that she had a nice healthy set of breast and some soft looking thick legs. The heels she wore exposed her tiny toes that had a fresh pedicure. Her hair flowed over her face covering just enough to not be noticed on first look. He could tell she was older but caught up in her thickness he never looked her directly in the eyes. The woman stepped to us and gave Angel a kiss and then thanked him for finding José.

"Follow me, sweetie," the woman's voice said softly as she turned and walked away.

Whoever this Spanish old head was she was phat! Her ass bounced from left to right in her purple Chanel fall ensemble. The heels added to her sex appeal as she pranced across the large aquarium underneath her giving José a full view of her backside from the waist down. Stepping into the area where the wet bar was located, she offered José a drink, but he declined. Then she tossed him a nice sac of some of the best-looking bud he had ever seen before. It was powder blue with white t.h.c. crystals all over it.

"What's this?" José asked in a curious tone.

"It's called poppa smurf," the woman replied.

José took another look at the bud then chuckled to himself. Leaving that area, the woman walked into the library and took a seat behind the desk while José continued standing. She could tell that he still hadn't recognized her yet and she knew why.

"Take a seat, José it's been a while since I've seen you. You're not in a hurry or anything are you? I hope not because I really need to talk with you about something and I hope you can help me out," she said with a cheerful attitude.

José wasn't in a hurry but what stuck out in his mind was the fact she said she hadn't seen him in a while. So, he took a closer look at her while she brushed her hair out of her face. With her hair and makeup done and a dress, heels, and accessories, she looked stunning. Not like she did when he saw her around the way. Noticing that he had recognized her she lit the room up with her beautiful smile. José couldn't help it as his jaw fell to the floor; he was fucked up!

"Angelina?" José said surprised.

"Yes dear," she responded in her always charming way.

"Is this your spot?"

"Yes, and welcome... mi casa su casa."

"Look at you... you don't look like that when I come into the store," José said still surprised to even see her dressed so provocative.

"Well, thank you for the compliment but I don't dress like this at the store because I'm working dear," Angelina responded.

"Damn, you Fucked my head up with this one... I thought I was about to be introduced to a movie star or something and come to find out it's Angelina who knew me all my life, wow!"

"Well, thank you... but do me a favor and never come here unannounced and never bring anyone here!" Angelina said seriously.

"I would never do that; I don't get down like that bring people to other people's houses. So, what's up? What's the reason you wanted to see me and why did you have that guy Angel come get me when you could have come yourself?" José asked trying to figure out the mystery.

Angelina sat there silently for a moment while eyeing José who was intently waiting on an answer.

"First, Angel is my husband and he decided that he would come find you instead of me looking around. However, I could've had Sammy tell you that I needed to speak with you. That may have taken to long and could have been too late. So, we came and found you," Angelina said becoming a little more serious.

"For what though?" José wanted to know.

Angelina began rubbing her hands together while having José roll up a cigarillo of the poppa smurf. After he was done pearling the bud, he sparked it and puffed a few times. He passed it to Angelina who hit the bud like a professional holding it in her freshly manicured nails then she spoke.

"José dear I think you have something that belongs to me," she said with a deadly demeanor about her now. Not knowing what she was talking about he was confused.

"José I'm gonna show you something first then we can talk... know that I brought you here today because I trust you. If I didn't, you'd be dead by now," Angelina spoke with not an ounce of compassion but strictly venom.

José looked shocked a little nervous and confused all in one once again. Angelina pressed a button under her desk and from out the wall, a 23" flat screen TV appeared. Grabbing the remote she pressed play and his mouth fell wide open! He watched in "HD" from beginning to end the gruesome murder of his old plug Fat Papi. The video showed a man entering the shop and talking briefly before opening fire on the mechanic Raúl while Fat Papi tried to cause some type of distraction and make a run for his weapon. It showed Fat Papi firing off a few rounds then taking cover. Next, it showed him raising up to fire again, but he must've run out of bullets. That's when the man who could now be seen clearly and looked familiar rose up with what looked to be a saw off shotgun blasting a round into Fat Papi that sent him flying unto the hood of a car. Next, what he saw made him flinch a little, the man whispered in Fat Papi's ear and then with the barrel of the shotie pressed to the side of Fat Papi's face the man fired. Nothing was left of his face except shreds of skin and meat. Angelina sat and watched José's demeanor and body movements for any signs of guilt. There was none and she was relieved. Angelina had removed the disc from the security room located in the back office of the shop the day she went to view the scene. José sat and watched as the man left the shop but was surprised to see she kept the video rolling. When he saw an image of himself appeared on the screen, he became uncomfortable instantly.

The next 10 minutes showed José, JoJo and Taylor taking money, guns and most importantly over $750,000 in drugs. Angelina finally stopped the video and sat silently staring at him playing with her fingernails.

"Do you understand why you're here now?" she questioned him. Still confused he shook his head no.

"José the drugs you took belong to me; Papi worked for me dear," she said clearing the air so that he knew exactly what she was talking about.

José's mouth fell open for the third time that afternoon. He couldn't believe that the kind ol' lady from the corner store was a major plug in the city and he never knew it. Plus, he realized that the work would now have to be returned to its owner.

"It was good while it lasted," he thought to himself.

"I thought y'all told me this would be beneficial to me coming here today?" José asked.

"And it could be if you're willing to consider what I'm about to offer you," Angelina said eyeing the youngin.

"What's that?" he asked suspiciously.

"I've done my homework and I see that you have a nice flow of traffic coming through Scott Street from 2nd up to 5th Street. I was also informed by Fat Papi before he passed away that you and your team was moving about three squares in 10 days all pieces," she said waiting for him to agree.

"Well, yeah but I've kinda sold a few of the whole ones since I had them," he confessed.

"That's good... I see you don't wait around, but what if I gave you Fat Papi's old clients and let you take over his operation?" she asked hoping he'd except.

"That sounds good but I don't know who Fat Papi was dealing with and what they were involved in so that may be kind of risky on my end by dealing with them if you know what I mean. What I was thinking was that you would let me hold that work and I'll knock it off then I'll bring you what I owe you," he said trying to convince her.

"How long will it take you to finish 30 bricks dear?" she asked.

"I'm not sure but I'll knock it off," he said confidently.

"That's what I'm saying, dear... see poppie moved all 40-20 coke and 20 manteca every three to four days," she sat with her hands folded for a second, "how about I help you move these squares, you continue to deal with your people as well and when you finished we can see how you feel. And if you still feel the same way then you won't have to do it again."

"How much do I owe you for the entire shipment?"

"If I'm not mistaken it was 20 squares of soft and 10 squares of manteca correct?"

"Yeah, that's right plus, 250 sticks already packaged," he stated.

"Alright this is what I'll do for you sweetheart just to make you see that I really want you and believe in you. Now, not even Fat Papi had it this sweet, but hey different strokes for different folks... I'll give you each brick for 145. That would make your total for the soft $281,000 and I would like $42,000 apiece for the other stuff so that would be another $420,000. That would be a grand total of $701,000. You can consider the packaged bundles and the money you found that had to be close to a $100,000 a gift from me to you," she said smiling while extending her hand.

Thinking about the once in a lifetime offer José quickly made his mind up.

"It's a deal but if I can't move that amount of work quick enough, remember I told you so."

"Honey don't worry you'll do just fine," she said taking a phone out of her desk then sliding it across to José.

"What's that for?" he asked inspecting the phone.

"Transfer all the contacts or call them, it doesn't matter just let them know you'll be picking up where Fat Papi left off. And if they question you anymore just say "Bella Bandido" and that should take care of everything," Angelina said with a smile now.

"Beautiful Bandit?" he asked looking confused.

"Yes, that's the name the streets gave me on my rise to the top. And the guys that you'll be dealing with I've known personally for years so you're okay. José listen, though you can have a lot more than Fat Papi ever did. To be honest, you could run the whole state plus, a few others as far as I'm concerned but you have to be loyal," she said returning serious looking.

"I'm loyal you'll see," José responded.

"Show me then," she said baiting him into the trap!

"How?" he asked.

"This guy I don't know but he killed my friend and I want him found very soon and I want him dead like yesterday! Take this disc and study his face and when you catch him, I need proof," she calmly stated.

José looked to see if she was serious and the expression, she gave confirmed that she meant it. The funny thing was the villain on the video had looked familiar to José he just couldn't pinpoint where he knew the killer from. Wherever it was, José was sure that he would meet up with this man and send him to his maker or die trying.

CHAPTER 12

They Want Ivan Dead!

The plane landed in Philadelphia exactly 4:45 pm. Priscilla and her family were just returning from Puerto Rico. The younger kids were still enjoying the recent memories of their vacation while Priscilla's thoughts were on whatever awaited her back in Murdertown. She hadn't talked with Alex in over a week and every time she tried calling him, she wouldn't receive an answer. She wondered if leaving her son alone to deal with a man or team she knew nothing about was a wise idea. The shuttle vans she reserved to pick her and the family up were on time, so they all loaded in and headed back to Wilmington. She tried calling Alex while heading South on 95 but she still didn't receive an answer. She began to fear the worst and it began weighing heavy on her heart. The more she thought on the situation the angrier she became. Priscilla was ready for war and she'd war with the whole city to protect her family. Her mind was made up as soon as she got home, she would call her oldest son, yeah, she was calling Amillio.

Alex has been incognito since the shootout with Ivan. He had switched up his car and was still on the hunt but knew now that he had to move in calculated steps. He knew his adversary was thinking the same way and Playing for Keeps, so it would ultimately come down to whoever was caught slippin' first. Alex had noticed that his mother had called him repeatedly but refused to answer until he handled his business. Lighting his third "dipper" of the afternoon Alex drifted into neverland and continued surfing through the 41 blocks of murder looking for his beef.

As soon as they landed and were on the road both Twins were on their phones calling Carlos and Dre. They love the conversation that the youngins had and couldn't wait to see them. The convo was erotic/mature which showed that Carlos and Dre were mature for their ages. They had made arrangements with Carlos and Dre to meet up someplace later that evening and the Twins couldn't wait! Carlos and Dre, we're excited as well they knew the two divas were feeling them and that tonight just might be the night!

The shuttle vans had just turned onto Franklin Street and were a half block away from Pleasant Street. Everything seemed to be calm in the neighborhood, the children played, the stray cats roamed, and no drama was occurring. When they turned onto Pleasant Street the block was still. It was quiet except for the empty chip bags tumbling across the tiny street and some middle-aged dude who looked like he was just walking through to get to his destination. The shuttle vans came to a stop in the middle of the block, the doors opened, and family began pouring out into the street. Priscilla had finally exited the van and headed to the house while Chomo, Edwin, and Hector grabbed the luggage. The older woman gathered the children together while bending over to pick up her toddler son Glady froze in a panic when she saw the same middle-aged man who was just walking up the block sprinting back down the block in her direction. Before she had a chance to say anything to warn everyone the first blast came causing everyone's earth to quake! POP, POP, POP! Everyone began screaming and running in all directions. The children scrambled for safety while Glady and her sisters took cover as well. Priscilla had tripped and fallen onto the steps just in time to see her son Chomo gunned down. Catching one to the chest and one to the stomach he dropped! The man ran up and stood over top of him and with no mercy and his eyes fired another shot into the back of his head. He then took off after Edwin and Hector who he was now firing shots at realizing he couldn't catch them he turned and sprinted back up the block were Priscilla and her daughters were now grieving and consoling their traumatized mother.

The man walked up to the group of women and said simply, "This block is taken I suggest you relocate. Oh, and Priscilla tell your son Alex when I find him, I'm gonna kill him," Ivan said savagely.

Remembering her son saying that the man who pulled the gun on him had a scar on his face. Priscilla knew at that moment that she had just come face-to-face with the man they called Ivan. For the first time since before her husband was killed Priscilla was truly scared. The look he gave her was that he would kill her as well, but something stopped him and because she didn't know what it was that's what she feared the most. Ivan jogged off and vanished in seconds. While holding the body of her deceased son she spoke to her daughters.

"Somebody go find Alex and tell him to get here now! Then one of you go and get Amillio on the phone!" she said screaming hysterically.

The sun was out, the weather was fair, and Prices Park was jam-packed. Northside day was in full effect and the sexiest women from that side of town were in attendance. Hustlers and playas politicked while the older folks played horseshoes and dominoes and the younger kids started up basketball games and jumped double-dutch. Dirt bikes and four wheelers engines revved loudly as the riders put on a show for the spectators. Numerous bottles of many different assortments of liquor from Amsterdam to Cîroc or Dom Perignon to Ace of Spades were consumed. Various types of "loud" smoke polluted the air and peoples lungs. Treasure and Hope were two of the most sought-after woman over North and they knew it. Since elementary even in their teens and twenties, men old and young from all over the city were after them. Down to earth and people-friendly, the sisters received love at a high volume. They weren't the stuck-up or conceited type so even females loved hanging out with them. "G.A.P. Gang" had four members who were Treasure, Hope, Fly Ass Kiesha Jenkins and their younger cousin Summer. At an event like Northside Day you knew the gang would be there. With Treasure, Hope, and Kiesha being equal to the queen of England in their community Summer would have been equivalent to the queen of Dubai in the City of Wilmington. The hustlers from North didn't really know her because she was from Westside on the Hilltop. She only came over North occasionally to hang out with her cousins, but with her man huggin' the block like a newborn baby she decided to join her gang at the event. G.A.P. stood for "good-ass pussy" and with all four women being natural squirters and pussy walls tighter than a pair of vice grips they all felt the name suited them perfectly. Do not for one second take a pretty smile and a cute face as a sign of weakness. On many occasions, they've had to turn up on a group of bum bitches here and there a few times just to show these hoes that they could stand toe-to-toe and go blow-for-blow. That alone has given them the reputation of beautiful brawlers along with all of them in college and working they're considered certified platinum dimes, young dimes at that! So, while the girls hung out and chit-chatted with numerous groups of people Summer would be introduced, speak, and enjoy the scenery. Summer was enjoying herself when she recognized a familiar face that she'd rather not see. Knowing she couldn't escape the encounter unless she left the barbecue which she wasn't doing she prepared herself for the shenanigans. She lowered her head and turned in the opposite direction and tried to step away before she was noticed. It was too late!

"Damn, sexy I didn't expect to see you here," Strap said in his arrogant tone. Summer turned to face him with a blank stare on her face.

"I didn't expect to see you either," she said bluntly.

"Well, now that you're here you might as well come over here and fuck with me and my peoples... who you here with?"

"My cousin's Treasure and Hope and my girl Kiesha," she said with her arms folded across her chest and head cocked to the side.

"Damn, why everything with you got to be with an attitude... a nigga can't even be nice to your stuck-up ass," Strap said becoming agitated.

"Because I really don't feel like talking to you but every time you see me you stalk and harass me until I stop and talk so now, I just go along with ya nonsense."

"Bitch, you alright but you ain't runway!" Strap said becoming sarcastic.

"I'm okay with that boo but if I'm not a model type then why do you keep on trying to talk to me when I've told you NO a million times," Summer said catching a slight attitude.

"Cause I'm trying to fuck... what you think?!" he yelled back feeling disrespected that Summer crushed him.

"Like, I told you before, you work for King that means you're a runner... runners never own the throne boo... with that being said you will never get to smell my panties and oh! They smell sweet as fruit punch. So, for the last time leave me alone!" she said with her hands on her hips and her head bouncing from left to right.

"Bitch Fuck you and that Lil Spanish Mothafucka you Fuck with... y'all need to get the fuck back on that banana boat and bounce!" he said yelling doing his best Tupac Shakur impersonation.

By this time, a small crowd had formed and were engrossed in the argument between well-known Strap and the pretty young dime.

"You keep talking bout my man but when we saw you leaving the restaurant you ain't have shit to say... my nigga ain't worried about you. How old are you? You're like 28 or 30, boy you're a has-been. You're sitting here arguing with an 18-year-old cause I won't give you any pussy... you wack and you need help, those are the signs of a pedophile!" Summer said with her finger in his face.

By this time, Strap was upset and tried grabbing Summer by the collar of her shirt but before he could the crowd jumped in between the two to break it up. That was the wrong thing to do on his behalf because as soon as he reached for Summer, Treasure, Hope, and Kiesha began punching on his ass. Fist and feet connected as the girls went for theirs. Strap managed to back slap Treasure sending her to the ground that made the other three go berserk! They attacked him like a pack of lions dismissing the fact that he was landing hard shots on them as well. The ruckus came to a calm when Straps right-hand man Code Blue jumped in between the scuffle with his torch pointed directly at the girl's chest. Everyone over North knew Code Blue from Concord Ave was a killer so they advised the girls to calm down. They took heed to the warning and stopped. Not feeling the vibe anymore, the G.A.P. Gang hopped in their cars and rolled out. Not feeling the shit that just went down she went straight 2nd and Scott to see her man. José could see that something was wrong by the way Summer and her peoples were hyped up. From the look of their hair, clothes and the few minor bruises he knew they had just got done rumbling. He thought it was some female or females, so he laughed at them. However, his smile and laughter quickly disappeared after she explained to him what happened. He wanted to go back over North at that moment but realized he would be outnumbered. It was way too many people just in case things went sour and shots were fired. Strap had violated in a major way so José knew that when he saw him it would be on site and whatever happens win or lose, life-or-death he would know not to Fuck with Spanish José anymore!

At first, the thought of going against the idea of dealing with Fat Papi's clients seems like the wise thing to do. Then once he contacted Fat Papi's players things took off. Between Fat Papi's clients, Rosé, and the two youngins from Cash Ave out New Castle the heroin was moving. The only problem was Poppies' clients were used to getting raw dope so when José cut a few bricks to stretch the work people complained. With Angelina supplying him now he decided to sell them as is and that was raw. The cocaine sold itself as well, Fat Papi's clients were buying two or three at a time and between the three he had bagged up in dimes and "ballgames" after three days he had only four bricks of coke left. Amazed at how fast the whole shipment was moving he knew that by Friday he would be to see Angelina again. And yes, he would be accepting the offer of moving the shipment like she suggested. With Carlos still murdering the block with the "loud" he seemed to still want more. So, José planned to surprise his best friend with a hundred pounds from Mac before the end of the weekend. He would take his own "spread" to grab the bud just to see that his man was good. Carlos wanted to sell weight and escape the block life fast and with the sudden change of events more than likely, they would all be disappearing from the block very soon. With the next shipment being 20 of both more than likely he would be given Castro five bricks of soft for 25 apiece and Dre would get five bricks of "d" for 50 apiece. Those prices were the best in the state if not the whole Tri-State and Delmarva region. Of course, he would show Dre how to cut it, but knowing his childhood friend he would be too lazy to handle the task. So, he would cut it himself and turn five into 11 and a quarter and have the girls bag and package it. That would keep everyone employed and give him some extra spending cash. Castro had even started dealing with some major players in block huggers down in Dover and Seaford Delaware. That was out of the county and that was considered downstate money. Most of those niggas had major paper to spend. The only downside was just like any other city if a nigga doesn't know you, they feel it's okay to snitch on you, so Castro had to play it smart. However, these Dover and Seaford niggas were good money and lived by the code so everything was cherry pie! The block was wide open and the squad took care of everyone and with money, cars and clothes on display in heavy rotation Scott Street had soon become the block to be on. By the end of the night or when the crowded block started to disperse José and the squad stopped by the Batcave to smoke, meet and to discuss the days' events. After the blunts were gone the squad parted, José went home, Carlos and Dre went to see the Twins and Castro got on Backpage to find a bitch to fuck for the night. Heading north on Route 202 towards Chadds Ford PA José headed to the new two-bedroom townhouse on Naamans Road Summer had found a day or two after someone broke into their old apartment. 1200 a month was worth it, it sat secluded in a quaint community of nine 1/3-acre home sites. If you didn't know your way to the house, you were sure to miss the turn or get lost. Checking his rearview the entire drive he was sure that he wasn't being followed. When he finally walked in the house, he was greeted by the smell of Lechon Asado and a soft ballad playing by Marc Anthony. She stood in the middle of the dining area in a yellow see-through Teddy with no panties on and her beautiful little painted toes on display. The site of Summer made him want to skip the food, but he was hungry. He was also sweaty too, so he went to take a shower first. When he stepped into the bathroom, he was surprised to see the tub filled hot and ready with a Dutch already pearled for him with a lighter sitting next to it. All he could do was smile, then undress and lower himself into the bath water. His body was finally gonna get the chance to relax and be at ease. He sparked his Dutch and tot away relieving all the stress of the days' madness. Just then the bathroom door opened and in walked Summer carrying his plate in one hand and an ice-cold glass of Orange Sunkist in the other. Feeding her man his meal while he smoked and they talked had Summer pussy walls sweating. Without warning, she stood up and let the straps on her Teddy fall to her side causing her lingerie to fall to the floor. José's dick grew hard fast and he couldn't wait as he extended his hands out to her to join him. She stepped in, then positioned herself over top of his huge dick, took a shallow breath and then lowered herself down onto the throbbing Jackhammer. He kissed her as she bounced up and down in the warm water until they both came.

The next morning, José was walking out the door while Summer was heading to work. With four bricks of coke and two of "d" on a Thursday, his mission was to move everything by that night. Before posting up he drove through the neighborhood checking out the cars and the city workers who could actually be the law setting up surveillance on his squad. Once he parked and hit the block it seemed everyone was on the same page because every one of them pulled up simultaneously. Each member of the squad greeted one another and then rolled up! Carlos and Dre told José and Castro about the Twins they had met and how their brother had gotten "earthed" last night on Pleasant Street. Not knowing the Twins or their brother José blew it off as another casualty. Castro thought back on the rumors of the family from out of town trying to run pressure on Pleasant Street and wondered but kept his thoughts to himself. José invited the squad to go out with him and Rosé to the Hookah lounge that Saturday. Castro was down but Carlos and Dre had plans. They declined saying they were taking the Twins out on a date. José decided to take Taylor and JoJo and invited MacLaden since he's been asking him to come fuck with him and hang out up top in Philly. Cooking one of the last four bricks of coke up to bag up in ballgames that morning came in Handy, José and Castro did their thing. José threw Castro one whole square since he said he could move it faster than he could imagine. Castro left heading out to New Castle and within three hours tops, Castro was calling José for two more. Wondering how and where his man was getting the shit off so fast, he asked him. And he explained that after cooking the square up and getting a few extra ounces his folks out in New Castle brought him out Saddlebrook and as soon as he dumped that his people Rudy Carter from Dover needed two squares of soft and they were paying 35 grand apiece if it was raw powder. José was impressed with his man but when his phone went off and MacLaden was trying to get his hands on some "d" for his people up North he knew today would be a good day.

Mac's folks wanted one for 70 but when José told him that he would give up two for a hundred, Mac's folks quickly changed their minds and purchased two. They even came to Wilmington to grab it and after they made it home safely, they had the work tested and found out that the product was A-1 they had made arrangements to meet up with José sooner than later. It was now late afternoon and all that was left was a square he thought about cooking it up and then fronting it to his block soldiers but then his phone rang, it was Castro. His homies from Seaford were coming up to visit him and they needed one so that cleared the order. After getting all the cash together instead of going to his moms, Taylors or JoJo's he went to the second safe house they purchased from the Sheriff sale. Only him, Summer, Taylor and JoJo knew where this house was located. Harding Avenue was in the cut and when José got there, he decided to call his girl and his friends to help him count the cash.

At 11:35 p.m. on a Thursday night after 4 ½ hours of counting the grand total was $1,785,000. The room was silent as it always was when they knew they had went in too deep. Placing $700,000 in a rubber band knot into a large duffel bag so that it would be easy to carry he went back outside to his SS Impala, then placed the money and the bag into the stash box. While sitting there he texted Angelina "I'm ready" she texted back "OK job well done dear I'll see you in the am" He went back in the house, grabbed the $1,084,000 and headed for the basement. In the basement he had two 7 x 2-foot Black and Decker floor safes built into the cement walls where he placed the million plus with the other 200 grand he had. He grabbed 20 grand, locked his safe, and then headed up the steps. Once he came from the basement, he gave each woman five stacks apiece and kept five for himself. They all got in their separate cars and headed home on the way all José could think to himself was, *"Damn I'm a millionaire at 18."*

He smiled to himself while mashing the pedal to the floor causing his muscle to come to life as it roared up Route 202. Turning up the volume to "Bag On Me" by A-Boogie he knew nothing could stop him now but himself. Niggas like Strap were not in his lane anymore and if need be a $50,000 bag will be put on his head to exterminate him but for the Fuck of it, he just might do it himself. When he touched Summer, it became personal, so it is what it is. For now, though, his focus was to find the pussy responsible for killing his man Fat Papi.

CHAPTER 13

The Goya Bean Cartel

"Que pasa Emilio?" Priscilla asked sincerely.

"Dimelo madre," Amillio answered.

"Te neseccitan aqui imediatamente," she stated.

"Voy en Camino," Amillio replied sensing the urgency in his mother's voice."

"Oh, Emillio estos vatos estan violentados en mayor medida. Ellos matron a tú Herman Edwin desde entonles ellos vienen aqui todos los dias," Priscilla said through heavy sobs and tears.

"Ma'ccual es el problems?" he said through clenched teeth after receiving the news of his brother's death.

"So nombre es Ivan y suprone que es un tipo peligroso," she replied.

"Donde puedo encontrar al tal Ivan?" he questioned.

"Le tienes que preguntar a Alex," she stated.

"No té preucupes Ma' yo me encargo de todo," Amillio said after consoling his mother.

Amillio didn't exactly know much about the city of Wilmington except for the Hilltop area. He knew nothing about this man named Ivan except for the fact that he had murdered his younger brother. And for that reason alone, he would be packing his bags and calling his men; they would be flying out of L.A.X. in a matter of hours. The Goya Bean Cartel are better known as G.B.C. in Southern California would be heading to Murdertown to kill Ivan and whoever was affiliated with him. Priscilla was relieved to finally hear that her oldest son would be there to handle the mess that Alex had started. She hoped Amillio would give Ivan a horrible death. The Goya Bean Cartel had made a name in the late 90s early 2000s from funneling drugs from Arizona and Mexico into Southern California. Many gangs tried entering their territory and they ended up either missing, shot dead, burned alive or stabbed to death. They went as far as raping women and then decapitating their heads. Amillio had inherited his mother's genes of a ruthless killer. The leader of his own drug cartel that prides themselves on violence and torture Amillio would just about go to war with anyone. He had no ties to his mother's operation on the East Coast but whenever she calls, which she rarely does, he comes because it's his mother. And with Amillio being more ruthful than his younger brother would he be the one to silence the man named Ivan? José couldn't sleep so he woke up early. With it being 5 a.m. he decided to slide down into the basement and watch the DVD that Angelina had given him. When he studied the man on screen, he was sure he knew the face but just couldn't put a finger on it. It had him a little-heated knowing he saw the face but didn't know where at. He was so caught up in his thoughts he never noticed Summer standing at the bottom of the steps watching the horrifying scene unfold on the TV screen.

"Babe, what are you watching? And isn't that Fat Papi from the garage?" Summer asked seemingly stunned.

José ignored her questions and told her to go back upstairs. She turned and headed up the steps when she vanished José grabbed his phone and screenshot the clearest view of the man. He would find out who he was very soon. Somebody had to know who he was and if he was still around the city José would find him. For now, he will wait the next few hours out patiently. Sometime that morning he'd be meeting with Angelina and he couldn't wait because he was ready to roll!

Alex walked into his mother's hideaway stone-faced after receiving the news about his brother Edwin. The hideaways were two multi-level Ranch houses Priscilla had in Smyrna built before they moved to Wilmington just for emergencies and situations like the one, she's facing. Pleasant Street and its activity have been shut down temporarily until the problem was resolved. It only slowed the cash flow down a little because the family had a lot of phone money. Alex could see the look of hurt and anger in his mother's eyes. He wanted to hold her, but he thought he would be rejected. Being the cause of his brother's death and showing up to see his mother two days later wasn't at all a sincere gesture. See, Alex used to be a cool fly guy type of poppie but ever since he started smoking them "dippers" he's been a totally different person. His anger has been the cause of so many street battles and wars that Priscilla has had to conquer in the past decade. She was tired of it and if it wasn't for Alex being her son, she would have probably killed him herself by now. Due to the fact that he's her own, he's still living but Amillio promised Alex a long time ago that if something ever happened to his mother over his foolishness, he'd pay the ultimate price. Alex stepped closer to his mother who looked to be off in a distant place. He cleared his throat to alert her that he was in the room when she turned to face him as tears streamed down her puffy cheeks. Alex finally let reality hit him that his brother was gone, he broke down and cried also. Priscilla extended her arms for her child to be comforted, even with all the wrong Alex may have done she knew he'd never do anything to harm his brother. She didn't say it but she was also relieved to see Alex alive as well. He had not answered his phone since she left for Puerto Rico. Seeing him there in one piece calmed her nerves extremely. With tears in his eyes, Alex apologized to his mother for all the havoc he has brought to the family. He explained to his mother about the shootout, how Ivan is still living, and the garage double murder. He told her he has not rested and won't until he kills him. He will avenge his brother's death if that's the last thing he did. Just then the room door opened behind them, Priscilla's eyes grew wide as ever with a huge smile to follow. When Alex turned to see what caused the sudden change of heart. There standing in the doorway with the same baby-faced killer look stood Amillio.

"Que pasa madre," Amillio said while walking towards his mother to embrace her. He then spun around and looked his youngest brother in the eyes with a cold stare and said in a sinister tone, "Where can I find this man you call Ivan?"

Alex knew that the war was officially on and with Amillio and him searching for Ivan it wouldn't be long before Ivan was found. And when he was, he would receive a gruesome death. Alex and his brother talked for a minute and then they hit the streets looking for Ivan.

Castro had been dealing with a few playas that spent nice dough. The New Castle money which people called county money seems to be more lucrative than the city money. Plus, it seems to be a lot more if one could target the right number of top players in the county, he or she could easily see a million dollars in about a year or two. The only downside to the county is you have to become associated with the crackers. Yeah, the White people, yes, they do spend the most cash hands down and most of a hustler's earnings come from them. Which is all good until they catch a charge and get to pointing fingers and down comes your Enterprise. Anyway, Castro had been running through the work and making mad money, but his major income came from his first hustle and love, gun running. Castro met with an unknown source once a month somewhere in Camden New Jersey and would get a shipment of 5 assault rifles, 5 to 10 riot pumps, and 20 to 40 handguns ranging from .38 specials to 50 calibers... minus the revolvers most of his arsenal came with extra extended clips and ammunition. Not to mention, every single one of these weapons were brand-new out of the factory. He sold weapons in Philadelphia, Delaware, and Maryland and he even had dealings with a few folks he knew down in Norfolk Virginia. Castro's strategy was to sell the guns quickly and sorry to say, he wanted to hit up every city and all the surrounding states where the violence and crime rates were high and then promote his product. One thing he was sure of was that wherever there were drugs you needed guns. And wherever there was beef there were guns. So, whatever price he put on his weapons when he went into the slums they would sell. Now with his new hustle doing well, Castro was about to spend his own cash on his next few shipments of guns just to see six figures of both guns and drugs apiece. His fortune was bound to grow and his team was just about strong as they ever been. He was comfortable and he had nothing to complain about. The way Castro saw things were that not a fucking soul could Fuck with his squad.

The meeting with Angelina was finished and now José was sitting on 40 squares of white girl and manteca. With everything being sold as is he would see a million, owing Angelina $700,000. He had plans to take the five bricks he would be fronting Dre and cut them to stretch the work. That alone would be an extra $300,000 profit. José called MacLaden and placed an order for a hundred pounds of L.A. Confidential that would secure Carlos as one of the heavier pushers of the bud in the city. With nothing but room to come up even more than what he already had, he skipped the lights and fashion for now and stayed focus on creating an Empire that has never been seen before. Taking half of the work to the second safe house on Harding Avenue and the other half to Taylor and JoJo's apartment he had the girls move two bricks over to Upper Oak Street to be cut and packaged. Just like always, the girls handled their parts faithfully. By noon on Friday in late September his phone had started buzzing like crazy. Castro called and he threw him the five squares he promised him. Plus, a few of Papi's folks called and surprisingly was buying more manteca today. By the end of the night, nine bricks of coke were sold and six bricks of "d" were gone. Only seldom did he think of the risk, his model was scared money don't make money, so he trapped like there was no tomorrow. By 10 p.m. the nightlife was in full swing, but José was tired as hell. With money still floating he didn't want to leave but his body was exhausted and he needed to rest. He took a mental note to find a few young hungry niggas to run the block while he politics and tries to expand. He knew for sure that his youngins Quan Showstopper, Vic-chow, A-1 Bry, Boo, and Dawger from the extension over South Bridge would definitely be down. He had been passing them little dime packs to hold the block down while the squad would be bagging up. That was months ago and with the squad all in position to move weight now, it was only right he let the little niggas see some of the cash flow too. Between Dawger and Quan Showstopper, those two heathens were a problem and most of the city knew it. So, when they all started running together the older cats would say the group of five were young & reckless and the name stayed with them. Now all José had to do was get them all on the same page as him and that was money. The only problem was how do you get a group of 15 and 16-year-olds to contain themselves after giving them a brick or two. José called Summer to let her know that he was tired and would either be home later that evening or early the next morning. Before calling it a night, he stopped by the liquor store and grabbed a bottle of his favorite Branson B. Cuveé and a box of blunts. Making it to his car he hopped in and headed to Taylor and JoJo's. When he arrived both girls were watching A Den of Thieves on the fire stick and eating cheese steaks and mozzarella sticks. José fell on the sofa between the two and grabbed one of Taylor's mozzarella sticks.

"I'm hungry, damn y'all should have ordered me something," he said while devouring the food.

"You should have called and told us you were coming and I would have ordered you something," Taylor said while biting into her cheesesteak still engulfed in the movie.

JoJo passed him one half of her cheese steak with no thought to it while caught up in the action. In exchange, he passed her the ozone of "sour" he had and two Dutch's. That was her cue to roll up. Tired and sweaty he decided to go take a shower. Stepping into the hot shower the water fell down his body relieving all the stress of the day. The shower was his sanctuary that's where he went to find peace and to get his thoughts together. After 10 minutes of quietness, his shower was completed. Stepping out to towel off he was startled when the bathroom door swung open. Standing naked, dick swinging, chest muscles flexing, JoJo looked on in awe! She looked him up and down for a good 10 seconds and he wasn't ashamed of his body, so he stood there and smiled. Um, she managed to softly echo not realizing that he had heard her. Grabbing his towel finally broke her concentration and it brought her eyes back to his, but the look in her eyes said something strange.

"Jo what's up?" he asked while wrapping the towel around his waist.

"Oh, I wa... I was coming to tell you to hurry up we bout to spark the weed... boy you got me stuttering," she said laughing it off.

"Stuttering for what? Once you see one you've seen them all... come give me a hug girl, my fault," he said extending his arms.

"No, it was my fault, I should have knocked first. I gotta stop doing that shit... you done got a bitch all wet "n" shit!" she said walking into his arms.

"Oh, you wet huh? Let me feel!" he said jokingly.

"Boy go head somewhere," JoJo said slapping his chest lightly then turned and walked out of the bathroom.

Before leaving she looked back, bent over and grabbed her ankles then smiled.

"Boy, you can't handle this wet... I'm Spanish we stay hot all day long!" she said before standing up and strutting back into the living room.

José drank and smoked a blunt with his homegirls and then decided to hit the extra room to catch some sleep. A mixture of sleepiness, loud and champagne had altered his thinking because the moment she climbed into bed with him all thoughts of friendship went out the window. He reached out and caressed her fluffy healthy-looking breast. Taking one of her light brown thick nipples into his mouth she softly gasped for air! He allowed his hands to explore her full body starting at the top running his fingers through her hair then bringing them down to gently touch both cheeks. They had finally made eye contact and the connection was undeniable. They shared their first kiss as his tongue explored hers, he could taste the sweetness of the watermelon Lifesaver she had eaten earlier. He inhaled deeply to take in her strawberry mango body wash, so soft!

He licked above and under her titties like a master of lovemaking. He softly kissed her midsection down past her dripping pussy to her beautiful toes, he began to suck each one individually; she grabbed for his half hard dick and began stroking it at a steady pace causing a moan to escape his mouth. As he made his way back up to her love nest the anticipation was building. The moment his tongue touched her clit she bucked like a stallion! Her back arched high and her moans were soft as love ballads. He sucked her in all the right places and it wasn't long before she was squirting everywhere. That turned him on, he wanted more so he continued to suck while inserting two fingers inside of her then lightly tapping her G-spot. She shot off another load of juices, this time it was further and stronger. With her legs spread wide open, she was now begging for him to enter her. Not until she tasted the light brown meat stick that resembled a 10-inch turkey sausage she sucked seductively bringing lots of spit to keep it extra wet as she moved from top to bottom. It was a challenge because of the length and girth but she relaxed her throat and took him all the way in. He was lost, it felt better than any headshot he had ever received. The way she played with his balls while sucking him off she had earned the nickname brain surgeon. He was ready and he wanted to feel her insides, he wanted to see if it was as tight and wet as he hoped it was. He prayed for a perfect fit and when he slid in it was a perfect fit! He began stroking at a steady pace while locking eyes with her and still passionately kissing her. His long strokes were harder and powerful, she was coming uncontrollably; she was loving every minute of it. She had wanted this for a long time and now she was getting it. He felt himself about to explode so he began pumping harder and faster until he couldn't hold back anymore. He released about a half-gallon of "nut" into his best friend now lover. They are both laid there in each other arms exhausted, he tilted her head upwards so that she could make eye contact with him so that she knew he was serious.

"I love you JoJo... always have and always will," he said kissing her lips.

Just then he was awakened from his dream with his best friend standing in the room in a one-piece Teddy with a smile but a confused look on her face.

"I love you too José... always have and always will," she said bending over giving him a kiss on the cheek then tossing that phat ass from left to right as she left the room.

In the hallway JoJo was stunned, she had been standing there watching José two minutes prior to him waking up. And she wasn't a rocket scientist, but she knew from the sound of things he was making love to someone but when he said her name, she knew he felt the same way as she did. She not only wanted to fuck him royally she was also very much in love with José.

The next morning, the silence between the two was awkward and Taylor picked up on it immediately. José would sneak a glance at her quickly then look away. He ate breakfast with his friends then reminded them that they were going to the Hookah Lounge tonight and that he would be back around 1 p.m. to take them shopping for an outfit. That brought the room to life. He grabbed his keys and then hit the door on his way home to Summer.

Miss Valdez was busy packing what little she had left and trying to keep Felix occupied at the same time. Romeo Santo blared through the speakers of her home stereo system while she danced around her living room. Happiness was all that she was feeling because she was finally moving away from the place that took her husband from her and corrupted her son. She would be leaving Wilmington in a matter of days and she was excited!

When José walked in his house Summer was cleaning up. In just a pair of boy shorts panties and a sports bra; her flat stomach, fat ass, and thick thighs were calling his name. After the dream he had the night before he gave her just what she wanted right there on the living room sofa; he fucked her good. Her juices ran down her ass crack and covered his thighs, they wanted each other and one night away from each other showed that. After they came together, Summer then informed José that she was going to Baltimore with her girls that night. That was cool with him because he had plans for the evening anyway. After lounging around the house until about 11:30 a.m. he kissed his girl and gave her a wad of 20s which she, in turn, gave right back stating that she had money and was okay. He then hit the door heading to Harding Avenue to drop off the money he earned the night before. Making sure he was straight for his outing to "K.O.P." he grabbed 20 grand to be on the safe side. Just when he was about to he hit the door, Rosé called placing an order for two more bricks. He grabbed them and rolled out.

After dropping Rosé's order off, he went to switch cars and to pick his two best friends up. Even when they looked average, they were beautiful. Switching cars, they hopped in his Marauder and with Taylor riding shotgun she plugged her phone up to his Aux cord and surfed her playlist. Knowing Hot Line Bling wouldn't be getting played in those wheels she decided on Meek Mill's Dreamchasers 4. She turned the volume up and rode up I-95

North nodding to Meeks versus while JoJo rolled up a Dutch.

An hour or so later, they pulled into the parking lot of the King of Prussia Mall. The three walked in the mall like they owned it, knowing they weren't the richest but damn sure wasn't broke either; they came to shop and have fun. José new he owed this little shopping venture to his friends. They were there for him anytime he called and would drop whatever they were doing to accommodate his needs. So today was really all about them. First, they wanted to window shop to view all the boutiques and all the nice designs. Not to mention, this was the first time ever that either of the girls has been to the mall, so they were hyped. José knew he had impressed the girls when he pulled this trick out of his sleeve. The first stop was at Neiman Marcus, the girls browsed through the selections of the high price designer outfits from Vera Wang to Michael Kors. It was so many shoes and stylish looks the girls wanted all of them. José advised them to take their time because it was so much more to see that they would regret buying something right now and seeing something later. They left Neiman's and José took the girls to Tiffany & Company where he had a surprise waiting. Sarah the Sales Associate had become acquainted with José over the last few months. José had brought Summer to the boutique several times purchasing anklets, tennis bracelets and rings. Today he wanted the girls to find a pair of earrings and they did fast! Taylor picked a gold hoop with princess-cut trimmed around the outside of the hoops. And JoJo grabbed a pair of customized letter "J" platinum and diamond earpieces. That light purchase cost José 2100 then out came the surprise.

Sarah placed two, one Rosé gold and one yellow and white gold link with matching heart-shaped medallions on the countertop. Taylor and JoJo looked at each other with confusion until Sarah informed them that the chains were theirs. They looked at José who had the dumbest smile on his face. They jumped on their friend so fast and smothered him with hugs and kisses. He had prepaid 1,500 and now he paid the remaining 1,500 to finalize the deal. The girls wasted no time placing the chains around their necks. Next, they stopped at the Sunglasses Hut a shop that had all types of frames and names. Within 20 minutes the girls had a pair of Gucci and Chloe shades, they cost another $1040. Now came the fun part, outfit and shoe shopping. Louis Vuitton and Chanel had some fly shit, but it didn't speak the message the girls were trying to send so they kept looking. Coach and Burberry had a plain older woman look so they dashed out of there quickly. When Taylor walked into the Jimmy Choo boutique, she knew she had found the spot she wanted to be in. She grabbed up a skirt and blouse, dress and slacks and hit the dressing room. José and JoJo were her panel of judges and after an hour of debating and fussing she ended up with a cream and silver mini dress that hugged all her curves. It rested on her thighs softly and it exposed her large breasts giving the viewers something to imagine. With the back and right shoulder being exposed completely this gave the dress not only a sexy but elegant look as well. Content with her outfit she surfed for a pair of heels. And with Jimmy Choo being known for a fly shoe game it wouldn't be hard. Finding a cream ostrich skin 4-inch heel she was happy and ready to go! The dress cost 1150 and the shoes were 675. So far José had only blown a cool 6500 give or take. Gucci had all sorts of things and while JoJo looked around José spotted a new fall selection of Gucci loafers and sneakers for his and hers. At 700 apiece he got four pairs, two for his friends, one for him and one for Summer. Not really liking what she saw they left. JoJo was picky and wouldn't just throw anything on. That's the traits of a bad bitch word was all she would to say. Now, while the females were picking their brains out over what to where he knew where he was going. Walking past the Armani Outlet just as he expected the girls wanted to stop in. He kept walking after seeing Angel the day he first met Angelina at her home he knew he wanted to rock something similar. The Versace Outlet was very upscale and sectioned. One side held the men's attire while the other side shelved the women. Now, it was his turn to shop, instead of buying something expensive and flashy he looks and he took the weather into consideration. Beings though it was late September he grabbed a gray and gold Versace sweat suit with a large Medusa head in gold on the front of the sweatshirt and Versace written in gold letters around the waistband. He also found a gray and gold Versace baseball cap to match. He went as far as grabbing a pair of the Versace socks as well. Of course, they were gray but what took the cake was the low top gray and white Versace sneakers that resembled the "95" Air Max. Those mothafuckas were soft and for $1,800 they better had been. Just like that José was done. He spent $3300 in 30 minutes, he rubbed it in his friends' faces on how quickly it took him to find an outfit. JoJo was stuck! She didn't know what to get but after seeing José grab the gray sweat suit, she secretly wanted something to match his lay since she was going with him that night. After changing in and out of outfit after outfit she found a charcoal gray dress with diamond studs running along the neckline and a slit up the left side wrapped around the ensemble. It exposed most of her thighs and if you caught a certain angle you might have seen the pussy since she rarely wore panties. The shoes she wanted were a silver peak-toe wedge heel that complemented her outfit well; her outfit and shoes came to a little over 2 grand and she was ecstatic! With everyone having the things they wanted José took the girls back to Wilmington and treated them to lunch at The Melting Pot. The restaurant was low-key and private, but the food was extraordinary and it always received raving reviews from the local food critics. It was a little expensive, but he wanted to spoil his girls today and that's what he was doing, and the day had just begun. While eating the girls informed José that the coming August, they'd both would be leaving for school. They were both accepted and will be attending Spelman University majoring in Agricultural Science. José was quiet for a minute and the girls watched him closely and then a smile appeared across his face. He knew they both wanted to go to the university and was happy that they were going.

"I guess I gotta make sure y'all are okay while y'all are down there," he said.

After they ate, he gave the girls money to get their hair, nails, and feet done. His phone was buzzing and money was calling. So, he dropped the girls off, switched cars with JoJo taking her tinted out Camry, and was out and about getting cash!

"Girl you crazy as hell ain't that much mothafuckin' trust in the world. He's always with them, he gives them money and neither of them bitches are ugly! I don't care if they were friends since the sandbox days ain't no way in the world I would let my man especially a nigga as fine as José be staying the night over a bitch house," Kiesha Jenkins said in gossip mode.

"Girl that's because ya ass ain't never been faithful... so of course you're gonna be insecure when it comes to ya man. All I'm saying is he's taking care of shit the way he's supposed to and he hasn't given me any reason to think he's doing anything so I'm not going to start assuming now. Besides, I've hung out with them plenty of times and they both had dudes at the time so why get all suspicious now," Summer said making her point.

"José is good to Summer and he's known them forever and we know he's in love with you so all that shit Kiesha is blabbing about pay it no mind girl," Hope said slapping her cousin's hand to reassure her of her man.

"Yeah Summer, you know what they do for him... that's why he's always with them. You get all the rewards and have to do no work, I would love that shit and would not complain," Treasurer spoke up.

"All I'm saying is love or not which I'm not gonna say he doesn't love you cause I know he does but pussy is pussy and dick is dick. When you bring them two together for a period of time you have a lot of fucking going on. Remember this, they will smile in your face... all the time they're trying to take your place... those backstabbers," Kiesha said in her best Lil Kim impersonation.

Summer trusted José completely, but after hearing Kiesha ramble on about trust, dick, pussy, and fucking she couldn't help but wonder if José has ever slipped up maybe once and slept with one of his friends. Determined not to let that deter her evening she floated down I-95 South heading for Baltimore to shake her ass all night! The evening had arrived and Scott Street was jumping! Instead of posting on 2nd the crowd migrated up to 5th and Scott. Waiting for everyone to arrive José politicked with an associate of his. Pooda was a little money gettin nigga as well but a few years back José got into a messy situation and Pooda could've easily been a stand-up guy and lightened the load which was weighing heavy on José shoulder. Instead, he avoided José and his family which ultimately brought tension. Not one to act off emotions José kept his cool resurfaced and started chewing more than ever. Never beefing over small shit was the reason José decided to cut him off from his circle, sell him no weight, and keep it at general conversations. The gray and gold Versace sweat suit and sneakers were plush! Everyone complimented him on the outfit that they had never seen before and with his eyes being hidden behind a pair of Versace shades along with his 24-inch Cuban Link in so many words he was a stunner! Taylor and JoJo pulled up next stepping out for the night looking marvelous! Their hair, makeup, nails, jewels, and dresses were perfect. As they stood there with José all the little block niggas tried doing the silliest things to get their attention. It didn't work, their attention was on fly ass José who looked like a half-mill in their eyes. Castro pulled up wearing an all-black Armani sweater and black Armani skinny leg jeans with a pair of all black Hierarchies. Fly as Fuck, he still tapped his waist signaling that he had his cannon on deck. Taylor and JoJo both padded their purses with smiles informing him that they were carrying as well. It was only 9 p.m. so they still had plenty of time, so José and Castro grabbed two bottles of Branson B. Cuvee' and rolled up for the meantime. Taylor and JoJo stood around looking cute while smoking their personals and being arm candy for their friend. MacLaden and Bunny pulled up and stole the fucking show in a black on black Maybach on 22s. Bunny looked finger licking good in her pink blazer and pants set that looked to be transparent revealing her lace bra that covered the little that it did. The O.G. Diva that she was she commanded all the attention and was receiving it. The block was starting to look like a scene from a dance show on Telemundo. Mac was flauncing heavy his Gucci suit that was tailored and fitted just right with the platinum and silver pinstripe enhanced the diamonds that covered his chest, wrist, fingers, and ears. Blunts were passed and music blasted loudly while the 5th St crew continued to make money. With so many people out and about the law didn't even bother stopping to harass anyone. Just when the block couldn't get any liver four foreign B.M.W. Audi Maserati and last but not least Rosé came pulling up in his snowflake white S-500 Benz on duce fours. Niggas and all the bitches heads turned and mouths dropped especially Taylors. She had a thing for Rosé she known him for a while, and they knew each other but always kept it neutral. Rosé stepped out blasting "Made Niggas" by the legend Tupac Shakur. Even after Labor Day Rosé broke the rules and made it look good rocking a all-white linen shirt and slacks by Fendi with a white and gold buckle Fendi belt to match. His shoes were baby powder white and were made by Havana Joe. His multi-colored iced out necklace and wrist wear made it look like he had Sponge Bob Square Pants on his neck and wrist. His crew was in full swing and was ready to party. José introduced everyone to each other and everyone became acquainted. Shockingly Rosé invited Taylor to ride with him for the night. She accepted since she was riding alone. She was all smiles as she gave her best friend JoJo a high five! With all the foreign cars on the block, you could have thought you were at an international car show. With José still driving his Marauder, Rosé and Mac began joking about him needing to step his wheel game up.

"Nigga you gettin' major paper now and you still pushing American," Rosé said pointing towards the Mercury.

"I'm not in a rush to go big time Jay-Z," José said sarcastically.

"A Benz or Beamer is boss, a Lex is playing, a Bentley or Rolls is big time but a Mercury my man is underprivileged," Mac said breaking the cars down into sections.

"Don't get it fucked up niggas, the bag is long enough to cop a wraithe I'm just not ready to get indicted yet…trust me when I tell you when I drop it won't be none of that shit it's gonna talk money somewhere around a half nigga!" José said getting arrogant!

"Word up, Word up right José!" JoJo chanted supporting her friend.

"And my bitches are gonna push Benzes and Beamers," he said grabbing JoJo around the waist pulling her closer to him.

Bunny had noticed how touchy-feely José was being but wrote it off reasoning that the bud and drink had him feeling friendly. She also knew that the boy was young and getting money so he was gonna fuck but she just hoped he would at least part ways with her cousin first. Knowing that wasn't going to happen, she played her position and enjoyed the night. It's almost 10:30 and everyone was in party mode and ready to go so they all hoped in their cars; Taylor riding with Rosé of course and José handing JoJo the keys so that she could drive. Before they pulled off, she leaned across the seat unintentionally and kissed him on the lips; he smiled like always and blew it off. Playa Circles throwback "Duffle Bag Boy" thumped hard as she pulled off. José leaned his seat back grabbed her hand tightly and closed his eyes. JoJo was all smiles all in less than 24 hours José made her feel wanted, desired, and like a star!

"What time are you coming poppie?" Jesenia asked becoming impatient with Dre.

"We'll be there soon, we gotta make a quick stop and then we're coming straight to the both of y'all… I hope y'all looking sexy and staying the night with all this damn rushing you're doing?" Dre commented.

"Yes, we're staying the night, but I don't know about sexy... my outfit is cute, but I definitely don't have any panties or bra on! Now hurry up and get here!" she shouted into the phone.

"No panties or bra? Oh, damn senorita, I think I love you," he said laughing.

"Come on boy before we get cold feet and change our mind."

"Give us 30 minutes and we'll be there," he said and then hung up.

The Twins had waited and had made Dre and Carlos wait longer than they expected, but tonight they planned to throw that pussy on them so good that they would never think of walking away. With a little help from the Twins close friend ecstasy the two homies just might fall in love. Summer and the rest of the G.A.P. Gang were in Baltimore having the time of their lives. A lot of touching and dancing, it was cool though no one seemed to be over aggressive so all the little feels on the ass and thighs were consensual. Of course, the girls had all the niggas in the club in their faces. They had so many bottles sent to them you would have thought they were VIP (Very Important People) Some tall yellow nigga with ocean waves spinning across the top of his head was on Summer, but she kindly declined. Kiesha wanted the young baller herself so to get his attention she did the grimiest shit one could do. She dropped a gram of molly in Summer's drink. In no time, the drug took effect and Kiesha was touching Summer and she was kissing her back. They had begun to put on a show and her cousins were stunned not knowing what happened to their cousin. The wavy hair kid made his way over to the girls and in a matter of minutes after talking they were leaving the club with Summer leading the way holding Yellow Man's hand.

CHAPTER 14

The Bandits

Sammy had stepped out to run to the store for his mother. Miss Valdez was in the kitchen making chicken enchilada when a knock came at the door. Thinking it was Sammy and he must've left his key because he had just left no more than two minutes earlier without asking who it was, she opened the door. That was the first time she had done something like that and it was a huge mistake. Two huge cannons were pointed directly at her face as the masked men warned her not to holler by placing their fingers to their mouths telling her to shush!

"Where's the money?" the masked man asked.

"I don't know what you're talking bout!" Miss Valdez screamed.

"Bitch stop lying now where ya son keep the money and drugs?" he said grabbing Miss Valdez by the hair dragging her causing her to yell loudly, "SHUT THE FUCK UP!" the man said before punching her in the face closing her eye instantly, "yo go search this bitch and see if you can find the shit and hurry up we ain't got all night!"

"Please, he doesn't keep anything here... just leave... you're hurting me." The second mask man returned with nothing in hand but a Puma Sports bag with about seven grand in it.

"Yo, this is all I found and this ain't shit but five to 10 grand," the second intruder stated.

"Fuck where the Fuck is the Shit at!" he hollered punching Miss Valdez repeatedly in the face causing blood to fly everywhere.

"Yo chill, what you doin?" the second man said pushing the first one.

Miss Valdez was lying helplessly in a small puddle of blood trying to gain strength to sit up. Just then in the blink of an eye, a loud crash hit the floor and both bandits spun around aiming. Jumping the gun instead of hesitating the second bandit fired! BOOM! The shot threw Felix's tiny body across the room slamming him into the China cabinet. By the time, his miniature frame hit the floor, he was dead! Miss Valdez struggled to get on her feet and make it to where her son laid. The gunmen stood silently with their guns still aiming. The first mask man wanted to finish her but was convinced by his partner that they couldn't be identified. Upset because of the outcome they hit the door and vanished in seconds. Miss Valdez sat crying uncontrollably holding her deceased 10-year-old. She called 911 and then she tried calling Sammy who didn't answer. Not reaching any of them she tried calling José and he answered, just then Sammy walked in to see the dreadful scene.

"I blow a bag a day, I don't do nothin' fugazi… I blow a bag a day, I walk the mall and go crazy." Future's hit was blaring through the speakers at the Hookah Lounge as the crowd of 13 in total made their way to the VIP section. Rosés folks grabbed another 10 to 15 bitches so the party looked like it was in the VIP. With about 25 people in total and Rosé, Mac, and José all putting up, it was about 10 bottles of Cîroc, five bottles of Patron, five bottles of Hennessey, five bottles of Crown Royal, and 12 bottles of Dom Perignon all the drinks were covered for a cool 20 grand! They started talking money and things got really heated in boss fashion though. First, who would buy out the bar for a light 10 grand? Rosé covered that with ease while Taylor looked on in amazement. Mac then took 10 grand cash and threw it in the middle of the crowded dance floor that sent the crowd into a frenzy. It was all love as the two giants held their dates close talking shit to

each other.

"All I'm saying is why you copp the S-5 if you could've grabbed the 550?"

Mac said feeling cocky, "Must ain't have the paper huh playboy?"

"Nigga you dumb, I could've dropped a Bentley if I wanted but I decided to wait until my birthday to spend close to a mill on his and hers for me and my new boo," Rosé said in his playa demeanor, "nigga its 2017 and you pushing a Maybach them shits are old as hell, you better sale that shit to Deals On Wheels."

"I got rid of the Ferrari Spyder and copped this so that I could spend more on this yacht I'm bout to copp," Mac said boasting.

Rosé was silent for a second too long.

"Damn, I hope you ain't catch feelings, my dude?" Mac asked.

"I don't catch feelings… I catch flights, privately on G-5's compliments of the plug; we can go to breakfast in France on the a.m. if you want," Rosé said shooting back.

The woman sat back and enjoyed themselves while they kept going on making all sorts of bets.

"Who ya favorite football team?" Rosé asked.

"Who you think… Eagles nigga!" Mac contested.

"Man, I fuck with the Goat… Brady and the Patriots," Rosé said.

"They good but they ain't fucking with my boys!"

"Bet it… 10 that Patriots make it to the bowl; if not, I owe you double," Rosé said.

"No bet… you crazy, that's Brady. I'm not betting against him on some shit like that, but I bet you 50 that if my boys make it to the bowl we gone win!" Mac said confidently.

"Fuck 50… how bout this, if the Eagles and Patriots meet in the bowl and the Eagles win I gotta buy Bunny here a house and if Patriots win you gotta by my boo Taylor here a spot," he said making the bet more interesting.

They had both girls' attention now and have every reason to.

"Where and how much?" Mac asked.

"Anywhere they want and it has to be a buc fifty!" Rosé said raising the bar.

"It's a bet… see you February 4th nigga!" Mac said cockily.

Carlos and Dre pulled up to the Twins' house in Smyrna ready to finally meet up with the girls, feeling that everything they had patiently waited for would be happening tonight. The two friends had a serious problem that really needed to be resolved but decided on dealing with that later. For now, they would be entertaining the Twins and seeing just what the night might bring. When the Twins exited the house, they both had on the smallest and tightest miniskirts and both wore pairs of come fuck me boots. The two friends planned to do just that, fuck them in their stiletto boots.

Hugs were exchanged and heavy kisses followed; the first spot they stopped was Dover Downs. At first, they hit the casino blowing money fast on the blackjack and craps table. It wasn't until the Twins got hot on roulette that they started winning money. They won about a stack off the game, so they were pleased.

After gambling, they decided to hit the night club that was also located at the establishment and just like the sexy hot Latinas they were, the Twins turned heads on the dance floor! They were hot and Carlos and Dre were moving to the beat right along with them. Exhausted and hungry, the foursome hopped in Dre's 2015 Acura SUV. Riding all the way back to Downtown Wilmington, Dre knew the girls were used to eating the ordinary Spanish dishes, but he wanted them to get acquainted with their surroundings. Being a product of his environment Dre took a liking to good ol' fashion soul food. Kameelah's had the best soul food in the county. You could say her meals were down to earth and you could tell she put a lot of love into each dish. He was sure they would love it especially her mouthwatering saucy wings with the garlic parmesan sauce with the macaroni and cheese, the seafood salad, and a side of crab balls.

After getting their meals, Dre pulled up on 11th Street to the Du Pont Hotel. This hotel's starting rate was 700 a night and that was for the bland rooms. Carlos and Dre went in and spent $2,500 apiece to get one of the luxury rooms, those weren't even the suites, but they had living rooms and jacuzzies though, so it was good for the night. The moment they stepped into the room the food was tossed to the side and the freaky festivities began. Carlos nor Dre was aware that while they were at the club the Twins spiked their drinks with a triple stack Louis Vuitton ecstasy pill. All four of them were rolling off a beautiful high and now all Carlos and Dre wanted was to see and taste those beautiful bodies.

Summer was in rare form as she climbed into the back of the light skin wavy head kids Hummer-H2. Kiesha followed right behind her friend pushing her dress up around her waist and pulling her laced thong completely off. Kiesha's tongue parted Summer's pussy lips causing her to squirt instantly. Kiesha sucked her clit with style and grace causing her friend to gush once more, but this time harder. Yellow Man the name the girls gave the light skin wavy head kid joined in by mounting Kiesha from the back fucking her good. The feeling was intense and the molly maximized the pleasure of his thrust! Knowing she was wrong, but it felt so right Summer switched positions and sat on her friends face riding the hell out of it while taking Yellow Man's dick in her mouth and swallowing it whole with ease. She was in a zone as a puddle formed underneath her from her constant flow of juices that she was squirting out.

After minutes of that head, Yellow Man wanted to feel her insides, so she laid on her back but not before she made him put a condom on. Then he proceeded to fuck her small pussy. Kiesha was riding Summer's face while she got fucked for a good 20 minutes. He rolled her onto her stomach with her ass totted in the air just a little. While he long stroked her, Kiesha played with her nipples sending her over the top again. She started throwing her ass back as hard as she could squirting uncontrollably. With beads of sweat falling, her mind was far from thinking of José. Getting one last nut before he came was her mission. The only problem was with her performing so good she tuned everyone around her out that she never realized that she was being recorded. How would José feel if he was to ever see the video of his wifey fucking like it was a sport.

Once the little fuck session ended, Summer pulled her dress down minus her thong which she left as a souvenir to Yellow Man fixed her hair, grabbed Kiesha's arm and headed back into the club with her cousins who were disgusted following right behind her.

Mac and Bunny grabbed two bottles and found spots on the sofa and enjoyed the tunes while the crowded VIP section "turned up." Rosé paid special attention to Taylor and yeah, she was feeling him, but she knew better than to be a victim of a hit and run. So, she carried herself like the young diva she was, not to pressed to be in his presence. She did let him get an occasional feel on her butter-soft ass here and there, but that was about it. He wanted her badly and by the imprint showing through his slacks, he wanted her right there. She nonchalantly patted his groin area and told him to be patient and one day his wish would be her command. She gave him his first kiss of the night that tasted like cinnamon and all he could do was grin! He grabbed a bottle of Peach Cîroc and found a seat, then he pulled Taylor down onto his lap and she excepted without hesitation. The DJ had switched the mood up and spun DeJ Loafs-Me Hennessey & You and fellas were looking for that special lady for the night. Sitting alone in the corner singing along to the song JoJo seemed to be enjoying herself. José watched her from a distance watching Rosés folks take shots at her only to get declined. The atmosphere was good, the liquor was flowing, and the perfect song was playing. So, José grabbed two cups, a bottle of Hennessey, and walked over to her. A smile spread across her face when she saw him standing in front of her looking handsome as ever. He lifted the bottle and cups up with a huge grin on his face she signaled for him to come and sit next to her. As soon as he did, he poured two shots and then placed his arm around her. The liquor had to be talking for him because he opened up to his friend. With the Henny in his system his swag was on 100 and as he whispered in her ear the game came fluently as his first language Spanish.

"Joanni you know we've been friends forever and you always held a special place in my life and heart."

"I know José but when did you start calling me by my first name?" JoJo said with a smile on her face.

"Well, technically I started calling you that in 3rd grade when you came to our school from New York… but I'm being serious right now… I've been thinking of you a lot lately and…"

"Thinking about what boy? I hope not that dream you had this morning," she said letting him know she knew he was dreaming about her.

"Look Jo… I have a girl that I care about, but for some reason, I feel like I want you to but it may mess up our friendship," he said confessing his true thoughts.

"José, I love you just as much… and you may have thought I was playing when I told you that you could have this anytime you want, but I wasn't. Because I'm your friend first, I'm patient but whenever you're ready you let me know and I'm all yours. José I just hope you don't have me waiting forever cause ya girl be getting mad lonely sometimes word up! In so many words José I'm not giving this wet away to anyone until you tell me you're ready."

"Well, how do you know if I'll ever be ready?"

"I don't but that's your loss if you never find out. José ain't too many bitches out here thorough as me and Taylor. We ready to take a charge, move the work, and buss our gun for ya fly ass. Is Summer gonna do that?" That's what you need to ask ya self. From now on when you look at me consider me your wife and she's just a side bitch cause I let her borrow my man, but when I'm ready and I mean really ready for you to come home I know what to do just to get to ya heart. Remember José, I've known you forever," she said looking him directly in the eyes.

Without thought, José leaned in and tongue kissed her with much heat and passion. She returned the kiss with the same energy as he griped her up in his arms. She loved the affection that he was showing and he was a great kisser. All Taylor could do was shake her head at the two friends. She knew this pot had been brewing for years and now it was at its boiling point. José knew that down ass Joanní would be his he didn't know when, but he could feel it. She sat on his lap and they kissed for the rest of the evening while she sipped Dom P. through a straw and he drank Henny. It was about 2 a.m. and the lounge was closing and as they began walking out, he spotted a familiar face! With Taylor and JoJo aware of what was about to go down they kept walking out of the lounge to the car. Castro, José, and Mac walked across the room while Rosé and his crew played the background just in case shit got hectic. Not even paying attention, Strap never seen José come down the side of his face with the straight razor he had hidden in his sneaks. Caught off guard, Strap couldn't stop the blows or the blood that was running freely down his face. His man Code Blue got into the action only to have Castro and Mac send a flurry of haymakers his way they dropped him. Security rushed to break up the chaos quickly and then kicked everyone out. In the parking lot, the madness escalated quickly Strap and his crew plus a few shooters from Northside were going at it with José, Castro, MacLaden, Rosé, and his partners. Before anyone could make it to their cars to grab anything Taylor and JoJo set it the Fuck Off!

"POP, POP, POP, POP, POP, POP, POP, POP, POP!"

The females were gunning for anyone who wasn't in the VIP section with them. All they know was José had to get out of there and that's what they did. When José was in the car safe and the smoke had cleared two bodies, one guy from Northside and an innocent bystander were dead.

"We lit that shit up for you boy word up!" JoJo said hyped as shit.

"Girl I love ya sexy ass! Look at you catchin' rec in a dress and heels…that's what the fuck I'm talking bout," he said leaning over the seat kissing her on the lips more natural like it was a regular thing.

On the way down the highway, José noticed that his mother and brother had been blowing his phone up all night which was unusual. Thinking something had to be wrong he would call early in the a.m. since it was so late. Just when he was about to fall back, relax, and enjoy the rest of the ride his phone rang and he knew something was wrong. She never called this late, let alone is awake this time of the morning. After the second ring, José answered and couldn't believe what he heard.

"José they kil… kil… killed Felix!" Miss Valdez shouted on the other end of the phone.

"Wait, what, what you just say? Ma what are you talking about?" José said sounding confused and alarmed.

"They came here tonight looking for drugs and money… they beat me badly and then when Felix walked in the room they turned around and shot him!" she said hysterically replaying the events over to her son.

"I'm on my way mama," José said in a defected tone.

José thought that it was a dream but knew that his mother wouldn't play like that. Forty-five minutes later, José and JoJo walked in his mother's house and the tears came automatically. His mother's left eye was closed in her face and lips were swollen beyond recognition. Sammy sat there silent ice grilling his younger brother. He knew the reason those people came was for José's money and drugs and if it wasn't for his mother, he would have punished him for it. He walked over to the spot in the dining room that had the bloodstain to remind himself that this wasn't a nightmare and that his baby brother was dead. He cried, he dropped to his knees, and let the tears flow from his face. JoJo came to his side to console him, but it did no good because his soul was hurting. Memories flashed through his mind rapidly as far back as Felix's birth. Sammy knew his pain and put his anger to the side and went to comfort it his younger brother.

"Why Felix why yo! Why not me for all that!" José sobbed.

Miss Valdes loved her son but reminded him of her the saying that she always would tell him and his deceased father.

"José, I kept telling you that the streets don't love no one and when they destroy everything around you then it will be your turn. José, Baby you need to leave the streets alone. They even took his favorite necklace you gave him off his neck," she said wiping away his tears.

"What, they took his necklace... them broke ass bitches I swear if I find out who did this, I'm killing them personally. Jo let ya girls know I've got 25 grand for information on who done this. Ma call Corletto Latino, I'll pay for the funeral I want the best for my lil man. All-white everything, a buggy, and all, Word," José said disguising his hurt with anger.

That night José and JoJo stayed in his mother's house and slept in the same bed for the first time and didn't do a thing. Early the next morning, the movers were there ready to move Miss Valdez to her new home. With so much joy that should have come with moving into her new home at the moment, she only felt grief. Heading out the door he kissed his mother and promised to find out what happened. His mother objected to his plans and told him to leave it alone, but she knew by the look in his eyes her son wouldn't leave it alone even if it cost him his life. All she could do is pray for him.

Dropping JoJo off at home, they talked for a second and once again he kissed her like it was a regular thing. All he thought about was her saying, "I'm ya wife and she's your side bitch." He smiled to himself and then pulled off, when he got home Summer hadn't made it back from Baltimore yet, so he just lounged around the crib. He received a text from Angelina sending her condolences, she must've found out from Sammy. While he sat in the crib his phone was alerted that he had a video text. When he opened the message, his mouth fell wide open! Shit couldn't have gotten any worse for him, but it did. You know what they say, bad things come in threes so with Felix's death, the video he just watched, he wondered what was coming his way next, only the Lord knew.

Strap left the emergency room on a mission. He wanted José dead so badly that he made a few calls then slid through Scott Street searching. Only people outside where the kids playing out front and their mothers. Strap was also dropping a bag on him. He needed to find Rakmeef and Twink.

Summer walked in the door around 2:30 that afternoon without a worry in the world. She was upbeat and jubilant like her usual self. So, when she went to kiss José on the lips and he moved his face away she was caught off guard. Thinking nothing of his gesture, she took it as he was deep in thought and wanted to be left alone. José set on the sofa with a stone face as flashbacks of his younger brother and mother kept appearing in his mind. Climbing the staircase to his bedroom he flopped down onto the bed and once again let the tears flow. Summer stepped out of the bathroom with a towel wrapped around her body and noticed José crying. She came and laid aside him to try and figure out what's wrong with him.

"Babe, what's wrong?" Summer inquired.

José ignored her, as she begins wiping away the tears from his face. She didn't know what was bothering her man but knew it was serious because José was never known to cry.

"You clean now huh?" he managed to say sarcastically through his tears.

Summer didn't know what he was talking about, so she blew it off and continued to try to find out what was wrong.

"José what's wrong babe?" she asked more concerned than before.

Through the tears, he managed to explain to her what happened. Some putos came into my mom's house last night looking for drugs and money. You know I don't keep nothing there, but some dumb ass went in there and beat my mom badly and then when Felix walked in the room, they shot him... these niggas killed my little brother," he said balling in tears.

Summer's mouth fell wide open in shock and this belief. She thought that she was hearing things but knew that she wasn't from the tears and look all over her man's face. She immediately began crying along with him. She loved Felix like a brother as well now he was gone so soon. They comforted each other for a while, trying to be each other's strength. That's when Summer tried going down to give him some head to relieve some of the built-up frustration he had bottled up. He pushed her away. The push wasn't a shove though, it was a push and it made her feel some type of way.

"Boy, what's what is wrong with you?!" Summer asked shouting.

"Nah, what's wrong with you?" he shot back.

"What? What the Fuck are you talking about?"

"What you get into last night? And don't lie."

"You know what I did... I went to Baltimore with my girls, why?"

"Yeah, ya trifling ass girls... those skank hoes ain't shit, especially

Kiesha. I should've fucked her when I had the chance," he said with venom.

"What… what you say?" she asked sounding angry.

"You heard me; I should've fucked her when I had the chance… I mean shit, why not share… you fucked her right!"

"What are you talking about José?" she said sounding nervous.

Without another word being said José fidgeted with his phone then tossed it towards her. When she pressed play and saw herself riding Kiesha's face and sucking Yellow Man's dick she fell to the floor instantly and began balling out in tears. She had remembered the night before and she couldn't take back what had happened and knew that she had to have been drugged because she would have never been involved with the shit under normal circumstances. From the outside looking in, it looked like she was very much enjoying herself. And it looked that way to José as well. He grabbed his phone from Summer and went to leave. She tried to stop him and explain herself, but it was no use, everything she tried saying fell on deaf ears. She tried grabbing his arm but when he spun around with his fist clenched tightly, she let him go. She has never seen him like that and before he walked out the door he turned and spoke words that would haunt her for months to come.

"I guess my all wasn't enough… it's all good though, I'm done with ya trifling ass… you scum cum guzzling whore," he said and then shut the door behind him heading to his best friend's house.

Summer laid in a puddle of her own tears for close to an hour trying to get her strength up to get up. Knowing infidelity was never a part of the plan when it came to her and José's relationship; she knew that she had made a major fuck up.

First, she wanted to find out who spiked her drink, then she wanted to find out who in the hell recorded the video. Last but not least, she wanted to know why Kiesha would even indulge in some shit like that knowing she was her girl and that she didn't get down with the girl on girl thing. After talking to her cousin Hope for about an hour, she found out that Kiesha had spiked her drink with "molly" and had set the whole ordeal up with Yellow Man to have a threesome with the two girls. She didn't know who recorded it but was certain that Kiesha probably played a part in that as well. *"I should've fucked her when I had the chance,"* replayed in Summer's mind. *"This bitch Kiesha has been out to get my man the whole fucking time,"* she thought to herself.

Summer and Kiesha would definitely be meeting in the park for this one. The park is where the girls went if they felt they wanted to handle something with one another. *"And this was worthy of a trip to the park,"* she thought.

"I'm gonna beat this Black Bitch Ass I swear on my unborn seed," Summer said fuming and still tearing at the eyes.

CHAPTER 15

The Abandoned House

José laid in the extra room of Taylor and JoJo's apartment feeling out of it. Castro, Carlos, and Dre had reached out to him, but he ignored their calls. He had his girls go meet with Mac at his place to grab the hundred pounds for Carlos-knowing he would have to surface he wanted this time to be airtight. Someone knew something for them to run in his mother's he thought. He just couldn't figure out who would go that far as to kill a 10-year-old. The only name that rang a bell was Rakmeef and Twink, two vicious stickup kids from Eastside. He canceled that thought because he hasn't seen them snooping around plus, they didn't know what he was doing to even be on his trail like that. It just wasn't making sense but what's in the dark will come to light. When Taylor and JoJo got back with the loud José grabbed five of the bricks he had cut for Dre and placed them in his sports bag.

Next, he grabbed two bricks of soft out of the closet in the extra room and made his calls. Calling Carlos and Dre back, then Castro, he then called his youngin Quan Showstopper, and his Young & Reckless crew up. Wanting to make it quick he had everyone meet him at Chelsea's Tavern on the Market Street Mall. Once everyone arrived, he explained the string of events that took place in the past 48-hours. Even the infamous sex tape he let everyone in attendance view.

After a quick lunch, he hit Dre with the five bricks of manteca and handed Quan and Dawger the two bricks of soft with specific orders to pump on 2nd and Scott only since it was already jumping. Outside Castro gave the lil niggas a bag full of guns as a gift. And just like that, they were off to the races! Taylor popped her trunk and had Carlos unload his gift! His eyes became as big as dinner plates.

"I told you I didn't forget about you," José said hugging his friend.

"You owe me a hundred!"

Carlos was cool with that because he knew he could see at least 240 grand selling all the weight.

"All I want is for my main niggas to do what y'all been wanted to do an that's sell weight... with this ain't no need to be on the block anymore."

Taylor and JoJo made runs for him all that day while he mourned. The next morning, he was out knocking off what work he had left and just like clockwork on the 3rd day the work was gone. With his youngins breaking shit down and Dre getting accustomed to selling weight he still had that money out, so he took that from his stash and paid Angelina. The first few times they met at her house, but then she started having it delivered to his second safe house on Harding Ave. With this shipment, he planned to step his game up, so he hit up all his folks throughout the city who was involved from North, East, South, and West; plus, New Castle, and Dover. After politicking with some old friends, he had a good 15 players alone grabbing hard anywhere from nine to a whole thing at a time, if not more. Then between Fat Papi's folks Rosé, MacLaden's people, and the three players he knew who copped at least a square at a time, these shipments were about the fly. Now, the question was, could Angelina cover the order because in two days José finished the work and without one front except to the Young & Reckless. Now, he was back to see her again twice in one week. He insisted that she double the order and with no thought, José had 80 bricks being delivered later that evening. It was only Wednesday and it was on with 40 apiece, he went ape shit! Instead of 25, he dropped prices on the soft to 23-5 and for the "d" 49. Every dollar off was a profit to the hustler and he would still see major cash flow. By Friday, 60 bricks between "d" and coke were sold in two states and three counties. The same thing happened on Saturday money came but he called it early and took a half day. He had been staying with his girls since leaving Summer, he thought of her time to time but left it at that. He had other things on his mind like seeing his little brother for the last time tomorrow. Damn it was Felix's funeral.

We gather here to celebrate the life of young Felix Valdez. He was taking away from us here on this earth and called to join our Heavenly Father in Heaven. I knew your probably asking the question right now, why Felix was chosen to be the sacrificial offering and not us. Well, let me tell you that God is forever knowing and what we may feel as unfair or not right might be a part of God's ultimate plan to reach those left behind. Don't think that young Felix is suffering because right now he's looking down on us in pure joy surrounded by the host of Heaven, the angels and God Almighty Himself! His spot is secure but how about you, now is your time to get yourself right with God so that when your day comes you to will be ready to face God… He lies me down in green pastures… as the minister recited the Lord's Prayer and the casket was being lowered into the ground all strength was lost. Everyone in attendance broke down and cried. Miss Valdez had to be held by her two sons while they wailed too. It was such a sad time for family, friends, and everyone had to be each other crutches. José crew, Taylor, JoJo, Angelina, Angel, Mac, Bunny, Rosé, Felix's friends from school, teachers, and other family members. Summer even came to say her farewells, José saw her as she tried to give her condolence, but he walked right by her. Her heart ached but she managed to hold back her tears. Instead of going to the repass with the rest of his family and friends he went to Silverbrook Cemetery somewhere he hadn't been in years. The only person that would just be quiet and let him mourn without telling him everything would be okay was his deceased father. Silence sometimes is the best remedy for pain and sitting at the cemetery for close to an hour having a conversation with a ghost he finally came to a conclusion. He could hear his father's voice saying to him, "José life goes on... Felix is okay and he forgives you. Son, if your gonna play in this game be the best at it... I want you to be 10 times better than me. Have no mercy cause your first sign of weakness could be your last day of breathing. Kill or be killed son, make me proud. Oh, and last but not least, it's the ones closest to you that pray on ya downfall." José got himself together and before he took it in, he went through Scott Street and it's a good thing he did!

Quan Showstopper and Vic-chow were hugging 2nd and Scott like gorillas tending to their newborns. Nothing had slowed up, to be honest, the Young & Reckless crew had generated more cash flow. With Quan and Vic holding the morning down and Dawger and A-1 Bry smashing the night shift and they, all played the late-night shift; Scott Street looked like Blue Hill Avenue. Boo was the poison waiting to kill anyone who infiltrated or tried to infiltrate his crew's wall. Just so happens on the specific day the crew was put to the test and just like they're named they were young and reckless! As the crew ran back and forth making sells, two cocky looking men with serious mean mugs and diddy bops came walking towards Showstopper. Vic-chow was making a bud sale but Boo and Dawger picked up on the men approaching then directed their full attention to the situation.

"Who got some chow out here?" the shorter of the two men asked.

"I do, what you want old head?" Quan Showstopper replied.

"Who got the hard too?" the taller of the two asked.

Not feeling neither of the men's approach, Quan asked where they were from.

"Yeah, I got both but what you trying to get? Cause, I only got a fifty of both."

"Let me get all that shit lil nigga!" Code Blue said attempting to pull his torch out.

Before he could get his weapon fully extended... POP! POP! POP! POP! Shots came flying from the opposite direction. Boo and Dawger were on point and that gave Quan just enough time to make it to safety and pull out his own cannon and bus at the perpetrators.

"Yo Strap you good?!" Code Blue hollered over top of the gunfire.

"I'm good my nigga... I'm trying to kill one of these lil niggas!" Strap hollered.

The shootout went on for a good five minutes and soon sirens could be heard approaching in the distance. Knowing it was time to go Code Blue and Strap let off a flurry of shots to make an escape. As they fled in one direction the youngins took off in the opposite, only to run into a police squad car. Before the two officers had a chance to get out, Quan sent two .40 cal shells through the front window causing the officers to duck and take cover. That half second was all the youngins needed to disperse like a cloud of smoke back into their neighborhood never to be seen for the rest of the day. While José was turning onto Scott, he saw a squad car approaching fast, then out of nowhere two shots rang out causing the police to slam on their brakes and come to a screeching halt! Next, he saw his youngins scattering across the block in all different directions then disappeared. Instead of going to the block where squad cars, unmarked vice cars, and detectives were now questioning residents and searching for clues. Everyone on the block knew that the youngins were José's youngins so they didn't know a thing. José texted Quan and Dawger and within a few minutes, they were texting him the address to their location.

Arriving on Chestnut Street entering the basement from the sidewalk, Quan could see the look of anger and frustration on his old heads face.

"What happened?" José asked calmly.

"Two niggas… older niggas walked down on us suspect asking for some chow, so I was about to serve him until his man was like who got the hard too? I felt something was fishy, so I asked what they wanted and the short nigga tried to pull out… that's when shit got messy," Quan spoke menacingly.

"So, they tried to rob you? All this time and now they tried to rob y'all," José said sounding surprised.

"Yo José I don't know what's up, all I know is while we were shooting it out, I heard one of those niggas ask his man… I guess his name is Strap if he was okay," Quan said remembering more detail.

"You said Strap?" José asked getting heated.

"Yeah why, you know him?" Quan asked.

"Yeah, I know the bitch ass nigga. I'll take care of it… y'all lay low for a few days, y'all hot as shit. Why y'all shoot at the police?"

"Shit that was to make them pigs think twice about getting out of that car," Quan said laughing.

"Y'all lil niggas crazy… but check, fall back for a while until the heat dies down. I'm going out of town for a week; be ready when I get back," he said dapping all of his youngins then headed out the door.

The thought of Strap coming through his block made it clear that he and his team wanted a war so that's what he's gonna get. Peace of mind was very much needed and instead of surrounding himself with friends he wanted to be with family, so he called his mother and brother and told them to pack a few things. It never rained, it's sunny and with it nicknamed the City of Angels he felt Los Angeles California would be a nice place to visit.

Rakmeef and Twink have been floating through the Westside heavy ever since Abbee had put them on to that grimy ass fiend Ramone. Plus, they had just received a contract on some young nigga named Spanish José from Scott Street. The contract was for 30 grand and they could keep whatever they found in the process. Finding any work was out of the question because for 30 grand this would be an assassination. Meantime and between time, Twink's younger cousin Bree had been assigned to foot patrol over Westside. She had been on the beat for two days before she had finally run into Ramone. His gay ass, as usual, was running around with a purple halter top and black tights on with purple Ugg Boots looking like a fucking freak. Knowing the freak boy would be game to a free bundle or two of the fire dope Bree knew that luring him in would be easy. Now that she had him, she had to keep him close and the best way to keep a blade around is to treat him how he wants to be treated and that's like a stone-cold Bitch.

"Hey girl, what's up?" Bree said to Ramone.

"Oh nothing, girl trying to sell this ass so I can get my fix!" Ramone said in his best Big Frieda impersonation.

"You ain't sick, are you?" Bree asked.

"No, not yet girl but if I don't make some money fast, I will be," he said rocking back and forth from foot to foot.

"Look, I just moved around here and I got some fire "d" I'm trying to get off and if you help me, I would definitely take care of you, feed you, and keep a couple ones in ya pocket," Bree said trying to convince him.

"You got some "d" girl? Why didn't you been say something? What's the name of it?" Ramone asked rambling on and on.

"Deathwish and my folks said the shit is guaranteed 10. You wanna try?" Bree asked knowing the answer.

"Hell yeah girl and if it's any good we gonna make mad loot today girl!" he said becoming hype.

"You gotta phone?" Bree asked.

"Yeah, why you gotta contact number?"

"Yup and take two of these an let me know how you like it girl," Bree said dropping two bundles of heroin into his palm, "now don't do the whole bundle because the shit is powerful."

"What name you want me to store you under?"

"Cyn, that's short for Cynthia girl."

"I got you Cyn, just be close when I call, you know these fiends don't like waiting too long."

"Alright, just call me," Bree said walking off.

Bree walked away feeling that the rat would be exterminated soon so she checked to make sure her safety was off her baby nine-millimeter and headed up the Hill towards Scott Street. This mission was a little more serious, she didn't know what this kid José looked like, but all she knew was he was Spanish and for 10 grand he had to die. So, if she got a chance to hit him and she could get away with it, then it's off with his head. When she made it to Scott Street, she was surprised to see that the block was a ghost town. Not a soul was in sight so she lingered for a while hoping to spark up a conversation with someone that might know José to get more info on him. Luck was not on her side this day cause as she sat out on the block alone smoking a blunt, not a soul appeared. Twink had hit her phone and she gave her cousin the rundown on Ramone and how things might happen faster than they thought. After ending the call with Twink, she began floating around the Hill until her phone rang. It was Ramone and he needed five bundles, so she went to meet him. Bree had posted on Scott Street a little too long because at that time any unfamiliar faces male or female was considered suspect. And the pretty light brown skin shorty, was a face that had never been seen before, so Castro watched from a distance but took a photo mentally.

Detective Baldwin had finally reached Ramone who had scheduled a meeting the next day with Abbee to speak with him. All Abbee kept thinking of was leaving for rehab the next day, so when she called him and said that she wanted to party later that evening he didn't refuse. For now, he wanted to get five bundles of "deathwish" so that he could have some to sell himself. At 20 a "b" the five he was copping he would surely double his money. Ramone didn't know Cyn, but he loved her for having some of the best dope he's had in a while. Plus, the sample bags that he gave out had the fiends coming back looking for more, so Cyn would definitely have to be around when the sun went down. That's when money came in abundance and if she had enough the night would be lovely. Abbee had been a part of the plot to take Ramone out and her job was to get him to the abandoned house. And with most fiends, wherever the product was, they would follow, even if that meant walking into Hell and back. This time though, he wouldn't be returning from his trip to Hell. The past week or two Abbee had cut back exceptionally on sniffing dope but hadn't completely stopped yet. She had converted back to her first love which was smoking loud. At first, the chow was too strong and would put her to sleep every single time she smoked it. Now, she's getting used to it again and she's blowing like a champ! Since she slowed down and she's eating more and Rakmeef has even turned her out to getting her pussy ate. He has had Nyomi basically with them every day as their personal sex slave. The trio had heavy several hour sessions of sensual threesomes, one on ones basically whatever came to mind. Abbee was happy to be back with the love of her life.

The sun had finally set, the zombies were mobile and Bree was in her mode. Standing on someone else's block with no worries in the world, she was trapping around 10 she had received a text telling her it was time. And just like clockwork Ramone who was in full homo swing received a call from his girlfriend Abbee.

"Hello-Hello!" Ramone answered girly.

"Yeah girl, where you at?... yes, I know where that's at... who you got with you?... how many?... girl you're a mess... Oooh! Girl, I got this new shit called Deathwish and everybody is loving it... 250 a stick... you want two... well, my peoples is right here with me, is it okay if I bring her... okay good, we'll be there in 20 minutes... okay see you then," Ramone said excitedly, he was about to get his party on.

Twenty minutes later, Ramone was riding shotgun in Cyn's bombed out Nissan Maxima pulling up to the lone abandominium on Rodman Street.

"This girl sure knows how to find a nice get-a-way," Ramone said whispering.

By this time, Cyn wasn't saying a word and followed as Ramone led the way to the rear of the house. After a few knocks and a few seconds of waiting, the door finally opened and there stood Abbee. Wearing only a thong and a bra even Ramones gay ass was starting to get a hard-on. She finally led them in letting him walk pass first then barely making eye contact with Bree. Abbee let them to an upstairs room that was vacant, the other rooms seemed to be occupied with what seemed to sound like fucking. Abbee had a look of hatred on her face but even in the dark, it could be seen.

"So, where's the good shit at girl?' Abbee said.

"My girl got it; you got the money?" Ramone questioned.

"Yeah, let me go get it out of the other room."

Abbee had walked out and the whole time Ramone was talking to Bree, he never noticed that her facial expression and body demeanor had changed until he looked up in the dark and realized that he had a gun pointed directly at him. He almost pissed on himself, Ramone wasn't sure what could have caused this change of heart, but he wanted to know quickly. I think he got his answer when Abbee and a butt naked Nyomi walked back in the room with Rakmeef and Twink behind them with two Louisville sluggers in hand.

"Nyomi, go take a shower boo and hurry up, I don't want you to miss out on all the fun," Rakmeef said stroking his bat from top to bottom.

"Hitting the light switch on the wall brought the room to life but the sad thing was everyone's eyes read death even Ramones. The silence was eerie until Abbee finally spoke.

"So, Ramone what time is that meeting with your detective friend tomorrow?"

"Wh... I don't know what you talkin' about," he said nervously.

"Yes you do boo... they know everything so just admit it," she said flatly.

"No, I told you it was a reward and we could split it if you told."

"So, you really gonna try to lock up my soulmate, my love, the father of my deceased child so that you can get a reward and get high?"

"No... I'm sorry, I swear... I won't say a thing if you let me go please," he said beginning to cry.

"Oh sweetie, I'm not gonna stop you from leaving, I have nothing against you except that you're a fucking below the earth dirty garbage eating no morals or values Rat! I can't say what they have planned for you though."

Just then, Nyomi walked back in the room still naked and wet looking on as if she was watching a new Stephen King horror flick. Abbee walked up to Rakmeef and pulled his cannon off his waist then told him while giving him wet lips and tongue.

"I'll hold this while you take care of that."

That's when the brutal beating began with Twink taking a swing of his bat to Ramones's midsection. The force of the swing caused him to bend over and clutch his stomach. That only gave way to Rakmeef crashing his Louisville slugger on the back of his head painting sections of the wall with blood. The screams that once fell from Ramones mouth had now ceased as he laid twitching on the floor in a pool of his own blood semi-conscious.

The beating was awful as you heard bone after bone Snap, Crackle, and Pop! What used to be his skull and face had been crushed and beyond recognition.

Almost 15 minutes later, with signs of death due to the piss and shit stench that invaded the air, Rakmeef and Twink who were now out of breath, tired and covered in blood kept crushing whatever bone that would give way to the force of the bats!

Finally, the torture was over and Ramone laid dead in the middle of the floor in an abandoned house. Just as planned, everyone had a part as Twink passed Nyomi the straight razor with orders to cut his fucking throat wide open from ear to ear. And without hesitation, she bent over still naked and sliced his throat. When she looked up though something was terribly wrong. Abbee, Bree, Rakmeef, and Twink stood with grim expressions on their faces. Somewhere in the equation, the plans had been switched and with Abbee pointing the gun at her chest, she knew that she had also been set up! Fear and confusion were written all over her face as she tried to hurry to her feet!

"Ny boo, you thought I was really okay with you bouncing ya ass around me and you fucking my man! You thought by sucking his dick on call you could take my place? This is my man boo and you better know that the Bolivian Barbie doesn't share her men. And since you thought it was okay to seduce my man in my face you gotta go," Abbee said in her strongest Latina accent ever.

"But I thought…"

Before she could finish her sentence… Pop! Pop! Pop! Pop! Pop! Abbee sent five shots into Nyomi's chocolate frame. She crumbled, there was no chance of survival. Nyomi's life was cut short all because of some good dick. Abbee was the Queen in Rakmeef's s castle and everyone close to him knew it. So, if one happens to come along and ever tried to dethrone her, they would meet an untimely death.

Now, that the rat was dead their mission was some young kid named Spanish José from the Hilltop. If they found him, they would become 30 grand richer if not then on to the next. Bree would play foot patrol on the Hill until she could get more info while Rakmeef and Twink hit up other spots getting more cash and drugs.

Abbee was leaving for rehab in the morning and would be gone for four to six months. Rakmeef promised to be there every weekend to see her and make sure she wanted for nothing. Taking his gun back from Abbee they left the abandoned house with two dead bodies inside.

Reaching the spot in Fairfax everyone dropped off their weapons and took showers to rinse away any evidence of foul play. After getting dressed, the bandits headed out to New Castle to stop by the Wawa to grab a bite to eat and a few snacks. Coming through the city late night was a risk sometimes because of the law and the fact that most of the time they had cannons on deck. This night Bree was the only one strapped, but had it tucked in the stash box. While they rode, they never noticed that they were being followed. It wasn't until they were about to pull into the Wawa parking lot that all four noticed the unmarked cars coming down the road towards them with more coming up fast behind. They knew it was too soon to be about the bodies earlier that night, so they assumed it was for some old shit. The vice squad had the car surrounded as they barked orders for all the passengers to exit the vehicle with their hands high. Before they had a chance to separate them, Rakmeef kissed Abbee reminded her that just because he was about to be taking that she was still to go to rehab in the morning.

"This is for our family… go get clean babe," he managed to say before being handcuffed.

After the girls came back 29-negative, they were uncuffed and released. By this time, a brown box style Caprice pulled up and Rakmeef and Twink's heart skipped a beat when they saw the occupant. Walking over to Rakmeef and Twink Detective Baldwin spoke as if he had solved the case beforehand.

"Good evening boys, long time no see… I see you two losers are still up to your tricks."

"What the fuck are you talking bout?!" Twink screamed.

"You know… body snatching, your asses are done this time."

"We don't know shit, ain't see shit or hear shit… that's all we gotta say!" the two said in unison.

"Take them to headquarters, I'll be there soon," Detective Baldwin said then turned and walked away.

Bree and Abbee stopped at the Wawa anyway, Bree never noticed the man watching her from his car in the parking lot. Castro was late night tricking with one of his many flings and stumbled across police jumping out on two of the city's most vicious stickup kids, Rakmeef and Twink. What caught his attention wasn't the arrest of the city's top goons but the same light brown skin shorty who looked like the Urban Vixen Kira Andrea. Now that he connected her to someone, he wanted to know her business on Scott Street and he was gonna find out. What Castro didn't know was that while he kept his watchful eye on shorty and entertaining the female with him, he was being watched as well. It was only a matter of time before shit got real for him and his team.

Since murdering Alex's family member, Ivan had been in the shadows. He only came out in the nighttime and he's always strapped with at least his .40 and a Mac-10 at all times. Rumors were still spreading that Alex was looking for him. Now the streets were saying he was also running around with some gang banger from Cali looking for him. They had even come to the store looking for him, Angelina felt it would be wise to let Noel and Sammy run the store until this was handled. She made a call and within hours three truckloads of poppies were in Wilmington ready for whatever. To make their point known, Amillio shot a few of Ivan's closest associates so that the word would get back to him. By now, the Goya Bean Cartel was causing major problems on the Hill and something needed to be done. The mission was to force Ivan out of hiding or shoot and kill so many people that even his own blood would lead them to him. Ivan had been playing I declare war for years and with many different people, so this wasn't any stress in no way to him. For now, he had better plans and that was meeting up with his new friend LeLe. They had spoken to each other quite a few times since they met and now tonight, she was inviting him to her condo for drinks, dinner, and a movie. When he arrived, she was playing the soft sounds of Mark Anthony. He was very impressed with her layout; she had several paintings of historical people and times in the Latin culture. The one that caught his eye was the one of Oscar De La Hoya standing over top of his opponent with a mean mug on. The caption at the bottom read "A fighter never quits!" The emerald pink with platinum trim Persian rug accompanied by matching platinum coffee tables. With floor to ceiling windows and her being on a higher level gave you a wonderful view of the city's skyline. That cocaine white three-piece sectional that was handcrafted in Morocco was elevated off the floor to give you that Royal Highness feel. As she gave him a tour of her living quarters, he really got a feel for the woman standing in front of him. You could tell a woman lived there; it just had a woman's touch. Entering her bedroom, he was loving it, it looked real comfortable. The black and gold silk bed sheets by Gorgio Armani laid perfectly on the Queen size Tempur-Pedic mattress that sat high off the floor making it somewhat complicated for LeLe to climb on top sometimes. In the middle of the bed laid a black and gold laced negligee with garter belts and heels to match. Ivan being the outspoken guy he was simply asked what was on his mind at that moment.

"Damn can I see you in this right here mami?"

"If you behave yourself you just might... and you might see a lot more!" LeLe said smiling at him.

They drank shots of Patron while chasing it with flutes of cupcake Moscato. This was LeLe's idea and by the fourth shot she was tipsy and becoming flirtatious. Ivan played it cool and respectful, never taking the lead or becoming over aggressive. He was patient while she prepared a Mexican dish called Bisteck A La Mexicana. While waiting he viewed the many portraits, she had on a glass stand. His mouth fell wide open! Here he was staring directly at the man he was trying to kill, Alex! LeLe had walked back into the living room and Ivan inquired about a few other pictures before targeting in on the one in specific.

"Yo LeLe, who's this guy?" Ivan asked curious.

"Who him?" she said pointing to the picture, "that's my youngest brother Alex he's a sweetheart," she said openly giving up the tapes.

He was beefing with a man whose sister he was about to fuck and could eventually lead him to his target. Things just started looking brighter for Ivan, but for now, he would eat this wonderful smelling meal and see LeLe in this negligee of hers, if not that then hopefully naked!

CHAPTER 16
Two Weeks Later

Rosé had taken a strong liking to Taylor and since the night he met her and hung out with her at the Hookah Lounge he's made it his business to see her once a day. He's sent flowers to her job, took her out to lunch, and he's even invited JoJo out to dinner with them a few times. He tried hooking JoJo up with one of his mans, but she shot it down before he even got started. She had her heart set on one man and that was José. Even after the gifts and kind gestures she still hadn't invited him into her home yet. He figured it had something to do with José, so he didn't trip. Tonight, he was planning to continue his great adventure by taking a private jet to Las Vegas to see Mariah Carey and Chris Brown perform at the MGM Grand. Then the next night, they attended a UFC event. Taylor was really into the hand to hand combat thing, so her panties were of course soaked by the action. After a few hours of gambling and drinking, they hit up a few boutiques and like always he's splurged on her dropping a cool 15 grand on her purchases. This took the cake and finally, Taylor had let her walls down. The feelings she had for him, she felt it was time to start showing them. Knowing it wouldn't come close to the amount he has spent on her, she pulled out her Visa Gold Card and grabbed him a pair of Original Penguin bedroom slippers and a Fendi sweater. It only cost $500, but it was the thought that counts and the fact that she has never spent a dime on a man made it special. When she handed him the bag his expression went from content to excited! His face reminded you of a kid on Christmas morning opening his first gift. See, Rosé has always been the provider and most times he never received anything in return. So, this simple act of kindness said a lot about her and made Rosé grow even more interested in her.

On the jet heading back to the east coast, Rosé turned on his iPhone playlist and searched until he found the perfect song. As soon as he found what he was looking for he connected his phone to the beats pill and let the song play while he walked over to her. He knelt down on one knee as Lyfe Jenning's "Must Be Nice" played in the background. Rosé parted her legs and he slid her one-piece wool sweater dress up her thighs and around her waist. Taylor was nervous and anxious, she wasn't gonna stop him from exploring her body, her white lace panties were extremely wet as he slowly pulled them down to her ankles. When she stepped out of them, he grabbed her calf muscles then extended both legs, spreading them east to west. And finally, had his first look at her fat, hairless, and barely tampered with pussy. He lowered his head in between her thighs resting his fat wet tongue on her clit. Her body shivered as goosebumps started appearing all over her. He sucked and she came tremendously! Her nut was thick and creamy and Rosé was loving the taste of her juices. Rosé now had her on her knees in the seat as he lashed his wet tongue up and down her asshole. She couldn't help but to moan out in pure pleasure as his tongue ran from her ass or pussy. As soon as she started begging for him to put it in her stomach he stopped. He got up from his knees, wiped his mouth, and then smiled. Then he took a seat and made a drink. Taylor was out of breath and spent! She was also upset, she wanted some dick, and he was playing! She did what any respectable woman would have done, without saying a word she pulled her dress down, tossed her soaked panties that smelled like mango Fusion in his face, crossed her legs, made a drink, and then got on Instagram! She had a plan though if he thought he was leaving her pussy throbbing he had another thing coming.

A few hours later, the jet landed in the New Castle County Airport. Instead of riding shotgun Taylor asked if it was okay if she drove. He was cool with it, but he had to be feeling her though because no female has never has ever pushed the S-500 before. And personally, her little frame looked sexy as hell pushing that big body Benz down Route 13. Instead of heading to Wilmington, Taylor hopped on I-95 heading South, within five minutes they got off on the Basin Road exit. Soon Rosé knew where they were headed as she pulled into the Sheraton Hotel that sat along I-95. They walked into the four-star establishment hand to hand walking up to the reception desk. Wanting a suite on one of the higher floors to overlook the interstate, she went into her purse and paid for this rendezvous. On the elevator ride up it was silent until Rosé pulled her into his arms and began kissing her with rhythm and skill as his hands roamed her body. No words were spoken until they entered the room. The kisses began and slowly but surely the clothes started coming off, within minutes Taylor laid naked on the bed while waiting for Rosé to remove his pants. She started rubbing on both nipples unknowingly as she watched his dick grow quite huge by the seconds. With his boxers still on she could see that he was well hung, Rosé went in headfirst finishing what he started on the jet. She was cumming and soaked as usual now she wanted him in her throat. When she pulled off his boxers her heart fluttered as she gazed at the piece of meat that had to be a foot long at least three fingers thick. She knew she wasn't ready for this, but she wanted it, so she engulfed her mouth around as much as she could. From the sounds of it, it must've been feeling good to her as well. After sucking the hell out of his dick and was sure that it was hard as a lead pipe, she wanted to feel that shit in her tightness. As she laid back and spread her legs apart staring him in the eyes as he mounted her, she revealed a secret that was sure to seal the deal between the two. And I'm sure Rosé wouldn't mind that one bit.

"I hope you're not just doing all this so that you can get some pussy Roho," Taylor said genuinely.

"Nah, if I just wanted pussy, do you think I would have let you push my wheels? Or you think I would have flown you to Vegas? Jet fuel ain't cheap! And do you think a shot of pussy is worth 15 grand if so, you're smoking dippers. I did what I did to show you that I like you Taylor and you're something special... you deserve the best. I know it's still early but I'm trying to show you that I want you and not just sexually but mentally, emotionally, and physically... now let me have you! Now, that you've heard my true feelings and my personal secrets, what secrets do you have to tell me? And don't blow my shit by saying you have some shit you can't get rid of," Rosé said seriously looking her in the eyes.

"Boy, how can I have some shit I can't get rid of if I never had sex Rosé. What I'm trying to tell you is, I really really need you to take your time and to be gentle baby because contrary to what you might believe looking at all this soft ass, flat stomach, and busky titties I'm still a virgin boo! Yes, I'm the only 18-year-old virgin left on earth. Oh my God!" she said covering her face.

Rosé couldn't believe his ears, he struck gold and now he had her and wasn't letting her go! Looking into her eyes, he sucked on her lips then he entered her slowly and gently; her eyes began to water from the slight pain she felt. He slowly started stroking her and the feeling started to become amazing. She quickly fell in love with his thrust and for the first time ever she felt the wonderful pleasure of lovemaking.

Carlos and Dre had been doing their thing hard and still made plenty of time to spend with the Twins since they were both moving weight now. What had the two homies fucked up was when they found out that the girls were involved in the pill game. At first, they thought that maybe the Twins received a prescription and flipped the script every month to earn extra money for themselves. It wasn't until they hung out with the Twins that they found out they were as heavy in the game as they were. Their cars had stash boxes carrying about a thousand pills at any given time. They rode around busing sells for a hundred perc thirty's at a time and that was a small sale. They made more stops than one could imagine. Between the girls making sells and taking Carlos and Dre to make their own sells it seemed like their cars were stopping every 10 minutes. The homies had been to the Twins house in Smyrna a few times where they lived with their elderly mother and other family members. Because they never visited the homes on Pleasant Street, they never knew the sweet elderly woman was really the ruthless and cold-blooded killer Priscilla Reyes. And that she had brought her family out of town and was now running pressure on the small-time drug dealers on the hilltop. José was still out of town and he wasn't answering his phone, so Dre and Carlos decided to hit the block to make up where the Young & Reckless crew had fell back. Since that shooting occurred on Scott Street the police presence had increased drastically including vice and detectives. It was obvious that they were looking for something, they just didn't know what yet. The first thought that came to mind was the youngins but from what they knew no one in the neighborhood said a word. The only people that could identify them were the law whose car was shot up, but that shit happened so fast and the youngins disappeared so quick that they doubted that they could positively identify any of the youngins. Detective Stevens sat two blocks away with his high-powered binoculars during a daytime investigation. He had recently been assigned a major case being though he was a sergeant on the governor's task force. The man he was looking for hasn't been spotted since he started the investigation a week ago. He knew that this was his stomping grounds because he knew the young Black kid personally. For Detective Stevens the case was memorable because it was his first arrest. Twelve-year-old Kevin Gaines was stopped and found to be in possession of a Ruger 9mm with an extended clip that held 25. The gun looked bigger than the kids' 12-year-old frame.

Now, six years later and an upcoming purchase of 350 weapons, 200 assault rifles, and a 150 handguns Castro was considered the region's largest arms dealers. And now, Detective Stevens was assigned to follow him and as soon as the deal is made, he will arrest him. The only problem was catching up to him so that he can start his surveillance. The only people on Scott Street today were two Spanish kids and a young Black girl who had just walked up. Luckily, the boys weren't doing too much hand to hand transactions and when they did, they would either walk around the block or slide into an alleyway. They didn't know that the block was now under investigation for two things. The shooting of a police car and gun running that would more than likely alert the Feds due to the fact that he's crossed state lines over a dozen times. It's just this shipment was the biggest that either state had seen in a long time so they wanted to stop him before the guns could hit the streets. With that many guns, one man had enough weaponry to take on the Wilmington, county, and the state police!

While Carlos and Dre were on post, a sexy little light brown skin shorty who resembled the urban vixen Kira Andrea walked up on them. You could tell she loved the same thing they did with her thuggish demeanor and turned up lip but with her cute ass, innocent eyes, and body that was thicker than a pot of oatmeal, you could still see the beauty in her. What no one knew about Bree was that she was far from a stud or butch who only loved pussy. She loved dick as well, it just wasn't often that she fucked a man. You had to be a rare type and it wasn't that many of them type around that's why she always stayed with a female. She was bi-sexual and when the right nigga came along, she would have no problem throwing that fat ass of hers back or even giving him a threesome with the woman of his choice.

"What's up y'all, what y'all doing?" Bree asked the two.

Looking at each other as if to say, is she talking to us cause I don't know her, Carlos and Dre looked stunned.

"Shit chilling, what's up with you?" Carlos asked.

"Shit, trying to find somewhere to smoke this chow and since I see y'all two handsome ass poppies I said what the hell and came to see if I could sit here with y'all," she said making it sound believable.

"Roll up, I feel like getting high anyway... you drink?" Dre asked.

"Yeah, a little why? You gettin' a bottle?"

"I mean all we drink is that Branson B. Cuvée," Dre stated.

"That's the new champagne that just came out... I tried it once, it was good! Get it if you gonna get it," she replied twisting the Dutch up!

They walked to the L.Q. on Lincoln Street and had small talk about this and that, like did she have a man; the answer was no and where was she from. She kept all her answers short but not to the point where she looked suspicious. After smoking a few blunts and sipping a little she handled what she came to do and that was find out if either of the two were José and if not, find out who he was. If one of these poppies were him beings though neither of the poppies were strapped, she was gonna pull out and blaze his ass up right there on the spot.

"Yo, I just moved down on Jackson Street about a month ago and I came through here a few times and the shit be jumping... the young boys be turned up! Y'all need to put a bitch on so I can get some paper," she said seriously.

"Yeah, it doin' okay... but it might be a little too much for you sexy," Dre stated.

"Boy thank you but don't let the pretty face fool you," she said turning up her lips.

"Nah, but I gotta holla at my folks and if he okay with it you can pump this gas out here for me," Carlos said.

"Ask who ain't this y'all strip? I mean I keep hearing bout this poppie named José and his crew and y'all both poppies so I figured one of y'all was José," she said hoping one of them confirmed her suspicion so she could torch his ass.

"Nah shorty, I'm Dre and that's my man Carlos... José is our boy but soon as we talk to him, I'll definitely put you dee with the team," she said in laughter.

"Where he at cause I'm trying to eat too boo," she says sounding more seductive.

"He out of town right now, but just stop back through here in a day or two; he should be back and I'll holla at him for you."

"A'ight, That sounds like a plan. A'ight y'all I hope you aren't bullshitting me," she said putting her hands on her hips.

"We got you," they both said in unison.

Just then both Carlos and Dre's phone rang, they had to go and make some drops. So, they hopped in Dre's Acura SUV and pulled off. Bree stood there and watched while they pulled off. As soon as they were out of sight, she got on the phone and called Rakmeef who had really been laying low after him and Twink was questioned about the double murder they committed a few months back. To make matters worse, a week after that which was last night, they were both taken in for questioning for the double murder of Nupmi Evans and Ramone Sanchez. After giving her team the new leads, she hung up. Wanting to get a bite to eat before taking it down for the night she stopped at KFC on Union Street. While she was on the hunt, she had worked up an appetite but what she didn't know was that she was being hunted and the hunter had a strong craving to find out what she wanted with his block or his crew. She stood in line ordering her meal and walked in the fly looking 19-year-old who was wearing a pair of PRP jeans, a pair of black ACG boots, and a black and gray *"Without Loyalty There's No Trust"* long sleeve shirt. Flexing with just enough ice to cover his upper body and to drop the temperature of a few degrees Castro knew he was that nigga and the way he walked and talked expressed that. When Bree looked over her shoulder and seen him, she had to do a double take. The pulsating sensation she immediately had between her thighs informed her that she was physically and sexually attracted to the brown skin wavy hair thug who stood about 6'3. Not realizing that she was staring now with a picture-perfect smile she felt embarrassed when the cashier had to raise her voice to get her attention to receive her food. She grabbed her tray of food and found a seat to enjoy her meal. From the looks of it the way he was staring he liked what he saw also. At times like these, this was when the female that she was came out of her. From the batting of her eyes to the feminine way she handled her food and ate it. Being the cocky and confident man that he was he walked up to her with his swag on a million and sat down across the table from her. Sliding into the booth with arrogance sent chills up her spine. Damn, she wanted to jump across the table and fuck him right there, but that wouldn't be lady like, but damn, it had been a long time since she had been with a male and at that point in time he was really working on her G-spot!

"Y.S.L. huh," Bree stated nibbling on her biscuit.

"What?" he replied.

"Your cologne is Y.S.L. right?" she asked being more direct.

"You're good... I like that... I can see you know ya shit and have a great sense of smell. What's ya name?" he asked sipping his Cherry Coke."

"Breanna, but you can call me Bree. What's ya name?"

"C-note, but just call me C."

Once the meal was finished and they exited the restaurant she was impressed with his truck. So, when he offered her a ride, she excepted it. She said that she only needed a ride to Jackson Street where her car was parked. On the way to her car, Castro wanted to see if he could crack the safe. And with just the right amount of charm, he just might be able too.

"Look, sometimes I can be kind of blunt but you're sexy as shit... you look the model Kira what's her name?" he asked stuck on stupid.

"Kira Andrea... I've heard that a lot, but the funny thing is I've never seen her. I hope she's bad as hell!" Bree said smiling from ear to ear.

"She is trust me, maybe if we ever get the chance to hang out, I'll show you a photo of her... so, I've seen you around the Hill lately. What you live around here?" he questioned.

"Yeah, something like that."

"So, what do you do?" he asked.

"I mean I trap a little... I got my hands in a few things... but where you be at, I never seen you around."

"I'm city wide baby girl, something that could be beneficial in many ways."

"City wide huh... so, what you know a lot of people?"

"A few... not everybody but enough."

"You know the boy Spanish José from Scott Street?"

"I know him, but I don't fuck with him like that... he be on some sucker shit when it comes to his prices on the weight. Why what's that your baby dad or something?"

"Nah, nothing like that... I'm just looking for him for my own reasons." Castro had now given her his full attention as they sat parked on Jackson Street.

"What you gave him some nana and he vanished?" he said jokingly tapping her thigh.

"Nah he... never mind."

"What? It's no big deal to me, I don't fuck with him nor do I talk to him," he said pushing her to continue.

Looking as if she really was deciding on whether or not to speak, she said fuck it.

"I mean you don't fuck with him anyway, so it doesn't matter if you know, I guess. I'm looking for the wet back mothafucka because apparently, he got into some shit at the club with some niggas from over North and the nigga put 30 grand on his head. Big Homie from North called up my folks from over the Eastside to cash the check. So, that's why my ass is over here looking for him. They said he be on Scott Street, so I went through there strapped ready to blaze his ass, but he wasn't out there; I ran into his folks. That's why you seen me at KFC because I had just left from off Scott Street," she said running the whole tape down to the enemy.

"So, who is ya folks? I might need them to put some work in for me."

"You know Rakmeef and Twink... Twink is my cousin but Rakmeef is like family too."

"Nah, I never heard of them before... I'm from Middletown boo."

Hearing all this made Castro want to kill that sexy looking bitch right there, but he had other plans for her. First, he had to put his man up on the check he had on his head then off Rakmeef, Twink, and this bitch, then finally give Strap a going away party!

"So, when can I see you again sexy? Maybe we can shoot up to Philly and hang out for the day if that's okay with you," Castro said throwing the charm back on."

"Anytime you want, just take my number and call me whenever I'll answer I'm always free... but you better call for real," she said before getting out of the truck and hopping in her Maxima then pulling off.

Castro called José who still wasn't answering but left him a message to call him back A.S.A.P. that it was important, life or death. Castro knew that it was about to be a war so he would definitely be grabbing this upcoming shipment in a few weeks.

"If these niggas want a war then a war is what they'll get!" he thought to himself.

JoJo was the only person José would answer for. Knowing his squad had enough work to hold them over until he came back JoJo was left to handle the rest of the buyers. Taylor was a part of the original plan, but she had been staying out Rosé's house lately, so JoJo rocked out. She didn't mind because he gave her profit off every brick. So, she had earned a nice sum of change while he was gone which she planned to take straight to the bank. She even dropped the whole 1.5 million that took her and Taylor about a day and a half to count multiple times off to Angelina that covered the whole 80 brick shipment. She even met with the delivery guy at the house on Harding Avenue to receive the next 80 brick shipment. She only sold to those that José specified and with him coming back in one day she alone ran through 50 bricks in a week. With 30 left plus what she made off the last flip, JoJo had made 40 thousand for herself and she was okay with it. Now, she wanted José to come back so he could see how good she did it all by herself!

It has been over three weeks since José left Summer alone in the house crying in the foyer. She had tried reaching out to him, but he would ignore her calls and send her to voicemail. She had caught up to Kiesha Jenkins and fuck making it to the park, Kiesha caught her ass whipping on site. Treasure and Hope had to pull Summer off her. Blind to what was about to happen, she pulled up on her girls thinking it was just another day. Summer wore a pair of sweatpants, a T-shirt, some comfortable sneakers, and her hair was pulled back into a ponytail. The second Keisha walked up and spoke Summer went off! She beat her, kicked her, ripped her shirt off exposing her titties and then snatched patches of hair out of her head. Her cousins felt sorry for Kiesha but didn't get involved because they knew she had violated Summer and for an act of betrayal like that no sympathy could be shown. Summer trashed Kiesha for a good 10 minutes and then spit in her face! The satisfaction of getting Kiesha back still didn't ease the pain she was feeling. So, immediately after the fight she hopped in the car, pulled off, and began to cry. All she wanted was to hear his voice and she couldn't even get that. She went back to her house and cried herself to sleep. When she awakened, she tried to watch TV but Richard Gere's movie "Unfaithful" only brought more tears about. She tried calling José for the thousandth time luckily, she got an answer, but it was his mother Miss Valdez letting Summer know that José had left his phone with her and she didn't know where he went or when he would be back. Strangely hearing his mother's voice somewhat eased some of the hurt she was dealing with. Stressed beyond the limit, she crawled her way up the stairs to her bedroom to grab a towel to go and take a shower. When the hot water cascaded down her body mixed with the steam, she felt relieved a little. It had been so long since she felt this touch and it was driving her crazy. Her hands played around her clit for what seemed like forever causing her legs to almost buckle. She kept imagining that it was José but once again after a few nuts reality sat in and the tears fell from her eyes once again. Laying in her bed with just a T-shirt on all she kept thinking of was if she ever had the chance to talk with him, she would explain everything to him with her proof, being her cousins to verify. Tears and sleep had become a ritual for her so by 10:30 that evening she had dozed off again.

An hour or so later, she woke up from her umpteenth nap of the day.

Thirsty as hell from being dehydrated which probably came from all the crying, Summer dragged her way down the steps into the kitchen to get a drink. While devouring the fruit punch she noticed that she had left the television on in the living room. When she went to turn the television off, she damn near pissed on herself in excitement when she saw her man José sitting on the sofa with a smile on his face. Unknowingly, she jumped in the air in excitement then ran and jumped in his lap and just like the past three weeks her tears fell.

"I'm soo soo sorry baby... I was trying to explain to you what happened," she said in between sobs.

"I hope you're ready to talk because I'm still pissed with you though."

"Yes, I'm ready to talk babe... I love you and I would never betray your trust."

So, for the next 30 minutes, she explained all the events of that night and how it was all set up by Kiesha. She couldn't stop apologizing for falling victim to something she should have been alert of.

"Do you believe me baby? Please do, because I'm not lying," she said sympathetically.

"I been knew you were set up Summer and that it wasn't your fault, but with my brother's death, this shit, and everything else I just needed to get away from everyone. So, I took my mom and Sammy on a vacation... just the three of us to get our thoughts right."

"How did you know that I wasn't lying and that I was set up?" Summer asked curiously.

"How do you think? Hope texted me damn near every day explaining the situation and swearing that you didn't know a thing... and that she was gonna kick my ass if I didn't respond to her texts," he said laughing.

"That's my girl, all in my shit!"

"You need to thank her because you know I can be stubborn... I heard your sexy ass got a nice two-piece combination too... give me a kiss." And for the first time in three weeks, she finally got the chance to be intimate with her man. She was in Heaven once again and she didn't want to come down just yet.

"Summer you love me?" José asked sincerely.

"Yes, I love you José and I will be there for you no matter what," she said tearing up again.

"I'm gonna hold you to that too... now let's go to bed because I've been fiending for your soft ass," he said gripping her round soft ass.

"Come on baby, I need to feel you inside of me right now!"

José was back and first things first, he called a family meeting. Everyone was to be in attendance. He only had to collect from Quan and Dawger for the two bricks that he threw them plus the 122 grand from Dre for the last 2 ½ bricks of "d". They met at Joe's Crab Shack for lunch, everyone was there, and everyone seemed ready to get back to work. The squad was shocked to see Summer join the meeting a few minutes after everyone was seated. In her hand she was carrying a large gift-wrapped box with two miniature size boxes on top of it. José had made eye contact with JoJo who looked away quickly. He knew that she was probably feeling some type of way and planned to talk to her after the meeting was over.

"So, what's new family!" José said charmingly.

"Shit, chilling, chilling," the crowd responded in return.

"I know everyone's been trying to contact me, but I needed to get away for a while to clear my mind of all the drama that's been going on."

"I see you ain't clear it enough," JoJo said eyeing Summer up and down.

José caught the subliminal message and blew it off. Now, he was sure that she was upset and would have to make it up to his friend.

"Look, I just got a new shipment plus I still have 30 left, 15 apiece. So, Castro, what can you handle? I was thinking 10 this time to start. Dre, I'll give you another five since you seem to be doing fine with that. Don't take ya time though because I'm trying to move the whole 80 in a week if possible. Taylor drop five squares off to the girls and have them handle that plus, I want you to give them this bonus for working so hard. Quan, I'm hitting ya crew with five joints, just make sure two is all dimes and two is all ballgames, the last one sell what the hell you want just as long as the money is accounted for. Carlos, you got that dough cause if you ready I'm gonna place an order today, but I'm gonna need 120 so that I can see something. JoJo, I'm proud of you, you took care of everything in my absence and so far, everything looks good... I do wanna talk with you after this meeting though. Look, it's October and you know what that means, indictment season so everyone needs to be safe! Listen, money is being made and like I said regardless of how much money one person has more than the other, no one is considered the least. We are family and to show you that I love you all I brought y'all all a gift! That's why it took me an extra week to get back because I was thinking of y'all. Taylor, I hear you've been spending a lot of time with Rosé... that's cool but remember the agreement and if you wanna change the plans please let me know sis... Summer hand me them boxes babe." Summer slid the gift-wrapped box over to José who removed the gift-wrapping paper then removed the top.

Everyone sat in silence with high anticipation wondering what was in the box.

"Compliments of L.A. Jewelers these are for my fam."

One by one, first, he pulled out five 14 karat gold diamond bezzled links with iced out customized letter "A" medallions. He gave them to Quan Showstopper and his crew. They were hyped to receive the four thousand-dollar chains. Next, he pulled out four platinum and diamond bezzled 36" chains with iced out medallions that read "Affiliates."

The chains were not flashy except for the sparkle from when the lights hit them. For 15,000 apiece José thought it spoke a language of class. Handing them to his squad he placed the fourth one around his neck. Last but not least, he pushed the two smaller boxes over to Taylor and JoJo. When they opened the Kay Jewelers ring box two customized rose and yellow gold letter "A" flooded with VVS diamonds along the sides and over the top blinds the two. The pinky rings cost 10,500 apiece, the girls were speechless. José could see that everyone was happy.

"Now, it's time to get this money fam... I just blew a hundred grand and I need that back A.S.A.P.," he said in a joking manner.

"So, I guess the A stands for Affiliates huh?" Carlos asked.

"Yeah, because we're affiliated with some real major players and we can only rise from this point. I'm about to make a power move that should get us up for a regional take over so be ready cause when it's on it's on!" José said like the boss he had just become.

"Yo José, I gotta talk to you about that nigga Strap. I know you been gone but it's time to war baby!" Castro said changing the mood at the table.

What's up nigga? What's going on, let me know?" he asked.

"He put a check on ya head for 30 grand and he hired Rakmeef and Twink to cash it!" Castro informed him.

"Well, I guess it's time to throw him and them stupid mothafuckas a going away party," he said contemplating his next move.

"Don't worry, I got the drop on them niggas and they don't even know it," Castro assures him.

"Yo José, let us handle that shit, we'll let them bitches have it," Quan said becoming angry about the news.

"Nah, I some niggas that'll take care of it for us... I'm gonna holla at you about that before we bounce," Castro stated.

"A'ight well, I'm not gonna let any of this spoil my day so eat, drink and be merry for tomorrow we die!" José said in his best King Arthur's voice.

Everyone had said their goodbyes and left the restaurant except for José, Castro, and JoJo. Sensing that this show down with her was more on a personal level he handled the situation with Castro first.

"So, he got 30 on me huh? I should send them reckless niggas through there for a week straight catching rec huh," said José.

"Nah, I got some niggas from Concord Ave and the lil Black nigga Twizz from 30th Street. They call their crew the Body Snatchers, they been tryna wreak havoc on the city... I know they'll do it," Castro assures.

"How much?" asked José.

"I mean he dropped 30, so drop 40... I would to entice them," Castro stated.

"Look, since Rakmeef and Twink took the contact I want them gone. I got 40 for them two... 20 apiece. Put ya hyenas on them A.S.A.P.... as for

Strap this shit is personal, so I'll handle that... oh yeah, our little nigga needs some new toys, they had to get rid of them after firing at lighting Jack, plus I need a new one something with an extendo."

"I got you my nigga... I'll handle that A.S.A.P. I'll pay the 40 just give it back," Castro said.

"Nah, just come grab half on the am. and when it's done, I'll give them the rest... but how you find out bro?" José was curious to know.

"Rakmeef and Twink have been sending their folks through the block to find out who you were, I peeped her, laid on her, went at her on some cocky shit, and she was on dick. She started running the whole tape after I told her I didn't fuck with you... that's how I found out she fucks with Rakmeef and Twink," Castro informed him.

"Me and Taylor gonna kill that bitch word up! That bitch got the game all the way fucked up... she fuckin' with the wrong one," JoJo said fuming.

"You think you can handle that?" asked José.

"Boy!" JoJo said rolling her eyes.

"Yo José, I'm about to slide, I'll hit you in the a.m. to get that a'ight," Castro said exchanging hugs and dap then leaving the restaurant.

Moving his chair closer to her, for a split second, there was silence as he tried getting her attention by caressing her hand. She looked away refusing to look him in his eyes knowing the tears from her hurt would have fallen instantly.

"You mad at me Jo?"

"No... as long as your happy I'm happy... and if she makes you happy who am I to rain on ya parade."

"Jo, I just had to make sure... I didn't want to jump into the next situation out of revenge and things from the past could have easily affected the next relationship."

"Well, learn how to be alone José... what are you scared to be alone for a little to get your head clear then move forward. I'm doing it... I like, no... I love dick, but until the right nigga comes along I gonna have to do without. You're not gonna be happy until I lose all interest in you and go find a man who really wants me, then you're not gonna wanna fuck with me anymore... and don't think it can't happen cause it already is. Taylor is on the verge of being wifed up and my silly ass is still daydreaming that my knight and shining armor José Valdez will someday come move me out of this fucked up city to a gated community since I've been here since day one! What I'm not beautiful enough... tell me what it is?" JoJo said with a finger in his face.

"It's not that you're the most beautiful woman I know outside of my mother... I'm just scared to ruin a friendship that's been forever."

"How can you ruin it if you continue to do what you've been doing José... you know what, since you insist on keeping me in the friend zone that's what the fuck it is. Don't be mad when you see me hugged up with my new boo," JoJo said standing up to leave.

"Come give me a kiss girl," José said slightly tugging at her hand.

JoJo bent down and kissed him on his lips with just a little tongue action. José couldn't help but smile, even when she was upset, she still couldn't deny her feelings.

"I love you Joanní."

"I love you too José," JoJo said turning then leaving Joes Crab Shack. José sat there alone for a while pondering on his meeting. He then started thinking of his savings and knew that when he moved this next shipment of

80 bricks his stash would be either close too or over 2 mill. If he had the 2, he was gonna make the biggest move of his life, so he had to talk with Angelina soon. Meanwhile, he wanted to holla at Mac to grab another hundred for Carlos but until then he was going home to his baby girl Summer.

CHAPTER 17

The Deadly Shootout

Detective Baldwin couldn't prove it but was more than certain that the death of Ramone and Nyomi was the work of Rakmeef and Twink. And without the eye witness the double murder case had just went cold. Some way or somehow Baldwin knew that in the long run he would put those two assholes away for life. Since both double murders had no leads except for Ramone's eyewitness who is now a ghost. Detective Baldwin had been assigned to a joint investigation with Dt. Stevenson on Kevin Gaines who Baldwin knew very well since a juvenile and the Scott Street Boys. They went by the name of the Young & Reckless and one of the guys were responsible for firing shots through the windshield of a police cruiser. The mayor and chief wanted these guys arrested in convicted like yesterday. Through a few informants that Baldwin had on his payroll, he also found out that Scott Street was more than just a petty nickel and dime block. With over five bricks moving in a week just on the block, it's rumored that the head of the Scott Street Boys José was moving anywhere between 10 to 20 bricks a week. And that's only cocaine, he was rumored to have his hands in the heroin and weed as well. This is all the narcotics that's being supplied on Scott Street. The biggest question now was who in the hell was and where can he find José.

"What's good big homie," Jizzy said extending his hand out to Castro.

"Same shit... came to find a couple Body Snatchers. You know where I can find some?" Castro asked.

"They around... depends on the price tag and who they are," Jizzy stated.

"Well, I got 40 grand for this hit and it'll be a memorable victory."

"Forty's a green light but who is it?" Jizzy question.

"Them two Eastside niggas Rakmeef and Twink," he confessed.

"Them two niggas! Word, those niggas are washed up and they wanna go to war with you... they must wanna take a ride on the dark side. I got em, I'm gonna hit Ballout and Twizz and let them know we gotta job to handle."

"I need this shit done A.S.A.P. the sooner the better. Here take this... its 20, half now half later."

"A'ight big homie we on that shit when the sun goes down."

Castro pulled off of Concord Ave knowing these heathens would cause havoc on Rakmeef and Twink until they were dead or vice versa. With three days until the weekend and his biggest shipment due to be delivered Castro needed everything to be running according to plan. His next stop was to see José. When he arrived at José's spot, he found the living room loaded with what looked to be a hundred pounds of chow! Pounds and pounds galore had the house smelling like a weed dispensary. And of course, José had one pearled ready to be sparked.

"What up playa?" José greeted his friend.

"Same ol' same ol' looks like your back to business huh?" Castro asked.

"Yeah, I'm about to drop this shit off to Carlos then I gotta holler at Bella Bandido. I'm trying to make a move that might set me straight if all goes well... how bout you, ya work moving okay?" José asked.

"Yeah, I got some playas from Dover, you might wanna holla at... my man keep saying that they trying to cop heavy, but I told him I gotta see what you wanna do first."

"They cool people?" José asked.

"They straight, I've been dealing with their people for a while and it's always been good business... I'll co-sign it," Castro confirmed.

"I'll holla at 'em... set it up. Oh, I got that 20 for you too... what's up with the tools I asked you about?"

"I got some major shit coming through this weekend like 300 of them we gonna be war ready," Castro bragged.

"300! Be careful my nigga that's fed time for a long time if shit go sour," said José.

"I know, I thought of it but I swear if any shit goes down, I'm holding court in the streets and I'm gonna be the judge," Castro said dead serious.

"Respect, respect, you want me to send the lil homies with you?"

"Nah, the less they know the better off they are and besides, he's coming to Delaware so if anything goes wrong, I'm in my own backyard."

"A'ight, just let me if you need anything. Hey, before you leave look at this pic and tell me if you seen this nigga around."

"Nah, I haven't seen him before why what's up?" Castro asked.

"I'm looking for him if you run into him let me know A.S.A.P."

"A'ight, I got you," Castro replied.

Castro and José smoked a Dutch together then hit the door. José went to make the drop to Carlos then to go see Angelina while Castro wanted to find out what he could about Rakmeef and Twink, so he called Bree.

Every time José pulled in Angelina's compound; he admired the scenery. The way the landscape was neatly trimmed, the automatic moon lights that brought life to the whole estate then the mansion itself. After pressing the intercom once, the doors drifted open. He entered the semi-palace only to be greeted by Angelina in an auburn see through Dolce & Gabanna linen robe. Besides the matching thongs there wasn't much left for the imagination. Her nipples were erect, but she didn't seem to mind, the fact that she was exposed so José kept looking. The switch in her hips made José's dick grow automatically. His thoughts were on where the hell was Angel at. Knowing that you should never mix business with pleasure he reasoned that if she dropped her robe, he would hit it! All his wild thoughts came to an end when Angel came walking down the hall as they head to the library. This nigga Angel was wearing a Marvel Action Hero Black Panther costume growling at Angelina until he noticed José following behind her with a smirk on his face. Angels expression went from excited to bland, in seconds he knew that when it was about business with Angelina pleasure had to wait.

"Hello honey... sorry I'm dressed so inappropriate, you caught us while we were role playing. Angels a costume freak if you know what I mean... so José what can I do for you today?" she asked crossing her hands and legs.

"First, you don't have to apologize this is your house and I'm the one who interrupted y'all besides from what I see you still have a gorgeous body if I might say," José said suavely.

"Thank you honey," Angelina replied blushing from the compliment.

"The reason I wanted to meet with you so soon was because when I'm finished with this 80, I'm gonna be well off... and I kinda wanted to make a major power move if it's okay with you," he said trying to read her mind."

"What kind of power move did you plan on making dear?" she questioned.

"I was hoping you would give me 75 squares of white girl for a million and 24 bricks of manteca for a million as well." Angelina sat quietly and stared at José for a minute then spoke softly.

"That's a pretty big order, how do you plan to move all that?" she asked interested in his response.

"Well, you know I've got all of Fat Papi's clientele thanks to you, plus my local playas who clear the 80 in no time... but I've also been talking numbers with some playas from New Jersey, Pennsylvania, lower Delaware, Maryland, and Northern Virginia. The numbers that they're throwing around will just about double the regular order and will probably sell faster," he said laying out his plan.

"So, you want to spend 2 million is that right?"

"Yes, but I would also like you to front the same amount that I buy," he said looking her in the eyes again. She sat in silence staring at José once again thinking of a power move herself.

"Okay listen, I'm gonna to do you one better. I'm going to give you 100 squares of white girl for a mill, that's 10 grand a kilo... and as far as the manteca I'll give you 25 kilos for a million. Now do you think you can handle the front is the main question," she said sounding more serious than ever.

"Yes, I know I can... plus, I got people in position ready to move so I'm confident on this one," he stated with confidence.

"So, how long do you think it would take you to clear the order?"

"With me and my team moving from state to state and now that you lowered prices, I can too. It should take me no more than two weeks tops if not faster to clear the whole 250 brick shipment."

"I remember when you first started this a few months back you weren't certain if you wanted to be involved... now look at you, I'm glad I could help you change your mind. You know you're the youngest millionaire I know, I'm proud of you and I will do anything to see you rise. So how much will you be owing me?"

"Um a hundred bricks… 25… two million dollars in less than two weeks."

"Okay José dear as soon as you're done with the shipment, I'll make your dreams come true," Angelina stated smiling ear to ear.

"Thank you!" José shouted and ran around the desk to give her a hug while she was still barely dressed, "oh, I have been asking around about the Fat Papi situation, but no one seems to know him."

"It's okay for now, focus on your money. Oh, but I knew I had something I needed to talk to you about that was urgent… your boy Castro is Calienté, fall back from him for a little while. I received a call and he's got some kind of arms deal that's coming up that won't be successful; if you know what I mean."

"Damn this nigga hot! I gotta holla at him and let him know not to Fuck with that deal," José said it out loud to himself.

Angelina had just informed him that the New Jersey Governor's Task Force had joined forces with the Delaware Task Force in a joint investigation to sell 300 firearms to Kevin Gaines a.k.a. Castro then arrest him in Delaware the upcoming weekend. The deal was arranged to take place in Wilmington where Castro is already a convicted felon, so if he's convicted, he would get at least 10 years in the state prison. With the amount of guns involved in this purchase even if the state dropped 250 firearm offenses with 100 charges pending and each one carrying three years apiece; he would still be facing 300 years. With loyalty being everything, José put whatever needed to be done on hold and had to holla at his man A.S.A.P. If he was under investigation, then we could all be under investigation was José thought.

"Damn, what a perfect fucking time!"

Slurp, Slurp, Slurp, Slurp was the sound of Bree sucking on Castro's dick like sucking dick was about to go out of style. As he drove through the city behind his tint, she did what she had been wanting to do from the day she met him. Her level of lust was at an all-time high when it came to Castro. It had been at least two years since she had sex with a man and for some reason, she wanted to feel him up inside of her. When he pulled into the Doubletree hotel parking lot his phone rang. So, caught up in the mouth and lip service he was receiving he pushed the button and sent the caller to voicemail. After swallowing his load, she let him know that sex was rare for her, so he had to take it easy. Beings though she was the opposition he would dig in her slow in deep, his mission was to make her fall in love with him so that she'd be willing to do whatever he asks of her.

After three hours of sexing and heavy orgasms Castro and Bree lay naked smoking a stuffed Dutch and sipping Branson B. Cuvée. Noticing that he had missed over a dozen calls he scanned down his call log and seen that José had called at least eight times and left a voice message. When he listened to the urgency in his voice, he knew that whatever he needed to speak to him about was serious. So, he called him back right then and there. He wasn't prepared for what he was about to hear. When José answered and began explaining the ill situation that his friend was about to walk into within a matter of minutes Castro eyes squinted, his jawbone had tightly locked and he clenched his phone firmly. All will to fuck was gone and the wheels of wisdom began rolling in his mind. As he listened, he started forming a plan in his head that would secure his freedom and get the ultimate payback on the whole law enforcement agency. Castro was a fucking monster when provoked and he had just been provoked. Looking over at Bree who seemed to be under his hypnotic spell he instantly had idea that would kill two birds with one stone. After hanging up from José he called Taylor and JoJo.

"Yo hoe what up!"

"Fuck you nigga, what's good?" JoJo replied.

"Remember that situation you said you were gonna handle for poppie?"

"Yeah, you talkin' bout the Lil Bitch, right?"

"Yeah, it's a green light for this weekend."

"A'ight set it up... I'll push her shit back myself word up!" JoJo said animated.

"I'll keep you posted, just be on standby... I'll holla at you later."

Castro hung up his call then pulled Bree on top of him and slowly guided her down onto him. She came instantly and Castro continued to blow her mind. Bree was lost and turned out and she didn't realize how deep the shit she had stepped in really was. After another hour of fucking thanks to the S.W.A.G. pill Castro wanted to test the waters to see if she was game for anything, he asks of her.

"Bree you know I fuck with you shorty."

"I hope so cause I only fuck niggas I really like and I like you."

"I like you too... but I need a favor boo!"

"What?"

"I gotta make a move this weekend, but I'm also supposed to meet with my people, but I can't. So, I wanted to know if you could meet with him for me and let him know that I can't make it and I'll have to reschedule."

"That's it? I can handle that... if you want, I can make the deal for you."

Castro thought for minute, this would be an easy way to get her out of the way then changed his mind when he thought of setting someone up to be locked away.

"Nah, that's cool... just handle that small part and we'll get up later that evening."

"Okay 'C' just let me know when and where," Bree said so gullible.

With Angelina calling in reinforcements Ivan was moving around more freely. He still watched his back but with some extra help he wasn't so tensed. Knowing that he held a trump card in this war with Alex he knew if things ever became critical, he would ultimately make Alex come to him.

Cruising down Lancaster Avenue around the Lancaster Court, Apartments area, Ivan pulled into the Shell gas station. Deciding to take his truck through the car wash for a good cleaning he went into the store to pay for the service. While walking back to his truck his intuition kicked in as a chill went through his body. Just as he turned to do a survey of the area, shots were being fired in his direction smashing into his truck.

"POP POP, BOOM BOOM, POW POW!"

With no time to think his killer instinct turned on as he spun around hitting back, he took one to the shoulder! His adrenaline was pumping, he felt the pain, but the shot never slowed him down. Alex and Amillio tried cornering Ivan in, but was unsuccessful due to Ivan's war strategy of stay low, keep firing, and stay moving. Losing blood fast he had to get out of there quick but leaving his truck with his license and registration was a no no! Realizing that they wouldn't be able to finish him off right then and there, they quickly got ghost.

Ivan rushed back to his truck where on lookers tried assisting him. He ignored them as he got into his truck and mashed out! Getting on his cell he called Angelina who in return called her private surgeon and had him pull over somewhere secluded where she could meet him then take him to get his wound attended to. Waiting for Angelina to come pick him up, Ivan cursed himself for slipping. That could have cost him his life and now they understood the severity of the situation; he would no longer wait for Alex. He was now the hunter and Alex, Amillio, and whoever else that was with them would be dead soon.

By the time Angela had arrived, she had made the call to go through Pleasant Street and take out everyone! When she finally received a call back while Ivan was being treated for his gunshot wound, she was happy to hear that 10 men in total, eight men from Pleasant Street and two of her own were killed in a shootout that had taken place about an hour earlier. No one knew if any of the guys were the target all they knew was that several of the guys wore chains with the letters G.B.C. on the medallion. Ivan had recovered and was ready to hit the streets on a hunt for the two dead men walking but Angelina gave him strict orders to go home and rest. So, Ivan took her advice and had her drop him off at his condo. Instead of going to his place, he went up LeLe's Place. When she answered the door, she was concerned about the sling that held his arm up. She pampered him the whole night until they fell asleep.

Rakmeef and Twink had just come back from dropping a care package off to Abbee and was now pulling up on 9th and Kirkwood. Always, before they exited their vehicles, they scanned the area for anything suspicious or out of place. Nothing seemed odd, the only thing happening seemed to be some teenage boys talking with about three girls in front of the corner store. Getting out of the car heading to the 'crib' Twink wanted to run to the store real quick to grab a Sunkist and a couple Dutch's. Passing the youngins who weren't paying him no mind as they fondled the girls asses, Twink stepped in the store. Rakmeef stood on the sidewalk minding his business waiting on his partner to come out the store. When Twink stepped out of the store he began walking towards the crib lost in his own thoughts. He had not one worry in the world until he saw Rakmeef eyes widened and started reaching for his torch! It was too late, Twizz sent the .40 caliber hollow round through the back of his head causing his skull to burst like a water main line, he dropped. Rakmeef began firing in blind rage as he watched his partners body twitch uncontrollably on the cement. Jizzy and Ballout was firing in his direction as the girls they were just with were ducking and screaming. Rakmeef wouldn't let up as his extended clip kept sending shots at his opposition. Just when Jizzy, Ballout, and Twizz were about to make their escape, Jizzy turned around and caught one smack dead in the center of his chest. God must have been with him because Bree knew for a fact that shot hit him in the chest and dropped him, but he got up and took off running.

When they were gone, Rakmeef and Bree ran to the curb where Twink's lifeless body laid disfigured. Tears ran from Rakmeef's eyes like a faucet. Bree stared in shock at her cousin who she had just got off the phone with was lying dead, she broke down and cried.

Across town, Jizzy had took a slug to the chest, but somehow survived. He was rushed to Riddle Memorial in Pennsylvania where he underwent several surgeries but pulled through. After being questioned by local officers a few times and sticking to his story of being an innocent bystander in a shootout they left him alone. Jizzy was in the hospital for a month and a half and when he came home the city was a war zone.

"Poppie where are you right now?" Jesenia asked Dre.

"Out making moves mama why, you okay?"

"Well, yeah and no... mama wants to meet with you now, we have something to discuss with you... so hurry up and get here."

Dre didn't know what was going on but from what he heard about Ms. Reyes if she asked to meet with you it's best to stop what you're doing and see what it is that she wants. Pulling into the driveway he noticed Jesenia's older brothers in the yard drinking with a few other guys, not knowing her brothers like that he gave them a head nod and kept it moving towards the front door. Jesenia met him with a hug longer than normal and a passionate kiss. She took him by the hand and led him through the rather spacious house. When they entered the den there doing an older woman's hair was Glady who smiled at Dre then continued on with her mission.

"Girls leave me and this nice-looking young man alone for a minute," Priscilla said in a motherly tone. Jesenia looked at Dre who looked confused but was comforted when Priscilla patted the seat right next to her and told him to take a seat.

"You're a very nice-looking young man... how old are you?"

"Thank you, I'm 19-years-old," Dre said politely.

"Jesenia likes them young huh," Priscilla joked.

"I mean I'm mature for my age I think."

"I hope so, cause we soon will see just how mature you are young man...

do you have any kids or do you like kids?" she quizzed.

"I mean I don't have any just yet, but I want kids one day... I guess you can say I like kids," he confessed.

"I'm glad to hear that young man because your world is about to change forever."

"What?" Dre asked.

"What do you do to make a living?" Priscilla asked.

"I do a little of this and a little of that," Dre replied.

"Be more specific please," Priscilla said reading between the lines.

"I'm in the import, export business."

"So, what do you import and export son? And before you answer, remember honesty takes you a long way in life," she added.

"Well, since you put it that way, I move and transport heroin Ms. Reyes.

"Oh, you're a street level drug dealer huh?" she questioned.

"Not quite, I'm pretty established. I've been doing this for a while now."

"Well, that's good to hear, so you wouldn't mind joining the family business since you are somewhat considered family now," she stated.

"Family Business? Family... Ms. Reyes what are you talking about?"

"Come here young man," she said taking his hands in her palms, "when you first meet people who you're attracted to you tend to make foolish decisions. And I don't know if you call getting my daughter pregnant foolish, but your decision to have unprotected sex has brought you into my family. I run a family business of the same ventures you're into so I'm asking you if you would like to join us?"

"Thank you I appreciate it, but I deal with my family as well and things are going good for me right now so I'm okay... but pregnant wow!"

"Yes Andre, Jesenia is six weeks pregnant and I hope you plan on taking care of your responsibility."

"Yes, I plan to," Dre said excited.

"Well, in a few months we'll be having a baby shower so let your family and friends know dear."

Dre was speechless as thoughts clouded his mental and began painting several pictures in his mind. A little Dre was soon to be a permanent fixture in his life and now he wanted to start planning for his seeds entrance into this world. By the time his son or daughter arrived he planned to retire and start a legitimate business. Buy a house for Jesenia and his seed and fall back on his hard-earned savings. Dre had a reason to call it quits and walk away, but will the ghost of his past come back to haunt him?

CHAPTER 18

The Ambush

Quan and his Young & Reckless crew were back on the block and back to getting money. Things were not the same though raids, jump outs, foot chases, and surveillance had been set up. One would think more money was lost than made on 2nd and Scott. That wasn't the case though, cars were purchased and sells were directed to different locations within a four-block radius which was still convenient for the customer. In the long run, after Quan and his crew were snatched up for the shooting and questioned, they were released. Knowing that they were hot, they would move everywhere drug-free. As long as they were not caught with the drugs or guns on their person, they were okay. During the questioning of a few of the lil homies, they all seemed to notice that the law kept asking about Castro and José. They made sure that both of the big homies were aware of it as soon as they were released.

José sat at the dinner table with Summer, MacLaden, and Bunny having a general conversation. José and Summer were invited to Macs for a dinner meeting that would help José stretch his empire into not only Philly but upstate Pennsylvania as well. With the connections Mac planned to introduce José to, he would move 20 squares of manteca every two weeks and close to 50 kilos of coke in two weeks. This was a nice portion of the work gone and with the four other states and the playas he dealt with the new shipment just might be gone in a week or less. If things went the way he planned them to go he would start piecing together the next part of his empire which is the entrepreneur shit! While José introduced his host to the astonishing taste of the Branson B. Cuvée laughter and giggles filled the room. Remembering that night he had to ask Bunny something, he pulled out his phone and started searching until he found what it was that he was looking for.

"Hey Bunny, let me ask you something," stated José.

"What's up cuz?" was Bunny's reply.

"Do you know, or have you ever seen poppie before?" José said sliding his phone across the table for Bunny to view it. Staring at the flick for a second with a smirk on her face she giggles!

"You jokin' right... boy you know I know him... stop playing dumb. You act like you don't remember him now," she stated obviously.

"I don't," he shot back.

"Yes, you do... remember when you first started grabbing bud from me, that was the poppie that was with me... that's Alex from Pleasant Street. Why?"

"Oh Shit! I knew I knew that mothafucka... oh he's that out of town family that's trying to run pressure on the hill."

"Yeah, that's why I stopped fucking with him, he started beefing with Ivan because Ivan pulled a gun on him and he went berserk. Started saying that he was gonna kill Ivan and his team. I don't think he knows Angelina is not the one to fuck with so when he started talking dumb, I parted ways cause when the bullshit pops off I don't wanna be nowhere around. Why what you looking for him?" she questioned.

"Yeah, he the one who killed Fat Papi!"

"Not un!" she shouted.

"I might need ya help," he stated.

"Just let me know when cuz and its esta lavista baby!"

José was glad he had finally found out who this puta was; now all he had to do was put a plan into action. This was the same nigga that the old head Ivan must be warring with he thought. There's no way he would be expecting José to pop his top so since this shit became personal, he would pull the trigger himself. He also heard about Twink's death, but Rakmeef was still roaming. After they were gone, he would pay Strap a visit personally. José never wanted war just money and if it was a way to turn things around, he probably wouldn't. It's the things a man goes through in his life that will ultimately define the character of the man he is. So, he embraces every war, grieves every lost, prays for better days, and cherishes every moment. With all that being said, every day he goes harder than his last and sets the bar high so no one will ever think for a second that Spanish José was your typical everyday hustler cause he wasn't. Having no face to put to the name made it damn near impossible to stick anything to him. Sunday morning his dreams would come true, he would have enough to cover just about any dealers order he came in contact with. The stage was set for a tri-state and Del Marva take over and with the love and loyalty he planned on spreading, you just had to love him. If you didn't, it was only two words that could describe that type of jealous, envious nigga, and that's pure hate!

Brandywine Towne Shopping Center on Naamans Road was the meeting place. Once they met, they would drive to a storage unit located on Philadelphia Pike where the deal was supposed to take place and Castro would be arrested. Captain Lane Johnson and members of both New Jersey and Delaware Governor's Task Force had surveillance on both spots. Detective Stevens would be the arresting officer while Detective Baldwin assisted. Planning to meet at 1:30 p.m., Captain Johnson who was a 20-year Vet sat waiting in his navy-blue Chevy Suburban anticipating the siege. When it was 1:28 p.m. and there was no sign of Castro the authorities began to wonder if he would show up. That's until he received a text asking where he was parked and what color vehicle, he was in. He alerted everyone to take their positions and be ready. That's when a bombed-out Nissan Maxima slowly pulled into the parking space next to the Suburban.

Minutes later, a woman who looked to be in her mid-twenties stepped out of the car. She approached the driver's side window where Captain Johnson awaited her arrival.

"Hey, you're Jacoby, right?" Bree asked leaning into the window.

"Yeah, that's me, why what's up and where's Castro?" he questioned sounding irritated.

"Oh, he sent me here to let you know that a family emergency had come up and he's sorry that he couldn't make it but to definitely let you know that it's still a go and that he would like to reschedule as soon as possible."

"Shit! He knows that I move around a lot and I'm not sure when the next time I'm gonna be able to make it out this way... tell you what, how bout I give you the merchandise and you make sure he gets it, I know he'll pay me whenever I see him so that's not a worry," Captain Johnson said trying to lure her into the trap.

Knowing this could be the perfect opportunity to show Castro that he could trust her she almost decided on making the deal. Then she remembered him saying not to bother it and knew if she did that would show signs of noncompliance. So, she left it alone and quickly declined the officers offer. Seeing that the deal was now up in smoke, Captain Johnson said his goodbyes, then pulled out of the parking spot, and drove off. Having to wait until Castro called to reschedule Captain Johnson drove to a Mobile Mini Station where the agents had another briefing to discuss more intel and further surveillance.

After this meeting, Captain Johnson got on I95 and drove to Vineland New Jersey where he lived with his two daughters and beautiful wife of 15 years. Home is where he found peace from a hectic world and the life of a police officer. Captain Johnson had plans to treat his three women to a night on the town. First, he would take his teenage daughters and wife to dinner at the restaurant of their choice then when that is completed, they would catch a movie. As they all loaded into the car Captain Johnson smiled at the only three things in life that makes him rise from his sleep every morning and go out and catch the bad guys. Over dinner, they laughed and joked like close families do. His daughters explained to him how school was going and the activities they were involved in while his wife was jubilant about the promotion she had just received at work. Indulged in what mattered the most at the time, which was his family, Captain Johnson never noticed that he was being watched.

As they left the restaurant in full swing and happy to be together none of the girls nor Captain Johnson saw the ambush that was waiting to happen! As they walked through the parking lot to the car Detective Johnson glanced over his shoulder out of habit, but nothing seemed to be out of place, so he hit the locks and everyone got into the car. Before anyone even has a chance to secure their seatbelts rushing directly at them with a modified AR-15, with an infer green beam was a hooded man with a Donald Trump mask on his face. He leaped on the hood of the car with skill and finesse. Captain

Johnson and his whole families eyes widened in fear, he knew he had no chance and that he was marked for death but to protect his loved ones, he would lay down his life. He tried reaching for his Glock 40, but he was too slow and it was too late! TAT, TAT, TAT, TAT, TAT, TAT, TAT, TAT, TAT, TAT, TAT, the body armor piercing bullets penetrated him and his wife's body effortlessly causing their bodies to jump and shriek uncontrollably in their seats. The two teenage girls began screaming hysterically, the masked man jumped off the hood and made his way to the back door. At gunpoint he forced the girls out of the car and to get face down on the concrete. Then he returned to the driver's side door and swung it open. He looked over at the deceased woman slumped in the passenger seat then turned his focus to the captain that was about a minute from eternity. While Captain Johnson fought to stay alive and his lungs fought to breathe, when Castro pulled the mask off his face you could tell death was seconds away! Pulling Captain Johnson's Glock from his hip he placed it to his temple and said, "You were better off killing yourself than to come fucking with me." Then he let off a round bombarding his skull causing flesh and blood to paint a bloody scene.

Once he completed what he set out to do he vanished in the dark. Castro head back to Delaware, he had one more thing to handle, but first, he needed to get in contact with José.

Bree had handled that errand that Castro needed to be done and was now waiting for his call. She would have tried spending every second of the day with him if it was possible. The way he made her body feel when she was cumming was unexplainable and he was so attentive to her needs. Day by day, she began carrying herself more womanly, from light makeup, her hair and nails done to more revealing clothes. When she actually wore women's clothing, she was stellar. The innocence in her eyes easily masked the demon that laid deeply in her soul.

Around 11 that evening after checking on Rakmeef who was crushed from the loss of his best friend she headed home thinking she would see her Castro that evening. Tired and sleepy from all the running around she had done earlier in the day she laid down to catch a quick nap. Before she could doze off a text message alerts her phone.

I want to apologize for texting so late... I've had a busy day and thank u for handling that for me too, if it's not too late I would like to see u... If not, it's OK I know it's kind a late, but I need to hold u close to me.

Bree suddenly gained a surge of energy with a smile included. She texted back immediately "O.M.W." after getting the directions to the location where he wanted to meet. Bree jumped out of bed and went to take a fast-hot shower. Blue Raspberry Body Wash was her choice for the night. Castro had never eaten her out but with the scent of berries flowing through his nostrils and a freshly shaven pussy, she hoped and prayed that his mouth wanted to go deep sea diving tonight. To entice him even more, she threw on her number 80 San Francisco 49ers jersey minus the bra and thong. Once he got a view of her tonight, he would want that pussy to be in house! She hopped in her car on her way to the location that was sent to her phone.

Arriving in Bear Delaware a little before one am. She drove into the driveway of a modern three-story townhouse. When she exited her car standing at the door in all black everything with an iced-out diamond necklace was Castro. Bree had a tingle between her legs instantly and the pulsing sensation needed attention automatically. When she reached the top step, she was lifted into the air by her ass cheeks and greeted with a kiss. She wrapped her thighs around his waist, she was wet, and she wanted him. Letting her down, he followed behind her admiring the peep show she was giving as she pulled the jersey up partially exposing one cheek at a time. They entered the living room where two champagne flutes and a bottle of chilled Moët sat. Handing her one of the flutes that were filled with the bubbly, she sipped her glass. Castro gulped his bubbly down after Bree sat back on the sofa then spread her legs wide open exposing her Georgia peach. Just like she hoped and prayed Castro went headfirst into the pussy. She was in heaven as her head began to spin and the beads of sweat began to form. Before she could figure out what was happening because of the awesome tongue massage she was receiving her breathing became more complicated then everything went black! Castro moved from between her legs and wiped his mouth, then a knock came at the door; knowing who the visitors were he opened the door to welcome José, Taylor, and JoJo to his honeycomb hideout!

"Yo nigga where that bitch at? JoJo asked satanically.

"She in the living room but you ain't doing the bitch here!" Castro expressed.

"I got a nice spot to do this shit... put her in the car and hurry up. How long does that shit last for?" José asked.

"My peoples said it's a date rape drug called Barbiturates on the street they call it Buns for sure it's suppose to last six hours," Castro said explaining the drug.

"Good, this shit won't take half of that... make sure you grab her phone and ditch her car out in the boondocks." Castro lifted her motionless body from the sofa and carried her out the door where his squad followed right behind him.

Rosé had been calling and texting Taylor all night. The only response he received was a text from her saying that she was with JoJo and José and she'd call him later. Rosé tried not to show his frustration, but he was a little upset. He knew José and the girls relationship and from several talks with Taylor he also knew her involvement with him. Not wanting to complicate or compromise the arrangement, Rosé wanted to have a sit down with José to let him know how he really felt about her. He wanted to remove her from that situation all together and put her in his spot in Middletown until she left for school in August. Knowing his childhood friend, he would be okay with it, but you never knew when money and drugs were involved. He tried calling her phone once again only to be sent to the voicemail after the first ring. Not liking the rejection, he called José's phone and after one ring he answered then said hold on.

"Yes dear," Taylor answered.

"What's up with you, why you keep ignoring my calls?" Rosé questioned.

"Babe I'm busy handling something, when I'm done, I will call you... better yet, I'll come to you."

"A'ight," Rosé said sounding defeated.

Rosé was well off and he could easily have retired if he wanted. A few years older than his friend, Rosé had well over a million cash tucked away and had been promoting events on the side to generate lucrative legitimate money as well. With things looking up for him all he wanted was for the girl he had fallen for to let him take care of her and to keep her safe. What he failed to realize was that Taylor and JoJo were loyal to José and José only. So, if he wanted a chance at whisking her away from the city, he had to convince José to convince her that walking away from the family would be beneficial to her in the long run.

"Wake up sleeping beauty," Castro said in a sinister tone.

Bree woke up from her drug induced slumber looking around the room in bewilderment. She noticed that she was naked and was handcuffed to a rickety old bed with a steel frame that sat in the middle of the floor. The abandoned house that José had purchased for one dollar from the Sheriff Sale was used for these specific reasons. With the house being located on 2nd Street in Chester PA chances of someone finding a body back there probably wouldn't happen for at least a year or two. Pure fear was written on her face when she realized that Castro expression was far from charming.

"Babe wh... what's going on?" Bree asked in total confusion.

Castro stood silent ignoring her attempts to figure out his intentions. That was until the basement door opened and several footsteps descended to the bottom. Bree looked at the three people standing in front of her strangely. No one said a word and the look of pure hatred spilled from the two females eyes. She tried connecting with Castro once again, but it was useless as he stared her down like she was a federal informant.

"Castro can you please tell me what's going on?" Bree asked again visibly shaken.

Castro finally spoke after he bent down to wipe the sweat from her forehead, "Bree everything will be okay, just relax and let it flow."

"Castro can you please take me out of these cuffs... you have people staring at me... I'm scared babe."

"Do me a favor and stop calling me babe bitch!" Castro yelled. The response frightened Bree as her eyes began to water.

"I want to introduce you to some of my closest friends if you don't mind. I'm sure you don't know them, but you will soon become acquainted with them all. These two lovely women go by the names of Taylor and JoJo. They have a surprise for you Bree," Castro said solemnly.

As if on cue both Taylor and JoJo went into the backpack they had brought along and pulled out one brown and one black 19-inch dildos apiece. Bree's eyes grew wide in terror as the mischievous smirks formed across their faces. Tears fell from her eyes as she pleaded for mercy for whatever reason, but none was shown. Castro and José grabbed Bree by both of her ankles spreading legs as far apart as they could go to the point her ass was off the mattress. She began kicking her legs wildly, but it was no use, they overpowered her. They let her kick until she tired herself out. Bree tried fighting the inevitable, she had been raped by her father at the tender age of 10 until she was 17 when she had run away. That's why she took a liking to woman and rarely entertained men because she really hated them. Opening up to Castro was rare and now she regretted ever doing so. Taylor and JoJo moved in like a hungry wolf pack stalking the prey. Without hesitation, they shoved the plastic imitators into Bree's pussy and asshole at the same time causing her to lose her breath and damn near faint. With no lubrication she was far from pleasure island as the pain tore through her private parts. The blood was visible and the screams were horrid as Taylor and JoJo continued to punish her little holes. After an hour of fucking her brains out literally and sore arms Taylor and JoJo took a five-minute break then went back to assaulting Bree's now battered twatt! Bree was on the brink of passing out when JoJo pulled the dildo out while Taylor continued. With no protection JoJo threw haymaker after haymaker to Bree's face. It didn't take long to swell her lips and close both of her eyes. Blood stained JoJo's knuckles while a few of Bree's teeth had disappeared from her mouth. She could barely speak as they released her legs from their grip; she could be heard mumbling and now Castro thought it was time for the grand finale!

"Why... why me C?" Bree managed to mumble. Becoming infuriated, he grabbed her swollen face then shouted at her!

"Why! You wanna know why! I'm gonna tell you why bitch... look at me," Bree struggled to open her eyes, but he had her attention, "now look at him... Bitch do you know him?" She shook her head no.

"So, tell me why you would want to kill a man you don't even know and hasn't done anything to you?" She looked on confused and Castro picked up on it, "Bree this is the reason you're about to die... the man standing in front of you is the man you were looking to kill. Bree this is José," Castro said calmly for the first time that night.

Her eyes grew wide in fear as she tried apologizing through distorted mumbles. She knew why she was in the position that she was in. She was hunting for José to kill him and the whole time she exposed her hand to Castro thinking he was genuine; she actually was sleeping with the enemy. Tears rolled as she prepared to face her maker and in a blink of an eye JoJo stepped into her view raising her torch. Her eyes expressed fear and just when she accepted her fate and closed her eyes JoJo fired six shots sending the last of the seis right beneath her left eyebrow. A single tear dropped from everyone's eyes as they watched the tortured body lay lifeless. José wasn't into killing females, but Bree had intentions on taking his life. The sad thing was if she really needed money, he would have easily put her to work so that she too would have seen the love that José so easily showed upon those close to him. It was too late now and nothing could bring her back. The only thing to do now was move forward and pray that him and his will survive the war they're in right now.

Taylor walked in the door close to 4:30 a.m. and trying to be unheard she tip toes through the dark in stealth mode and quiet as a mouse. As she climbed each step of the staircase her attempt was to slide into the bed next to her man, but she was unsuccessful. As she reached the top unknowingly, she bumped into a figure sitting in the dark. She was more than startled, she was scared as hell. The way she damn near jumped out of her skin proved it. Rosé grabbed her around the waist and sat in silence as he tried collecting his thoughts. He then took her hand and led her into the bedroom; flicking the lights on sent a slight sense of panic throughout his body but after quickly assuring that she was unharmed and not injured he became angry. Her blood-stained body and clothes informed Rosé that she had been involved in some brutal shit that evening. That was just what he didn't want, he respected José but his love for Taylor had outgrown the love he had for his childhood friend. And he wanted her out now! He couldn't think straight when he was out in the streets making moves and his unofficial girlfriend was also in the streets move making just with another team. He didn't look at it like a smack to the face for José and he hoped he didn't either. He just felt that with him having his own name, a legacy in the streets and wealth, there was no need for her to have to even be involved in none of the nonsense that the streets had to offer anymore. He thought of the bond she shared with JoJo as well and considered letting her come along then blew that idea off. That would really ruffle José's feathers, besides the look in JoJo's eyes magnified love and loyalty for José only so it was no use. JoJo would ride to the depths of hell and shoot it out with Lucifer himself for José. She was José's true wife and better half; he was just too blind to see it. If he had his way though, Rosé would be removing Taylor from the part of life that could only bring heart ache in the end.

Instead of going home José texted Summer to let her know that he would be home early in the morning. He and JoJo pulled into the parking space in front of the house and sat there for a moment. The whole ride was in silence, he could tell that the torture had really affected her in some way. JoJo was younger than José by only a few months, so she was also 18 but she had become an adult long before that. See, JoJo had lost both parents when she was only 10 to a drug overdose that her mother had a few months after her husband died from a heart attack. JoJo was sent to several group homes over a period of two years where she experienced the reality of being a ward of the state. It wasn't until she was about to turn 13 that Taylor's mother adopted her. With the mental and physical abuse, she had been through in the states custody it was hard for her to love and trust anyone. The only people she cared for was Mrs. Francine Taylor's mother, Taylor, and the little Spanish kid her and Taylor knew since kindergarten. José Valdez had been their friend since the sandbox days. He would walk the two girls home from school every day and would even have to show his loyalty to the girls every now and then. And when a stupid ass would disrespect them, he would be sparring in the middle of the street defending their honor. Soon the roles switched, Taylor and JoJo were beating bitches up for their friend as well.

Over the years, as they got older and their bodies matured, their hormones started raging out of control and it was obvious that they both had an attraction for one another. Out of respect for their friendship, they would laugh it off as teasing each other. Lately, that had changed and it was no more denying the fact that what was supposed to happen was gonna happen sooner or later. José had to admit it that since the night at the club his feelings for her are at an all-time high. And he wants to be with her more now than ever, he just didn't want to leave Summer. Love had a crazy way of working things out!

"You okay Jo?" José asked while rubbing her shoulders.

"Yeah, I'm cool... it's just... did you see her body lying there? I started envisioning myself there. What if I end up in that position? I mean, I have done a lot of fucked up shit to people you know. I just want to go to school so that I can relax a little. José, I'm tired of this life, but I do it because I love you and will be there for you even if it meant me losing my life. All I want is you and me, a son for you and a daughter for me, a house far away from this bullshit and happiness," JoJo said with tears in her eyes.

José could feel her pain and could also see the hurt in her eyes. She was in love with a man who she thought the world of, but he didn't feel the same way.

"It's complicated Jo... you know... Summer and you. Sometimes I wish I never met her so that I could be with you every day," he said confessing the truth.

"Then my sister has fallen for ya boy Rosé... I'm the only one alone and it hurts babe," she said without realizing what she called him.

"I know and I promise I will take care of you forever... just give me a minute to clear up somethings. I don't know how we got here but now that we are, I promise I will never hurt you or leave you alone again."

"José can you do me a favor? Since I know you're not gonna comply with what I really need you to do... cause I'm really vulnerable José," she said turning to look directly at him. Knowing that he could be setting himself up he asked the question.

"What can I do to help ease your pain?" he asked sincerely.

"I just want you to hold me for the remainder of the night in your arms and maybe a kiss from the man I love." José smiled from ear to ear as he felt sudden comfort from her words like he always did.

"I would hold you forever girl if I could, but for tonight I'll just hold you til you fall asleep."

"What about my kiss?" she joked wiping the tears away from her eyes.

José leaned across the seat and gently kissed her on the lips while tilting her head sideways. A smile formed on her face instantly.

"Joanní I feel wrong though, even though I'm just kissing you I'm still cheating. It feels good and natural and it feels so right," he tried explaining.

"José if loving you is wrong then I don't wanna be right... now can we go in the house cause I'm tired as hell and I just want you to hold me. Baby, I just wanna feel ya touch," JoJo said more intimate than she ever had before. Eventually, they made their way into the crib just like he promised he held his best friend in his arms until she fell asleep.

Angelina listened intently as the governor explain the ambush on the lead officer in the Kevin Gaines firearms case. The F.B.I. had now become involved in the manhunt for the cop killer and had joined forces with both New Jersey and Delaware task force with hopes of getting a lead and ultimately bringing someone to justice. They had no suspects, leads, or motives but every recent case that Captain Johnson was assigned too would be the starting line. This would only put Castro under the watchful eye of the feds which could bring heat on José, Angelina, and whoever else that's at the top of the food chain. This worried the governor and Angelina, but she believed that José was wise for his age and trusted he would make the right decision. Now, all she had to do was inform her young protégé of the unwelcomed company that arrived.

CHAPTER 19

On the Hunt for Ivan

Alex and Amillio were still on the hunt for Ivan after hearing about the eight-man massacre on Pleasant Street. Things have changed slightly though, the ones who were doing the hunting at first, had now become the hunted. Never knowing that she was dancing with the Devil, Ellé never knew that the war her family was in was with the man she was sleeping with and seriously catching feelings for. She had wanted Ivan to meet her family on a few occasions but he either declined or had something to do. Blind to the fact that he never wanted to join her family functions she thought he was just as busy as she was running his several businesses. On many occasions when Ellé went to visit her mother, she never knew that he'd followed her in one of his unmarked cars. Finding the hornets' nest was simple and after a few days of lurking around, he spotted both marks. After doing his homework, he found out that the Cali looking fool was Alex's older brother named Amillio. He ran a crew out west called the Goya Bean Cartel that Ivan was well aware of. He knew that they weren't strong enough financially or physically to war with Angelina's Bella Bandido Cartel so that was the least of his worries. He only wanted to eliminate his targets before Ellé caught wind of his involvement and cut him off, set him up or worse kill him herself. With all these thoughts running through his mind he wanted them snuffed out immediately.

Carlos had been running his bud operation smoothly with no worries in the world. He had come to the point in the game where a hundred pounds would be gone in a few calls and less than a week. He needed more and he wanted to grab more but selfishness made him tuck his money and let José continue to grab instead of putting up the equal amount with his friend so that he could make more. Besides the price that José was asking for couldn't be beat. Glady had offered to plug him into his family but he refused the offer. Being the thinker that he was he did put a nice sum of money towards the Twins pill operation and was now in the mix with pills as well. He knew Dre and Jesenia had a baby coming and Dre had plans on falling back soon as the baby was born. So, he planned to go hard until that day came. Glady got into Carlos Infiniti with her 12-year-old nephew Nelson. Carlos was about to take them to grab a bite to eat that's what he did on slow days. He would pick his girl up and they would get a meal and talk about the days' events.

"This is fresh Carlos!" Nelson said from the back seat holding up the rose gold chain.

"What's fresh about it? Do you know what kind of chain it is?" Carlos asked.

"I don't know what kind it is but I know it's gold and that's Jesus face!" he said confirming his decision.

"That's a Cuban Link with a Jesus piece on it... you like?" he asked a young Nelson.

"Hell yeah!" Nelson excitedly shouted forgetting that his aunt was still sitting there.

"Watch your mouth boy!" Glady scolded him.

"I'm sorry," he pouted.

"Chill mami he a'ight he just excited... tell you what lil man if you like it you can have it... it's yours!"

"Man thanks, Carlos you're the best!" Nelson said blown away by the gift he just received.

Carlos was that kind of guy who never cherished anything. With that being said he was like a double-edged sword along with the good he did he also had a bad side. Hopefully, he would at least change his way of thinking before it causes his demise to be a very deadly one.

Rakmeef had been calling and texting Bree all day and still hadn't heard a word from her. It was unlike Bree not to answer his calls since Twink was killed. She normally answered after two or three rings so after a day and a half with no response he began to worry. His villain ethics kicked in and he blew it off as her chilling with the new nigga she met and was fucking or something. Feeling naked without his crew he needed to start recruiting some young fresh talent. Shit had got personal after Twink was killed. He didn't know who did it, but after hollering at Strap that changed. He found out that a young crew who went by the name the Body Snatchers from Concord Ave. may have been responsible. Strap wasn't a hundred percent sure it was them or why they did it, but word was floating around that the youngins were shot and he remembered Bree saying she had shot one of them in the chest, so he narrowed his decision down to the Body Snatchers. The way he felt he didn't give a fuck if he didn't have a crew, he was gonna handle this shit himself and A.S.A.P. He needed a way to get close to them and couldn't think of one until his phone rang.

Summer was heading out the door when José walked in the door with light colored blood stains on his shirt. He wasn't injured but she was curious about whose blood was on his shirt. Not wanting to be late for work but still concerned, she stopped in her tracks and started in with a million questions. Sensing that she was alarmed he kissed her and assured her that he was fine.

After a few more minutes of are you sure and concerned stares, she was convinced everything was good and she left for work. Grabbing a trash bag then headed upstairs to the shower he placed the evidence in the bag with plans on dumping it in a dumpster on his way to Harding Avenue. He took a quick shower, got dressed, and then went to the safe house on Harding Avenue. The work was all gone and that was the first time that had ever happened, but he had a good reason though. As he counted the last of all the cash that his safe contained, he impressed himself with a total of 2.15 million dollars. As he loaded the money into his duffle bags, he called Angelina who was waiting for his call. Gathering all the cash together José hopped in his SS Impala and headed to Angelina's.

Arriving 40 minutes later, he was startled when Angelina answered the door wearing a similar negligee to the one, she wore on his last visit. The only difference, which was a big one was that underneath the royal gold see-through robe she wore nothing. José couldn't resist, he had to look. Her busky breast sat high with full attentiveness and her thick lips that sat between her thighs looked so tight and warm. For a woman in her middle to late 40's she looked immaculate. Instead of entering the home, he stood frozen like a deer caught in headlights with two duffle bags that contained two million dollars. Instead of speaking, he handed the two bags to her and continued to watch her.

"Come in silly... you're standing there lost in space. Hasn't your mother told you that it's not polite to stare? Speak boy... I know you've seen way better tits and ass than my old behind," Angelina said in a joyous manner.

"Oh, I'm sorry... hello. I mean, from where I'm standing nothing looks old. I mean seriously, you can give a lot of these younger females a run for their money... you're hot! So, where's Angel?" José asked sounding curious.

"Thank you honey, I can tell you're a ladies man... you must have them young ladies going crazy... but Angel is in New York City for the weekend visiting family and taking care of business for us," she said tapping him on the chest.

"Oh, okay that sounds good for the both of us," he said giving her a high five.

Grabbing the duffle bags, José followed her to the outside kitchen located on the back of the mansion. As she took a seat in the lounge chaise she fumbled through the bags of money. Excited by the enormous amount of cash she touched her body in a seductive manner.

"Seeing this amount of money makes me wet José," she said eyeing him.

"Shit, it makes my dick hard!" he said licking his lips.

Silence fell between the two as they locked eyes. Unknowingly José was visibly rubbing his crotch while Angelina was massaging her inner thighs. Taking the lead, she stood to her feet and dropped her robe. José never ever mixed business with pleasure but this attractive older woman with a body of a goddess with equal power somehow had turned him on. She pranced to him, took his hand to help him to his feet, and then began unbuttoning his shirt. Next, she undid his jeans and began pulling his boxers briefs down pass his thighs. As they stood naked in the early December chill, she grabbed his hand and then guided him into the heated Jacuzzi that was awaiting them. Once again, she took the lead by kissing him first on the lips then moved to his neck and then to his chest. She did what no other woman had set out to do and that was seduce him. She stopped for a brief second then spoke in her native dialect sounding erotic while continuing to kiss him.

"José dear you are to never and I mean never mix business with pleasure. That could be a sure way to get set up... and I care too much for you to see that happen," she said still kissing him.

José couldn't wait as he lifted her on top of his throbbing pipe. Between the mixture of her juices and the Jacuzzi, she was wet, and she was in ecstasy! She rolled her hips back and forth while he occupied himself with one of her delicious looking breast in his mouth. After a while of sexing and apparent goosebumps from the cool weather, she stopped lifted herself off the dick and took his hand then led him into the house. She stopped in her tracks, turned, and stated calmly but with sternness and power.

"José dear this is a one-time thing... if Angel finds out he'll kill you so please understand that it cannot be any kind of attachment. This is a weekend fling that will happen once. I wanted this more than you so after this it's back to business as usual."

"I, I, I mean whatever you feel, I'm with whatever and yeah I'm definitely in agreement with this being a one-time thing. I never mix business with pleasure. Since we've already started though we might as well finish," José said pulling her into his arms squeezing both of her soft ass cheeks.

"That sounds like a winner," she said kissing him then leading him to the queens quarters.

Angelina and José sexed for the next couple of hours. She seduced her young lover who in return released his youthfulness on her which sent her into a state of convulsions. The sex was mind-blowing for both of them and when they finished, they laid cuddling having small talk until she interrupted the convo with a matter that needed both of their immediate attention.

"Papi you need to be careful; I spoke to the governor earlier this week and strangely Captain Johnson from the New Jersey Governor's Task Force was ambushed and he and his wife were killed this past Saturday," she said trying to read his body and facial expression. Having no clue who Captain Johnson was, José looked confused.

She continued, "José, Captain Johnson is the officer who was investigating your friend Castro."

José's mood changed instantly as he sat up in the bed. He listened as she explained the dilemma that not only José and she faced but a few people in high positions, such as the governor himself faced as well.

"Apparently, someone ambushed the officer while he was with his family when they were leaving dinner. They shot him and his wife over 20 times in close range. This all happened the same day that the deal with Castro was supposed to take place. I'm not assuming anything, it's just funny that I tell you of the setup and he winds up dead as a doorknob. So, you know they're investigating the murder... but what has a few people worrying is since it was an officer the Feds have picked the case up. They have no leads so they're starting with all of his most recent assigned cases. Which means, they will be watching Castro which could lead them to you, which ultimately can lead them to me and my friends. That's what none of us wants so I'm telling you this so you can make arrangements to slow your friend down for a while until things die down."

"Damn! This nigga! I'll take care of it; I'll just have to put him on floater status. He's gonna be upset but he'll get over it; we can't afford any bullshit right now!" he said fuming.

"Whatever you do remember darling that one wrong move could cost us all," she said taking him into her mouth at the same time.

"I will," José stated leaning his head back drifting off into the land of ecstasy.

Once the wonderful sex session was completed José felt refreshed for some reason and ready to hit the strip to check on his youngins. As he got dressed Angelina assured him that his shipment would be delivered early the next morning so he should be ready. Leaving Angelina's José first checked the magazine on his torch then slid through Scott Street. Before getting out to holla at his youngins he had to get in contact with Castro!

Agent Brian Kramer shuffled through the file that sat in front of him while receiving an Intel from both Detectives Stevens and Baldwin. Agent Kramer had been assigned to Kevin Gaines a.k.a. Castro's case and was leading the investigation with the help of the two local detectives. Anxious to hit the streets to find out what he could about Castro he wanted surveillance immediately on him or whoever hangs around him. That would mean focus on Scott Street and the heavy flow of narcotics being moved out there. Detective Baldwin informed Agent Kramer of the rumor about the large amounts of drugs being sold and supposedly ran by a young man who goes by the name of Spanish José. Kramer had a plan to stir up things in the city of Wilmington while he was in town. His main focus was to find out if this Castro guy had anything to do with the murder of Captain Johnson but if he could stumble over an organized drug ring that would be great too! Cruising through the Hill behind the black tinted out Chevy Tahoe, Kramer viewed the different crews on the different blocks, possible informants, and the occupants of either the high-priced fashions or luxury cars. Driving or just having a $125,000 car parked on the block where the houses don't cost but $80,000 tops and being occupied by a young Black male or female who have no job, not an entertainer or sports player, and didn't inherit millions it's somewhat a dead giveaway to the profession. Along with the thousands they spend on jewelry just to be seen it isn't hard for the government to build a case on them. With years under his belt, Kramer can spot a corner boy, a weight pusher or a supplier just off the way they move. What Agent Kramer was unaware of though, was that the Affiliates weren't just your ordinary crew. And the youngins they had under them were down for the cause and would ride til the very end. Just like Detective Baldwin informed him when he parked a few blocks away and watched for himself he noticed the heavy flow of traffic. Kramer had to admit the way the young teens interacted with the kids and people on the block you would have thought they were hangin' out. The way they would slide into the alleyways then direct sells off the block made it impossible to actually get any footage of a sale being made. Kramer would have to put a couple of stops-n-frisk, jump outs, and a good ol' fashion raid on the block. With those being the usual tactics, he would still do video surveillance and take photos of multiple transactions if he could catch any.

Over on the Northside, Twizz, and Ballout were posted like stop signs doing what they do best, politicking with the bitches. For the middle of December, the weather was fair, a little chilly but for the most part, it was sunny and nice out. The triple fat goose down winter coats concealed the heavy artillery they both were holding. As they interacted with the young girls whose flirtatious antics could have probably gotten one of the young girls screwed in a nearby alley a thick Latina who had to be in her 20s came strutting down the block like a supermodel. Her strides along with her power walk caught everyone's eye as the hip huggin jeans and snug fit Peak Coat revealed the mami's light brown eyes and her golden high lights that were hidden by the gold and white Polo knitted hat. With much sass and confidence, the mami stepped in between the little girls and Twizz with a hand on her hips and a jubilant smile on her face.

"Yo, do y'all know where I can get some bud from?"

"Yeah, I got some, but who you?" Ballout asked her.

"My fault, my name Bree I just moved here from V.A... I'm just tryna get some chow so I can blow it down," the mami stated.

"A'ight... I got it sexy but you gotta walk me and around the corner, I don't have any left on me."

"Come on then... it looks like it's hot round these parts," she said.

"You good, ain't been no shootings so they ain't sweating us," Ballout said smiling at the attractive Latina as they walked off.

Using her beauty to her advantage, she interlocked her arm with his and put a little more switch in her walk to make the young girls envious who watched in disgust.

"What's ya name cutie?" she asked.

"Who me?" replied Ballout.

"Yes, you silly... who else am I talking too? Ooh it's kind of chilly, can you keep me warm?" she asked getting closer to him.

"Ballout... is my name and yeah I can keep you warm," he said wrapping both arms around her squeezing her a little tighter, "I gotta go in this alley to get it for you, you can either wait here or you can... on the other hand, wait here." Before he could step away into the alley, she grabbed his hand and placed it between her warm thighs and spoke music to Ballout's ears.

"I don't normally do this but I'm feeling ya swag, you look like you gotta big dick and I'm horny as hell," she said massaging his crotch area.

"So, what are you saying?" he asked.

"Well, I was hoping I can suck ya dick or something?"

"Where at?" he asked sounding confused.

"I mean, we could go in this alley silly if you want."

Without a second thought, he led her into the alleyway anticipating the head service he was about to get. The December chill mixed with the warmth of her mouth was all that kept running through his head. As he leaned back against the wall the mami quickly relieved his growing meat stick from his jeans and hurriedly took him into her mouth. The slurps and the pressure from her jaws let him know that she was far from an amateur as she wet his pipe like a water faucet. She was on a mission to taste his nut on her tonsils and she wasn't stopping until she had completed her task. So caught up in her matrix, he relaxed and let his eyes close, as she continued to blow his mind. While under her spell he heard the first of many gunshots! BOOM, BOOM, BOOM BOOM, POP! BOOM BOOM! Out of instinct, he reached for his gun as his eyes opened wide. Forgetting that his jeans were down around his ankles he went to pull them up and headed out the alley. Before he made it to the end of the alleyway two shots POP POP! Crashed into the back of his skull dropping him instantly. Abbee stood over top of him and fired another round to his back and then ran out the alley towards the shooting. Running to the top of the block she saw Rakmeef shooting it out with the dark skin kid who had the scar in his head. Never realizing that Abbee was on the opposing team and creeping behind him when the Beretta 9mm sliced through his goose puncturing his heart; Twizz looked to the heavens for an answer then gave up his soul. He dropped and out of habit she fired a couple more rounds into his face and body. Rakmeef ran to her side taking the gun from her pulling her in the opposite direction of the mayhem. Knowing it wasn't wise to stay together they decided to split up and it was a good thing they did because as soon as Rakmeef pulled onto Concord Ave. witnesses began pointing the suspect out to officers as he tried riding pass. It didn't take long for the officers to begin pursuing the suspect and one of the first officers in the pursuit was senior Detective Baldwin. He led them on a high-speed chase up Rt. 202 into Fairfax where he hopped out the car firing shots at the officers striking one of the uniformed pigs in the stomach dropping him. Making it to his apartment he cursed himself for getting trapped. He knew it was over, but he also knew that they wouldn't be taking him alive!

Just as promised the shipment arrived the next day early in the morning. José and JoJo eyed the 250-brick shipment in amazement. Now that he had his biggest shipment ever it was no time to contemplate on his next move, he had to move it. With connections all around the tri-state thanks to a few key players in his circle and his Delmarva playas he would be moving up and down the interstate more often which meant more risk but also meant more money. As if she was reading his mind like only a soulmate could, she volunteered her services.

"You know I don't mind making drops for you José," JoJo said sounding serious and ready.

"Girl look at you… thanks, Jo but you know I'm not putting you in the lion's den like that. I love you too much to risk ya life for a few of these. You can have whatever you want just ask… so with that being said, why would I risk your life like that when I don't have too?"

"I can have anything huh?"

"Yeah, what you want?" he asked before realizing what he was saying.

"You know what I want… I want you!" she said plainly.

"JoJo you have me… truthfully, you have me more than Summer does, you're with me more than she is. The only thing you don't have is the magic stick," José said jokingly pointing to his crotch.

"I mean, that's not all I want but a sample would be nice."

"If I do that then our whole situation is gonna change and I don't want that."

"What, me holding ya work for you being ya dumb young girl… it's cool that's all about to change. You ain't gonna be happy until a nigga swoops me up and my ass is ghost!"

They stood in the basement silent for a moment trying to read each other's thoughts. It was obvious that JoJo was beginning to explore her other options or was thinking of doing so. He couldn't feel any type away; he understood her feelings for him and with him having a situation it was only right to let her go. He was feeling selfish, he wanted her all to himself, but he didn't want to commit to her, so she was leaving.

"Come give me a hug girl, I feel where you're coming from so I gotta be okay with whatever you do," he said hugging his childhood friend, "so you leaving to huh?"

"José I'm not leaving, I just wanna be happy too!"

"And you have every right too, so go and be happy Jo," he said looking into her eyes, "you know my birthday is coming up soon."

"I know boy... you turnin' the big 19, so what you gonna do?" she asked.

"I don't know but I'm thinking bout taking everyone on a little vacation, we gonna live it up if I decide too."

"Ya birthday is on New Year's, what kind of vacation are you talking about?" she questioned.

"All I know is somewhere hot!"

"Sounds good to me," JoJo said kissing him passionately.

"Oh yeah, it's time to go house shopping... this house will be paid for with all cash. The new one will hold the majority of the work. The other one is for you since Taylor is in love now."

"Boy you know she was a virgin!"

"Oh, he got her head fucked up!"

"Seriously, but what about the apartment?"

"We'll keep that as another stash spot in the city since it's not hot."

"A'ight cool, I'll get on it right away"

"Hey JoJo, I love you... always have always will."

"Love you too boo... word up!" she said with a convincing smile.

While securing the work Rosé called placing an order for five bricks, ready to get back to work he grabbed the five bricks of manteca and was about to inform them that he was back in the game.

CHAPTER 20

Time to Hit the Road Hard

With only $150,000 in cash to his name and close to 6 ½ million in drugs and a debt of $1.85 million dollars it was time to hit the road hard. He wanted this shipment done in two weeks tops if it would take him that long. That meant no more Scott Street for José or Castro and if Dre was the thinker, he knew his friend was he would expand as well. The only work that he would be fronting was the work he paid for personally and that was going to his team only.

When he pulled up to Rosés hideout in Middletown, he wasn't surprised to see his friend Taylor standing in the doorway waving to him and JoJo. She didn't want to admit it but she was happy to see Taylor it hadn't really been the same around the apartment since she's been involved with Rosé. JoJo hopped out and ran to meet her friend who was excited to see her as well. José sat and watched the two embrace as a smile crept across his face. The look was unconditional between the two as if it were years since they've seen each other which was not the case, it had only been a few days. The more he studied the two-reality set in and he finally understood what JoJo was missing, companionship. Taylor exuberated happiness, peace, and love that he had never seen in her before. His friend was in love and the high that she was on wasn't gonna let her come down. It was clear that JoJo had witnessed her transition and wanted to feel the same feeling as her friend. José came to grips with himself and had to admit that his two naïve childhood friends were now two young beautiful women who also had desires to be loved and just like young chicks they were ready to leave the nest to explore the world. José joined the family reunion and tried squeezing the life out of the girls. Entering Rosés place let José know that he would soon be upgrading to a pad more lavish and definitely more modern. Rosé and Taylor were exceptional hosts as they served Peach Cîroc, Granddaddy purple haze, diced mangos, and pineapples while awaiting their dinner to finish. Taylor and JoJo had girl talk while José and Rosé did what most young man with money do, talk shit to each other! José excused himself and went to the car to grab the work for his friend. Returning with the package they handled the deal and had more small talk until Taylor and JoJo announced that the food was ready to be served. Over brunch things seemed all well until Rosé made the comment these bitches! The room became silent immediately, everyone focused their attention on him. José didn't know where this was going but cursed himself, for not having his torch on his hip. He may not have had his, but he was sure JoJo had hers as they interlocked hands beneath the table wondering what was about to take place. Even Taylor had a look of confusion on her face trying to figure out what caused the sudden outburst!

"These bitches will use and abuse you if you let them… they will fuck ya best friend and do all kinds of trifling shit. You could buy them the finest clothes, the most expensive jewelry just to show them that you enjoy their company then after that they will take from you, lie and steal from you. Those bitches are ungrateful and don't deserve to be pissed on if they were on fire! You my dear are a real jewel… a diamond in the rough and I want to give you all that I possibly can and as of right now hopefully in the future even my last name," he said leaning to give Taylor a kiss on the lips.

"That's why I called you here tonight José and JoJo because I know that her loyalty lies with you two and I will never try to come between what y'all have. So, I'm asking the two of you if y'all could somehow trust me enough to provide and take care of her, protect and honor her to the point where I can take her away from these dangers of the streets and pamper her like the queen she is."

A single tear fell from JoJo's eye as she tried to hold back her emotions. She could tell that the feelings Rosé and Taylor had for one another were mutual regardless of what anyone felt or had any objections it wasn't gonna stop these two from being together. The simple fact that he was asking her two closest friends made the moment even more special. JoJo was happy for her sister and the tears proved it.

"Why are you asking for our permission... we ain't her parents' nigga," José said throwing his hands in the air busting out in laughter, "It's all good fam as long as you take care of her and don't put her in harm's way, we good. She's more than a friend, she's a sister... now all we gotta do is find her a man and all will be happy," he said pointing to JoJo who didn't find his last remark amusing.

The drive home was a silent one José could tell JoJo was in deep thought and decided not to poke at an open wound. He knew what was bothering her but at the time he didn't have a sensible resolution, so he kept his comments to himself. Reminding her of the upcoming week and the task it presented she was ready. After dropping her off he went to the house with Summer and lounged around for the remainder of the day. Knowing it probably wasn't the wisest decision he ever made he shockingly asked Summer if it was okay if JoJo moved in with them. After explaining the ordeal with Taylor, she stunned him when she was okay with it. Now all he had to do was convince JoJo to come. Scanning through the channels he stopped on the Channel 6 Action News where the anchorwoman Sharrie Williams had some breaking news on a developing story that was taking place in Fairfax Delaware a small town in Wilmington.

"Sharrie, apparently a man has the Wilmington and New Castle County Police Departments at a standoff... he's been barricaded in this building for over two hours and the officers haven't contacted him yet. We're not sure of all the details at this moment, but what we know is that the man whose name we don't have at this time is the main suspect in a triple murder that has left two teenage boys and a Wilmington police officer dead. Oh, we just got the name of the man inside the building, his name is Zy'Kim Harris and he goes by the name of Rakmeef... the local police are very familiar with the man and at this time he's wanted in the connection of the three deaths. Authorities have made several attempts to correspond but have all been failed attempts. The SWAT, ATF, and the State Police are on the scene now... the apartment building has been evacuated but due to no interaction with the suspect authorities are not sure just what apartment Harris is in. As the details come in, we'll keep you posted on the development of the story. This is Christieilleto reporting with Channel 6 Action News. Thank you."

José looked on in disbelief as the scene on the television unfolded before his eyes. At the time he didn't know that the two teens killed were his contract killers but knew Rakmeef was up shits creeks and wanted to see how the standoff would end. He rolled up a Dutch and poured himself a shot of Bombay Sapphire as he stayed glued to the television like he was about to watch a motion picture. He wondered how this would turn out for city's legendary villain. Would he surrender and spend the rest of his natural life in prison or would he cut his life short and die with honor like the outlaw

Billy the Kid.

Rakmeef scrambled around the three-bedroom apartment loading up his weapons, smoking chow laced with dipper juice and a few lines of raw cocaine. So amped up he almost didn't realize that his phone was ringing due to the comatose state he was in and the loud sound of Jadakisses verse on 24 Hours to Live. It was true indeed that Rakmeef knew he had less than 24-hours to live but was gonna give the local authorities hell before he checked out. Answering his phone brought him back to reality as he heard the soft sniffles of Abbee on the other end of the phone.

"Baby are you okay? This shit is all over the news Rakmeef," Abbee said with sobs in between words."

"Yeah babe, I'm good but you know the outcome of this already. I ain't sitting in no cage for the rest of my life… so, ring the alarm cause it's about to go down!" he said sounding like a true gangsta.

"Don't say that baby… I need you more than ever now… no, we need you more than ever Zy'Kim."

"You only call me by my government when somethings wrong… Abb I'm gonna be fine I'll see you again."

"Promise me… promise the baby," she said crying uncontrollably.

"What!"

"Zy'Kim I'm pregnant… I was going to tell you tonight, but I didn't get a chance to. That's why you gotta make it, but I know you... you're not sitting in nobody's cell for life."

Rakmeef became silent for a minute internalizing the Information he had just received his high school sweetheart the love of his life was once again carrying his child and he knew he wouldn't be around to even look his first child in the eyes. Tears fell from his eyes as he totted the sour filled Dutch.

"Damn Abb when you find this out?"

"Earlier this week baby!" she said excited to inform him of the news.

"I love you girrl! Listen, I got 300 for you and the baby at the spot over Eastside. The combination to the safe is 8.25.11. Take that and get up out of DE A.S.A.P. Remember to tell my seed that before he or she even got here that I loved them unconditionally and that their dad was one of the most feared mothafuckas in the streets of Wilmington Delaware. Babe do me a favor, don't watch the news anymore tonight because I don't want you stressing over shit... now blow me a kiss babe!"

"Smoooch!" She blew her man one last wet juicy kiss.

"Now go and get that money before shit get hectic and you can't get to it... plus, I got a surprise in there for you. I was waiting until after you completed rehab, but I guess I won't be around to see that. Remember Abbee, no drug is stronger than the love that a child has for their mother... this child is gonna need you... I'm gonna need you to raise this child in a drug free environment. You can do it now, make me proud... you hear me?"

"Yes baby, I love you and I promise to put my all into this child. Now if you're gonna go out, you better go out in style. Make them bitches remember ya name... Zy'Kim it's time for the 4th of July," she said giggling through her sobs and tears.

"Fourth of July huh," he chuckled knowing what she meant, "a'ight babe, it's time for me to go... remember what I said... this child is gonna need you," he said wiping the steady flow of tears that was streaming down his face.

"I will... I love you Zy," she said then hanging up the phone.

Rakmeef finished smoking his chow and snorting a few more lines of coke then put on his full body armor including head and finger protection as well. Knowing from the looks of things he was outgunned and outnumbered but he had a few tricks up his sleeve. Walking into the master bedroom he entered the walk-in closet and retrieved his military-issued tactical briefcase. Opening it up he smirked to himself as he glanced down at the six grenades, two infer red beams and two warhead missiles designed for the government famous AT-4. After loading several drums full of ammunition, he grabbed his two modified AR-15 assault rifles then headed out the door ready to go to war!

Castro was on his way to José's after receiving a text that they needed to talk and to come to the crib A.S.A.P. Castro arrived at José's and was greeted at the door by Summer. He walked into the living room to find José engulfed in the news segment that was on the television.

"Yo, what up bro?" José said giving this friend dap and a hug.

"Shit, chasing paper and closing in on this million bucks fast!" Castro said in an eager tone.

"Right though... yo, you see this shit on TV... ya boy Rakmeef is done for real, that nigga done killed two teenagers and a cop, now he's barricaded himself inside the building.

At that moment the two pictures, one of Twizz and one of Ballout appeared on the TV screen then a picture of the slain officer as well.

"Oh Shit bro, those the two little heathens I hired to off them niggas... damn he must've caught them slipping... I bet this nigga gonna go out like a bitch and surrender... it's too much anticipation and hype for that nigga to go out blazing!" Castro shouted.

"Bet a stack that nigga go out hard... I don't like the nigga, but the dude is a fucking soldier... he gotta go to war with them fucks to leave a legacy in the streets," José said making it a bet and not a life or death situation.

"Yo, so what did you wanna holla at me about bro?"

"Oh yeah listen, apparently the officer that you were supposed to do the deal with ended up dead and the law ain't feeling that shit. My connect said the F.B.I. has picked up the case and because they have no clues their starting point will be with his most recent cases," José stated dropping the bomb on his friend.

"So, that means they're watching me... if they're watching me that means they could be watching us which is not good."

"Exactly, so what I need from you is to go into drifter status. I need you to stay off of Scott for a while. We don't need them trying to link anything back to the squad or stumbling over something they never knew about. I got enough work to keep you occupied though. I need you to hit 95 with me to move some of this shit. I'm gonna hit you with 25 joints to start with, is that cool? I hope so cause that's all you're getting right now," José joked.

"That's straight... you want 25, right?" Castro questions.

"Nah, give me 20... that'll be 300 grand you owe me. I'm letting you still move out because I love you like a brother and I know you want that paper but bro you gotta be careful and you gotta move cautiously."

"I got you bro... I'm gonna fade the black," Castro reassured his friend.

"So, what's up with ya people from Dover... what's the verdict?" José asked.

"I talked to my folks and he said his man Skinny Kev is always trying to grab at least 10 to 15 every week. Plus, I told him 30… but if you giving them up for 20, I'll tell them 25."

"Twenty is for you and a few others not everybody!"

"I was gonna let you have him though, besides, you want me to fall back so I'm going out of state I'm only coming through to grab... you know, cop & go baby!"

"Cool but re..."

"Oh Shittt, look at that Shit!" Castro shouted.

"Pay me nigga, I told you!" replied an excited José.

Strapped down with six grenades, two AR-15's with two 100 round drums and a rocket launcher along with body armor that covered him from head to toe. He walked into the hallway then said a quick prayer asking God to forgive him for his sins then it was on! Rakmeef lifted the AT-4 on to his shoulder and pressed the button starting the war! BOOMMM! The missile shredded the building door into pieces as it traveled to its target, the SWAT teams armored tank. The impact of the missile almost lifted the tank from the ground as it severely damaged the tank. On cue, multiple rounds were fired into the building that now seemed to be blocked by a cloud of dark gray smoke caused from by explosion of the missile. After a minute or so the authorities stopped firing only to witness another missile launched into a cluster of police cars sending a few cars flying the air and an even bigger explosion. With the smoke on his side, Rakmeef rushed into the courtyard tossing grenades one after another into several crowds of officers sending the fatality rates up sky high. Blinded by the smoke, the officers were at a huge disadvantage and wasn't aware of the grenades being thrown in their direction until either they or a fellow officers body parts went flying high in the sky. The officers shot but were unaware due to the dark cloud that Rakmeef had the body armor on. With two grenades left, he tossed both back to back in the direction of Detective Baldwin's car. He automatically started firing one of the AR's as he stepped from out of the smoke finally making himself visible to everyone in attendance. TAT TAT, TAT TAT TAT, TAT, TAT TAT, TAT, TAT TAT, total mayhem had taken place in Fairfax as officers were dropping and being wounded by the most feared stick up kid in the city. It was obvious that the authorities were frustrated and annoyed by the fact that he had killed multiple officers and at that present time they had no way to stop the man. Behind the armored helmet, Rakmeef shouted obscenities taunting the authorities to bring it on! He knew making it to his getaway dirt bike and escaping was a slim to none chance, especially with the weight of the body armor slowing him down. Then once he stripped out of the armor, he would be a sitting duck so as he finished off the first drum, he started moving towards the wooded area behind the apartment complex. Still taking shots to the armor but still moving, Rakmeef was determined not to stop for a second. When a round from a .50 caliber assault rifle hit him, he went flying landing into a nearby tree hard! Survival mode set back in as he regained his composure, got back to his feet and began firing rounds from the other AR-15 as he disappeared into the woods.

Abbee made it to the house over Eastside in record-setting time. Making sure that the coast was clear, she entered the house cautiously as she went straight to the basement where the safe was located. Turning the knob to execute the combination to unlock the safe, she opened it up and just as he said there neatly stacked were rows of hundreds. Along with the money sat a .40 caliber Glock and a little plastic bag that read Kay Jewelers. More concerned on getting out of there, she hurriedly placed the money in the backpack that sat at the bottom of the safe. Once all the money was stuffed into the L.L. Bean hiking backpack she looked into the bag. A small gift-wrapped box with her name on it made her curiosity suddenly grow. When she opened it, her eyes became glossy as the tears clouded her vision. Rakmeef had purchased a 2.5 karat titanium engagement ring with a customized diamond trim with her name engraved on the inside. The rock was a pink diamond that was shaped in the form of an octagon. It was beautiful and Abbee loved it, she called Rakmeef who surprisingly answered after two rings.

"Zy'Kim I love it!" she shouted into the phone trying to over talk the sounds of gunfire that could be heard loud and clear in the background.

"Oh, I can see you got the ring huh? I got that for the only woman who ever mattered in my life... you're my favorite girl," he responded while still firing rounds.

"I'm glad I caught you in time... Zy nobody will ever take your place, I swear to God baby," Abbee said beginning to cry once again.

"Yo Abb I already know that that's why I gave you all that I did because I know I have your heart always like you got mine... now babe get up out of there and vanish... I gotta go, I gotta few more cops to kill I love you." That was all he said and then the phone went dead.

Listening to her fiancée, she grabbed the Glock then went back upstairs. When she reached the living room, she was met by two men who looked to be dope fiends with two 14-inch steak knives in their hands. They must've seen the news and figured it was over for Rakmeef then decided to break in the house expecting it to be empty. The look they had on their faces were the looks of sheer desperation, fiending, and stone-cold lust. With Abbee being away at rehab for over a month she had definitely gotten her weight up and to the two junkies, she looked like eye candy. Raising the knife then stepping towards her had put her back against the wall.

"What you got in that bag and what you trying to get into?" one of the intruders asked licking his lips.

Without a second thought or hesitation, she removed the Glock from her waistband firing several rounds into both men. Without an ounce of remorse, she stood over top of both motionless bodies and fired a shot apiece to each man's face then slid out the back door in route to her apartment to retrieve her small stash then make her way to the train station then vanished from Wilmington Delaware forever!

Time was running out and so was his ammunition. Including the 30 or so shells left in the drum he also had one fully loaded magazine left. Knowing the law wouldn't be stupid enough to just rush into the wooded area not know what's awaiting them he had a few minutes alone at last! He could hear someone on a bullhorn commanding him to come out with his hands up but that wasn't gonna happen. Knowing he had just about reached the end of his road he quickly stripped out of his body armor and made a dash deeper into the woods until he made it to his dirt bike. He was sure he had them by a good distance but knew it wasn't no escaping the ghetto bird which was the eye in the sky. Relieved that he made it to his bike he pulled out a Dutch rolled with sour and coke and sparked it like he didn't have a problem in the world. The coke sent him to the matrix as he looked at his phone screen viewing a picture of him, Abbee, Twink, Bree, and Nyomi.

That sent a surge of anger through him knowing that if his team was there it was possible, he could've made it out alive. Once the laced weed was gone, he lit a fully soaked dipper and went deeper into the matrix. He was shaken from his altered state of mind when he heard the bloodhounds closing in on him. He hopped on the dirt bike, started it then peeled off like Jeremy McGraff in his prime. Rakmeef maneuvered through the woods like an expert with his gun in hand. As he came closer to the exit point, he began letting shots off as he came into sight of the law. Speeding and firing was a brief distraction until a sniper aligned a perfect headshot while others attempted to stop him fired, POP! One single shot to the side of his head sent Rakmeef's body slumped over in one direction while the bike went in the other. It was over, the cities most feared stick up kid Zy'Kim Harris aka Rakmeef was dead!

CHAPTER 21

The Early Bird Always Got the Worm

The early bird always got the worm, so José was up and ready to move. He left the house before seven that morning stopping by Harding Ave to grab up some work to cover the crew's order first. He was giving Castro 25, Showstopper and the Young & Reckless crew 10, and Dre would get 10 of manteca. Between MacLaden's PA connects, Skinny Kev, and his folks, the playas he met through other business associates from Maryland to Virginia that should cover at least hundred bricks of coke and close to 20 in dope. Fat Papi's playas still grab about 80 squares of both total. Not to mention, Rosés five a week.

After stopping by the stash and grabbing 50 bricks he went to JoJo apartment to drop the five bricks of coke off then went to distribute the work to his team. Making a quick pitstop, he stopped by Angelina's to check on his brother. Sammy was happy to see his brother but playfully scolded his younger sibling for going M.I.A. once again. As usual, they embraced, talked about how their mother was coming along since Felix's death. And they reminisced about their youngest brother. The moment was grim at the mention of his brother's name, he felt he was the reason why his brother wasn't here any longer due to his involvement in the streets. He still hadn't received word on who was behind the home invasion which extremely had him vexed. The streets would have normally been talking but no one seemed to know nothing about it. While having general conversation José was stopped in mid-sentence once he looked over his shoulder and saw entering the store the man of the hour. The man he was looking for was standing right behind him. He reached for his torch and out of instinct and not thinking, but Sammy quickly pulled him to the back of the aisle out of the sight of the two goons.

"José chill bro, you can't do that in the store... what's wrong?" asked a concerned Sammy. Ignoring his brother José calmed down stepping back from his killer mode.

"Stay back here until I return... please José," Sammy begged before rushing back to the front of the store.

"What can I get y'all?" Sammy asked the two men.

"I'm looking for a friend of mine named Ivan... I heard he works here from time to time," Alex said snooping around the store.

"Ivan... Ivan, he doesn't work here he helps out around here from time to time, but I haven't seen him in about three weeks or so... if you leave ya name I'll let him know you stopped by when I see him," Sammy said sensing something wasn't right.

"Amillio... tell him Amillio stopped by," the older of the two men spoke up.

Once the men left the store, Sammy rushed to the back of the store with a worried look plastered across his face. His concern for his brother was evident. All he was concerned with was José safety and by the way, José was about to react he knew it was a major problem.

"José what was all that about man!" Sammy asked sounding a little shaken.

"Don't worry about it bro but what did they want?" asked José.

"He said he was a friend of Ivan's, but I doubt it, I wasn't born yesterday... they gave off a funny vibe."

"Ivan... hmm a'ight bro I gotta go... I'll talk to you later tell ma I love her," José said darting out the door.

After making his drops José called Angelina who informed him to come to her house immediately. An hour later and reassuring her that the man who came into the store looking for Ivan was the man that killed Fat Papi. Angelina had Ivan on the phone who was in route to her home as well now. When Ivan arrived, he was surprised to see young José from around the way lounge at the wet bar pearling a Dutch of poppa smurf. Angelina joined the two gentlemen and discussed the problem at hand, Alex.

"What's up, what's going on mamasita," Ivan addressed his boss.

"It seems your little friend has stopped passed the store again."

"When?" he questioned.

"Apparently today... now I let you handle this because you said you could and would but he's starting to make his presence known a little too often and it's starting to rub me the wrong way. I had my friends handle the block war, what else do you need me to do... do I have to hold your hand and walk you through this? I hope not because this isn't your repertoire. Now, what I need for you to do is eliminate this problem A.S.A.P.... to make it easier for you José here has a simple and easy way. Oh, before I forget to tell you, ya friend Alex is the puta that killed Fat Papi," Angelina said sounding more frustrated than angry or bothered.

"What... how you know?" Ivan questioned.

Angelina hit the play button on the remote and the horrific scene of Fat Papi's final moments played. Ivan's head fell low as he witnessed his cousin's execution play out. The room fell silent as all eyes were on him. For the first time in the meeting, José finally spoke up.

"I gotta way to get at the pussy but you gotta keep a cool head because my familia will lure him to us. I'm not sure if the other dude will be there but I'm assuming if he does it'll be a shootout and she can't be caught in the middle. So, if you're willing to move on my cue, he can be dead in less than 48-hours. So, what's the verdict?" José asked seriously awaiting an answer.

"I'm wit it, just take my number and when you're ready hit me up papa. What you doin out here tho youngin?" Ivan asked curiously.

"Now see, you're asking too many questions... no, but he's the youngest team member we have... these were the sticky fingers that found poppies stash. If I must say tho he's made me proud since joining us."

"A'ight, that's what's up... glad to see you handling things like a young O.G.," Ivan said giving the young gee a salute and dap.

Accepting the recognition like the humble gee that he was his only expression was a smirk and a slight nod of the head. With his phones blowing up it was time to pack up and hit the highway, money had to be made, and his first stop was Pittsburgh to holla at his old friend Titanic. Saying his goodbyes, he left Angelina's then headed to Harvey Ave to grab a brick and a half of "d". He wanted JoJo to ride with him but thought twice. With the secret stash box, he should be good, but you just never know and with that in mind, he wasn't gonna risk his friend's freedom and life by taking her to an unknown place. When he arrived at JoJo's she was home on her lunch break snacking on a fruit salad. She noticed José grabbed the five bricks and was packing a small suitcase.

"Where are you going ugly?" she asked.

"I gotta go outta town for a night or two."

"Once again, the question was, where are you going?"

"Oh, I'm going up to Pittsburgh."

"Who you know of there that you're taking all that?" she asked more concerned.

"My man Titanic from Clayton Street lives up there now."

" I don't know him and I don't want you going all the way up there by yourself... I wanna go then," she demanded.

"Nah, it's too risky... I need you here just in case I need you to make some runs for me around here."

"No José, I don't like this... you never went that far before especially with all that stuff I wanna go." Grabbing his judge and Glock 40, he looked her in the eyes.

"I'm okay Joanní, I promise."

"Please! Let me go José Please!" she began begging.

He walked up placing his arms around his friends shoulder kissing her forehead. He tilted her head up looking her in her glossy eyes and spoke soft assuring words to her.

"I'm gonna be alright… Jo, I gotta travel if I plan on making enough to take care of all of us when this hustling shit is all over… I definitely need to be rich if I wanna keep my future wife laced in the finest. Oh, did you start looking for those houses yet?"

"Not yet."

"Alright well... when I come back, I want you to come move in with me and Summer. I don't want you here by yourself and I'm not taking no for an answer you hear me?"

"Yeah, but I have something to tell you," she said looking down at the floor.

"What JoJo?"

"I've been talking to someone and I like him... but I swear José I haven't slept with him and he has never stepped foot in here!"

Silence fell upon them and you could feel the tension rising quickly. He released his arms from around her and stood there quiet for a second.

"Are you happy? Do you like him?"

"I mean he's nice and I'm happy but only because I need to get my mind off you José."

"Joanní if you're happy I'm happy too."

José didn't want to admit it, but he was crushed. His childhood love had been spotted and captured and because of his own situation with Summer, there was nothing he could do but accept it.

"So, do you still want me to move in with you now?" she asked nervously.

"Of course, your my sister always... remember one could never take my spot in ya heart and vice versa,' he said kissing her lips palming her ass lifting her up onto her toes.

"Okay, but what about the other stash spot. You still want me to get that right?"

"Yeah, but oh I need you to call the travel agency and book a trip for the crew all seven of us... but make sure you call them niggas up and let them know that if they wanna bring their girls they better drop that money off A.S.A.P. Book Summer for me, call Taylor and tell her that if she wants Rosé to join us they need to break bread too. I'm covering my team only."

"So where are we going?" she asked excitingly.

"Qualia."

"Qu... Qu what!" she shouted.

"Qualia... it's a tropical island in Australia. The resort is at the tip of Hamilton Island."

"I've been online looking and it's a private island to get there we're gonna have to take a private jet and all that other boogee shit so y'all better love it cause I'm paying a grip for the eight of us as it is."

"Thank you, José! I've never been on vacation!" she sounded excited.

"Girl please, when it's finally time I got a special place I'm taking you too."

"Where?" she asked curiously.

"Laucala Island."

"What! Where the hell is that and how did you pronounce that?"

"Don't worry, when it's time all will be revealed nosey," he said tapping her on the nose then smiling, "look, I gotta hit the road I'm trying to get there and get back so keep ya phone close just in case I need you."

"Okay, I'm ready... remember, I'm ya ride or die and I love you... sometimes I think more than myself. You think it would be okay if I went out there with Summer tonight?"

"Yeah, go ahead, I'll call her and let her know you're coming."

"Thank you boo... I love you," she said wrapping her arms around his waist pulling him in closer and giving him her tongue to taste, "be careful," she said before releasing him.

José couldn't do a thing except stand there and shake his head. Getting himself together, he shook off the feeling to fuck his best friend right then and there. Grabbing his bags, José walked out the door as JoJo watched her friend worrying if this move was a good one. All she could do was pray that he made it back safe. Before he could hit the highway MacLaden's Philly Peoplez put an order in for five birds of "d" and five birds of soft. So, he shot to the stash house, grabbed the work and was out! With 16 ½ bricks and two guns he knew he had to follow the laws of the land. That meant doing the proper speed limit, no drinking or smoking and make sure all his lights and signals were working. He reached Philly in no time. He handled his dealings with them and before he left a call from Skinny Kev from Dover came through, so he arranged to have JoJo make that drop. He wanted 15 at 30 apiece since it was the first time dealing with dude, he took it but let him know the next flip and so on would be 25 a kilo. Since JoJo was going to handle that move, he had her tuck the 325 grand and let her pocket the 75 grand for herself. He also had her drop 10 off to Castro for his playas in Norfolk VA. After those dealers were taken care of, he was back on the road heading to Pittsburgh PA. All he could think of on the ride there was why would he come this far from home with close to 200 grand of work on him? He reasoned with himself and said fuck it, if it's time to go then so be it but they better come correct cause if they don't it might cost them their lives.

Quan Showstopper had just turned 16 and for his age, he was living the life! With him being the youngest of the five, but the most dangerous his flamboyant persona attracted women both young and old. He stayed surrounded by women if it wasn't the woman from the block it was the young girls who hung out with him and his crew after school or after work. With the crew just getting 10 bricks in, Boo went straight to work whipping up the moon rock. Deciding to take a chance "Show" and Dawger even bagged up 50s and hundreds of powder cocaine. Surprisingly, the demand is high which led to more ounce and weight sales starting to come. Today was just like any other day as Vic-chow met with Carlos to re-up on his loud pack while the others floated back and forth doing what they do best, make money. With about a quarter brick of powder, a half of brick of ballgames, and A-1 Bry sitting on about 20 sticks of dope along with five handguns and an assault rifle they were in motion. The block was jumping, Dre and Carlos had slid through to check on the youngsters and make sure things were running smoothly while José and Castro were out of town. "Show" had just pulled up on the block in his brand new 2017 Porsche Cayenne S hopping out looking like a million bucks and when the loud blast was heard then everyone went deaf! Out of nowhere, police squad cars and unmarked tinted Tahoe's came from every direction. It was a raid and everyone tried fleeing! Parents and kids were detained even a few of the girl's houses were ransacked in the process. Nothing was found in the houses though simultaneously all the crew's residents were hit at the same time. With José and the rest of the squad schooling the youngins, nothing but a couple of grand, and maybe some bud for personal consumption was there. Now, if they would have found out about the Batcave or the Hornets' Nest the names the "Reckless" gave their chill spots then they would be in trouble. Boo and Dawger where strapped but when they raided, they flew out of there like a bat out of hell only far enough get the guns off of them. Once the authorities had everyone detained, they started searching the area.

After an hour of searching trash cans, under cars, alleyways, and backyards they came up with 72 ballgames, two handguns, and an assault rifle. It was unlawful to do but with Federal Agents on the scene, they even searched Carlos, Dre, Show, and Vic-chow's cars. The total amount of money was a light $15,000 which none of the suspects cared to argue about getting back. With no rule nine indictments, they really had no reason to hold them but decided to take them down for questioning to see if they could find anything out. The main person they were looking for had been MIA and they had no idea where in the hell he was at.

After finding the drugs, guns, and money Agent Kramer and Detective Baldwin wanted to find out who this mysterious man José was as well. Thinking Carlos are Dre might be the man, José they took a shot at them only to find out through Delaware State driver's license that neither of the two was him. Downtown at the Federal Building they tried scaring, lying, threatening each member of the squad and crew, but it was useless, not even the youngest member said a word but their names.

Once they were released, everyone was relieved but was now on high alert. Everyone was once again on the same accord but the question everyone wanted to know was, what did Castro do for them to have his picture asking about his whereabouts? And, the million-dollar question was why in the hell did they keep asking us who the hell was José! Before they could relay the message back to José news that the block had been raided had already reached him. Once he made his drop he would call and find out the details.

JoJo was meeting Castro on Chestnut and Scott Street when she saw the whole raid take place in front of her eyes. Castro had pulled up just in time to witness the seizure, knowing what the cause may have stemmed from Castro got the hell out of dodge with JoJo following right behind him. Making the exchange at the Adams Four parking lot when she gave him the work, she hit Rt. 13 making her way to Dover to meet Skinny Kev and Castro was heading down South to Norfolk Virginia to poly with the country folk. Money had to be made still so as soon as everyone was released Carlos collected everyone's phone after having them get all their most important contacts out of them. He told everyone to go grab new phones immediately because he would be getting rid of the old ones. He instructed Quan and his team to leave the block alone until they spoke to José but move only through the phones until further notice. The wake-up call wasn't really the raid but the joint investigation between the feds and the local authorities. The federal government conviction rate is damn near 100% so either two things had to happen, everyone could fall back and not make money or continue to grind until they came for the team. And the way they were all seeing cash everyone agreed it would most likely be the latter one. Dre had a totally different outlook on things since he had a baby on the way now, he wasn't sure if he wanted to risk any more of his freedom if he didn't have to. He had close to a million in cash plus, he could easily invest into the pills with Jesenia or just slow grind with the dope downstate. Whatever he chooses to do, he knew that his decision would have to be made soon before he hustles with Glady, so he was closer to a million than Dre. He made a nice sum of cash of the chow a half-mill to be exact plus, a nice number off the pills. Hustling was all he knew so the way he saw things was his destiny would be either locked away for life or a pine box. He embraced it like a lost love that has finally come back to him. Carlos was the definition of a product of his environment and he wanted it no other way.

The GPS tracking device on José phone directed him straight to the front door of his destination. When he arrived at the three-story townhouse, he called Titanic to let him know that he had arrived. Opting to keep the work in the stash and retrieving his judge he hopped out heading for the front door. Instead of his friend greeting him he was met by a hot Latina who had to be the twin sister of the sexy seductress Cubana lust! Standing in the doorway in a white sports bra exposing her nicely toned stomach, a pair of white laced boy shorts panties, and a pair of Chanel peek toe fluffy bedroom slippers.

"Come in poppie," she said extending her hand so she could take his.

She was beautiful and José wanted her but wasn't sure if she was his friend's wife or something he at least claims to be.

"You must be José, nice to meet you I'm Marisol," she said smiling ear to ear.

When they walked into the living room there sat three more Latina women smoking chow, counting money, and dressed in the same attire is Marisol.

"Damn what y'all having a sleepover?" José said jokingly.

"You can call it that... this is José y'all," she said introducing him to her girls, "Titanic will be down in a few minutes sexy. You want anything to drink?" she asked holding up a bottle of Coconut Cîroc.

"Nah, I'm good... so what you Titanic girl?" he asked.

"No way, he the biggest whore I know, he's like a brother from another mother though, he makes sure we good around here and we move out for him when it's needed. He is fucking all my girls tho, why you ask me that?" she asked cheesing from ear to ear. You like what you see poppie?"

"Yeah, you can say that... I'm gonna be in town for the night so I'm tryna go have some fun and I need a guide. I was hoping you could show me around."

"Well, handle what you need to handle here then we can go somewhere to enjoy the Pittsburgh nightlife."

Just then Titanic came walking down the stairs into the living room. He hugged his old friend who he was so happy to see! At 5'10 José was six inches taller than Titanic; he was standing at 6'4. The two young men caught up on the latest things like old buddies do. Marisol and her friends were great hosts as the three other girls got naked and danced for the men. However, Marisol made herself comfortable on José's lap playing in his wavy hair while they talked about everything. Now, it was time to get down to business, so Titanic sent Marisol to the basement to retrieve the cash. When she returned, she was carrying a plastic Nike clothing bag. She gave the bag to Titanic who pulled knot after knot out of the bag until 20 wads of cash sat before them. Titanic had Marisol and the girls began counting the money out until they were sure the total was $201,000. With everything seeming official, José excused himself and went to the car to grab his other torch and the work. Coming back to what he just left they were ready to seal the deal. The only thing that needed to be done was to test the potency of the work. So, Marisol pulled out a testing kit and within minutes the test was assuring them that they had some A-1 powder and some raw dope. Everyone in the room was hyped by the test results. See, the darker the color the more potent and the dark blue color verified that they had some of the best work the streets of Pittsburgh had seen in a long time. José was nonchalant he knew what he had on his hands and was sure he would never get any complaints. Placing his cash back in the Nike bag he went back to his car then placed all but three grand in the stash box. With the business behind him, he went back to join his friend and the mamis.

So, do you want a drink now poppie?" Marisol asked.

"Yeah, I'll take one... but T look, you know if you meet me halfway or come to me, I'll give you the soft for 20 a key."

"What about the "d"?"

"You gotta grab more than 10 for that to drop only 500... that's A-1 so I'm only dropping that if my number drops but hey who knows what tomorrow may bring."

"I see you like my peoples go ahead and take her out... she needs to go somewhere; she don't do shit but get on my nerves all day anyway."

"I mean, if she wants to show me around the town, I'm with it, I'm leaving tomorrow around one in the afternoon so if we gonna go we need to leave it's already 11."

"Nigga! This Pittsburgh this ain't DE the city just starts jumping around one in the morning, so have fun!"

Before anyone could change their mind, she was up the stairs in a flash getting dolled up. A half hour later, she appeared rocking a pair of black True Religion fitted jeans that hugged her curves like a roll of masking tape with a black and gold turtleneck sweater also by True Religion that was complimented by a black with a gold trim Christian Louboutin red bottom stilettos. She looked sexy mixed with a little Latina spice and the Black Cartier spectacles gave her the educated look as well. She was ready, so they hit the town first for sightseeing then stopping at a few local grub spots tasting different varieties of food like the pizza and cheesesteaks. They were just talking getting to know each other better and getting a feel for the natives of Pittsburgh. Next, they hit the local night club which was the hotspot for the younger crowd. Wiz Khalifa was performing that night, so it was alive! They danced very close and sexy and the temperature was definitely rising between the two. Getting a spot in VIP for 1600 plus, a bottle of Cîroc for 300, they fell back and became more acquainted with each other. It didn't take long before the flirting turned into touching, touching turned into sucking, and then it was time to be out! With Cîroc and chow in his system instead of riding around, he decided to stay Downtown and get a room at the Westin Hotel. As soon as they hit the door what was taking place in the club was occurring again. She surprised him when she removed her sweater exposing her perky breasts then removed her jeans revealing a fat bald pussy. Without a second thought, he stripped out of his clothes. They stood there naked lusting at each other's body. Marisol went to take a shower when she returned José stood wrapping his muscular frame around her little frame. At 6'4 and 225 lbs. and in tip-top shape she felt like she was in Heaven when he lifted her then slid her down onto his dick and fucked her every way possible until they both were sweaty and exhausted. That was the best shot of pussy he had in a while. Why was José so foolish not to wear a condom?

CHAPTER 22
Priscilla and Angelina Meet

Priscilla and her two daughters Yari in Silvia out were out and about shopping and enjoying the day. Christiana Mall had a number of new boutiques that the girls wanted to explore. With so much drama in the streets and still mourning the death of their brother and son, a trip to the mall for a little shopping spree seemed like it would be a stress reliever. The girls stopped by the Steve Madden boutique purchasing purses and other materialistic things. The next stop was Forever 21 then they stopped in Macy's buying Polo, Tommy Hilfiger, and Nautica gear for the kids. After grabbing each of themselves pairs of Columbia and UGG boots, they were tired and hungry, so they went to the food court to get a bite to eat. With everything from Cinnabon to Ruby Tuesday's, they all decided on Chipotle. Once they received their food, they took a seat to enjoy the meal. Leaving the family business alone, for the time being, they talked with their mother about modern-day girl talk, fashion, music, movies, and male crushes. That was suddenly interrupted when four brolic men circled the table. A startled look appeared across the three women's faces, that look turned into fear when suddenly from out of nowhere Ivan pulled up a chair and made himself comfortable. No words were exchanged for a good minute, then the look of the Devil spread across Priscilla's face, she was no longer scared she wanted his head. Then a lady who looked to be in her mid-40s walked up and patted Ivan's shoulder signaling for him to excuse himself from the table. Even in jeans, boots, a winter coat, and a skull cap she looked elegant. Her makeup was flawless, her jewelry was expensive, and her approach and demeanor spoke power! She took a seat without saying a word as she stared at the once beautiful elderly woman, she extended her hand and spoke to Priscilla and her daughters.

"Hello, my name is Angelina, nice to meet you."

Priscilla's mouth damn near hit the floor. She had heard stories about the woman who was supposed to have had sole control over the largest distribution of coke and dope from Connecticut to Delaware. Her empire was at least triple the worth of Priscilla's and her power was somewhat unimaginable. Priscilla wasn't even sure if this was the same person, the infamous Angelina, the head of the east coast cartel better known as the Bella Bandido Cartel.

"Bella Bandido?" Priscilla asked cautiously.

"Si!" Angelina replied smiling.

Priscilla covered her face with her hands trying to cover the mixed emotions she was having. She knew she was no match financially for her opposition, but she could never let the blood of her own child be shed and go on punished.

"Nice to finally meet you senorita," she spoke coldly.

"It seems we have a problem; you and your family have come in town with the impression that it was okay for you guys to set up an operation that was already established way before you got here," Angelina spoke reasonably.

"Listen, when me and my family came here the block was dead… no cash flow, not a soul spoke of Pleasant Street. Now, that we brought it back to life your friend over there wants to bring me and my family trouble… and I can't stand him for that," Priscilla said raising her voice and slamming her fist on the table.

Both Yari and Sylvia were visibly shaken by the verbal encounter that was sure to come because they knew their mother wouldn't back off.

"Just because you see that a block is empty doesn't mean it wasn't occupied... that block held four houses of mine that had over 10 million in drugs in them at the time. So, when you and your little family came in and opened a 24-hour drive-thru for the latest drugs, then decided to buy up all the damn houses on the block and when they finally decided to raid your block that also puts my houses and my 10 million in drugs in jeopardy. Now that's where we have the problem, Ms. Reyes," Angelina said with the authoritarian of God in her voice.

"So, what now?" Priscilla asked already knowing the answer.

"You need to relocate... and to make things cordial, I'll beat whatever price you're paying now."

"I don't think me and my family will be relocating anywhere and I don't want anything from you! Your guy killed my son and you think I'm sweeping that under the rug, never! Listen, in this line of work two things will either happen jail or death and for the death of my son jail would be too easy for him. So, he's gonna die... if it means it will cost me my own life which I've lived a long and successful life so be it; my sons will cause havoc in my honor," she said getting up from the table to leave.

Angelina sat there watching the elderly woman wobble to her feet to leave with her hands folded together trying to keep her composure.

"Well, since you put it that way it's your guys funeral, not mine!"

Angelina mumbled under her breath then raised up from out of her chair then left in the opposite direction.

José was back and things were still moving like usual. Castro was in and out of state like they planned and José stayed away from Scott Street as much as possible. After talking with the Young & Reckless crew they moved their operation from 2nd to 5th and Scott. Still having access to all the same spots just more blocks to roam on, that made the disappearing act more frequent.

By the end of the two weeks, José had knocked off his shipment. He was surprised with himself to see how he maneuvered around the highway patrol, Feds, haters, and still alive and free to talk about it. Along with the money came the risks but the money he had just seen off that last flip he was content with taking the risk. Pulling into his driveway he noticed Summer and JoJo's cars in the parking spots. When he walked in the sound system was blasting Ivy Queen and the aroma of the food smelled wonderful. Summer ran to her man and wrapped her arms around him planting a kiss or his lips, JoJo stood off in the distance with a half-smile on her face. José felt the discomfort, so he walked up to his friend giving her a hug too. Nothing was awkward about the threesome sharing the house together. Out of respect, José tried to keep his sex life to a minimum whenever JoJo was home. Summer picked up on it and would literally throw the pussy on her man sometimes forcing him to fuck her. She would put on a show with her loud moans and hollers, then seldom she would brag to her house guest about how amazing and how big and thick her man was. JoJo would play her little game by waving her off also letting her know that José was like her brother and that she didn't want to vision any of the things that Summer was talking about. Truthfully, she really wanted to know, it made her pussy swell and when she was alone in her room at night playing with her clit making herself cum it was evident that she wanted him or for that matter a man inside of. Out of respect for José and Summer she never let her thoughts control her because if she did, she would have dropped to her knees and sucked his dick royally. That would make any man wanna fuck especially with her having a cute face, small waist, and perfect size ass to palm. Even though she was hungry as hell her new friend was occupying most of her time now when she wasn't working so her toys, fingers, and his conversation kept her content for the time being. They all gathered in the living room watching Netflix eating quesadillas while Summer and JoJo gossiped about what was happening at work. José sat and listened like he was watching the evening news. He couldn't help but admire the beauties that sat in the room in front of them.

"So, Summer what's going on with school?" José asked.

"Well babe, I think I'm doing good but because of the holidays and work I've been slacking on my studies, but I should still be making the Dean's list."

"That's good boo... look if you make the Dean's list both semesters you can get any Benz or beamer you want... deal?"

"Are you serious? Babe if I make the Dean's list, I want the G-wagon!"

"What! Girl, I don't even have the G-wagon."

"José you did say she could get any kind she wants," JoJo added teaming up with Summer to remind him of his words.

"Alright... but you better have straight A's," José said firmly."

"Straight A's... that's light work you better check my resume," Summer said boasting.

"I know that's what I'm scared of... and you and Taylor are going to Spellman next year right? What y'all taking up that Agricultural Science still?"

"Well, since she has moved on, I'm not sure I wanna go there anymore."

"Well, where are do wanna go? I hope you wanna stay here to help me run this shit!"

"Sorry for ya! I'm out of this bitch dog. My mind is on something new. I want to go to New York and attend the New York film Academy. It takes 2 to 4 years but if I go overtime, I should be done in 2 to 3 tops."

"You sure that's what you wanna do Spellman is a great school," he said trying to convince her to change her mind back to her original choice.

"I'm sure… I wanna do movies, videos, documentaries, and shit like that. I wanna be involved in the entertainment business and I already got accepted so I'm feeling like this may be my true calling," JoJo said becoming excited just speaking about it."

"Well, have you found anywhere to stay?" José asked.

"Not yet, I still have time though, but I'm looking to live in Manhattan so that I can be close. I'm not trying to do a lot of driving in New York City."

"Just let me know and I'll help you find something suitable. Did you book the trip yet, my birthday is next week?"

"Yup, and you owe me 50 bands!"

"I got you in the morning."

"We leave Philadelphia International next Friday at 7:30 a.m. Once we arrive in Australia, our private jet will be awaiting our arrival that will take us to the island. Everyone decided to bring a partner, so we'll be flying in a G-650, that's top of the line, so happy birthday! Oh, but one more thing, I decided to bring my friend along," she said nervously.

"That's what's up I guess we'll get to meet him but what trip and what island are you talking about?" Summer asked in a puzzled manner.

"Girl, he didn't tell you? That boy reserved a private island for a week in Australia for his birthday! That shit cost 50,000 for five days but everything is included and I mean everything! Spa, golf course, nightlife clubbing, deep sea diving, nature walks, and they even have a little shopping district. From the pictures I've seen online for it to be a private island they sure have a lot of things to do. And it only caters to 40 people at a time so for an island that size we'll basically be alone wherever we go. To put the icing on top of your birthday cake we will all have our own tour guides and the travel agent said the locals say they have some very good smoke. Bam!"

"Did you get it for my birthday?" he asked.

"Yeah, we leave next Saturday on New Year's Eve."

"Good, Good, alright well, I'll give you your money in the am. What about the new house for the work?"

"The Sheriff Sale is Tuesday, the listing said they had a house in Richardson Park and one in Belvedere. They should be less than 30."

"You know, you got a lot of property in your name girl."

"Shit, I ain't got no tenants living in them, so a bitch ain't making no money off them!"

"You right, but you makin' money though."

"Word up!" she said excitedly.

"Look, continue to do what y'all been doing and y'all both have my support. The sky is the limit and as long as you two shoot for the stars the world could be y'all's."

For the rest of the evening, José and his girls parlayed, smoked, and joked enjoying each other's company. I guess the living arrangement actually would work out for the threesome.

The next morning, when José woke up, he was feeling groggy and the answer to his problem was a nice hot shower, so he headed straight for the bathroom. Still half asleep, he opened the bathroom door surprising the hell out of JoJo who was drying herself off after an early morning shower. She stood there exposed and silently letting the towel hang to her side. Her wet and wavy mane lay delicate or her soft smelling skin, her young perky C-cup breast stood tall with thick brown nipples to complement them. Her flat stomach, soft and thick looking thighs that seemed to be barely tampered with, and that yellow ass of hers were screaming out to be spanked. Her tiny pedicured toes wiggled in anticipation and nervousness, she wanted it to happen right there and then. Through his shorts, it was evident that José had become aroused by the sight of her.

"Is Summer still here?" José asked walking towards her."

"No… she left for work already, I gotta get ready too."

Shortening the space between them they could feel each other breathing. A kiss was exchanged between the two, their hands roamed each other's body parts. Moans escaped JoJo's mouth as José lifted her, causing her to wrap her legs around his waist. Thinking wisely, she quickly jumped down stepping back with a flustered look on her face. Grabbing her towel and wrapping it around her body a chill ran through her body, trying to shake off the urge to fuck her friend.

"José you know I want to badly! I just want it to be special if we ever do it."

"This wouldn't be special; this would be wrong." She invited me into her house.

"I'm too thorough to do some foul shit like that... I want to, trust me I can't tell you how many times I thought of you but if we do it, it won't be a one-time thing or an occasional rendezvous. Trust me, this pussy so tight and wet you're gonna want me every night and that's what I want. So, until I can have that I'm willing to wait, cause trust me when I tell you, mark my words, one day I will be wifey. I've put too much time in to be overlooked. I'm the most thorough chick you'll probably ever meet. I should have the title, Queen Joanní Valdez. Until then, I'll just wait," she said kissing him and then walked out the bathroom.

José had mixed emotions as he stood there with a serious hard-on. On one hand, he wanted to throw a tantrum fit because he wanted some early morning nana and couldn't get any. On the other hand, he suddenly found himself falling deeply in love with his friend. It may have been the thrill of the chase that made him want her more. Whatever the case was, he no longer wanted his friend he needed her. She was right and he began to realize over the years she has proven that he loved Summer unconditionally, but he was deeply in love wit Joanní.

The Reyes family was in full attendance except for Ellé. The unexpected run-in at the mall had Priscilla furious but also on edge. For Angelina to have known she was gonna be at the mall that meant she was being followed. She really didn't care at that time, all she wanted was blood! Fuck the money or power side of things, Priscilla was the Black Widow and she knew Angelina was equivalent to the Black Mamba guess it would ultimately come down to who struck first. She planned to bring more reinforcements in just in case things went bananas! The Twins, Yari, and

Silvia also wanted a piece of the action ready to war with anyone bringing trouble to their family. They definitely weren't naive to shootouts and drama back in Redding PA even the daughters had a reputation of shooting first then asking questions last. That was one of the main reasons Priscilla moved her family away to save them from the indictment the state was trying to build against them.

Alex and Amillo wanted to kill anyone involved with Ivan and his crew, that meant Angelina too. Edwin and Hector were also on the same page, their concern was for their mother and sisters. So, when the opposition decided to cross the line and approach their mother all rules were broken which meant everyone who was against them were in danger. Priscilla understood how everyone felt about the situation, but she had to remind her children that the women they were attempting to war with was a dangerous and deadly woman. Her moves were calculated and if she executed a hit it was almost 100% guaranteed to be completed. She explained that Angelina was not a myth, the Bella Bandido Cartel was the opposition and the family had also heard the stories but for family, no one in the room cared. They knew they only had each other and all were willing to sacrifice their lives. Yari slid her phone to the middle of the table giving everyone a chance to view the scene. While her mother and Angelina exchanged words at the mall Yari discreetly, while acting like she was messing around on her phone snapped off a picture of both Angelina and Ivan. Everyone got a good look at their targets, now they were ready for war. They wouldn't wait for them to come for any of theirs, they were gonna strike first! Alex finally apologized for bringing anarchy to his family once again. By this time, the family was passed that, they wanted war and it was final. Alex had received a call from his old friend trying to get five pounds, so he had to excuse himself from the meeting. Amillio would have gone along but stayed back with his mother making plans to have more of the G.B.C. members to fly into town. Once they arrived and Priscilla acquaintances showed up in Hellaware another name for the state, would be plagued with death.

"Largo hora no ver," Alex said to his old friend.

"Si... yo, been busy lately... still trying to get paid you know me," Bunny said feeling upbeat like her normal self, "so what's going on with you?"

"Shit, still getting money as well, but looking for this pussy that's scared to face me in the streets," Alex spoke cockily.

"Who?" she asked.

"That pussy Ivan and that bitch Angelina. They approached mama and my sisters at the mall so now it's on sight when I see either of them," he said sounding deranged.

"Alex, I like you that's why am telling you, you should leave well enough alone. That lady is a sweet woman but if you push her, she has the power to make everyone around you disappear. And Ivan is a killer... that's why when you said something about it before I kind of fell back because I know what those two are capable of and I don't want any parts of it. Alex, I'm only telling you because I like ya fly ass and if drama could be avoided why not fall back," she said in a caring manner.

"I feel you Bunny, but they approached my mother and Ivan killed my brother. It could never be peace now. One of us has to go and I'm okay with it as long as somebody feels the raft of the Reyes family."

"Well, let's not talk about that now; I'm happy to see you and I missed you," Bunny said grabbing at his crotch area. With no hesitation, he removed his man pipe from his jeans letting Bunny suck the life out of him. Unnoticeable behind the tinted windows, Alex pushed the button to recline his seat as Bunny's head began bobbing up and down swiftly and exotically. His phone rang, when he saw his brother Amillo's name he ignored the call, then laid back enjoying the sensation his dick was feeling. Alex grabbed the back of her head and closed his eyes as she became more focused on making him erupt in the back of her throat. While lost in her utopia, Alex was blind to the fact that Bunny had managed while still sucking him genuinely to maneuver herself to unlock both the drivers and passengers side doors. With him lost in his own fantasy world, he never saw the two shadows creeping up along the side of the car. He didn't expect a thing until the driver's side door swung open! He jumped but it was too late, the .40 cal was aimed at his face. He didn't recognize the young boy off hand, but he quickly remembered he was the same young poppie that Bunny had introduced him to months back. José had a killer look in his eyes as he aimed his torch ready to fire. Alex knew Bunny had set him up to get robbed once she grabbed the bag from the back seat then took his phone. He vowed to kill both of them when the time presented itself.

"You got that papa... you can have that, that's lightweight. I could've thrown you 50, lil nigga," Alex said in an upset tone.

"You know who Fat Papi is?" José asked.

"Who! What the hell are you talking about youngin," Alex said beginning to fidget in his seat.

"Fat Papi you Bitch Ass Mothafucka!"

"Nah, I don't know him young... what's this about?" Alex questioned.

"Well, the man you killed at that mechanic shop that was my folks and it was his family," José said directing his attention to the other side of the car.

On cue, Bunny opened the door getting out walking away from the car. When Ivan bent over with his pistol in hand looking into the car you would have thought he just saw the soul leave Alex's body.

"Now see poppie, I told you to relocate but you didn't listen. Now look, I told you that you could not fuck with me, now you're dead!" Ivan said spitting venom with every word.

Alex knew his life was over but instead of going out bitching and crying, he gritted his teeth together then reached for his cannon.

BOOM, BOOM, BOOM, BOOM, BOOM, BOOM, BOOM!

The execution was fast and the shots entered his face and body leaving another corpse on the streets of Murdertown.

After the shots seized, Bunny appeared leaning into the car to finalize the plan. She whipped the straight razor across his throat swiftly causing a massive blood flow, then took his phone, then snapped a few pictures, and then bounced. After making a clean get-a-way, José took Alex's cell sending a group text to everyone in his phone. The picture texted was of Alex's deceased body with a caption that read, "We told you to relocate... Ha! Ha! Ha! You can find him on 11th and Scott puta!"

Before José had a chance to disassemble the phone into pieces and get rid of it the phone was alerted over a dozen times. They never even bothered to view the comments, piece by piece as they drove, he tossed the pieces away! When the pictures first came through the phone, she didn't recognize the person. Never thinking that it was her son because he had just left no more than an hour earlier; she was lost.

When she heard the rest of the house erupt into an uproar with cry's and screams; she felt her heart drop. She knew then that she was staring at her son's deceased body. All the children entered the room with sobs and tears, Priscilla couldn't hold back her feelings anymore, she broke down crying uncontrollably. Yeah, Alex was the hard-headed one, but he was also the protector and now he was gone. Priscilla took this hard, she loved Alex just the same as the others but Alex despite his rugged persona he was a momma's boy. He stayed under his mother and wouldn't leave her side for the world now he was commissioned by God to leave his family behind. Amillio cursed himself for letting his brother go alone in the midst of a war. It may have gone down differently if he was by his side, but he wasn't so his younger sibling was gone forever. Hector, Edwin, and Amillio hopped in their wheels on their way back to Angelina's corner store. If she was there, she was dead, if Ivan was there, he was dead. Basically, anyone around the store was marked for death! It was a good thing no one was at the store when they got there, but you know they planned to return very soon!

José got dropped off at his car and Bunny got dropped off as well. Knowing he needed to get out of them clothes instead of going all the way home he stopped by JoJo's apartment changing into an all-black True Religion sweat suit and a pair of black Timberland Chuckers. Getting rid of the evidence by disposing of it in a nearby apartment complex garbage dumpster he was in the clear. With a week until they left for vacation José went ahead and put his order in for the same thing. When it arrived, he did what he did best and that was hustle hard and flawless. While he was gone, he planned to have Showstopper and Dawger handle all his local runs. He would leave them with access to a hundred bricks, but not in their hands. He would have Janay, Hope, and Treasure make drops to them whenever they needed them too. For now, he was up and down the interstate making drops to skinny Kev from Dover. Kev was climbing the ladder slowly but surely increasing his order every time he called. He even had Castro slide down to Rockville Maryland with him to check his associate Keith out. Keith was major, dude was a high-ranking military official who worked in the Pentagon but pumped birds of coke on the side. He moved anywhere between 10 to 20 birds a week and he was willing to pay top dollar if it was brought to him. So, like the businessman that he was José and his man was on the road again. As soon as he made it back to Wilmington, he was back out the door heading to Salem New Jersey to holla at another business associate "Fat Man" and then he headed back to Pittsburgh to see Titanic and Marisol. Just like the first time they met up, he and Marisol sexed. Afterward, he was back on the road heading home.

By the weekend, José had moved over half of his shipment. He was in hustle mode and he felt like the snowman Jeezy with all the white he was selling. José was moving enough blow and dope in a month to supply the whole Pennsylvania state and the two largest counties in Delaware. New Year's Eve was a day away and before his trip, he wanted to see his mother and brother. Pulling into his mother's driveway, he sat in the car briefly thinking about how his life had changed in six months. Heading into the house, he found his mother watching a Bible study on TV being preached by Evangelist Billy Graham. On the coffee table were several scattered pictures of Felix, his mother was still grieving, and it hurt his heart to see her hurting. The sad part about it was he still hadn't found out a thing about the murder and now that Rakmeef and Twink were dead he might never find out the truth.

"Hey ma," José spoke catching his mother off guard.

"Ooh boy, you scared me," Miss Valdez said jumping up slightly, "come give me a kiss boy... I missed you. Why didn't you stop by on Christmas?"

"I'm sorry ma, but didn't you get the gifts? I gave them to Sammy for you," he tried explaining.

"Yes, I got the gifts and they were beautiful but that still doesn't excuse you from not stopping by to see your family on holidays. We are all we have and the road you're traveling, tomorrow's not promised. So, I'm not asking you anymore I'm telling you that you better make it your business to start stopping by here every couple of days and calling me at least once a day to let me know that you're breathing José! I'm scared for you boy and it's not fair for you to do me this way," Miss Valdez said finally venting to her son.

"I'm sorry ma... I have been tripping but I'll start checking in more often. Look, if something tragic was to happen I have something put to the side for you and Sammy."

"José, your money will never be a replacement for your being... the only way you can make me happy is walking away from the streets for good."

"I am ma... I am soon, I promise. You and Sammy need a car... I'm gonna give him my other car so that y'all have some transportation alright?"

"Okay dear," she responded.

"Where's Sammy at anyway ma?" José asked.

"He's at work."

"Okay, before I go home, I'm gonna stop by to see him."

José and his mother hung out around the house for a few hours enjoying each other's company. As usual, Miss Valdez fed her son until he was stuffed, they caught a new movie on the fire stick called Proud Mary that his mother was so intrigued by. Taraji P. Henson did her thing in the action movie. Miss Valdez tried to mimic certain scenes from the movie, when the fighting started, causing his mother to become animated numerous times throughout the flick. When it was time for José to depart you could feel his mother's entire mood change. She went from an upbeat jubilant mother to a silent concerned parent. When José got into his car, he saw the worry all over her face as she stood in the door waving him goodbye. He knew he was killing his mother slowly and wished there was another way but then his phone rang and that's when he realized, this way was the only way and would continue to be the only way until either he had a life-changing experience, or he hit the Powerball!

Since the beef between Alex and Ivan, Angelina had switched up drop spots for her deliveries. Knowing that at any time her operation could be compromised with a sudden shootout or homicide she felt cleaning the basement out would be the wisest thing to do. She also has had Sammy running the store night and day with the help of Noel and his younger cousin Kachito. She would stop by to check on things but since Alex had been popping up at the store she stayed away. Today she stopped in with Ivan at her side to collect the earnings for the week. Everyone except for Sammy was strapped so when Amillio and his two brothers walked in the store looking suspicious everyone was on high alert. The moment Ivan appeared from the back of the store the war was officially started! When Ivan and Amillio locked eyes nothing else needed to be spoken, shots were fired!

CHAPTER 23

The Double Funerals

Dre had called José trying to re-up so now José was on his way to buss that move before heading to the house. The Young & Reckless crew was also ready, so instead of going to JoJo's apartment, he shot over to Harding Avenue. He had Dre, Quan, and Dawger meet him at the North Quarter Restaurant and Lounge. The lounge was located on the 2nd level where Treasure and Hope were the bartenders, so everything was cool and they had the green light to handle business in the back room, which was the VIP. Dre had taken José's advice and started moving around in Federalsburg and Chestertown Maryland. With the baby coming, instead of spending his own cash he would let José throw it to him now. Remembering that they were all leaving the next morning he was about to decline on grabbing the 10 squares of manteca, but José had brought them and didn't plan on leaving with them, so he took them while passing him a bag containing 480 grand. He excused himself then left without a trace. Show passed him the backpack with 200 grand in it and in return, José passed them the 10 bricks of soft. Giving them the numbers to the people who would drop off the work as they needed it and informing them to only sell weight until sundown for safety precautions seemed reasonable. He also reminded them that it was a strong possibility that they were under investigation, so they needed to move carefully. Before they all left the North Quarter, José dropped a $5,000 apiece to Treasure and Hope for the lookout. Rolling through the same streets he once ran up and down making hand to hand sells, he now was a street king. José could have easily at the age of 18 been on any volume of cocaine cowboys. As he cruised down West 4th Street he acknowledged friends and associates with head nods and hand gestures while he thumped Jay-Z's Hard Knock Life. With close to 700 grand in the car, his intentions were to drop the cash off at the stash house but it was no time to think about that, it was time to shoot. Yeah, he was about to Spaz the Fuck Out!

POP POP POP, POP POP POP POP POP POP!

BOOM BOOM POP BOOM POP POP BOOM BOOM BOOM!

Amillio fired first followed by Ivan blasting back then Angelina letting off a couple of rounds. Objects were flying around as both sides traded shots trying to eliminate the opposition. Hector got off a good one sending a rhino to Noel's stomach killing him instantly.

POP POP BOOM, POP BOOM BOOM BOOM, POP POP!

Sammy was scared as hell with tears in his eyes when Angelina came to his rescue firing round after round while getting Sammy to safety. Once she was sure that he was okay, she returned to the gun battle. Angelina looked like a Murda Mami the way she slung the shots! Kachito had been hit in the shoulder which caused him to lose his weapon that made the situation grim looking and you could see the look on their faces that they needed a miracle. The store looked like a natural disaster had just hit it. Even with the fear of dying clearly on his mind Sammy grabbed Kachito's gun and began firing as if his life depended on it. The sudden rush of bullets was not only a chance for Angelina and Ivan to reload but it caused the three brothers to retreat from out of the store. Still firing back into the store caused the somewhat quiet and calm block to erupt in mayhem. As the trio tried to escape, they were surprised from the blind side when shots were fired at them! BOOM BOOM BOOM BOOM!

"Fuck Y'all Mothafuckas! Die!" BOOM BOOM!

The sound of José's judge made the earthquake as one of rounds exploded into Hectors back leaving a hole the size of a tennis ball through the front and back of his body. His life had come to an end but that didn't stop José from catching wreck! As the .45 burst, Amillio and Edwin locked eyes with José who was trying to kill them. José ambush gave Ivan and Angelina time to come out of the store firing as well. Amillio and Edwin had managed to make it out alive, but now they had to tell their mother another one of her children were slain. José main concern was his brother and until he made actual contact with his brother, his nerves would not settle. When a trembling Sammy exited the store, José embraced his brother who was still visibly shaken. Knowing that the law was in route, he had to evacuate the premises quickly. With Angelina being the owner of the store, her and Ivan would stay behind to answer the questions of the law. She advised José to leave and to take Sammy with him. Angelina knew a few of the department's top dogs so everything should be okay.

Leaving the scene in a hurry, instead of taking Sammy home he took him to his house where he could calm his nerves and get himself together. For the first time in his life, Sammy took a few puffs of the weed while sipping on some Branson B. Cuvée. After the weed took effect, Sammy began to relax a little more.

"Bro what the hell was that about?" Sammy asked José.

"I don't know Sammy; all I know was that you were in there and I had to make sure you were alright. My main concern was you and you only," José spoke seriously.

"I was scared as hell bro... I did shoot back though. Man, you should have seen Angelina, that woman is bad with a gun!" he said becoming a little excited.

"I bet she was... Angelina is a good woman, but you might wanna find another job, things may get a little hectic for a while," José said honestly.

"Man, she's the only person who will pay me like that... she pays me enough to hold me and ma down."

"If you find another job and you need help, I got you... you act like I'm gonna see you and ma on the streets. Let me show you something."

José left the house returning a few minutes later with the bag and backpack. He emptied the rolls of money on the floor in front of both of them. Sammy's eyes almost bulged out of his face seeing that amount of cash.

"Bro how much dough is that!" Sammy asked.

"Seven hundred thousand large!"

"Damn, I never saw that much money in my life!"

"Sammy, when I tell you it's more where that came from, trust me bro it's way more... you and ma don't have to worry, I got both of y'all. And if something ever happens to me, I have a stash growing by the weeks for the both of you."

It began getting late so Sammy was ready to head home. When José handed him the keys to the Marauder and told him that it was his now, his brother was blown away. Sammy headed home while José waited for his girls to arrive home. The next morning, the trio were up and ready to roll out! Instead of driving, they had the shuttle van pick them up and take them to the airport. Everyone arrived on time and formal introductions were given, so now, everyone seemed more relaxed. Carlos and Dre introduced the Twins who looked like the model Elba Everlasting. They seemed down to earth; Castro brought along one of his jump offs who he probably invited just to show off then fuck! Who could blame him, she was bad! She had an exotic look, you could tell that she was from another country by her skin tone, features, and a strong accent. He was a good actor when he wanted something because the way he catered to the woman and showered her with affection was flattering but his crew knew him all too well. That's when a 6'3, 200 lb. well-built basketball playing looking dude approached JoJo giving her a hug and a slight kiss on the cheek. All eyes were on the dude especially José's, but he couldn't make it to noticeable that he was grilling him.

"Everyone this is Jamal!" she said so happily.

"Jamal, this is my family and friends," she announced.

Everyone greeted him warmly, come to find out that Jamal was a sophomore at Villanova University that started at the point guard position for the basketball team. After having a brief conversation with him for the most part he seemed to be a good guy, so he was welcomed with open arms. They all boarded Delta Airlines heading for Australia. They were ready to have some fun in the sun.

Since the raid on Scott Street, Detective Baldwin, Stevens, and Agent Kramer had been very active in patrolling the block. Even with the heat being turned up it had become difficult to snag anyone from the Scott Street Boys. They had been damn near invisible, only showing their faces briefly then routing. All the block money and small weight sales were on their phones, so a majority of the cash was still accounted for. Just like the smart thugs that they were Showstopper and Dawger took 4 ½ and recruited a few youngins to post up on the block. Sad to say, they were even younger than they were, so if they were to ever get caught it would be a slap on the wrist. With no solid evidence on Castro for the murder of Captain Johnson he was only wanted for questioning, but he had vanished because he hadn't been seen or heard from since the day the deal was supposed to take place. In his gut, Kramer had a feeling that Kevin Gaines was the man, but without any evidence, it would be hard to make it stick. After going to his last few addresses only to find out that he didn't reside at any of them, Kramer became overwhelmed. The only good thing that came out of the investigation was after weeks of searching and looking a reliable informant had given him the last name of one of Castro's partner which was Valdez. After weeks of wondering who he was, Kramer finally had a full name, José Valdez. A quick search of Deljis showed that José had been locked up as a juvenile back when he was 13. The picture was old and he looked like a little boy, but nonetheless he had a picture. Now Agent Kramer had a face to match the name. He finally knew who this Spanish José from the Hill was.

Detective Baldwin had been swamped with new cases. Over the last few months while working the joint investigation with the feds, a double murder that took place over Eastside in one of the row homes which they have no suspects for. The Felix Valdez homicide and apparently a drug war that's brewing between the Reyes family who he is well aware of and Ivan Santana's crew that left two of the Reyes men dead within a weeks' time. He tried questioning the Reyes family but hasn't come up with anything. Ivan Santana was questioned by the Chief of Police himself, but nothing ever came out of it. So, until he hears anything from his higher-ups he'll just keep searching for clues. One thing that did catch his attention was that at the scene of the corner store shooting, rumor had it that someone named José killed Hector Reyes. Sharing that information with Agent Kramer, they thought it was a coincidence that the same José who was supposed to be moving a large amount of narcotics in the city could possibly be the shooter of a suspected mid-level drug dealer. If that was the case, then Hector's death could have been an attempted retaliation that went wrong. His younger brother Alex had been brutally murdered a week earlier and now him. The only problem the law had was when they went to question the witnesses, they heard the whispers and rumors, but no one dared to make a statement. Knowing Ivan's involvement in the underworld and his level of dealings that have never been able to stick, why no one knows Detective Baldwin and Agent Kramer thinking hypothetically thought that perhaps maybe José might have dealings with Ivan somehow. Keeping an eye on Ivan would now become a priority just to see if this José character has any dealings with him. Baldwin, Stevens, and Kramer felt that if they were patient, they just might find out all they needed to know. Maybe even ultimately find out who's supplying them!

Qualia was beautiful, the weather, the water, the scenery everything seemed great! If it was possible to live there it wouldn't have been a question, the whole squad would have packed up and moved out of the country. Island life was much more tranquil than any living in the states, city, or country period! The music even tends to affect the soul better, everything about the island spoke peace and that's just what everyone needed especially José.

On the first day, everyone enjoyed the beach and the sapphire-colored water. They hung out and danced, playing flag football the women verse men. At the end of the night, they all met at the campfire where they ate, fried fish, and told stories about growing up in the city. José even noticed that Jamal and JoJo were hitting it off well. Secretly, he had to admit that was the happiest he'd seen her in a while and even though he felt a sting of jealousy he was happy for her. Even though she knew he wouldn't say it, she kept telling herself that she wanted to be happy as well, so she continued to enjoy her vacation. The next day of the vacation was spent on the beach of course then the group along with their tour guides went snorkeling and deep-sea diving with dolphins. That was probably the highlight of the vacation, the next couple of days consisted of nature walks on the islands exclusive nature trails, spa treatments for both the women and men, more clubbing, and of course Hella shopping. On the last day, everyone mainly lounged around the beach relaxing and smoking. From a distance, José watched his squad in their companions. They all looked so at peace; it was a shame they had to return to the harsh realities of life once they stepped foot back on American soil. Summer seemed to be living out her dream of seeing the world as she lay on the beach with her eyes hidden behind her Ahdash frames. Making her happy was never a complicated job, all she wanted was to spend time with her man. So, now that they were on this exclusive island for a week where they've been sexing multiple times a day and walking hand in hand like a king and queen, he was sure she felt liberated and satisfied.

Nightfall had arrived and the stars and moon illuminated the whole island. With less than 12-hours left in paradise and a colossal of problems awaiting his arrival, José walked along the beach contemplating a strategy that would keep him and his team out of harm's way and free! While treading the sand he was stopped in his tracks when the two silhouettes that were no more than 50 feet in front of him seemed to be engaging in a very explicit sex session. At first, he was about to turn around and leave thinking it was probably Castro and his friend, but after seeing her throw her ass back and drop her head in ecstasy the way she did he slowly made his way closer to get a better view of the action. As he got closer, he could hear her moans clearly, they were sweet enough to cause his blood to flow. Still unnoticed by the two dark figures the lovers performed like newlyweds. When he came within five feet of the action and he finally locked eyes with the sex kitten who was arching her back and grinding her ass so erotic into this man's crotch area. The dude wasn't Castro and the woman wasn't his jump-off. His heart dropped and fire shot throughout his body as he stood frozen watching JoJo, who was now eyeing him seductively while she continued the performance of her life. Jamal hadn't noticed what was taken place due to his focus being on her body. She turned up even more when she realized she had the one spectator she always wanted watching her. José stayed in the dark watching until she hollered out in passion that she was cumming then collapsed. José finally walked off into the night fuming. He finally came to the realization that he not only loved his friend but that he was very much in love with her and didn't want her with no one else. He went back to his villa and made love to Summer until the sun came up. Everyone was packed and ready to leave, before leaving the island JoJo tried pulling José to the side to speak with him. He just gave her a cold blank stare then waved her off. She knew he was upset and decided to leave the issue alone for the time being.

Once they boarded the jet and they finally were airborne, José closed his eyes and got some much-needed sleep. It was best that he got his sleep now because in just a few hours once he's back in the states if he was ever caught sleeping it might just cost him his freedom or even worse, his life!

The double funerals for Alex and Hector Reyes were very sad and emotional. The tension was very high and everyone in attendance wanted blood. Alex had been shot in the face so many times that he had a closed casket while family and friends had the chance to view Hector's body. Priscilla tried her best to keep her composure, but it was useless. Every time the choir would sing a spiritual song she would break down and cry. Associates from Reading, Los Angeles, and family from Puerto Rico even showed up. With so many cold killers lurking around the city something was bound to pop off. About 15 new members from the G.B.C. even came to town with the G.B.C. Priscilla's Redding Los Angeles, and her brothers from Puerto Rico in Wilmington, it was sure to be a Murdertown! At the Gracelawn Cemetery where the burials were taking place, as the pastor spoke his final words before the two brothers were lowered into the ground total pandemonium broke out! Two white cargo vans that looked to be delivery vans came to an abrupt stop causing the entourage attending the funeral to look. All within a few seconds, the side doors swung open and out came four masked men letting off multiple rounds from the banana clipped AK-47's they were firing. People took cover, kids ran, and several bodies dropped! The small caliber handguns that the attendees of the funeral had were no match for the war weapons that was causing grief along with panic. As long as the drama was lit and casualties were caused including the death of a seven-year-old little girl, Ivan was cool. The four men hopped back in the van and quickly escaped without a trace!

CLICK, CLICK, CLICK, was the sound of every associate and every adult family member that was linked to Priscilla loading up weapons preparing to hit the streets of Wilmington, to put it simply, kill! Every block that was rumored to be supplied by Ivan or Angelina would be fire-bombed if anyone claimed to be soldiers of the cartel they would be shot on the spot. Houses used as stash houses would be robbed and burned down. The little information she had about Angelina and Ivan was minor, but it was enough to send a message. With more than 10 carloads of goons riding out on the hunt and Angelina having a small army patrolling the streets it was sure to be a blood bath. Once all the men were gone still dressed in black Priscilla was surrounded by her daughters and other female family members. She knew she could end the war by just packing her family up and leaving but with all that had taken place, running away was not an option. Ellé was never involved in the underworld dealing of her families business and only running the families legitimate businesses, Ellé never really knew who the woman Angelina was. But when her sister Yari showed her the picture she damn near had heart failure when she saw the photo of the man her mother somewhat feared. The man they called Ivan was the same man she was currently sleeping with, but his name wasn't Ivan it was Hoviare! Her head began spinning and she was confused there was no way she could tell her family that she was in love with the killer of her two brothers. Then it all hit her like a ton of bricks, the first day he came to her condo and ask who Alex was after seeing him in the pictures. Then he never wanted to attend any of the family functions she invited him too. She felt so stupid but ashamed as well because whatever spell he had her under she still wanted to be with him. She had to get the hell out of there, fast!

Normally, José was the kind of guy who would let bygones be bygones but with all the madness surrounding his life at that present time and a plan to dead all his problems from the past it was one task that had to be completed. Before placing his next order to Angelina, he wanted all issues handled so he called a meeting to first collect his cash from the Young & Reckless crew, then to discuss what he wanted taken care of. After tossing the idea around for a while with the squad a plan was formulated now all it had to be was executed.

That night Ellé cried repeatedly while Ivan held her close. Knowing what she now knew was detrimental to her life and relationship. If she told him that she knew everything he wouldn't trust her and might ultimately kill her. She was willing to keep her affairs away from her family to keep him. It had been a while since she was sexually active so when Ivan had come along, he blew her mind and she wasn't ready to give that up just yet. Ivan thought it was just the tears of attending her brother's funerals, but it was really because she was so hurt and confused. That night they made love and Ellé fell asleep in Ivan's arms like she normally would do.

Since losing his whole team in a shootout with Rakmeef and catching a shot to the chest, Jiz had been staying under the radar. When Boo, Showstopper, and Dawger came through to holla at him he knew it was on again. What the Reckless crew needed from Jiz was simple, so he pointed them in the right direction. The crew stalked the three-story brick house for the better part of the day into the early evening hours. Around 7:30 p.m. their patience paid off when the target was seen pulling up in front of the house. They wanted to cut him down on the spot but when the elderly woman appeared walking with a cane was escorted to the front door by the target the trio paused. As soon as the elderly woman disappeared into the house with the target the Young & Reckless went into action taking their positions. About a half hour later, the target exited the house heading to his car. He never saw Boo come from out of the alley on the side of the house until he snuck up behind him calling out his name causing him to jump!

"Yo Blue!" Boo called out. Blue spun around startled to find a .44 desert eagle aiming at his face.

"Yo Blue!" Showstopper and Dawger shouted.

When Blue turned to face them, he damn near shit himself when he saw Dawger holding a sawed-off shotie and Show holding a .40 caliber. Before anything could be said a slug penetrated the back of his skull dropping his body on the spot. Already dead and gone, Show and Dawger took the pleasure of pumping more rounds into his limp body on his mother's walkway. The young hyenas made it back to Westside in the Batcave then smoked a Dutch in the memory of Code Blue, Ha! Ha! Ha!

CHAPTER 24

One Month Later – February 2018

With a net worth estimated at close to eight million if not more José and the affiliates were all well off. Even JoJo had a kitty that had her sitting comfortably on $350,000 in drug money. Since the vacation, José treated her like a sister and nothing more or less. He was certain that he wouldn't let anything come between them and he meant that. While he was out of town, she made all his local runs which earned her nice savings for herself. Tonight, everyone came to hang out with MacLaden and Bunny at his plush pad to attend his Super Bowl Party. You know the night was going to be interesting since like they both hoped for the New England Patriots were playing against the Philadelphia Eagles. Rosé and Mac both bought $150,000 cash for the bet! The bet was that the loser had to buy the winners girl a house and from the kickoff, they were at odds. A few times things got heated but it was all love overall. At the end of the game, the Philadelphia Eagles were crowned the Super Bowl Champions. Rosé passed off the buc fifty with no hesitation and a smile. In return, Mac handed the money to Bunny that he just received from Rosé then took his stash and handed it to Taylor as a gift. She was surely confused.

"What's this for?" asked a puzzled Taylor.

"It's a gift... your about to go away to school, right? We real niggas so we do real shit... homie too thorough to take his money... it was a friendly bet to me," MacLaden said shaking Rosé hand.

Rosé had a newfound respect for Mac and a bond was formed from that very moment. José, with the approval of Mac introduced Carlos to him personally so that his friend could now rise to his highest potential. The sky was the limit for the Affiliates and only they could stop themselves.

"You still going to New York for school?" José asked JoJo.

"Yeah... why what's up?"

"Did you find a spot yet?"

"Nah, you said you were gonna go with me to look at some."

"I will just let me know when you wanna go."

"Alright... José are you mad at me because of what you saw on vacation?"

"Joanní for the umpteenth time, if you're happy, I'm happy," he said walking away.

Three Months Later - May 2018

Time had passed and things had died down a little, but the law was still hunting. With both Carlos and José in and out of town, it was damn near impossible to catch up with the two. They tried shaking Carlos down but with Carlos having more dealings in Kent County with the bud and pills he was another person they had trouble keeping track of. With Dre falling back even more than before, his circle had become smaller. His dealings were with a selected few and that's how he wanted to keep it. Quan, Showstopper, Dawger, Boo, A-1 Bry, and Vic-chow were living out their street dreams. With the respect and reputation that the youngins have they're like young entertainers. Leaving Scott Street to their youngins now they moved on to bigger and better things thanks to José. The local and feds have still been pressuring them with random stop & frisk but the most they ever get is maybe an ounce of chow which is a misdemeanor, so they ended up getting a $100 fine and then released. Instead of using their money on foolishness, the Young & Reckless with the financial backing of José invested their money into buying music equipment and starting a record label. The first artist will be none other than Dawger the Madman. With a few mixtapes, videos, and shows they've done they had a nice buzz! Only time would tell where the Writers Block Ent. Group and the Young & Reckless might go!

Five months into the new year and José was truly a made nigga. He was with a major cartel that had money and power. He was slowly expanding into uncharted territories that could possibly bring him more money. After having numerous meetings, José finalized a deal with a grape vineyard in Cali to start the production of his own delicate champagne. With hopes of having it on the shelves in the next year and a little promotion from his artist, his champagne might be the next big drink that the world is talking about! He also met with his friend from high school and now play director Richard Jackson to discuss the possibility of Richard directing one of the many plays José has secretly written over the years. José first love was writing and with him willing to place a few hundred thousand dollars to see his writing come to life he'd gladly front the money. She didn't know it yet but if everything went as planned after JoJo finished film school, he planned to give her whatever she needed to produce her first film. His hands were finally about to see some legal money and if things went his way, he would triple his worth plus some! With the 3rd house that was purchased from the sheriff sale, José had three ceiling to floor safes placed in the walls. No one but him and JoJo knew about that spot since Taylor was no longer in the equation. He would change the location of his money and keep the work at Harding Ave. Things seemed to be looking up, now he had to holla at an old friend.

Sitting on the corner of 27th and Tatnall in his 2018 S65 Mercedes Benz José bobbed his head to Beyoncé and Jay-Z's Drunk in Love while waiting for Summer to come out of the corner store. While waiting on her, his youngin who used to live around the way was walking pass. Never noticing José sitting behind the wheel of the huge spacecraft so when he heard his name coming from the driver side window, he was shocked.

"What up lil homie?" José asked.

"All tryna eat... you know I just came home bout two weeks ago. Look at you though I heard you doing ya thing."

"A little suttin' you still pumping that reggie?" José asked the dark-skinned chubby kid.

"Yup, and I'm doing alright too. Why what you got something for ya youngin?"

"I might, depends... you do me a favor I do you a favor."

"What kind of favor?" the chubby kid asked.

That's when Summer got into the car looking like a supermodel, modeling high-end fashions. The kid was stuck on her beauty, all José could do was laugh!

"I'll let you know, just call me... I will tell you this, it's 10 lbs. of loud in it for you free of charge if you do it," José promised.

"That's why I fuck with you cause you always look out for ya peeps. I'll hit you in a day or two," the kid said giving José a pound then walking away.

Marisol had hidden her pregnancy of three months very well. At 22 with no future except the drug game her life didn't seem aspiring. With her first child on the way and refusing to tell her child's father the news because of fear that he might reject her and the child, she kept her pregnancy to herself. With all the stress of a soon to be mother, having the secrets she was holding in and her newfound habit for sniffing both a little coke and dope here and there; it was surely not healthy for the baby that she was carrying. With José meeting up with Titanic at least twice a month, she wondered when she would tell José that he would soon be a father. She had plenty of opportunities to tell him but every time he came to town, they would make love then he would leave. She would have to tell him sooner or later.

Dre and Jesenia were sending out all the invitations for the baby shower and were so excited. She was now six months pregnant and was having a boy with everything in order, the baby shower would be in two weeks at the extravagant Christiana Hilton Ballroom. The two soon to be parents were so happy and in love, nothing could separate them. In less than 100 days they would be the proud parents of a baby boy and Dre will finally be walking away from the street life to focus on raising his son and taking care of his family.

Carlos and Glady had been rolling thick as thieves since the first date and nothing has changed. With the bud that Carlos was now getting from MacLaden and his partnership with Glady on the pills, him and his mamasita were handling business like two corporate giants in the Urban communities. With the truth being revealed about her family and Carlos mentality that his ending would either be jail or death, he knew he had finally found his ride or die chick!

Ellé and Ivan were still together and even with the thought that he was responsible for the deaths of her brothers, she pushed that to the back of her mind. He still refused to attend family gatherings with her and secretly she knew why. She felt bad because whenever she looked at her mother, she could see the pain in her eyes still and she knew she held a secret that would open the floodgates to her happiness.

José hollered at his man Mac and grabbed a quick 10 lbs. of "girl scout cookies" then called his youngin who was more than ready to do a favor. After giving the youngin the plot, José just waited patiently to receive the call stating that he finally had the green light.

Since the death of her three sons, Priscilla had been seriously thinking of walking away from Wilmington while she still had family left to tell her story. With her age being a disadvantage and losing so many loved ones behind the mayhem that was really over nothing. She could easily pass the crown down to one of her daughters but thinking of the risk factors she erased the thought from her mind. With her having millions in cash, her children all having comfortable stashes, and Ellé investing money into stocks that have been bringing the family as a whole seven-figure payoffs from time to time, she could retire. And her family should still be wealthy for at least the next 50 years and that's well after she's gone. Priscilla knew from the beginning that she was no match for Angelina but refused to bow down to another woman in front of her daughters, now the fatalities weren't in her favor. Just when she was about to call a mandatory family meeting in walked her oldest daughter and son.

Strap was still moving his couple bricks a week and living an imaginary dream where he was the man! After the death of Code Blue, Strap moved more cautiously and with a lot smaller entourage. He didn't know who to trust since there were no suspects. So, to eliminate the worry and hassle of who, what, where, and why he's been mainly rolling dolo and only once the sun went down. He was parked on 29th and West waiting for the young boy Lil Black from 27th Street to come grab this ounce and a half of "hard" from him. He had just hung up the phone from him, so he sat listening to the Jadakiss and Fabulous mixtape Freddy vs. Jason. He knew that Lil Black was walking so he knew it would take a minute but it's almost 15 minutes and he was only two blocks away. Just when he was beginning to get impatient, Lil Black bent the corner then paused throwing up his index finger signaling Strap to give him a second. Then he began walking towards the car again just as Black was about to hop in the passenger seat a tap came on the driver's side window startling Strap. When he turned, he was looking directly at a hooded man dressed in all black, so he reached for his cannon. It was useless, José released at least 10 black talent shells into Strap's body throwing him violently from the drivers to the passenger seat. To seal the deal, José blasted one last shell through the side of Strap's face. José reached in the car grabbing his cell phone then dropped an ounce of powder to make it look drug related when it actually wasn't. It was personal, he disrespected his girl, tried to come through his block and catch wreck, then last but not least, he tried to put a check on his head. So, in José's eyes, Strap got everything he had coming his way. Black and José skated off into the darkness using the shadows as their allies. Once they were far away from the scene of the crime José disposed of Straps phone then made it to his car. At the car, José reminds Black that he didn't know a thing about Shit! After he assured his old head that he was blind and didn't see a thing, José grabbed 10 pounds of chow from his trunk of the Impala then handed it to the dark-skinned chubby kid. They both said their goodbyes and went their separate ways.

May 18th was the birthday of Ellé, but instead of spending the day with her family like she normally did she decided to celebrate with her man. Instead of letting him arrange the day's events she put together a little shopping spree first which mainly included jewelry shopping along with other clothing and shoe boutiques. Next, they walked down South Street in Philly holding hands like most of the other couples were doing. They enjoyed themselves and the time they were spending together. For the first time in a long, Ivan let his guard down by leaving his torch in her SUV while they shopped and sightseeing. Leaving South Street, Ellé wanted to give Ivan a sample of what was to come later in the evening once they were finished clubbing for the night. On the top floor of the Four Seasons Hotel in Center City, Philadelphia, Ellé had the suite reserved for the night. When they entered the room, she stripped naked then took Ivan in her mouth immediately. She put on an all-star performance as she rode his dick better than ever before. He pushed her legs back as far as they could possibly go then proceeded to drop his anchor in her until it touched her bottom. She fucked him back like the porn star Chyanne Jacobs as he hit that ass from behind. Once they both came, just like the adult she was she went to the bathroom, cleaned herself up, got dressed, and was ready to leave. Before they left the room, she promised him that if he loved that then the episode tonight would be unforgettable.

Castro had just come back to Wilmington from making a run to Hampton, Virginia where he met with his older cousin Bootsie. When he made it back to town, he immediately went to switch from his SUV to his 2018 Porsche Panamera Sport Turismo. People had seen him in his Audi truck which would be easier to spot. Then with the feds looking for him, for only Lord knows what he felt he needed speed just in case he had to escape in a hurry. Springtime had arrived which meant less clothes and more skin it also meant family cookouts and block parties. With the sun shining and nice weather every block in Wilmington was live! So, just like every other major player throughout the city the Affiliates were having a block party for the whole Scott Street. Carlos, Dre, the Twins, and even Mac came through with Bunny who felt odd knowing the Twins were the younger sisters of Alex. Anyway, it wasn't her place to speak on it so she kept her mouth shut like the O.G. Diva she was. Rosé and his team showed up with so much chow you would have thought there was a weed dispensary located on the block. Taylor and JoJo pulled up banging the new Cardi B album in JoJo's new cherry red 2018 Jaguar XE 25T. The food was smelling wonderful and the kids were having so much fun jumping around in the bounces, thanks to José. This cookout even had a large assortment of seafood from shrimp, crabs, clams, Alaskan crab legs, and oysters along with steak, burgers, fish, deer meat, and the usual shit that's at a bar-b-que. The D.J. had the block in full party mode as he spun the latest hits plus, including a dance contest and things that would get the people involved. That's when Summer stole the show pulling up in the 2018 Mercedes Benz G-550 with José riding shotgun. That was the gift he promised her if she got straight A's and made the Dean's list and she did just that! Getting out, sporting Versace's new Spring collection he looked like an affluent young gangster. He really had the block excited and had the kids in mass hysteria when he opened the rear door then began passing out Super Soaker water guns to everyone. Everyone chipped in so the alcohol run looked like Scott Street had a liquor distributor out there. Bottles of Branson B., Cîroc, Henny, E & J, Patron, 1800, and Crown

Royal Apple were the drinks of choice all in liter sizes. Of course, there were a couple of cases of Seagrams Jamaican Me Happy's for the women. All was good and no one had any real major beef to worry about. Just as the sun started to set Castro pulled up stepped out cocky as ever. They all knew it was a bad idea for him to be out there, but the block was live, the weather was nice, and he wanted to hang out with his squad too, so today he was willing to take a chance. They ate, smoked, drank, and laughed together just as they did before they had the money. This is what made everything they'd been through as a squad worthwhile. Just when things seemed to be dying down Quan Showstopper and the crew showed up with about three carloads of bitches, it really got turned up out there! Castro, feeling like he had hung out enough for the night decided it was time to bounce but before he left, he wanted to holler at José about grabbing some work in the morning. So, they went in hopped in Castro's wheels to discuss business. Before they could even close the doors and get comfortable the lights colored the sky bright. From both ends of the block Vice, squad cars, and F.B.I. Agents swarmed the area. They left the entire block party alone but surrounded Castro's car with guns drawn. Without question, Castro was taken into custody by Agent Kramer while Detective Baldwin asked for José identification. Once he saw the name on the ID, he began putting the face to the name then everything came to him like a revelation, they caught two birds with one stone.

"Spanish José... you're just the kid we're looking for. You wouldn't mind coming with us to answer a few questions, would you?" Detective Baldwin asked.

José and Castro were hauled away from the block and just like that the block party was over!

Domingos Bar and Lounge was the party spot Ellé had decided to stop by to celebrate. Located in North Philadelphia the bar wasn't a huge or lavish establishment it wasn't even mediocre. Domingos was more of a neighborhood bar that catered to the locals mainly the Dominicans from the area. The hustler's hangout, however, Ellé chose that particular spot in the hood because everyday life had consisted of five-star restaurants, snobby associates, and rather extravagant outings. Tonight, she wanted to let loose and live free, she wanted to let her hair down and party with her people. Taking shot after shot of Patron, her hips were winding to the salsa music that was loudly playing. Ivan even two-stepped to the music showing much attention to his woman who was loving the feeling of his hands roaming all over her body. 1800 was Ivan's drink of the night, instead of buying shots all night he purchased a bottle and got smashed. Ellé had stopped drinking beings though she was the designated driver for the night. About 2 a.m., Ellé stepped into the early morning air feeling vibrant with a staggering Ivan following behind her. Heading to her Lexus Jeep Ellé got in while Ivan hopped into the passenger seat feeling the effects of the liquor. Before she put the key in the ignition, she turned to face a half-asleep Ivan. Without ever knowing what happened, Amillio sprung up from the back seat smothering Ivan's face with a cloth soaked in chlorine. He struggled to free himself which was useless. After breathing in the potent chemicals, he passed out!

CHAPTER 25

Ivan's Demise

"Mr. Gaines my name is Agent Kramer and I'm with the F.B.I.... you've been a hard man to catch up too. First, let me inform you that you're not under arrest you're just here for questioning," Agent Kramer said sternly.

"Questioned for what?" Castro asked.

"The murder of Captain Lane Johnson of the New Jersey State Police."

"Who?" asked Castro. Agent Kramer shuffled through the file that sat in front of him searching for the information.

"Jacoby," Agent Kramer stated.

"Captain... State Police... smh," Castro said lowering his head.

"Yeah, we're aware of the dealings you had with Captain Johnson, but never had enough to make it stick, but we're not here for that. I'm here investigating his murder. So, where were you at on Nov..."

"To be honest that was so long ago I'd be lying if I told you I knew exactly where I was. So, to keep myself clear of any misconceptions I'm gonna say that I can't really recall," Castro said sticking to the story.

"It's funny you don't remember but it's a coincidence that Captain Johnson and his wife were murdered on the same night that you were to buy the guns."

"What guns?" Castro said smirking a little.

"Listen asshole, you might find this funny but there are two girls without their parents because someone felt the need to execute them and if you had anything to do with it, I won't stop until I take you down," Agent Kramer said becoming irritated.

"You wanna know what I find funny? You just told me that I wasn't under arrest that I'm only here for questioning then in so many words assuming that I had something to do with the deaths of Jacoby and his wife. Is it because I'm Black with a criminal history? How are you so sure it wasn't a White person?"

"You wouldn't mind being in a line up, would you?" Kramer asked.

"Sure, why not, I haven't done any wrong."

After the line-up and the daughters of Captain Johnson not able to identify him, Castro was released. Not before Agent Kramer promised him that he'd be seeing him again very soon.

Detective Baldwin, Stevens, and Agent Kramer surrounded the small gray desk that José sat at with a nonchalant look on their faces. First, the detectives tried questioning him about the murder of Hector Reyes which José denied any involvement in. They tried lying, telling him that people placed him at the scene, but his response to the fraudulent lies was if you have the evidence to prove it then charge him with it. After two hours of flip flop, good cop bad cop they had no other choice but to let him go. José knew they had nothing on him, so he played it cool, but when Agent Kramer from the F.B.I. introduced himself and spoke José listened.

"José my name is Federal Agent Brian Kramer; I'm with the F.B.I. originally I was sent here to investigate and question your friend Kevin Gaines. However, in doing so I think we may have stumbled onto something even bigger than a double murder. Your crew, all the guys wearing the chains saying Affiliates like the one you have on now and the ones their all wearing in these pictures I've gathered. He said sliding the pictures onto the desk.

"I know what y'all are doing and this is my first and final warning if you wanna be home to see a new year I suggest you find a new profession because if you don't I'm gonna take everything you and your little crew has worked so hard to get including ya girl... ya know their the first to go when you catch time," Agent Kramer said patting José on the shoulder.

José left the federal building wondering just how much they knew. It didn't matter, he was in too deep to look back now with 500 bricks being sold between dope and coke he was willing to accept whatever came with his fast life. Leaving the federal building feeling that he might be followed he walked from Downtown Wilmington back to the Hilltop where he could elude any authority figure that was following him.

Ivan was awakened from a smack to the face. When his eyes finally opened and his clouded vision cleared, he realized that he was in serious trouble. In the pitch dark he could tell that his hands had been elevated above his head as he hung from what seemed to be a ceiling. Struggling to free himself was a waste of time as the cuffs locked tighter from all the excessive movements he was doing. The last thing he remembered was being in the club with Ellé! Where was Elle was the first thought that came to mind. And as if he was thinking out loud his question was answered when the light came on then in walked Ellé only this time she didn't have her same everyday lovable expression, she had a more bland look. She stood in front of him for a few seconds silent trying to control her anger.

"Who is this?!" Ellé shouted holding up a picture of Alex and Chomo.

"You know who they are so why are you asking me! I never knew they were your family if I did, I would've squashed the beef," Ivan said convincingly.

"You're a lie! That's why you ask me who he was that night at the condo when you saw his picture. That's why you never attended any of my family functions... and just think I was in love with you... but now, that doesn't matter," she cried.

"Listen LeLe, maybe I can talk to your family and we can work this out," he said trying to cop a plea!

"Work it out, ha! You killed my family, her sons. As much as I love you and wish this could be worked out, I'm sorry there's nothing I can do," she said wiping her tears then kissing Ivan one last time!

As Ellé left the room in walked Amillio and none other than Priscilla Reyes carrying a medium size chainsaw. Ivan's eyes grew wide but never bitched up or said a word but Bella Bandido.

After 30 minutes of kicks, punches, smacks to the face, and elbows to the groin Amillio was tired and finished. Amillio left the room leaving his mother alone with Ivan. She stood there in a one-piece overall with a grim look on her face. Priscilla unzipped the overalls stepping out of it standing naked in all her glory. The once-promising body that was to die for was now shaggy and worn from old age and kids.

"You killed my soul... you've taken from me what I've created. You caused me a great deal of pain, but good things come to those who wait," Priscilla said slowly yanking the string on the chainsaw to start the engine. Knowing his death was eventually near, instead of crying he embraced death with a smug look on his face and a slew of obscenities.

"Bitch, once Angelina finds out about this your whole family will be dead within a weeks' time! I'm Ivan you don't know who you're Fucking with! You can kill me now and I'll be waiting in Hell for you Bitch," Ivan spat, "sorry Ms. Reyes, killing me is not gonna bring ya Pussy Ass sons back so kill me cause I ain't scared to die," Ivan said spitting in her face.

"Good, cause I'm not scared to kill you... now you're gonna die!" Priscilla said swinging the chainsaw into the side of his leg cutting it off at the knee.

For the next hour or so, Priscilla chopped Ivan's body into pieces in the basement of an old abandoned row home in the Strawberry Mansion section of Philadelphia. Ellé was a little hurt but her family ties outweighed any love she ever had for an opposition over the years. This wasn't the first time the situation occurred, but she sure hoped and prayed that it would be the last time.

Using her better judgment, Priscilla decided to move her family to the Eastern Shore of Maryland where she purchased some land then had trailers placed on it while she had her mansion built. Before she completely left Wilmington alone, she had to send the Bella Bandido Cartel one last going away gift. Chandelier Ballroom was beautiful, the decorations and colors represented the soon to be arrival of a brand-new baby boy had the guest in awe. Everyone from Dre's family to friends attended the gathering. You would have thought Babies R Us had packed everything in their warehouse into the ballroom with all the gifts that Taylor and Jo brought alone. José and the rest of the squad including the Young & Reckless had another large assortment of clothing, accessories, and jewelry. The Reyes women were there along with the children who ran around having a ball! A few men showed up, but they were older men who had no involvement in the families affairs. Both parties were introduced to each other and everything seemed to be wonderful. Everyone was enjoying themselves and as usual Latin people danced, ate, and then danced some more. Priscilla watched from afar at the young team of wealthy young drug dealers. She had to admit they were successful at what they were doing. Knowing they were from Wilmington and that Angelina's operation was based there she wondered if this group in some way had any ties to her. Today was a special day, so she decided to enjoy the event but took a mental note to ask Carlos and Dre if they knew Bella Bandido. José and Summer lounged at one of the tables watching the action that was happening on the dance floor. Jesenia was being the best hostess she could, she even came to conversate with José and Summer while nibbling on finger foods. The kids ran back and forth tossing balloons in the air. For a brief moment, José drifted off to thinking of Felix and how he would have enjoyed himself today. A single tear fell from his eye, Summer noticed but Jesenia didn't as José discretely wiped it away. Nelson, Jesenia's nephew came walking up to his aunt hugging her and politely introducing himself to José and Summer. The well-mannered kid was also dressed down rocking the latest True Religion spring attire. The chain he wore stood out beings though the kid was so young rocking an iced-out Jesus piece.

Amillio had planned to head back out west after they killed Ivan, but he wanted to make sure his mother was out of town first and he wanted to attend his sisters baby shower. With this being a family gathering and it being a private event in Kent County he left his guns at home and came to enjoy another family gathering. Just as he walked into the lobby he walked into José and his entourage who seemed to be in a hurry to leave. Once they locked eyes, Amillio reached for his piece but remembered that he didn't have it. José instinctively pulled his torch out causing everyone following behind him to draw their weapons also. JoJo and Taylor stood on both sides of Amillio waiting to blow his top off. The commotion caused everyone inside of the hall to come out into the lobby causing everyone to panic in fear from the scene that was about to unfold. The Twins, Priscilla, Carlos, and Dre rushed to the middle of the quarrel with hopes on defusing the situation.

"Yo what the fuck is going on?" Dre spoke up.

"This puto killed Hector," Amillio hissed.

"I didn't kill that nigga intentionally, y'all were shooting at my brother at the store."

"Ivan's ya brother?"

"Fuck no... Sammy the youngin that works in the store. All I'm saying is that shit wasn't meant to happen, that shit was between you, Angelina, and Ivan but my brother was there so shit got hectic. If you can't except that we can do whatever right here and right now," José stated ready to blow.

"Yo José calm down bro," Carlos spoke up.

José looked back and forth between Carlos and Dre saying nothing. It was obvious something was running through his mind, but he kept quiet. José lowered his gun then turned back to face Amillio.

"Look poppie, no disrespect and I apologize about ya brother, but my advice is to leave well enough alone cause this ain't what you want!" José said convincingly.

"Excuse me young man, do you know Angelina?" Priscilla asked.

"Yeah why, who's asking?" José spat.

"No one important," she replied.

"Yo, we out... Carlos, Dre I'll holla at y'all soon," José spat.

"Yo bro, you don't gotta leave we can work this out... where you goin?"

Dre asked.

And if looks could kill Dre would have been dead on the spot but José kept his cool and responded like the Gee that he was.

"I gotta go bro... I have to attend to some family issues." That was all José said before turning his back on his friends and walked out.

After three days of noncommunication, Angelina had finally received a text from Ivan who has been M.I.A. In the middle of a war, he knew it was a priority to check in on a day to day basis, so she planned on telling him off when she saw him.

The text read: Angelina shit got hectic, I might've offed the old woman so things might get crazy, be on point. I'm at the condo come through A.S.A.P. we really need to talk.

Not liking the sound of urgency in his text, she phoned Noel to have him meet her and Angel at Ivan's place. Both Angelina and her husband grabbed their torches then headed to the Riverfront Condos.

A half hour later, they pulled into the parking lot of the condo with Noel pulling in behind them. They went straight to Ivan's place on the 9th floor where they didn't receive an answer after knocking on the door several times. Luckily, Angelina had a spare key that Ivan had given her in case of emergencies. When they entered the condo, Angelina had an eerie feeling, but nothing seemed to be odd or out of place. Checking every room only to realize that Ivan was not there and that gave the trio a bad vibe. At first thought, she figured that he may have stepped out for a second and would be right back. She decided to call his phone and she still didn't get an answer but strangely she heard a phone ringing on the other side of the front door. Listening briefly to the rings but still, no sign that Ivan would walk through the door made the three of them pull out their weapons and cautiously walk to the door. Angelina called the phone once again which began ringing again. She signaled for Noel to open the door while she and Angel held a steady aim and ready to blaze whatever happens to move on the other side. Noel opened the door slowly not knowing what to expect. When he had it opened fully sitting on the welcome mat was a large size storage box with Ivan's phone placed on top of it. Stepping into the hallway briefly, Noel scanned the perimeter looking for anyone suspicious. Seeing the box, Angelina and Angel feared the worst. Noel retrieved it and brought it into the house placing it on the coffee table. In her line of work, death was a part of the game and beings though she received a text and not a call, found a box with Ivan's phone she could only imagine what was to come when she removed the top from the box. Beings though Ivan had become somewhat family to her she wanted to see what was in the box before anyone else. When she removed the top, a single tear fell from her left eye. All she could do was bow her head, the man that was assigned to protect her with his life, plus helped her move thousands of bricks over the years had been brutally murdered. Ivan's head that was badly swollen to the point of unrecognition from obvious head trauma was placed in the box with his dick in his mouth. They all sat there in silence for a minute trying to collect their thoughts. The sting of death was finally felt and Angelina was hurting from it.

"I want that family killed... I want their house burned to the ground. I want to attend their funeral," she spoke in between sniffles.

The box was a giveaway Angelina knew that they were being watched but at that moment she could care less. If her life was on the line when she left the condo then so be it, she knew she would take a few to Hell with her!

A few days had passed since the baby shower, José had spoken to Carlos and Dre a few times but kept it short. They would come through and holla, Dre would come and re-up but that was it. Needing to clear the air on a few things with his squad he had everyone meet at the Delaware Canal where Angelina's 75-foot super yacht was awaiting them. For the occasion, José purchased five bottles of Louis XIII and five ounces of poppa smurf to smoke on. They cruised the Atlantic for a good part of the day, enjoying the sun and fishing. For dinner, they ate Lobster and potatoes washed down by more Louis XIII. By sunset the night air became chilly, so everyone relocated to the general area to lounge. The friends conversated about everything, it almost reminded them of the days in the Batcave. That's when JoJo called for everyone to come to the upper deck. José led the way with Castro, Carlos, and Dre following in suit. On the other deck, JoJo had five Dutch's rolled awaiting their arrival.

"I called y'all out here to smoke a blunt under the stars with y'all baby," JoJo said passing each member a Dutch, "we made it baby look how far we've come. All this would've never happened if it wasn't for my brother my best friend, man fuck that my soul mate... do you have anything to say poppie," JoJo said wrapping her arms around him then stepping off to the side.

"Yeah, I do as a matter of fact. Man, when we first started pumping, we used to dream about this secretly. It seemed like a long shot but with a little extra hard work and connecting with the right people we went from dimes to one brick, to moving close to 500 bricks a month, cocaine, and dope. Niggas can't fuck with my team; I call us Affiliates because we're affiliated with some major breadwinners and they look at us all like family. It's sad when family ain't family no more. When you provide and would die for and in return, they kill ya soul, they take apart of ya life and you never get it back until your dying day. We came in this as a team and the dream was to make enough money to fallback and retire without getting caught by the law... that my friends we've accomplished. So, with all the highlights of our rise to the top why would y'all betray me," José said putting his head down.

On cue, JoJo and Castro pulled out their cannons aiming directly at Carlos and Dre. Visibly shaken not knowing the cause for the sudden turn of events Dre started pleading asking questions that fell upon deaf ears while Carlos stood silent.

"You know what I'm talking bout, ask ya boy Carlos to remind you nigga!" José shouted.

"Yeah, tell him Los, refresh his memory," JoJo spat. Castro stood there ready to blow those two niggas heads off.

"What the fuck are y'all talking bout word!" Carlos spat standing in his big boi stance.

José went into his pocket pulling out the chain that he had given to Felix, that was taken from him in the homicide then tossed it to Carlos," he dropped his head and closed his eyes.

"See the night we went clubbing I found it strange that y'all didn't want to bring the Twins to party with us. I blew it off thinking nothing of it. I mean, y'all were my family I trusted y'all so I would have never thought of you two... but you know what they say what's done in the dark will eventually come to the light. And thanks to my little friend Nelson who pointed the finger directly at you Los everything is out in the open. I put all the pieces together connected the dots and came to the conclusion that you beat my mother and killed my little brother out of greed. I've given you two more than I've given my own mother. Thanks for everything, now give me my chain back." Carlos still standing tall tossed the chain back while Dre was on the brink of pissing on himself.

"I just wanna know one thing... if you looked at me like a brother then why?" José wanted an honest answer.

"Man, you thought..." BOOM! JoJo's shot shattered Carlos chest cavity.

"Fuck the excuses... excuses, excuses, excuses... excuses are for failures," she said spitting on her ex-friends lifeless body. Castro grabbed the body up and tossed it into the deep blue of the Atlantic Ocean floating to the bottom of the Abyss never to be seen ever again.

"Yo bro, I didn't want anything to do with it! I didn't know he was going to ya moms spot til we got there I swear... plus, I told him to chill when he got on that dumb shit. José, I'm sorry man, I never wanted anything to ever happen to Felix I mean, I mean he just snuck up behind me and... Dre caught himself."

"And what Dre?" José questioned.

"And I shot him... I'm sorry bro," Dre said lowering his head wailing with tears flowing heavily down his face, "at least I don't have to worry myself about who pulled the trigger."

"Damn Dre, you should've walked out."

"You should have told me bro!" José shouted.

"Yo José, my fault fam. How do you tell ya friend that you're involved in the murder of his flesh and blood?" Dre stated, "I wish I could take it back, but I can't and I regret that shit. Bro, you know I got my first seed coming soon and I need to be there to raise him... if you let me go, you will never see me again," Dre pleaded to José.

"Joanní, how far are we from land?" asked José.

"About 100 miles... or more!"

"Listen, only because of your seed pussy I'm not gonna kill you but I never wanna see you again... so with that being said, Castro," José said tapping his friend. POP! Two shots entered both of Dre's legs dropping him where he stood.

"AHH... AHH SHIT!" Dre screamed in pain.

"Shut up bitch... you're a sorry excuse for a friend," Castro said lifting Dre and tossing him over the side with the feisty help of JoJo.

"Yo José, it's dark out here... come on fam, what am I gonna do?" Dre cried.

"Remember, family ain't family no more and I kept my promise, I didn't kill you, but I did tell you that I didn't want to see you anymore... so you best to get to swimming. Adios!" José said turning his back on his ex-friend walking away.

Dre struggled to stay afloat as the yacht began to cruise away. In the middle of nowhere in the pitch darkness with two bullet wounds to his legs a hundred miles away from land, death was only a matter of minutes away. If he didn't die from drowning, he feared being pulled under and torn to pieces by a shark to the least whatever his death would be he was certain he would never get to see the birth of his first child.

48-Hours Later

"Bro what's up? I know I should've been here a long time ago, but I just couldn't face the truth yet. Ma is doing alright; she misses you like crazy and so does Sammy. Truthfully, we all do... Felix, I got the new 2K18 and every time I play it, I think of how you would crush me, bro! Shit ain't the same without you around and I blame myself for your death, so forgive me if it felt like I was avoiding you. I know you're up there with pop I know he's watching over you tell him I said hey," José said wiping his tears, " Felix, I'm sorry little bro, my judgment of character was way off. I let people around my family who I thought I could trust, but in all actuality, for money, I should've known not to trust anyone. In my mishap, it cost you your life and took you away and I won't see ever again until it's my time to die," he said sobbing, "if I could change positions with you right now bro, I would in a heartbeat. I would do that just to put a smile on ma's face. Since, I can't do that I'm gonna keep ya memory alive until my dying day, just to show you how serious I am about holding you down I brought you a gift." José pulled the Cuban link with the iced-out Jesus piece from his Polo Spring jacket placing it on Felix's gravestone.

"I got them niggas for you bro... you can go ahead and rest in peace. This belongs to you and now it's back to its rightful owner, I love you."

José sat at the cemetery smoking and drinking for a while until it was closing time. Leaving the cemetery José made a call to Angelina to place the order for his next shipment. He had business to attend and with all his distractions behind him, it was back to chasing change!

Having to murder his two best friends had really bothered José. It had to be done though they crossed the line and violated in a major way; the penalty for their actions could have only been death. JoJo and Castro tried getting his mind off it explaining to him that their death was justified. He understood how they felt, but these two had been there from the beginning.

He reminisced on how they used to split quarter bags of chips amongst the three of them. How they would split an order of fries three ways or when they all got their first shot of pussy. It would be hard to put in the back of his mind, but it had to be done. He had an operation to run and his altered thinking was clouding his judgment causing him to make mistakes that a person like José normally wouldn't make. Castro and JoJo suggested he take a break to get his thoughts together, but he refused. With Carlos and Dre out of the picture, it was time for Quan Showstopper and Boo to move up in the ranks. He wanted Dawger making moves in and out of state, but he was in the studio heavily and had a nice following so José wanted him to stay focused on the prize. Since the death of his two friends, José's life had been moving in slow motion. His timing was off a little, it was like he was missing a valuable link to a chain. Noticing the lack of progress in José, Angelina had a sit down with him. She shared the death of Ivan with him and in return, he told her about his best friends. She explained to him that in the game they played no one is loyal when it came to money, everyone has their own motive and the ones closest to you want more from you than your own blood. That's why it's best to keep a safe distance. She also explained that in this game errors will come but you have to learn from it and move wiser every day. Having a good heart will win you favor with the people but never let a person push over you or take a penny from you without asking first. Last but not least, never find yourself becoming excited with killing someone, that shows that you have a cold heart and dark eyes. It's a place reserved in Hell for people like that. José felt rejuvenated after talking to his plug. Now, all he wanted was to add another million to his bank account. Sticking to the script was simple so of course, money was stacked like the lottery.

On his last trip to Pittsburgh to holla at Titanic, Marisol informed him that she was four months pregnant. He was shocked, the news caught him off guard. He didn't know if he wanted to be excited or upset how would he break the news to Summer or would he tell her at all. So many questions for José to answer, whatever the outcome maybe he just hoped his decision making was on point. When he arrived back in Wilmington, he didn't have time to stop in politic. He could've easily sent JoJo to make the drop to Skinny Kev from Dover since the commute wouldn't take that long but since Quan Showstopper needed 10 bricks, he slid to Harvey Ave. to grab the whole 20 squares. Since the closest meeting spot was the Batcave he had "Show" meet him there.

Both Detectives and Agent Kramer weren't satisfied with their police work lately. The effort shocking and none of the snitches were willing to make a statement on José or anyone in his crew. Two missing persons reports were issued for Carlos and Dre by the Twins. They were last seen with José but there was nothing to prove that accusation so nothing could be done. Agent Kramer really wasn't certain that Castro was the killer of Captain Johnson, but he was a hundred percent sure that José and the rest of his gang were involved in a high level of drug dealings and trafficking. Until he could scrounge up some solid evidence he would have to wait until someone was willing to testify against the Affiliates or catch them in the act. At the end of the day, Kramer had a job to do and that was to capture the bad guys so back to the streets he went searching for the criminals.

With Kev calling constantly and Quan heading to Smyrna to holla at his folks who wanted a half brick, José decided to ride downstate with Quan.

Before getting on Rt. 13 "Show" wanted to stop at his stash spot which was one of his young girl's parents house to drop of his work. The less work the better off they were on the ride downstate. Quan's Dodge Demon was by far one of the fastest cars on the market at the time, but it could never outrun the speed of sound. So, when they saw the same tinted out Suburban following them that was on the scene the day off the block raid and when José and Castro got taken in for questioning, they wanted to boogie!

While patrolling the Hilltop area cruising from block to block Agent Kramer spotted Daquan Hargrove's Dodge Demon. With nothing better to do but harass the young punk, he planned to pull him over. Knowing his truck would never be able to keep up with the muscle car if the youngster tried to elude him, he radioed in for backup, then turned on his light!

José cursed himself for not taking his SS Impala that had the stash box. He would have never made a decision like this but with so much on his mind his judgment was off. He knew this mistake would cost him a lot so to be on the safe side, he got on his phone and quickly called Summer and JoJo letting them both know what might go down. Then he called his attorney Anthony Nash Esquire who informed him not to elude them or say a word, he would meet him downtown if necessary then he hung up. Quan Showstopper called his lawyer but before anyone could answer, the car came to a screeching halt in the middle of 4th Street as they were suddenly surrounded by members of the F.B.I. and the Wilmington Police. Everything was in slow motion from that point on. Agent Kramer approached the car with his gun drawn on a mission to be a dick. Asking for his license and registration, Quan cooperated giving him everything he asked for, so did José. With everything coming back 29-negative, they should have let the two roll, but Agent Kramer and Detective Baldwin took it a step further when they asked to search the vehicle.

"Hey, Show you mind if we search your car?" Agent Kramer asked sarcastically.

"Yeah, I mind... you can't search it. We gave you the proper paperwork and shit so why are you still fucking with us!" Show snapped.

"Regardless if you like it or not, we're gonna search this car today and if it's anything and I mean anything even a dime bag y'all asses are going to jail," Agent Kramer said more seriously.

José being the brain that he was pulled out his phone and began recording the whole ordeal from the time "Show" refused to let them search the car. He then sent a video text to Summer and JoJo asking them to save it until he spoke with them. Knowing the outcome of the situation José told Quan to step out and when he got to the federal lock-up not to say a word. "Show" was willing to take the charge for his big homie beings though he was loyal and knew José was a stand-up guy. José declined and told him they would likely both be charged but that everything should be okay. Even in the hour of despair, José tried to make the best out of the bad situation they were in.

As soon as they stepped out of the car they were detained. West 4th Street was overpopulated with spectators watching the city's biggest drug supplier and his youngin get frisk down. The moment they were pulled in the opposite direction of the car several agents swarmed in on it. José looked on as both duffle bags were pulled from the trunk. The agents went into the bags pulling brick after brick out revealing 20 bricks of 100% pure cocaine for every onlooker to view. José looked to the Heavens because he knew he was gonna need a blessing from God. Quan kept his head high promising the viewers who were posting his arrest on every social media outlet that he would be returning to the streets soon. José took a deep breath, lowered his head, and strutted away with confidence. Reality had just set in the game that he once played, made millions in, and achieved levels that many will never achieve or dream of was abruptly brought to an end. It was over!

To be continued...

ABOUT THE AUTHOR

J. Rice was born and raised in Wilmington, Delaware. His love for the culture of Hip Hop and personal life experiences has inspired him to pursue writing Urban Fiction Literature.

In 2011, he was diagnosed with two severe eye diseases; Uveitic Glaucoma and Cataract which caused him to lose his eyesight for four years (20/200). After, four major eye procedures and numerous injections to the eyeballs on December 31, 2015, his sight was restored. This miracle has given him the opportunity to follow his dream of becoming a published author.

J. Rice is currently serving a 7 ½ year prison sentence for firearm charges; he would love to hear your comments on his first novel. To contact him you can write to:

John Rice

H.R.Y.C.I

PO Box 9561

Wilmington, DE 19809

Please leave reviews and comments on Amazon.com after you are finished reading. Thanks in advance for your support!

www.ingramcontent.com/pod-product-compliance
Lightning Source LLC
Chambersburg PA
CBHW071148100726
47908CB00002B/293